Winter Maessen...

the Queen of Deception.

Is there anything real about you?

Such convincing lies that even you

believe them now.

Acolyte

WINTER BOOK THREE

KEVEN NEWSOME

Acolyte

Keven Newsome

2nd Edition

ISBN: 978-0-9989596-3-4

KevenNewsome.com

PRESS EPIC

To Sarah.
For teaching me to dream a bigger dream.

0

Last Year

Dr. Streffield waited behind his large mahogany desk, elbows on the glass-top and head in his hands. The grandfather clock ticked by the plate-glass window behind him, reminding him the time drew near. Nothing more was to be done. He had made his choice. Dr. Streffield firmed his jaw and raised his head. With a deep breath, he stood and approached the window to gaze out upon the Meadow.

Immediately he saw a black-clad girl walking toward the Ancient along the sidewalk from the religion building and the Chapel of Radiance. A surge of panic, tinged with a hint of hope, coursed through him. If anyone could stop these plans…if anyone could save him, save everyone…it would be her. He folded his arms and watched. What was she doing? Why was Winter here?

She slowed as she neared the Ancient, easing forward, and stood watching the tree. She turned slightly to face upfield, and then slowly circled around, always staring at one empty spot beside the tree, until she faced the administration building and the tree stood behind her. Dr. Streffield took a step back, afraid he would be seen. But Winter just stared straight ahead, never looking up. She reached out to the air. Her mouth moved as if talking. With another careful step forward, Winter knelt to touch the ground.

Another girl approached from behind Winter…a girl with red hair. Dr. Streffield hadn't noticed her until she reached the right side of the Ancient and stepped onto the path leading her around to Winter. He narrowed his eyes and crept closer to the window. Was she the one they were looking for?

The intercom beeped.

"Yes?" he asked.

"Dr. Streffield, your nine o'clock just called to cancel."

He nodded. The signal. Right on time. "Thank you, Ms. Warner."

The intercom clicked silent.

Dr. Streffield reached for the tablet on his desk and turned back to the window. Winter and the red-haired girl were running across the Meadow toward the administration building. Panic swelled within him, but that taint of hope came just a little bit stronger. He began tapping quickly on his tablet, hating himself for it. Maybe Winter really could save everyone.

Davis shoved through the surging crowd as the people screamed and rushed in the opposite direction. He bounced a little to see over their heads, perspiration dripping onto his glasses. The Union was close. Maybe he could still make it.

He pushed forward again, tripping over a man crawling on the ground, blood gushing from his arm. Davis paused to survey the horror around him. Bodies lay strewn over the ground, blood everywhere. He couldn't tell if they were dead or alive, but most lay still. The surging crowd thinned as the people fled in the opposite direction. Whoever, whatever, had caused this, Davis knew he ran straight to it. For a moment, he thought about going back, he thought about joining the fleeing crowd. But his friends were up there, and they needed him. He leaned forward and ran, the path now clear and straight, and more bodies revealed in the emptiness.

As he neared the Union, one of the glass front doors exploded with a deep boom resonating from within. He skidded to a halt as Winter, Peter, and Ayden limped through the wreckage. Peter pulled Ayden tighter against his side. As Winter jumped down the steps and turned toward the Arts Plaza, Ayden found her feet and stumbled down with Peter, the back of her pants leg saturated with blood.

"Winter!" Davis shouted as the others crossed the service road. He pushed himself to run faster and catch up.

Winter spun to face him from the far side of the road, her black hair swinging into her face. Blood glazed the bicep of her left arm and she held it gingerly against her body. "Davis! Get out of here!" she screamed.

"Come on!" Peter shouted back after passing her, hoisting Ayden higher against his side and hobbling away at what was probably their fastest speed.

Winter stood there, turning from Peter to Davis and back again, hesitant.

"Wait for me!" Davis shouted, before she had a chance to turn away again.

The shattered door frame and the remaining intact door to the Union both flew open. A man in a silver and black mask strolled out, confident and almost leisurely, but with all the deadliness of a coiled snake. He glared at Davis, then Winter, finally fixating on the other two still hobbling away. Winter just stood there staring at the man as he cocked his shotgun and lifted it to take aim in her direction.

Davis roared and launched himself up the steps. He slammed his shoulder into the man's side, bringing both of them crashing to the concrete landing. The shotgun clattered away. Davis wrapped his arms around the man and squeezed his torso. An elbow landed on

Davis's shoulder, but Davis ground his teeth against the pain and leveraged his legs to flip the man onto his face. Before Davis could push, the man twisted, grabbed Davis's wrist, and bent it almost flat against his forearm. Davis wanted to cry out, but he kept his mouth clenched, trying to remember the counter move he had been taught. The man shoved Davis forward, and then jerked back on the arm to pull him directly into the fist launched at his eye. Davis fell back onto the ground, black speckling his vision and pain like fire consuming his face. Rather than pounce on him, the man simply looked toward the arts plaza again. Davis wanted to stand, to roll, to do anything to get away, but as he tried to find his feet, nausea and dizziness sent him back to the ground. The man peered down at him again, black demonic eyes glinting beyond the mask, and then stepped forward to pick up his gun.

Peter forced two fingers through the tiny pellet hole in Ayden's pants. He yanked it bigger until the wound was completely exposed; the sound of the fabric ripping made a small echo through the auditorium.

"That's not going to last long…" Winter said.

Peter glanced over to her as she came back from the stage doors, a broom now wedged through the push bars. Another gunshot sounded beyond the door and someone screamed. He grunted and went back to Ayden. The skin was purple at the wound entrance, but the immediate area around it was beginning to pale. The entrance wound itself was nothing more than a black hole, but surprisingly small. Ayden trembled like a child just out of a cold bath, and she peered down at him with eyes big enough to be that child, her face pale and her normally spiky red hair matted down with sweat. Peter slapped a piece of gauze over the bleeding hole and placed one end of the medical tape on her thigh. Then he quickly wrapped the gauze down.

When he finished, he found another gauze pad from the first aid kit and shoved the gauze and tape into Winter's chest. "Do it as we go."

Another gunshot in the hall. Closer than the last.

Peter took Ayden by the arm, and yanked her to her feet. Then he turned to Summer. Summer's pleading stare told him more than he wanted to know, and everything he already knew. He stole a glance at the door to the sound and lighting booth.

"Take her," he said, grabbing Summer by the hand. "Hide. Stay quiet. He thinks she's with us, so we'll lead him away. Then get out, got it? Get as far away from the school as possible."

Summer nodded and took Ayden's hand.

Peter cast over his shoulder at Winter. She was kicking the contents of the first aid kit toward the sound booth entrance. "We'll get him up…" she was saying, but Peter tuned her out and leaned close to Summer.

"Do what you have to do," Peter whispered.

"Don't make me do this," Summer whimpered.

Peter sighed and shook his head. "You have to. It's the only way."

Winter stopped talking. Peter turned to her and nodded, as if he agreed with whatever she had said. If she found out what was really happening…

Summer stared with wide eyes at the double doors. Peter pointed over her shoulder. "Go!"

Summer shook her head almost imperceptibly.

Peter softened and let his arm drop. "It'll be okay. Do it."

Summer covered her mouth and ran across the stage with Ayden.

Winter slid to her knees in front of Agent Gains. Blood saturated his stomach and oozed onto the floor below. He lifted his pale face and met her eyes.

"You have to keep her safe. She's the key...she's special. Promise me you'll keep her safe. He doesn't know who she is, you have to ke...ke...ke..." His body shuddered.

"Keep her safe. Got it," Winter said.

"He's not alone. Others."

Dr. Streffield called up the school security protocols on his tablet. He punched in his override code and navigated to the fire safety systems. A single button glowed red near the bottom. EMERGENCY SOUND ALL.

"God forgive me," he whispered as he tapped the button.

The fire alarm blared through the building, and he knew every building on campus heard the same. Dr. Streffield slipped into his blazer, straightened the lapels, and left the room.

"Others?" Winter asked.

The man in the silver and black mask stooped to pick up his gun. Davis watched helplessly, his body still not responding. The man cradled the gun in the crook of his arm, stretching his back and popping his neck. Then he looked back down at Davis. His head cocked to one side, eyes glinting in what could have been a smile.

"Well done."

"S...Skotos. Dark magic. They could be anywhere."

Summer urged Ayden through the trapdoor to hide beneath the stage. She descended partially but paused to look back to the sound booth door. The door was cracked, and Peter watched her from within. Summer shook her head again, wishing for another way. But as Peter nodded, urging her to go forward with the plan, Summer knew she had no way out. She gazed into the dark hole and descended…purposefully and self-consciously leaving the trap door wide open, and praying God would forgive her.

"Don't trust anyone."

You have not heard, you have not known.
Even from long ago your ear has not been open,
because I knew that you would deal
very treacherously; and you have been called a
rebel from birth.
For the sake of My name I delay My wrath,
and for My praise I restrain it for you,
in order not to cut you off.
Behold, I have refined you, but not as silver; I have
tested you in the furnace of affliction.
For My own sake, for My own sake, I will act;
for how can My name be profaned?
And My glory I will not give to another.
Isaiah 48:8-11 (NAS)

1

Present Day

The bandage itched like poison ivy. Winter rubbed it with the heel of her hand, with no result. She stared at the white sterile wrap tightly covering where a pellet had struck her, and wondered if it would really hurt anything if she just ripped it off right then.

Winter made herself look away, dragging up a more important matter to try to divert her mind elsewhere. Why had she been summoned back to the FBI field office in Cherithville immediately after the hospital let her leave?

The pellet had passed right through her arm, and the hospital had only kept her a few hours, to clean the wound, pump her full of fluids, and kick-start an antibiotic regimen. She was anxious to go home, but the summons put an end to that hope. At the very least, she wanted to call her dad and tell him everything, but the hospital had taken all her things, and the FBI had confiscated them from the hospital…so she was without her phone. A uniformed Cherithville police officer as an escort kept her from running off to find some random phone to use elsewhere.

Maybe the FBI weren't going to let her leave this time. Maybe they were going to make her disappear. She quirked a half grin at the idea, at the irony of how many times she had wanted to run away and disappear, but now that it might happen she didn't want it at all.

The police escort had dropped her off in front of the apartment buildings and drove away, and now Winter stood at the bottom of the stairs, staring up, wondering if there might still be a way out. As she examined the minuscule security camera, tucked away in the corner and almost invisible to anyone who didn't know what this apartment really was, Winter knew if she turned and bolted it wouldn't take long before she found herself back at this place minus a great deal of dignity. She sighed, climbed the stairs, heavy boots thumping each step, and knocked on the door with a meek two knocks. It was immediately answered by a blond man with a firm jaw and a goatee.

"Hello, Winter," the man said. "Come in."

Winter stepped in and scanned the room. Agent Erickson sat in a dining chair pulled away from the table into the living room. On the couch waited Kaci, wavy brown hair pulled to one side of her petite face. Her parents, Chris and Beverly, sat with her. Beverly looked like an older version of Kaci, though Winter knew she was really Kaci's aunt. They smiled at Winter, but Winter only managed to tighten her mouth in return.

Across the room in another dining chair was Ayden, arms crossed, and face redder than her spiked hair. Her bandaged leg stuck out straight and she gazed at her exposed toes.

Agent Erickson stood. "Winter, this is my newly assigned partner, Agent William Golbeck."

The blond man grabbed her hand and shook it, then placed his other hand on her back to direct her to an empty chair beside Ayden.

She spun on him, eyes flashing. "Are you an agent or a kindergarten teacher? I'm not going to get lost finding the chair."

Agent Golbeck smirked and crossed back to his post by the door, eyes on her until she sat.

Erickson shook his head and returned to his seat. "Winter, Ayden…you probably don't know what we're doing here, so let me start by explaining that this is a briefing. The Williamses have frequent briefings with us, sometimes here, sometimes at their home, or sometimes at the field office we have in Grady. This is our time to discuss things that have happened, things that are about to happen, and how you fit into the plan."

Winter bit her lip. "Okay, sure. But why is Ayden here?"

Ayden jerked her head up. "Yeah. Why am I here? You're holding me against my will. I want a lawyer."

Erickson held his hand up and then rubbed it through his dark brown hair. "It seems we need to get serious real quick. Just take it easy, Ayden, I'll explain everything. After I explain, I'll make sure your options are clear, and you can make your own decision."

He looked at Kaci then back to Ayden. "The man who tried to kill you two days ago is called Xaphan. His real name is Robert Olsen. He's a serial killer that identifies himself as a Satanic priest, and we've been after him for almost fifteen years now. For reasons we don't fully understand, a little over eleven years ago, he attempted to kill Kaci while she was only in first grade. She is the only survivor of the Mordensfield Massacre, where her entire class was shot in cold blood, and hiding beneath the body of her teacher was the only thing that saved her life. He has been maneuvering to find and kill her ever since. Kaci has been with us in protective custody since that time, until we can capture him and those with him." He leaned forward and stared directly at Ayden. "This man tried to kill you yesterday, because he thinks you are her."

Ayden shrugged. "So it's over with, right? That man is dead. I was there." She glanced at Winter, a look that held a tinge of fear.

Winter shook her head. "That wasn't Xaphan. Xaphan is still out there, and he doesn't know anything different. As far as he's concerned, you're the Sandy he's been looking for."

"So?"

Erickson took a deep breath. "You are his target. There's nothing you can do about it. You can't reason with him, because he won't take the chance of you lying. Anything we do to put him off of you would only seem like clever misdirection. Even if we do manage to convince him of the truth—which we won't because our priority is to protect everyone—he still won't allow you to live simply because you've seen and heard too much about him. Like it or not, you're in this for good. And just like Kaci, we now have to protect you until he can be captured or killed."

"You...you mean I can't go home? That's kidnapping!"

"It's called protective custody," said Erickson. "You've seen him. You've spoken with him. And he failed to kill you. So he'll be after you now more than ever."

Ayden pointed to Kaci. "Why don't you just give her to him?"

"Ayden!" Winter said.

Ayden folded her arms and sat back with a snort.

Silence fell on the room like wool. Agent Golbeck stepped closer to the window and peeked out.

"So what do we do now?" asked Kaci, cheeks red and obviously avoiding eye contact with Ayden.

"We have a couple options," said Erickson. "One...we could pull everyone in this room and relocate you."

"You can't do that!" said Ayden.

"Yes we can," said Erickson. "Everyone here is over eighteen. We don't have to involve anyone's guardians at all. You simply disappear, and start over somewhere else. New name. New identity. New life. And a dedicated case handler nearby at all times. The Williamses are no strangers to the process."

Ayden put her head in her hands and started crying.

Winter put a hand on her shoulder and scowled at Erickson. "You said options."

He nodded. "The second option is everyone stays here. No one relocates. We put certain safeguards in place, and we use Xaphan's false assumptions against him to try and draw him out. Maybe we can actually end this."

"Be specific," said Chris.

"Priority one right now is Kaci," said Erickson. "We will place her and Winter in an apartment complex a short distance from here, that we can monitor constantly and respond to quickly. We can't risk bringing them to this complex because we suspect Xaphan knows our location. We wouldn't want to do anything to tip him off."

"What about school?" asked Kaci. "It's my senior year. I want to finish."

Erickson nodded. "We'll have an agent shadowing you at all times, just like we have the past three years. Our network isn't changing. But Xaphan's people were able to penetrate too far into Tishbe dorms last year and we want you off campus."

"What did you mean use Xaphan's false assumptions against him?" Winter asked.

"Xaphan thinks Ayden is Sandy," Erickson said. "We do nothing to tell him otherwise. Ayden goes back to school, checks into the dorm, except this time she'll have an undercover agent as a roommate. Ayden is shadowed everywhere she goes. We lay out the grid wider than we have in the past and hope that Xaphan comes looking for her. When he does, we'll be ready."

Winter frowned. "You mean use her as bait?"

"What?" said Ayden. "Are you crazy?"

"Like it or not," said Erickson, "you are the target. Be the target that stops this monster, or leave everything behind to start a new life in protection. But we can't unmake you the target. You're it. The Bureau is all in to stop him. We've got more resources allocated now than we've ever had before. You'll be safe. I promise."

Ayden pursed her lips and peered at the floor.

Erickson turned to Winter. "Your job is the most complicated, and we need you ready to protect Kaci, especially at night. That's why you'll be in the apartment with her instead of in the dorm with Ayden. For some reason, you are able to be there for Kaci when our agents can't get there in time. I'm not ready to admit anything supernatural yet, but there's something going on and we have to use it.

"On the other hand, we also need you to sell the red herring. The only people who know Kaci is the real Sandy are in this room…even the other agents involved in protecting Kaci have never been told why, and may not even realize they're doing it. Most of the agents just think they're watching Winter and her closest friends, and it needs to stay this way. Winter, you were reckless last year. You broadcasted everywhere what you were doing, and you had no clue that Xaphan was watching you like a hawk. Thank God you never found out the truth.

"Everyone that was helping you knows you found Ayden and believes she's Sandy, just like Xaphan, and you need to let them believe this. That means spending time visibly with Ayden so everyone thinks you're trying to protect her, not Kaci."

"I can't do that," said Winter. "Peter, Davis, and Summer are our friends. They can help us."

"Are you sure? Are you willing to risk their lives giving information that might jeopardize Kaci and Ayden? If we're going to draw out Xaphan, everything needs to point to Ayden; which means we'll be pulling some resources from Kaci and putting them to protect Ayden. Kaci will be more vulnerable than ever, and we can't risk even a whisper of her true identity. No one outside this room can know the truth. Understood? Because if they do, both Kaci and Ayden could die."

Winter shook her head. "We can trust them."

"It doesn't matter," said Erickson. "It's not a matter of trust. It's a matter of safely manipulating the situation so Xaphan can finally be trapped. We've never had an opportunity like this before."

Beverly stiffened. "If you're pulling resources from Kaci, how is she protected?"

"Like I said, Winter will be with her at night and an undercover agent with Ayden at night. During the day the assignments will be reversed. Winter will shadow Ayden while the undercover agent shadows Kaci. Everyone will be under the eyes of our network, but more emphasis will be given to Ayden since she is in the most danger.

"I know there are risks." Erickson surveyed everyone in the room. "That's why you have two options. You can willingly choose to participate in this plan or you can choose to be relocated and placed into protection…even you, Winter."

Erickson watched Kaci, as if waiting for her to speak for everyone.

"I'm tired of running," said Kaci. "Winter can stop this. I'm with her. If she stays I stay."

"I'm staying," said Winter, smiling at Kaci.

Chris looked at Beverly and she nodded. "Okay," said Chris. "We'll support Kaci in whatever she chooses. She's tired of running and so are we."

Erickson nodded and turned to Ayden.

"No," she said.

"Do you not understand…"

"I understand perfectly," said Ayden. "You want me to be bait, and you're threatening to kidnap me if I don't agree. Well, the answer is no. I won't do either." She stood.

"Ayden, it's no use," said Winter.

"Leave me alone!" She rushed toward the door, but Agent Golbeck blocked her way. "Let me out."

Golbeck frowned at her.

"We can't do that, Ayden," said Agent Erickson.

Winter stood. "Ayden, wait."

Ayden spun with her arms crossed, looming at least two inches taller than Winter.

Winter stepped toward her, trying not to flinch beneath what she recognized as a good representation of the same glare she used herself.

"Remember how it felt?" Winter said. "Remember how scared you were and how hopeless you felt? Kaci has been feeling that her entire life. This monster murdered her entire first-grade class in front of her. Her teacher died to protect her that day. Xaphan almost killed Kaci last year because of me, and if he'd known then who she was he would have won already. This is the reality of her life. And yesterday, without the help of the FBI, I was there for you. I helped you after you were shot. I found you in the forest. I kept you safe. Now, we're not alone because there's help. And I will still be there for both you and Kaci." Her voice firmed and filled with anger. "Don't let this monster win. Because if you walk out that door, he might be waiting at the bottom of the stairs. He might be waiting in your car. He might be waiting at your home. You will never get away from him. Even if you run, it's you he'll be looking for…not me or Kaci. You are his target, and he will do everything possible to kill you. However scared and hopeless you felt yesterday, it will never go away for the rest of your life unless you choose to take a stand now. You're not the type to run away from a fight, so don't start now. And nobody wants to leave, not me, not Kaci, not you. If you don't help, we'll all be taken away. That choice is yours." Winter folded her arms and glared back at Ayden.

Ayden tightened her eyes and stuck out her jaw. The seconds dragged by as Ayden tapped her foot. Finally she tore her eyes away from Winter and stomped back to her chair.

Erickson crossed to the dining room table and opened a lockbox. He pulled out two cellphones and plugged them into a laptop. After a few taps he looked across the room to them.

"Sorry we had to take your phones, but if Xaphan managed to tap into their GPS signatures, he'd have been able to find you in the hospital. We've reprogrammed them with new GPS IDs and encoded them to our network…as well as a few other goodies. Don't worry, I'm not erasing any of your contacts or photos. But everything that goes through your phone will be tracked from here on out and backed up to our secure server, so keep that in mind."

"What about them?" asked Ayden, nodding her head to Kaci.

Chris laughed and adjusted his glasses. "The FBI souped-up our phones a long time ago. We get new ones every year."

"Sorry about the battery life, though." Erickson came back with the phones and two small silver bracelets. "Without the ability to disable your location services and with the constant data uploading, it tends to put an extra drain on the battery." He handed a bracelet each to Winter and Ayden, a silver circlet, about a quarter inch wide and solid. It would have been more at home on Summer's wrist than Winter's. "You'll also need these. After the Olamel incident, we decided we needed Kaci to have a tracking device on her at all times. Hers is the tulip pendant. Yours can be whatever you like. But until you decide or provide us with something to modify, you'll wear these."

Erickson returned to his seat. "It's important that we keep up appearances for everyone. They don't know about Kaci, so we don't want to provide them with any unnecessary clues. So Kaci will go home as usual and will spend the summer under the watch-care of the field office in Grady. Ayden will also go home as if the FBI do not suspect Xaphan will be after her. There will be agents there to watch her, even though we're not even confident he knows where she's from. The same goes for Winter. Xaphan's entrenched here in Cherithville, so the most likely scenario is that he will recognize the normalcy of our actions and make his own preparations for everyone's return next fall. Agent Golbeck and I will remain here to monitor the progress of our own preparations and to listen for any movement from Xaphan in case we're wrong. We'll also be constantly monitoring everyone from here and be in daily contact with the agents assigned to you. Are there any questions?"

"Can I go now?" asked Ayden as she stood.

Erickson crossed over to her and grabbed the hand holding her bracelet. "You'll need to put this on." He wrapped it around her wrist. "Don't worry. Everything's under control."

Ayden huffed and stomped back to the door. This time Agent Golbeck let her pass.

Chris, Beverly, and Kaci stood. Chris walked over to Agent Erickson and extended his hand. "Thank you, as always," he said as they shook. "I'm sorry about Agent Gains. He was a good man."

Erickson nodded. "Yes he was. And he loved your family. I'll do all that I can to make sure you stay safe like he wanted."

As Kaci and her parents left, Winter moved to follow. Agent Golbeck held a hand out to her and shook his head.

"Winter, if you could stay a moment longer," Erickson said from behind her.

She turned back. "Why? What's wrong?"

Agent Golbeck closed the door, sealing her alone with the two agents.

"There's nothing wrong. But if we're going to accomplish our plan, your role is very important. It's also outside of civilian scope."

"So?"

"Last year you were limited. This year we want to free you to know and do what is necessary to protect Kaci and Ayden. I've been authorized to deputize you as a special officer, code name Butterfly, for this task force, with a Top Secret security clearance level so you will have access to the records and information you need. We've already done the background checks on both you and your father."

Winter blinked at him. "Are you serious? I don't know anything about that."

"You know enough. But we need to require more of you."

"Like what?" Winter's stomach lurched into her lungs.

Agent Erickson led her to the table, opened a file folder and pulled out some official-looking documents. "You'll be required this summer to become firearms and baton qualified. You'll also go through weapons retention, compliance and take-down techniques, defensive tactics, basic hand-to-hand combat, CPR and first aid, and scene security, with victim recovery and evidence preservation."

Winter's jaw dropped.

"These training courses are a conditional requirement of your deputation and you will be required to complete them before the fall term begins. An agent has already been assigned to you in Trenton Hills to mentor you through the process. Of course all of this, your deputation, your training, and your involvement is classified at the Top Secret level and you're not to mention a word of it to anyone without clearance from me. I'll be acting as your direct supervisor."

"Wait," Winter said. "Not even my dad? Or Kaci?"

"No. Kaci doesn't need to know about your training. You'll use the cover of a summer job with your dad. You'll have some salary to go with it, so it's not far from the truth."

Winter shook her head. "I'm not sure I want to do this."

"You don't have a choice. You agreed to the task and this is your role. If you think we're going to let you face a monster like Xaphan without being properly prepared next time, then think again. Are you in or not? I thought you wanted to catch him."

"I do, it's just…"

"Just what? You thought this would be easy?" Erickson shook his head. "There's a reason we haven't been able to stop him. You've come closer than anybody, which is why we want your help. With the proper tools and training, maybe the next time you face him you can accomplish what we can't seem to do."

Winter crossed her arms and stared at the document on the table.

Erickson held a pen out to her. "All you have to do is sign."

Winter tapped her foot and twisted her mouth. Then she reached out, snatched the pen, and scratched her name onto the form.

"Welcome to the war," said Erickson.

2

Winter turned her gleaming black BMW into the Hazelnut Woods apartment complex. She checked her rear-view mirror to make sure her dad didn't miss the turn. After only a moment, his Dodge Dakota turned in, trailer in tow. Winter looked back to the apartments, searching for building B and apartment 202. It was easy to find. A small rental trailer sat backed up to the curb, attached to Chris's small truck. Kaci and her parents were pulling boxes and furniture out. Kaci, wearing a red short-sleeve turtleneck, noticed her and waved, then hefted the box again in her arms and turned toward the apartment. Peter Strong jogged down the apartment stairs, empty-handed. He glanced once at her car, grinned, and then took the box from Kaci.

Winter found an empty parking spot an apartment away and jumped out to direct her dad to the empty space beside Kaci's rental trailer. As Steve began backing the trailer into position, Kaci ran up to her and wrapped her arms around her.

"How was your summer?" Kaci asked.

"Short. Wasn't expecting to have to move in the middle of July."

Kaci grinned. "I know. I think they were getting anxious. At least we'll have plenty of time to settle in."

Peter waved at them and grabbed another box to take upstairs.

"What's he doing here?" Winter asked. "He doesn't know, does he?"

"Of course not. But we've been talking the past couple of months. When I told him we were moving into an apartment, he insisted on coming to help."

"Talking?"

Kaci brushed a strand of wavy brown hair behind her ear and gazed at the ground.

"So, does this mean…?" asked Winter.

"Not officially," said Kaci. "But maybe. We'll see."

Winter chuckled. "Well, it's about time."

A loud metallic squeak made them both turn.

Steve was lifting the latch on the trailer doors and opening them wide. "It's not going to unload itself," he said.

"How much more of your stuff is left?" Winter asked Kaci.

"About half the trailer. Mostly just boxes now. If you two come help us finish, then we can all work on yours together."

"Dad?" asked Winter.

Steve shrugged. "I was about to suggest the same thing."

Before Winter could grab a box from Kaci's trailer, Beverly gave Winter a big hug. When Beverly released her, Winter found herself wrapped up by Peter. She couldn't help noticing from the smell that his hair had been freshly shampooed. His short goatee tickled the side of her face as he leaned over slightly…he was about as tall as Ryan.

Winter peered at Kaci, who seemed to be purposefully looking the other direction. Winter almost pushed Peter away to go talk to her, but Kaci was already hauling another box back to the building. Winter took a deep breath and let it go…she didn't really know what to say anyway. It was nothing.

Chris stood hunched over in the trailer, bringing stuff to the opening for everyone to grab. Winter took the nearest box and followed Kaci up the iron stairs to the open door of apartment 202. They entered into the living room, piled with random boxes, some balanced on a couch. The room extended to the right, where sunlight glistened through the sliding glass door of a small balcony overlooking the parking lot. A little in and to the left the dining room and kitchen waited, with a small square folding table leaning against the wall and counters covered in more boxes.

"That box goes in my bedroom," said Kaci.

Straight ahead, a short hall led to three doors. At the head of the hall was a bathroom. To the left and right were identical bedrooms. Kaci led her to the bedroom on the left, already full of boxes and the ingredients for a bed leaning against the wall.

Winter set the box down and then walked across the hall to check out her new room. Compared to Kaci's room, this room appeared naked, with nothing more than soft tan carpet underneath and an accordion-door closet to the right. A bare window on the back wall looked out over a parking lot like the sliding doors.

"Do you like it?" asked Kaci.

"It's nice," Winter said. "Much better than a dorm room."

"I know."

"This was such a great idea." Winter grinned.

"It was your idea, Winter?" asked Steve as he dropped a box into Kaci's room.

Winter shrugged. "Um, I suppose."

"Well, I'm proud of both of you," he said. "Getting jobs and a place of your own is a big step." He patted Winter and Kaci on the shoulders and went back outside.

"Come on," said Kaci as she turned to follow.

"Just one second," Winter said. "I need to use the restroom."

Kaci nodded and left Winter momentarily alone in the apartment. Winter hurried through the bathroom door and locked it behind her.

She stood in front of the mirror and took a deep breath, staring at a face leaner than it had been in years, but still decorated with a nose stud, eyebrow ring, and five studs in her ears. Dark patches underlining her sky-blue eyes had nothing to do with make-up. If she looked different to anyone else, no one had said anything. Maybe they were too busy counting her piercings.

She put a hand on her left shoulder and rotated her arm, wincing from the stiffness. Then she tugged at the collar of her shirt to inspect a dark purple and green bruise, fading already but still too noticeable to leave uncovered. It had only been a few days since her qualifying exam with the FBI made her an officially deputized special officer, and her body still wore the evidence of it. As bad as Agent Erickson had made the training sound, the reality was that he didn't tell her the half of it.

Winter reached down to the inside of her left ankle and pulled up the hem of her baggy pants. She checked the ankle holster holding her newly issued Ruger LCP, making sure it didn't need to be tightened. At only about five inches long and weighing less than half a pound, Winter often forgot she had it…until she kicked it with her other foot or the holster started itching again. Like it was doing now. And they found her a gun that was purple and black, as if it made a difference. Winter rolled her eyes every time she thought about it.

She shoved her fingers as far as she could beneath the holster and tried to relieve the itch, the real reason she had ducked into the bathroom, but it didn't do much good. So she checked the tightness of the holster again, tugged her pants back over the gun, and flushed the toilet in case someone was just outside.

The sun sat no more than a finger's width over the horizon by the time they finished unloading Winter's trailer. It was difficult to move around the apartment with all the boxes everywhere, but Steve and Chris managed to reorganize the kitchen area and set up the small table for pizzas. Steve, Chris, and Beverly sat on the couch and ate while Winter, Kaci, and Peter went onto the balcony, despite the heat.

"Where are you staying this year?" Winter asked Peter.

"Same as last year…in Edwards. Davis is going to room with me this year."

"Really? I didn't know that," said Winter.

Peter shrugged. "Yeah. We figured since we hung out helping you so much last year, it would save time if we were in the same place." Peter flicked his eyes to Kaci. "Um, sorry."

"No, it's okay," said Kaci. She smiled. "You don't have to tip-toe around me so much. I'm doing much better. You should know that."

Peter's face reddened and he peered out at the parking lot.

Kaci turned to Winter. "How's Summer doing?"

"Fine, I guess. When I call her, she's usually pretty short. Last spring really freaked her out. But she's coming back to school, though I think she's giving up the RA thing."

"Is she going to be in Divine this year?"

Winter shook her head. "Boon, I think. And I'm pretty sure her parents sprung for a private room, too."

"Must be nice," said Peter.

"Hey, lay off her," said Winter. "It's true she's not hurting for anything, but that's not her fault. Besides, we don't have to worry about another person overhearing anything we talk about. It can all be private. The way things are going, I'd be suspicious of any new roommate that came onto the scene."

Kaci frowned. "We should probably be suspicious of everyone."

"Everyone keeps telling me that…"

"To change the subject to something a little more cheerful," Peter said with a grimace, "when everyone gets back into town, we need to have some kind of party."

Kaci laughed. "A real party, Peter?"

Peter shrugged. "It can be whatever kind of party you like. You two plan it."

The glass door slid open behind them and Steve stuck out his head. "Winter? I need to be going. It'll already be well after midnight before I get home."

Winter hopped up. "Sure. I'll be right there."

As Steve went back inside, Kaci stood beside her. "My parents will probably want to leave soon too." She sighed.

"I'll tell you what," Peter said as he rose to stand with them. "While you two are saying your goodbyes, I'll get your beds set up." He smiled at them and led the way inside.

The goodbyes didn't take long, as it turned out. Steve had always been awkward with those kinds of emotional moments, and he was in too much of a hurry to pretend otherwise. After a quick hug and a kiss on the cheek, he once again told her to be careful and then left without looking back.

Chris and Beverly hugged them both, Beverly wiping her eyes dry, but neither of them made any real effort to linger. Despite their concerned frowns and obvious hesitation to leave, they weren't long behind Steve.

Back inside, Peter emerged from Winter's room, clapping his hands. "That was easy enough."

"Are you done already?" asked Kaci.

He shrugged. "Not much to it really. I hope I put them in the right places. If not, I'll help you move them before I go."

Kaci bit her lower lip. "You're not going already, are you?"

"Well, it's getting dark. I should probably be leaving too. It's an hour and a half to home."

"You could crash here, tonight," said Kaci. "You could take the couch. That way you can help us unpack some."

Peter ran a hand through his brown hair and grinned. "Yeah, maybe." He nodded. "Okay, sure. I'll just call my folks and let them know." He fished out his cellphone and started walking toward the balcony.

Kaci grinned after him, and when he slid the door closed, Winter asked, "Has he even asked you out yet?"

"No. We're just sort of…clicking, you know? At least it feels that way. You know, he didn't just call me. He came over twice. We stayed up late into the night watching movies. I've never felt this way before."

"I'm happy for you. It's about time you had something good going. Are you sure it's a good idea for him to stay? I mean..."

"Winter! It's not like that." Kaci looked away, face bright red.

Winter laughed. "Okay, sorry. Has he even kissed you yet?"

A smirk crossed Kaci's face. "No comment." She turned and hurried into her room.

Winter shook her head and grabbed another piece of pizza from the table.

She awoke that night with a jerk. A muffled voice floated down the hall from the living room, the same voice that permeated her dreams from the mouth of a shadowy figure, mocking her, always at the corner of her eye, but yet familiar. The tones dredged up long-dead feelings from her past.

A moment of breathing deeply and sitting up in her bed brought enough quiet to hear the muffled voice was real. She snatched up her cell phone with one hand and her gun with the other, using her phone as a flashlight to navigate the still-mostly-packed boxes in her room. When she leaned her ear against the door, she couldn't hear the voice any more clearly, so she pressed gently against the door to ease the pressure from the latch and slowly twisted the knob.

The door made almost no sound as she cracked it open. She could just see Peter pacing from the kitchen to the living room, talking in hushed tones into his cellphone.

"No, I told you," he said. "Not yet. Not here...Because she's not ready. Give me more time...Yes, I can handle it. I told you I could...Another month, maybe..."

Winter frowned and set the gun down on the nearest box, then eased into the hall and padded closer. "What are you doing?"

Peter snapped his phone shut. "Nothing. Just talking to my cousin."

"At two in the morning?"

"He works the night shift. I'm sorry I woke you."

Winter shook her head. "No, it's okay. I wasn't sleeping well anyway. New place and all that."

"I understand." Peter walked back to the couch and sat, placing his head in his hands.

Winter narrowed her eyes at his shadowy form. "Listen. I don't know what's really going on, but there's no need to keep it secret."

"It's nothing," he said.

"Didn't sound like nothing. You said 'she.' Who were you talking about? Me or Kaci?"

"It's not what you think."

Winter crossed her arms. "Then what is it?"

Peter didn't respond.

"After all we've been through together, this is what I get from you? Secrets?"

"I'm sorry, okay? It's nothing to do with you or Kaci. It's personal. And I'm not ready to talk about it."

Winter took a deep breath to force her frustration away. "Sure. I get it. I know all about the personal stuff. But if you hurt Kaci…"

"I won't. It's nothing like that." Peter turned on the couch and lay down. "I promise. When it's time, I'll let you know everything."

Winter backed toward her room, watching the dark shadow on the couch where she knew he was probably watching her. "Fine. I'm going back to bed. But I won't forget this, Peter. Remember that."

His silence was answer enough. Winter retreated to her room and lay awake for a long time thinking about that brief snippet she heard of his phone conversation. Every time it replayed in her mind, perfectly repeated in that unpredictable photographic memory she sometimes had, it was immediately followed by the voice of Agent Gains, imploring her not to trust anyone. But Peter? Could he really be keeping something that serious from her? What was going on?

Exhaustion eventually dragged her back to sleep…and back to dreams of that shadowy figure, now taunting her as she chased Peter, Summer, Davis, and for some reason Dr. Streffield through a maze of mirrors.

3

Four Years Ago

Winter slouched in the armchair by the wall and gazed at the floor of her dad's living room. Her backpack waited next to her booted feet and her hands clung together in her lap. She let a curtain of her jet-black hair swing forward into her face and then brushed the strands aside again.

A squeal outside made her look to the window. The school bus had arrived. Winter took a deep breath and watched it, knowing she should probably get up, but just not rousing the will-power to do so. Ten seconds passed and the driver blew the horn. Winter bit her lip, hoping her dad didn't hear it. Another ten seconds and the bus drove away.

Winter stood and crossed the room to the kitchen where her dad sat at the table drinking coffee and looking over the newspaper.

"Dad, I missed the bus. Will you take me to school?"

Steve peered up and firmed his lips. His eyes searched her face, but Winter was not too concerned. She had become good at letting everything readable drain from her face, not wanting anyone to know about the hell raging in her heart.

Steve checked his watch and nodded. "I'll be there in a minute."

Winter slowly turned and shuffled back to her chair.

Ten minutes later found Winter staring out of the window of her dad's truck as he shuttled her to Trenton Hills High School. He didn't speak to her, and that was fine with Winter. The mutual silence between them had long ceased to be awkward. Winter shouldered her backpack when he dropped her off and trudged the short sidewalk to the main entrance. A few students stood around talking, but when they saw Winter they studied her in silence. Winter kept her eyes on the sidewalk and ignored their questioning stares, but she could still feel them...the weight of their accusations, their hatred, their blame...like hammers on her back.

The hall was not much better. Her presence carved a path to homeroom, like the prow of a boat, as people stood aside to watch her, to whisper, to shake their heads. Winter summoned more numbness to protect her heart...what was left of it.

In homeroom, Winter found a vacant seat near the back corner. She slouched into it, set her backpack on the floor, and laid her head down on top of her folded arms. Still, the growing silence in the room told her everyone watched, unspoken questions hurled in her direction.

Winter heard a shuffle in the desk in front of her. She peeked up as Claire leaned toward her.

"Hey," Claire said. Claire scanned the room, and as she did everyone looked away and went back to their own conversations.

Winter lifted her head enough to set her chin on her arms. "Hey."

Claire found Winter's hand and squeezed. Then she turned around as the teacher called the class to attention.

After homeroom, Claire walked silently at her side to the lockers. Since they had been sitting next to each other in homeroom, they had been assigned adjoining lockers. Winter more than suspected Claire did that on purpose. But as they tested the lock combinations, even though they didn't yet have books to put in the lockers, Claire still didn't speak. She followed Winter to the door of Winter's next class and then proceeded to her own.

When lunch came, Winter found Claire waiting for her at the lunchroom entrance. Claire fell into step with her and followed through the line and to a table, again in silence.

When they sat, Winter frowned at her. "What are you doing?"

Claire shrugged.

Winter stiffened. "Seriously, why are you following me?"

Claire met her gaze, her cheeks reddening and her eyes tearing over.

Winter diverted her eyes and shuffled her food.

The lunchroom filled and the noise swelled. The sweet cafeteria smell mirrored the taste of the soy burger. Winter tried to ignore the people filling up the nearest tables, but knew they wouldn't stop staring. The people at the table just next to her had been staring since they arrived.

Near the end of the lunch period, two girls from the next table stood and plopped into chairs at Winter and Claire's table.

Winter glanced up and then back to her almost empty tray, for once at a loss for what to say to drive them away.

"Everyone wants to know," the first girl said.

"Know what?" Winter asked.

"What happened?"

The simple question shattered the numb casing around her heart. A lump grew in Winter's throat. The question hung in the air as the two girls watched her. Their voices were loud enough to draw the attention of the other nearby tables, and now everyone leaned forward to hear what Winter might say. Seconds ticked by as Winter stared at her cafeteria tray. In her peripheral vision, she saw Claire stiffen.

"What's wrong with you?" said Claire. "Can't you see she doesn't want to talk about it?"

The second girl spoke this time. "But she's the only one that really knows. The whole school wants to know what happened in that car."

Claire stood, her chair sliding back into the next table. "Do you want to know what happened? I'll tell you. They had an accident! And people we loved are dead!"

A tear fell down Winter's cheek.

"But what about prom?" the first girl asked.

"Just leave Winter alone!" Claire shouted. "It wasn't her fault, so stop treating her like it was."

"We…we weren't…"

"And if you can't respect that and you must know, then go read the stupid newspaper. Go ask the principal. Just stop hurting Winter!" Claire turned to the rest of the cafeteria. Everyone had stopped to watch and listen, even the teachers. "It's not important what happened in that car," she shouted to the whole silent room. "It's over. Move on. At least you're capable of doing that. Winter's going to have a hard enough time learning to live with what happened without all of you dragging it in front of her everywhere she goes. It may be all you can think about, but all she wants to do is think about something else. So have a little respect and find something else shiny to look at. Winter is not talking. Got it?"

The two girls fled back to their own table. A hushed form of conversation kicked up again in the cafeteria as everyone leaned together in obvious discussion and speculation of what Claire said. A few teachers nodded as if in approval and Claire sat down again.

Winter rubbed her eyes dry and tried to face Claire. Claire's red face glistened, and she quickly wiped at her cheeks. Winter offered her a forced smile, and Claire just nodded in return.

4

Present Day

Winter trudged toward the kitchen with her hand against her forehead. The summer hadn't been long enough…too much to do, too much to worry about. The FBI checked on them by phone or by meeting away from the apartment at least every other day, and as the preparations for the next school year were made, she had long meetings at the field office. Kaci got away from all of the meetings since they didn't want to risk drawing attention to her. But Winter suspected agents kept closer watch on them in the apartment building than they had originally been told.

Agent Erickson insisted on continuing Winter's training, taking every opportunity to go through all related case files, pointing out the potential leads, and explaining in detail how Xaphan managed to get away every time. The education she could handle, but the photos of Xaphan's murderous trail she could do without.

Now suddenly it was time for classes to begin again. And as usual, the dreams had started.

As Winter staggered into the kitchen, Kaci looked up at her from the table, crunching on cereal, wearing a T-shirt that revealed the old scar across her neck. "Bad night again?"

Winter nodded and plopped down in a chair. "It's the same dream. And I don't know what it means."

"Well, why don't you finally tell me about it?" said Kaci.

"Are you sure? I mean, you spent all last year avoiding this. I kinda got used to keeping it to myself." Winter stood and meandered into the kitchen for her own bowl of cereal.

"Yeah. I'm ready. I mean, it can't be avoided any longer. Last year I had to keep things quiet, not only for my own sake emotionally but because Agent Gains had told me to. But this year...we're in this together completely."

Winter sat back in the chair and took a mouthful of cereal. "It's about Claire."

"The girl you were friends with in high school?"

Winter nodded. "Yeah. The dreams have been about her. They've mostly been the same, but each time something small changes. First I saw her walking through Trenton Hills. Then I saw her walking along the highway I drive to get to Cherithville. Two nights ago I saw her running down Hoole Boulevard. But last night...last night she was just over there." Winter pointed to the glass door of the balcony overlooking the parking lot. "She was sitting on the curb across the street...looking over here."

"How did she look? Did she look mean or angry, or what?"

Winter shrugged. "She looked normal, just like the last time I saw her."

Kaci twisted her mouth in thought. "And how did you feel about it?"

"Happy." Winter smiled. "I mean...if there were any way possible to bring her into my new life with my new friends, I think it would be perfect. She was a good friend, even if she had some wrong ideas about life. She was there for me when I first moved. And even though I was horrible to her right after my mother died, she was still there for me, no questions asked, after my accident. I needed that more than anything at that time. To have Claire here and on our side…I don't know. It would be like my life was finally coming full circle and I could begin to reattach these disjointed chapters of my life. You know?"

Kaci grinned. "Well maybe that's it. Maybe you understand this dream stuff better than you give yourself credit. Maybe God's going to find a way for you to reconcile your past to your present."

"I don't know if I want that to happen, though. It would mean having to face a lot of ugly I left behind."

"We all have to face our ugly one day. You can't grow beautiful until you do."

"Yeah…maybe. Can't I just forget it though?"

"Ugly has a way of getting your attention, like a toddler with no concept of personal space."

Winter laughed. "Or an uncle."

Kaci snorted as she stood to take her bowl to the sink. "There is one other possibility. Maybe a simpler explanation for your dream."

"What's that?"

"Maybe Claire's really coming. Maybe she's quite literally going to become a part of your new life."

Winter let go of her spoon and peered at the table. "Yeah, well…that would never happen."

"Why?"

"It's a long story." Without waiting for Kaci to respond, Winter left her half-eaten bowl on the table and went back to her room to get ready for class.

The queue of vehicles on Hoole Boulevard going into the school crawled forward, and Winter impatiently tapped her fingers on the steering wheel. Students on foot trekking along the sidewalk, slightly hunched beneath weighty backpacks, made quicker progress.

Winter eyed her dash clock and huffed. "I thought being only a couple of miles away from campus wouldn't be so bad."

"We should probably leave earlier tomorrow," said Kaci.

"Do you think it would be quicker to circle around to the back of campus?"

Kaci shrugged, fingering the scarf around her neck. "Maybe. We'll try it one day and see. Does this look all right?"

"It looks fine. Much better than wearing a turtle-neck in the heat. Besides, you know how most of them are…they'll be too busy staring at me to notice your scarf. You look great. Relax."

Kaci bit her bottom lip and nodded.

With a quick check of her parking decal at the gate, and an admonition from the guard to get it updated before the end of the week, they made it through. The pace of traffic quickened, though most everyone was careful not to speed, with vehicles scattering into parking lots and down roads leading deeper into campus. Winter found a vacant parking spot behind the Union, pulled in, and gave Kaci a smile.

"Are you ready?" Winter asked.

Kaci took a deep breath and nodded. "Let's go."

The two girls walked next to each other along the service road between the Union and the Arts Plaza. As they rounded the Union and entered the Meadow, Ayden and a young woman with short blond hair descended the steps as if at random, though Winter suspected they had been watching for them from a nearby window.

"That must be Ayden's handler, Nadeen," Kaci whispered.

Nadeen flicked her brown eyes at them. She passed easily enough for a college student, though Winter knew she couldn't be nearly as young as she appeared. Dark eyebrows to match her brown eyes were the only clues suggesting she wasn't really blond. Nadeen let her blue backpack slide off her shoulder, and paused a moment to check something on the inside.

"Okay," said Winter. "Remember, just keep walking and don't make direct contact."

Kaci nodded and turned for her first class. Nadeen casually hunched up the backpack and followed on the sidewalk several feet behind, even allowing for a couple of other students to walk between them. No one would have suspected the whole thing had been planned.

Ayden never looked at Winter, either. Winter took large steps to get within a comfortable distance behind her. They took a sidewalk to cross diagonally through the Meadow, past the Ancient, and toward the opposite corner from the Union. Winter followed Ayden to the foot of the science building, slowing to watch her enter. Then she turned and jogged to her Ethics of Psychology class in the neighboring building.

At the end of the hour and a half of tedious syllabus discussion and introductory material, Winter rushed out of class expecting to find Ayden waiting for her at the top of the science building steps, but Ayden was already rushing down the sidewalk to the adjoining building for her health class. Winter sprinted to catch up, hoping anyone paying attention would just think she was late for her next class. Ayden reached the building long before Winter could catch her. Winter came to an abrupt halt, to the protests of the students standing just around her. She clenched her teeth and turned to cross the Meadow to the religion department for her next two classes.

Entering the religion department brought an unexpected wave of emotions through Winter. Dr. Cook's last moments replayed in her mind, as he waved to her and placed his things into the trunk of his car. She remembered the man in the silver and black mask as the gun pivoted to Dr. Cook…

Winter looked to the floor and sped up as she passed by the office, not daring to peer inside and risk seeing the new dean of the department. As she turned the corner into the hall, she didn't slow down until she arrived at the room for her Intermediate Greek class. She took a seat in the back of the mostly filled room, a room she had shared previously with Dr. Cook, and quietly took out her notebook. No one else in the room spoke either, most keeping their eyes on their desks or else busying themselves by thumbing through other syllabi they had already received from other classes. No one looked up. No one spoke. Everyone just sat there waiting, and Winter suspected everyone had similar emotions running through them as she.

An older man with long gray hair walked slowly in, scanning the students in the room and frowning as he sensed the mood. He set his briefcase onto the table at the front of the room, and tugged at his suit coat. After a quick introduction, he passed out his syllabus.

With Greek out of the way a little early, Winter waited at the foot of the religion department for Ayden. They were supposed to rendezvous in that nonchalant way here, and then meet with Kaci and Nadeen at the Union to swap back for lunch. Ayden's building sat opposite the religion building, and Winter watched it carefully, but Ayden never came out. Winter gave her an extra ten minutes past the expected time for classes to let out, and then took off to find her, careful not to run or stomp her away across the Meadow. She climbed the stairs to the second floor where Ayden's class was supposed to be, but found the entire floor already deserted. Just to be sure, she stuck her head into the room. The teacher still sat behind a desk, looking over some papers.

"Um, excuse me," Winter said. The teacher looked up. "I'm looking for a student that was in your class just now."

The lady smiled. "I'm sorry. I let the class out ten minutes early today."

Winter bit her lip. "Okay. Thank you." Ten minutes early.

Winter must have just missed her, but now Ayden had been wandering on campus for nearly twenty minutes without escort. What was the protocol if they missed a planned connection? Winter couldn't remember, but she was certain it wasn't to just disappear. She ran back downstairs and rushed toward the Union, trying not to draw too much attention to her haste and hoping Ayden would have had enough sense to at least go there. And if Ayden wasn't to be found, at least Nadeen would be. Winter could give the code and have this place swarming with agents within just a few minutes. That would teach Ayden to run away.

She entered the crowded building, full of the first chaotic day of students trying to get their lunch from workers who had forgotten what it was like to serve so many people at once. Winter scanned the recently remodeled interior—the faces waiting in line, sitting at tables, and sitting on couches—until she finally spotted Ayden's red spiky hair at a corner arm-chair near the windows. Winter crossed her arms and stomped over.

"What's wrong with you?"

Ayden pursed her lips and looked up.

Winter glanced around at the students nearest and lowered her voice. "Do you want to get yourself killed? Do you realize how dangerous it is for you to wander off like that? You're supposed to stick to the plan. You're supposed to wait for me. I don't care if you don't like this, I certainly don't, but at the very least you should have enough concern for your own safety to follow directions."

Ayden's face flushed crimson and she turned to stare at the floor, slumping a little further into her chair.

"Well? Don't you have anything to say? Is this all a game to you? Do you realize how many people died because of this monster looking for you? I've seen the pictures!"

"Ahem…"

Winter spun at the interruption, heart thumping, and realized she had nearly shouted those last words. Nadeen stood with her arms crossed and her eyes glaring. Kaci waited several feet away, face pale and eyes wide.

Nadeen's lips parted and she whispered through clenched teeth.

"If anyone has put us all in danger it's you and your loud mouth. Go away. I'll take it from here."

Winter huffed and went to Kaci.

After lunch, the morning separation routine was repeated at the foot of the steps, with Kaci and Ayden breaking away for their own classes, and Nadeen and Winter casually following behind. Ayden walked slower this time, almost dragging her feet, all the way to the religion department, where she was taking a Biblical history elective. Nadeen had obviously finished giving her the thorough tongue thrashing Winter had begun. They separated in the hall and Winter went to her Hermeneutics class.

After class, Winter found Ayden waiting in the lobby properly this time. Ayden scowled at her once, with narrow eyes full of rage, and started walking back toward the Union without waiting. Kaci and Nadeen were already there, standing apart from each other, and looking like they had absolutely nothing to do with the other and every bit as if they were waiting for someone else in particular. As Ayden and Winter approached, the switch was made, and Kaci and Winter walked back to the parking lot.

When Winter sank into the leather seat of her black BMW, she let her shoulders sag and leaned her head against the wheel.

Kaci closed her door. "Was it that bad?"

"Worst first day of school ever," Winter mumbled.

5

As Winter and Kaci walked toward the front of the Union the next day to make the escort exchange, Ayden leaned against a tree opposite the Union steps, arms crossed and staring at the ground. Nadeen waited at the foot of the steps, casting a dangerous glare toward the middle of the Meadow.

"What's going on?" Winter asked Kaci.

Kaci shrugged. "I don't know. I suppose we just stick to the routine."

Without looking at Nadeen, Kaci left Winter's side and started walking across the Meadow. Nadeen waited a few seconds, stole a venomous glance at Ayden, and then followed.

Winter slowed, waiting for Ayden to take the lead. But as Winter neared, Ayden fell into step beside her.

"Are you okay?" Winter asked.

Ayden didn't speak as they angled toward the middle of the Meadow and the Ancient. Today their destinations would be slightly different. It was back to the psychology building for a sociology class for Winter, but first they had to swing by the English building for

Ayden.

As they neared the English building, Ayden finally spoke. "Remember when you said I wasn't the type to run from a fight?"

Winter turned to her, almost stopping in the process.

"You were right," Ayden said and walked away.

Winter stood there watching as Ayden ascended the steps of the English building amid a current of other students. After Ayden disappeared through the doors, Winter rushed down the sidewalk to her own class. What had she meant by that? Would Ayden help now?

At lunch, Winter found Ayden waiting for her properly this time. They walked in silence beside each other to the Union, but Ayden followed her through the lunch line and to the table rather than breaking off and spending lunch with Nadeen.

"What are you doing?" Winter asked when they sat. She stole a glance at Nadeen who sat alone two tables over, occasionally flicking her gaze toward them.

Ayden shrugged. "I don't think it'll hurt anything. Everybody said me and you needed to spend time together, right?"

"What is it with you and breaking the rules? You messed up the routine yesterday and you're doing it again today."

"You're one to talk." The corner of Ayden's mouth lifted in a half smile.

"Whatever. But I'm still not sure this is a good idea."

Ayden shrugged and met Winter's eyes with her own. "I don't care. I need to talk to you."

Winter paused in the middle of chewing. "What about?"

At that moment, Kaci, Peter, and Summer arrived in a cluster, each carrying their own tray of food.

Winter got up immediately to hug Summer. "It's good to see you!

How was your break?"

Summer shook her bright blonde hair. "Busy."

"I know what you mean," Winter said as she sat back down.

Kaci and Summer took the two empty chairs to Winter's left and right, and Peter grabbed a chair from the next table and slid it beside Kaci.

"What's going on?" Peter asked, eyeing Winter and Ayden. "Wasn't expecting you two to be on sharing-a-table terms so quickly."

"We're just talking," said Winter.

"I need to work out some things," said Ayden. "That's all."

Peter nodded knowingly, and then took a big bite out of his hamburger.

Winter frowned at Summer. "Where's Davis?"

"He had to go to the financial aid office to take care of some paperwork," Summer said, her blue eyes sparkling. "He'll be here when he's finished."

Peter leaned in. "So what's the plan?"

Winter blinked at him. "Plan? What do you mean? There is no plan."

Peter waved his arms at everyone at the table. "Of course there's a plan. We're your team. Team Prophetess."

Winter clenched her eyes. "Don't call it that."

"We're helping you whether you want us to or not. So what's the plan this year?" Peter smiled. "There has to be a plan."

Winter took a deep breath. "The plan is the same as it was last year."

"Okay. Find Sandy and protect her." Peter nodded.

"No." Winter bit her lip and looked at Ayden, willing herself not to stare at Kaci. "Just protect her. That's why we were here talking."

Peter slowly looked from Winter to Ayden. "But you said in the woods that you were wrong. That Ayden's not her."

Winter shook her head. "I was confused and tired. I'm not sure what I was thinking. I didn't mean what I said."

"Ayden's her?"

Winter hesitated, trying to form her words just right to avoid lying to her friends. "She's the one we have to protect."

Peter nodded. "Great. So how do we do that?"

"I'm not sure yet. I've just been walking with her to class the past couple of days."

"Okay, I can help do that too. What about you, Kaci?"

Kaci quickly swallowed a mouthful of food and turned to look at him directly. "Don't think bad of me, please. I don't mind getting a little involved, but I don't think I'm ready to get that involved. Sorry."

Peter put his arm around her and squeezed. "We understand. You can be our constant source of moral support."

"Summer, you're being very quiet," Winter said.

Summer sighed. "Last year in the Raven, right after Agent Gains was killed, you said it could have been me in the tower." Summer peeked up at Kaci, face reddening. Kaci just stared at the wall behind Summer. Summer nodded toward Ayden and lowered her voice. "It was us last spring in the forest. I didn't know what was going to happen…I thought I was going to die." She looked to Winter. "I didn't really realize how dangerous this is."

"What are you saying?" Winter asked.

Summer shrugged. "I don't know. I…I just need some time to think. Sorry. I don't think I can be much help right now."

"That's okay." Peter smiled. "We'll just put you on the moral support team, too."

"What about Davis?" asked Winter.

"What about him?" Davis asked as he pulled a chair between Winter and Summer.

"Speak of the devil…" said Peter.

"Are you in this year? Are you going to help?" asked Winter.

"Why wouldn't I? I want to do more, actually."

Winter shook her head. "I'm not sure there's more to do. We just need to keep an eye on Ayden."

Davis nodded. "Do we have an out plan?"

"A what?" asked Peter.

"You know, a plan for if something goes wrong. How do we get her out? What do we do? We've never had an out plan before…could have used it last spring."

"You call me," said Winter. "And I'll tell you what to do. That's the out plan."

"Not really a lot of help," said Davis. "Can't you give us some idea right now? You know, just some general direction in case…oh, I don't know…one of us is running across a screaming campus trying to find you?"

"Just hide her and keep her safe until you call me. There are some things I'm not allowed to tell you, so you'll have to follow my lead in an emergency. That's the best I can do. Sorry."

Davis pursed his lips. "Okay. So what about at her dorm and overnight? Who's keeping an eye on her then?"

"Don't worry about that. It's taken care of."

"Taken care of?" Peter cocked his head. "How is it taken care of?"

"I can't tell you."

Peter leaned forward again. "How is it taken care of when none of us are in her building?"

"I can't tell you."

"Are we even needed? Or are we just part of some kind of elaborate plot? A red herring?"

"I can't tell you!" Winter huffed. "Just drop it okay."

Kaci put a hand on Peter's shoulder. "It's okay. I'm sure Winter knows what she's doing this year more than last. She seems to be in control, so let's just do what she says. Don't you trust her?"

Peter watched Winter a moment and then cast around the table. He and Davis shared a narrowed, knowing look, before he turned back to face Winter. "Yeah, I trust her. But she's not the only one who's been through a lot with this mess. It's time she trusted us too."

"I do trust you. All of you."

Peter shook his head. "From the very beginning we've all put our lives in your hands and we trust you completely. If it wasn't for you every one of us at this table would be dead. We've all been affected in more ways than one. I don't know what kind of gag order the FBI put on you or what they're up to, but it's time you stopped acting like you're the only one that matters."

Winter gazed at the table, a hole spreading through her abdomen.

"That's not fair, Peter," Kaci said.

"Isn't it?" Peter turned to her. "Then why do I get the impression that we're just pawns in a game Winter isn't telling us about?"

The hole filled with cold water. Peter was right.

"Stop it, Peter," Kaci said with a hint of tightness.

"You said you trusted her," said Davis to Peter. "Maybe you should back off. Winter's doing what she has to do. Like you said, we don't know what she's dealing with."

"She cares about us," said Summer.

Peter sighed. "I know. But she doesn't have to act like she's the only one who cares and the only one who can be trusted. She's not alone."

Kaci moved so fast, Winter didn't realize what was happening until she had finished punching Peter in the shoulder.

"Ow!" Peter protested, covering the spot with his hand.

Without looking at any of them, Winter stood and walked away. They were all right, and she hated keeping everything to herself. She needed to talk to Agent Erickson again.

6

Four Years Ago

Winter made a decision that first week of school. She was a Junior now. Only two years left and she could finally leave that place…maybe go back to her real home. Maybe start a new life somewhere else. Winter made the decision to focus all her energy on getting out. No more just getting by in class. No more half paying attention. She would do what she had to do…study, homework, projects, papers, good grades like she had when she was younger…anything and everything. No more excuses and no more bare minimums. She wouldn't risk not graduating on time or failing to open up as many doors as possible to escape in a little over a year and a half. At the very least this new dedication might give her mind something else to focus on rather than…

The classes actually came easy to her when she let them. She had been an all-A student at her old school, but just hadn't found the determination to keep it up at Trenton Hills. It didn't take her long to get settled into a routine of thorough note-taking, completing her homework, and studying ahead of time, a routine returning by instinct from her earlier years of wanting to be top of the class.

Claire followed her lead, applying herself in a way Winter had never seen from her. They talked little, but when they did talk it was mostly about things they might do once school was over. Winter's determination to cruise to graduation without causing any potential roadblocks had infected Claire completely.

After the first week, Winter stopped paying attention to the stares and the whispered questions happening when she walked through the hall or sat with Claire for lunch. But no one ever came back to voice those questions. That was part of the new determination...if she could get away from here, she could finally rid herself of the questions and stares and memories. Ignoring everyone but Claire became part of the new routine too.

During the second week of school, Stacy joined Claire and Winter for lunch. Her slightly Asian features were unusually red, and she stiffened as she sat.

A flicker of hollowness coursed through Winter, knowing what Stacy was about to ask. She could ignore the rest of the school, but Stacy would be more difficult. Winter had hoped Stacy would just write her off and move on with life.

"Just get it over with," Winter croaked.

Claire darted her eyes from Winter to Stacy.

"Don't worry," Stacy said. "I'm not here to ask you a bunch of questions you don't want to answer."

"Then why are you here?"

"I thought I was your friend, remember? Whether you still believe that or not." Stacy fidgeted with her hands and looked away. "I know what you're going through. I thought maybe I could help."

"You have no idea what I'm going through."

Stacy leaned forward, dark brown hair falling forward over her shoulder. "Why do you do that? Why are you trying to isolate yourself? Is it easier that way?"

Heat rose up the sides of Winter's neck. "Yes! It's easier that way.

Now just leave me alone!"

"You need to understand something, Winter, and it's time you got this through your thick head right now. You're not the only one who is hurting. You're not the only one who's lost someone they love. Three people died last spring, and this whole school is hurting, whether you want to believe that or not. Would it kill you to acknowledge that the world of pain doesn't revolve around you? I've seen more than one person wiping tears or crying unexpectedly in class. Even some of the teachers."

Winter folded her arms and looked away.

"Ryan was my friend," said Stacy. "When I became a Christian, for a time he was my only friend. All the Christian goody-goodies didn't want to accept me, and all of my old friends wouldn't talk to me."

The heat in Winter's neck turned to ice.

"Alison and I had been friends since kindergarten. We may have gone our separate ways over the past year, but it wasn't far enough to erase ten years of friendship. Most people liked her around here, even if she did go a little crazy at the end." Stacy's voice began to waver.

Winter looked to her and saw her eyes glistening and her chin quivering. Claire stared at the wall.

"Your parents are divorced, same as mine. But I never told you why. When I was little my older brother was killed in a car wreck. He was thirteen. It tore my family apart. It tore my parents apart. And they've never been able to let it go."

Winter sighed. "Stacy…I didn't know."

Tears rolled quickly down Stacy's cheeks now and she didn't bother to wipe them away. "That's right, you didn't know. You've been too wrapped up in yourself to know anything about your friends. Ryan knew. It's why we became such good friends. He understood me. And Alison knew. Her friendship through those years helped me through it. When are you going to realize that you're not alone, Winter?"

"I know I'm not," Winter said as she closed her eyes briefly. "I just can't..."

"Can't what? Can't think about other people whose emotions are just as important as yours? Look around you." Stacy waved her arm to the crowded cafeteria. "Do you know how many people loved Ryan in this place? Do you realize how many people in this school are hurting just like you?"

Stacy pointed to a table in the far corner. "Look over there. That's James and David. They were best friends with Ryan. Look at them, Winter!"

Winter bit her lip and looked.

"They've been sitting like that every day. They don't talk, they don't look up. They just sit there, eat, and leave. Do you see that empty seat between them? That's where Ryan used to sit. James asked Claire to prom. Ask Claire why they never went out again."

Winter glanced at Claire. Claire kept her crimson face pointed at the wall.

"Ask her," Stacy said.

"Claire?"

Claire turned just her eyes to Winter, both of them glistening. "He said he was too messed up right now for a new relationship. He couldn't handle it."

"Look over there." Stacy pointed to a table a little ways from James and David. Three girls sat there, unsmiling. "The one on the right is Erin. She used to date Ryan. Everyone knows she still had a thing for him. Every morning someone finds her in the bathroom crying."

Winter reached up and caught a tear running down her cheek. "Okay, Stacy. I get it."

"Do you? Look over there." She pointed to another table with three guys and one girl. "Phillip's friends. Look at them. They won't talk to each other, they won't even look at each other. They sit together out of habit. And Johnny's telling everyone he's going to drop out of school now."

"That's enough, Stacy," said Claire.

"Not yet," Stacy said. "Winter, have you even thought about Ali's grandparents? What must they be going through? Did you even think to go talk to them? Of course not. And let me tell you one more thing. I was at the memorials. All three of them. The whole school was. Even Claire. The only person missing was you."

"Please," said Winter. "Stop it."

Stacy sighed. "I'm not trying to hurt you. But you need to realize you're not the only one hurting. You need to stop acting like you're all alone in this. Please."

Winter shook her head. "What do you expect me to do?"

"I don't know," said Stacy. "Just…maybe, acknowledge other people for a change. Some of them want answers only you can give."

"Stacy, I can't…"

"I know you can't. But you don't have to hate them for it. Respect their pain, Winter."

Winter nodded. "Fine. I'll try."

Stacy smiled and rubbed her cheeks dry with the palms of her hands. "Thank you. Would it be too much to ask if I could start sitting with you at lunch? I'm getting tired of sitting alone."

Winter tried to return the smile. "Sure."

7

Present Day

Ayden barely spoke to Winter the rest of that week, but Winter could clearly see something weighed heavily on her. Ayden shuffled her feet and watched the ground more often than not, usually walking fast enough in front of Winter so Winter couldn't attempt conversation. But on Friday, while walking across the Meadow to their first class after the escort switch, Ayden slowed a little and peeked over her shoulder as if signaling Winter. Winter jogged the few steps to fall in beside her. Ayden scanned the Meadow for a moment, then grabbed Winter by the arm and pulled her toward the library.

"What are you doing?" asked Winter, jerking out of Ayden's grip.

Ayden grunted, but didn't stop taking long purposeful strides. "We need to talk. Alone."

"Fine. But I'm capable of walking by myself," Winter said, catching back up to her.

In the library, Ayden paused to search the building map near the entrance, and then headed for the elevator. Winter followed in silence, studying the library patrons for anything suspicious. She thought for a moment one student sitting by the coffee shop was eyeing them, but with a second glance he had looked away. Maybe he was FBI…maybe not. Before Winter realized it, she had unconsciously rubbed her gun with the opposite ankle. Once the elevator doors closed, Winter turned to Ayden, but Ayden pursed her lips and refused to acknowledge her. Winter crossed her arms and tapped her foot in the silence. On the fourth floor, Ayden led Winter to an isolated corner full of study tables. The entire floor was vacant, except for one worker behind a wall desk.

"Okay, what's up?" asked Winter as they sat down

Ayden clenched her teeth and spoke in a low voice, stealing occasional glances at the lone worker on the opposite side of the room, much too far away to overhear. "Nadeen called me helpless this morning. She said I had no idea how to protect myself and I needed to be thankful the government finds it necessary to keep me alive."

"Well, that was rude of her."

Ayden crossed her arms. "Well, I might have told her she was a horrible roommate."

"Why did you do that?"

"Because she is." Ayden leaned closer. "I'm not helpless. I can protect myself."

"Finally. Progress. So you've decided to stop being a victim?"

"I've decided to do whatever it takes to survive. That's why I wanted to talk to you."

Winter furrowed her brow. "What does that have to do with me? Nadeen could probably give you some training better than I could."

"I doubt that."

"What do you mean?" Ayden couldn't possibly know about her summer training, could she?

Ayden took a deep breath. "I saw what you did last spring. I don't know how you did it, but I saw. While everyone else was clinging to the tree, I opened my eyes and watched you. I've never seen anything like it in my life. It was like something from a superhero movie. I saw this spinning ball of water all around us, the wind was tearing through the leaves, the tree was floating in the air. And there you were, unafraid, fighting with that murderer. How did you do that?"

Winter shook her head. "A floating tree? Are you sure…"

Ayden slammed her fist on the table. "I know what I saw! Don't pretend it didn't happen. What did you do?"

Winter considered her for a moment, wondering how much she should tell. With Ayden being so convinced of what she saw, Winter couldn't just play it off. She sighed. "I'm sure you don't really want to know. It's complicated."

"Try me. Let's pretend I'm good with complicated. If I'm going to trust you and this Nadeen…" Her lip curled. "…then you owe me an explanation."

"Fine. I suppose it's time you knew anyway, since you're a part of this now. I have a special gift."

"You mean, super powers?"

"No," said Winter. "Not really. I'm a prophetess. I've been gifted from God with certain prophet abilities."

"Like telling the future?"

"Sometimes. But that's not all there is to it. In the Bible, the prophets did an awful lot of things that had nothing to do with telling the future. They were basically conduits for God's power. So they could do and accomplish anything God wanted them to do."

Ayden tilted her head. "Anything?"

"Anything. Even making a tree fly, apparently."

Ayden crossed her arms and chewed her lip. "So…this is all a Christian thing?"

"Sort of," said Winter. "You've seen it for yourself. And you asked how I did it. That's how."

"So all this God and Christian stuff is real?"

Winter nodded. "It's real."

Ayden sighed. "Well, I'm not sure I'm ready for that yet. I'll think about it. But I want to help. And I want Nadeen off my back. I'm not a helpless little girl, and I'm perfectly capable of defending myself."

"I'll talk to Agent Erickson. Maybe we can work out another arrangement that doesn't involve you being so closely shadowed all the time. Though I'm not sure it'll do any good."

"Anything's better than this," said Ayden.

"Erickson will probably think you're trying to find a way to run. He may even watch you closer."

Ayden shook her head. "I'm not running. I may be stubborn, but I'm not stupid. You were all right. This guy isn't going away, and I'm not going to rely on the FBI to keep me safe. I want to know more and do more."

Winter nodded again. "I'll try to talk to him."

Ayden checked her watch, swore, and grabbed her backpack. "We're late." Without waiting for Winter to follow, Ayden stood and practically stomped back to the elevator.

The next weekend, Winter and Kaci spent most of their time watching TV and wishing for something else to do. Thankfully, Saturday night Peter suggested the old gang get together for burgers.

Peter was the first to arrive at their apartment, a sack full of groceries in hand. He immediately went to the kitchen and put the meat in the refrigerator, while Kaci shadowed him like a puppy and grinned like a cat. All Winter could do was roll her eyes.

Davis and Summer arrived ten minutes later with a case of sodas. Where Peter and Kaci seemed giddy together, Davis and Summer stared at nothing and barely spoke to anyone, including each other. They sat on the couch, holding hands almost by reflex.

"What's going on?" asked Winter, as she pulled a dining room chair into the living room.

Davis shook his head and gave Winter a "you should know" look. Winter shrugged it off, refusing to believe what Summer had told them the other day. And even if that was at least part of the problem, Winter refused to let Summer spend the rest of her time moping like this.

"Summer, you okay?" she asked.

Summer glanced up, then pulled her hand away from Davis and started fidgeting with her own fingers. "I haven't been sleeping well."

Winter nodded. "Me either. Have you talked to someone?"

"Like who? A counselor?"

"Maybe. It doesn't have to be. You could talk to me. You know, like old times. Just the two of us."

"I don't know," said Summer.

"Hey Winter," Peter called from the kitchen.

Winter hesitated a moment, watching Summer's pale face continue to stare beyond her hands in her lap, and then looked at Davis, who also watched Summer with a creased brow and a red face. Winter took a deep breath and stood. Around the corner in the kitchen, Kaci and Peter waited for her just out of sight of the living room.

Winter crossed her arms and lowered her voice. "What?"

"Give Summer some space," said Peter.

"I'm sorry? Give her some space? She's my friend. She's been my friend for a while now, longer than you've known her. What's wrong with wanting to help talk her through this?"

Peter shook his head. "I just don't think it's a good idea right now. It's a little more complicated than you realize."

"What? So you've talked with her?"

"Maybe a little. But not too much. Just enough to know she's very confused right now."

Winter stepped closer. "Confused about what?"

"About everything. About the school, about what's going on, about being taken last year."

Winter grunted. "And that's exactly what she needs to talk through. That's why I'm trying to get her to talk. She can't keep things like this in…I should know."

"You don't understand," said Peter. "She's confused about a lot of things. But the biggest thing is you."

"What about me?" Winter frowned.

"She doesn't know what to think about you anymore. So you talking to her doesn't work. It's a bad idea."

"But…well…what about Davis? Will she at least talk to him?"

Peter shook his head again. "I think she wants to. But I've tried talking with Davis, and there's something going on with him too. I don't know what it is. I don't think you trying to talk to Davis would make any difference, either…much less trying to get to Summer through him. He's completely shutting everyone out, even her. I think that's probably part of Summer's issues."

Winter's mouth opened, but no words came out. She saw a look in Peter's eyes that said he knew more than he was telling.

Kaci reached over to rub Peter on the back and looked at Winter. "Give them some space. Let Peter keep working on Davis. I'll take Summer and try to get her to open up."

"But I haven't done anything," said Winter. A numbness closed in around her chest. "They're my friends. I haven't done anything wrong."

Kaci's face softened. "I'm sorry, Winter. I know it hurts. We're your friends too, and we're okay."

That glint in Peter's eyes…

"Look," said Peter. "Even if they are trying to push you away a little, I'm sure it's only temporary and I'm sure it's not really about you. So don't take it personally."

Kaci nodded. "Give them some time. They'll figure it out. Everything will be fine."

"That's right," said Peter. "And we're still here, so you're not alone."

Winter stepped back to where she could peer around the corner. Davis sat with his arm around Summer, and Summer laid her head against his shoulder. They watched TV and didn't seem to be paying any attention to what was going on in the kitchen. She looked back to Peter and Kaci, Kaci still rubbing Peter's back.

Winter shook her head as she looked back and forth between the two couples. "I've always been alone. I need to go for a walk." She turned for the door.

"Winter, don't be like that," Kaci said.

But Winter closed the door and ran down the steps before anything else could be said.

At the street, Winter sat on the curb in the deepening twilight, thankful no one had followed her, though she suspected someone might be watching from the balcony door. How could she explain how she felt? How could she express that seeing the four of them as couples mulched her from the inside out? Whatever. Better off alone and outside than a stupid fifth wheel.

Winter reached in deep and grabbed the hollowness she still kept hidden for times such as this, wrapping its safety around her heart. After all, things might have changed between her and God, but to everyone else she would always be the unlovable freak.

Her phone rang. She groaned, wishing she had left the stupid phone in the apartment. If Kaci was calling to convince her to come back, she might throw it *into* the apartment by way of shattering the balcony door. She clenched her teeth and dug it out.

Agent Erickson. She frowned and answered, filtering the emotion from her voice so it wouldn't tremble.

"Hello?"

"Winter, we have a problem."

"What's going on?"

"Ayden is missing," Erickson said. *"Her tracking bracelet was left in the room. Agent Garner has checked the dorm, and I've instructed her to stay in the room in case Ayden returns. But..."*

"But? What's going on?"

"There was some movement earlier this evening. Our people moved into position to intercept, but Ayden disappeared before anything hostile was identified."

Winter stood. "She disappeared? The first real test of her trust, and you lose her? You should have taken her in! What if they have her? What if she's hurt? How could you let this happen?"

"We have no evidence they have her. In fact, there has been no counter-movement to suggest Xaphan found what he was looking for or has been sufficiently deflected. It's most likely coincidence and poor timing on even worse judgment from Ayden. We're searching the entire campus right now. If she's around, we'll find her."

"Okay, what do you want me to do?" Winter patted her pocket and realized her keys were still in the apartment.

"Nothing. I'm just informing you of what's happening in case some of that movement comes your way. Keep the others safe. And if Ayden shows up there, contact me immediately, understood?"

"No! You need me. I can find her faster than you. And if they've taken her..." Erickson made a sound to object, but Winter plowed over him. "...you don't know they haven't! If they have taken her, I may be the only one who can find her."

"Maybe, but priority one is Kaci. She's your assignment, not Ayden. You stay there and keep her safe," said Erickson.

Winter chewed her lip and looked up to her apartment balcony, where light spilled out to the street, expecting the silhouette of someone watching her, but saw no one. Kaci was her responsibility...but so was Ayden. They all were, no matter what Erickson said. "And if you can't find her? What then?"

"Once we've exhausted what we can do and we begin to suspect the worst, I'll

send agents there to relieve you so you can help. But until then…"

"It may be too late by then, and you know it," Winter said over him.

"Lest you forget, I'm your supervisor. Stay there. That's an order." Erickson hung up.

Winter cursed under her breath and shoved the phone back into her pocket. With another glance at the balcony door, she ran up the stairs, and burst into the apartment. The others called to her as she came through, but she ignored them and jogged back to her room for her car keys.

On the way back out, Peter moved to stand in front of her, arms crossed. "What's going on?"

Winter hesitated and looked around the room. All four of them were at the table now, Davis standing and facing her, Kaci and Summer watching with wide eyes.

"I have to go," she said and stepped around Peter, their questioning stares on her back.

Halfway down the stairs she heard the door slam and hurried footsteps behind her. "Wait," said Peter. "I'll come with you."

Winter turned on him, willing herself to stare him in the eyes. "No, you can't. You have to stay here."

"Why?"

"Because…because I can't be in two places at once," she nearly shouted. "I have to go do something. I need you here to help protect the others. Just in case."

Peter shook his head. "That's not how this works."

Winter spun and continued down the sidewalk toward her car. "That's how it works tonight." She could hear him still following and started jogging the rest of the way.

As she opened the car door, Peter grabbed her shoulder. "I'm not letting you do this alone."

Winter shoved him in the chest with both hands. "Go away! I don't need you!"

"That's not true!"

She bared her teeth and narrowed her eyes, stepping forward with her fists clenched. "Don't make me hurt you."

Peter held up his hands and stepped back. "Fine. Whatever. Just call if you change your mind. We'll all come help. Probably even Kaci."

"I won't," she spat as she slammed the car door closed. The last thing she wanted was to get any of them hurt again. Let them have their couples' party. It was better that way.

Peter watched from the curb as she backed up and shoved the car into drive. She checked her mirror as she approached the turn out of the complex and saw him still watching. When he was out of sight, she took a deep breath and let it out in a long sigh.

So much for the hollow protection around her heart.

As Winter neared the campus of Tishbe University, her phone rang again. A quick glance at the ID told her it was Erickson again. "What?" she answered.

"Why is your car moving?"

"I'm coming to help," said Winter.

Erickson swore on the other end. *"I told you to stay with Kaci!"*

"And I told you that you need my help. Kaci's fine. She's with Peter. Peter loves her. He won't let anything happen."

"Are you sure you believe that?"

"Why wouldn't I? I would trust Peter with my own life. Kaci's safe. And Ayden needs me right now. I'm coming whether you like it or not!" Winter hung up and dropped her phone into a cup holder. If it rang again, she just might toss it out the window.

She neared the CLC building just outside the main gate, and slowed to pull into the parking lot. Winter turned out her lights and closed her eyes, taking deep breaths and trying to relax, the only thing she knew to do to help the premonitions come faster. But nothing touched the racing of her heart. She needed a premonition and she needed it now. "Come on, come on. Give me something," she said out loud, mentally pulling her conscience in the direction of premonition.

Nothing happened.

Winter opened her eyes and looked around the parking lot of the CLC building and the other homes and businesses lining Hoole Boulevard, holding back a string of curses at still not having control of her prophecy the way she wanted.

But maybe if she relied on instinct…maybe instinct was part of the prophecy too. Something in her gut told her Ayden was still safe wherever she was. But where would she go? And why would she leave her bracelet behind? Would she have taken her car?

No. She'd be on foot. Winter took another deep breath and tried to clear her mind again for a full premonition or vision or something more than just this gut feeling, but still nothing would come.

Then another thought occurred to her. Ayden would be on foot, because that's what Winter would do. *So where would I go?*

Winter slid her car back into gear, flipped the lights on, and headed for Divine Hall, Ayden's dorm. She parked in the darkest corner of the lot, clinging to the shadows as she got out. She walked slowly toward the back door, scanning the parking lot and the sides of the building for the deepest shadows near the back door, and then crouched there as Ayden might have done. From there she could see the outskirts of campus, where few buildings had been developed. Large open spaces indicated fields for intramural sports and practice fields for some of the more official school sports. But the one thing standing out the most in that direction, near the edge of all the fields was the basketball coliseum. Winter traced a broken path of shadows from the coliseum back to where she crouched, with few street lights in the way…an easy enough path to cross without being seen if one wished.

That's what Winter would have done. That's what Ayden did. Winter took a deep breath and started toward the coliseum, clinging to the shadows where her dark clothing and black hair easily made her nothing more than a shadow herself. Several people were out walking, seemingly casual, but the intensity with which they looked around told Winter they were searching for Ayden too. FBI or Xaphan's people, she couldn't tell. Either way, Winter had no intention of letting them know she was around. She moved only when sure no one could see her, clinging as tightly to the shadows as possible.

At the coliseum, Winter had to jog across a lighted parking lot to reach the next nearest shadow. At the edge of the building, she crept around checking for any open doors. The first two she came upon were locked. Locked doors usually didn't stop her, but Winter wanted to stay with Ayden's path as closely as possible, and knew an open door would keep her on the trail. The third door stood open against the jamb. Winter stole another glance around for the searchers and then slipped inside.

She carefully closed the door all the way, pre-turning the latch to minimize any sound. In the dark curved hall, only safety lights and the machine lights from refreshment stands gave enough ambiance to walk around confidently. Winter hesitated, looking both ways, trying to decide which direction she would most likely go if trying to hide. Nothing stood out, so she jogged forward to the stadium entrance and looked out over the bleachers and the basketball court a little below.

The stadium bleachers rose high on either side, with any number of dark hiding places. But Winter wouldn't have come in here…so Ayden wouldn't have come in here. Then her eyes landed on a long row of glass windows near the roof, where the press box and private rooms for the school's most generous donors hid. She saw a flicker of movement behind the glass, noticeable only in the shifting of a glare where an internal ambient light had been momentarily blocked.

Winter ran back into the outer hall and jogged the circumference of the stadium toward the windows on the other side. On the way she scanned the darkness for directional signs on the walls, and when she found one with directions to the press box, she veered aside and sprinted up the stairs. Two floors up, Winter followed the signs onto another curved hall built into the perimeter of the stadium, but this time it was narrower with numbered doors, a private corridor for invited guests only. She jogged around the hall again, briefly touching and twisting doorknobs, looking for the open door. When she found it, she stopped to take a deep breath before easing into the room.

Ayden sat in a chair at a pub table, looking out of the glass to the stadium floor far below.

9

Four Years Ago

The bell rang, still an old metal bell in the hallways and outside the building, but nothing more than a long tone on the classroom intercom speaker, signaling the end of the school day. Winter turned in her assignment, the first to the front of the classroom, and picked up her books to leave. She kept her head down and her books close to her chest as she threaded through the crowded hall to her locker.

Claire was already there, closing the locker door next to Winter's. She gave Winter a smile. "How'd you do on that English test?"

"An A," Winter said.

Claire shook her head. "I wish I was as smart as you. Have you always made good grades?"

"Usually. I guess the past two years weren't so great."

"I understand," said Claire with a sympathetic smile as she hoisted her backpack on to one shoulder. "Well...see you tomorrow."

"Bye." Winter turned to her locker and opened it as Claire joined the crowd headed toward the exit. She shoved in her English and history books, and took out her math book for her homework assignments, slipping it into her backpack.

When she closed the locker and turned, three people stood there waiting, two guys and a girl. She recognized them all from the cafeteria when Stacy had named them. James and David both frowned at her, James with brown shaggy hair similar to Ryan's, if a shade darker, and David standing half a head taller, and lankier as if he had been stretched. Beside them, standing eye to eye with Winter, Ryan's ex-girlfriend Erin, her pale skin blotchy red from what could have been too much sun, but the strain in her eyes said otherwise. She brushed her strawberry blonde hair behind one ear and shifted to stand on one hip.

"What?" Winter whispered, trying to meet them in the eyes without betraying the ice forming in her chest.

James looked to the exit. Winter followed his gaze and saw Claire leaving. Then he turned back to her. "We need to know."

"Know what?"

"You know what," said Erin, her voice quivering. "You're the only one who really knows what happened."

Winter clenched her eyes. "I can't talk about it."

"Can't? Or won't?" asked James. "Ryan and I were best friends since first grade. I need to know."

Erin took a step closer. "It's not fair. We've known and loved him a lot longer than you…" Her voice wavered and she turned away, sniffling.

James put an arm around Erin's shoulder. "What she's trying to say is that Ryan was very close to us. We're not trying to hurt you, but you owe us at least the truth."

"I…I can't…I'm going to miss the bus," said Winter. She tried to push past them, but David stood in her way.

"Not until you tell us," David said.

"If you miss the bus, I'll give you a ride home," said James.

The sincerity on James's face reminded Winter so much of Ryan that a lump filled her neck. She looked around the hall, trying to find someone who might help her, to rescue her before she did something stupid. But everyone remaining in the hall, mostly those who drove their own cars and didn't care when the buses left, had stopped moving to watch.

James saw her looking and nodded. "They all just want to know too. Look, we can go somewhere else if you like."

Winter's eyes stung and her throat constricted. When she spoke, it was not much more than a croak. "Please. I can't. Just let me go."

"Winter, we need to know," said Erin, almost panicky.

Winter shoved away the pending tears, forcing a measure of fire to take the place of the ice, and unleashed it with enough force to shove down the other emotions bubbling within. "Leave me alone!" She shoved past them and ran down the hall, away from the buses, realizing her mistake far too late to change directions. She found the front entrance instead, in time to see the first buses leaving campus, and cursed.

The alternative was to turn back and accept the offer of a ride home…and have to tell her story. Another alternative was to call her dad at work…and have to explain why she missed the bus. Neither would do… The fire within spread from her chest and cheeks to penetrate deep within her memories, morphing into the flames of a broken car and broken bodies, despite her efforts to keep them suppressed in the stone around her heart. She screamed and ran. She ran, not sure where she was going, just knowing she needed to get away…to think. To clear her head. To do something.

Maybe to die. If she could manage it. It might be the only real way to escape the onslaught of memories…the chirping of the tires, the crashing upon the roof, the spinning of the sky.

The twisted car.

The fire.

The screams.

Ryan's body.

No matter how fast or how far she ran, the memories would not set her free. But dying would make them go away.

When she found herself at the football stadium, she ran to the visitors' side and searched for a place to sit beneath the bleachers out of anyone's sight. She placed her back to one of the support beams, wrapped her arms around her knees, and laid her head down, ignoring the humid smell of half-dried mud and the more pungent aromas of discarded food from last week's game.

The more the memories flashed, the more they drained her. Despite a deep ache to kill herself, the emotional energy to face death was gone. All she could manage was to sit and just hope to rot away.

Long after all the sounds of departing school traffic had died away, she heard footsteps coming her direction.

Winter picked up her head to peek through the support beams and underbrush, but all she could make out was a humanoid blob, obscured through the foliage and the tears in her eyes. It wasn't until the person rounded the closest beam and Winter hastily scrubbed her eyes dry with the heels of her hands, that Winter saw it was Stacy.

"How did you find me?" Winter asked, her voice surprisingly strong and normal.

Stacy shrugged as she stepped to Winter's side and sat down. "This is where I would have gone. I talked to James. Believe it or not, he's pretty upset about what they did."

"Well, he should be."

"Try to cut them some slack," said Stacy. "They're really hurting too. People tend to make bad choices when they're hurting. They just want to know what happened."

"They know what happened."

Stacy shook her head. "They want to hear it from you."

"Too bad. I'm not going to talk."

"Maybe that's the problem." Stacy put a hand on Winter's back. "Maybe you need to talk. Maybe you need to get it all out. It's not healthy bottling it all up."

"You sound like Daniel," said Winter.

"No, I sound like good sense. The year your mom was sick, we all started down a darker path."

"Stop it."

"No. I'm talking about it whether you want to or not. We all started down a darker path…maybe it was teenage hormones, I don't know. But you had a real reason to bottle everything up and to hide your emotions. You refused to talk about it, but at the same time you wore this depression and anger of yours on the outside. It's like subconsciously you wanted everyone to know the pain inside of you, even if you were trying to hide from yourself."

"Maybe I just like wearing black."

Stacy shook her head. "You didn't when you first came. You changed the way you looked on the outside when your life started going down the toilet. That's a cry for help."

Winter snapped her head to face her. "What do you know about it? What do you know about your life going down the toilet? Come back when your mother abandons you, when your father hates you, and when you kill the first person you ever…" Winter laid her head back on her knees to hide the tears.

"You know, I've got issues, too. Maybe they're not as dramatic as what you've been through, but it's not easy having two parents who live in opposite cities, even if they do get along. I miss my brother…we all do, but we go on. We live. Do you know how difficult it's been trying to make friends at my dad's? Especially when he has two kids by his second wife. I'm the oddball. I feel like I don't belong there. But I go on. I live with it. And Ryan may have liked you…" Stacy put a hand over her mouth to stifle a sob. When she continued, her voice trembled. "But the reason I started going to church in the first place was because I liked him. Most of the time I didn't even think he knew I existed. He was a good friend, but he never saw me as anything but a friend. Not like he looked at you. I knew the first time I saw him with you in the hall."

"I don't want to talk about him. Please…"

"Well, maybe I do. Did you ever think of that? Maybe I need a friend to talk to. You're all I have, so don't flake out on me now."

Winter bit her lip and looked away.

Stacy sighed. "Things used to be so different. Ali and I were inseparable…always getting into trouble together, cheating on tests together, chasing boys together. I never told anyone this, but I crushed on Phillip first. We never went out or anything. But he was the first boy I actually liked, you know? Ali even helped me try to get his attention. But he liked someone else, so I moved on. Then in eighth grade he and Ali started dating. At first I was a little jealous, but I got over it. He became one of us. The three of us doing everything together. I'm not sure when Claire joined us, it was such a gradual thing. I think she had homeroom with Phillip. We'd be goofing off, and there she'd be in the middle of it. By the end of eighth grade our group of three became four. And then freshman year, you came. I never had so many friends in my life."

Winter lay her head sideways on her knees to watch Stacy.

"And then the summer before last year," said Stacy, "you went into grief shock, Claire went somewhere I didn't want to follow, Phillip and Ali hated each other, and Ali went bat-crazy. I lost it all. You were all gone from me, just like that. I didn't know what to do. I knew Ryan…kinda liked him a little…so I followed him to church, and I found something there. I found a true love and acceptance that I didn't know existed."

"Stop…" Winter whispered.

"Winter…" Stacy's voice shook and the tears spilled from her eyes. "Ali and Phillip and Ryan are gone. Claire is…gone too. You're the only friend I have. Please don't shut me out this year."

"I just can't listen to the church stuff and I can't talk about him."

"Fine. But I need to know I'm not alone, that I've got someone I can talk to. You're it. Please be it. I won't bring up any of those things. I promise."

Winter took a deep breath. "Okay."

"And I want you to know that you're not alone either. You can talk to me. You can let it all spill out. Things like this have a way of building pressure and it'll eventually blow, whether you want it to or not. But if you wait too long…Winter, I don't want to lose you, too."

Winter sniffed, her list of suicide options flipping through her mind, riding a surge of fresh guilt. "My whole world has changed too much, too fast. I need to figure out how to process it before I can talk about it. Does that make sense?"

Stacy shook her head. "Maybe the right way to process it is to talk about it. Let me help."

"Okay." Winter nodded. "But not today. I'm not ready."

Stacy squeezed Winter's hand. "I'll be here when you are."

Winter nodded again and looked away.

"Do you need a ride home?"

Winter smiled.

10

Present Day

When Ayden heard Winter enter, she jumped out of her chair and spun around, terror crossing her face in the darkness.

"What are you doing?" Winter asked. "Everyone's looking for you."

"How did you find me?" Ayden lowered back into her seat.

Winter crossed the room, a small private box with a bathroom near the door. Plenty of chairs and couches filled the room for fans to watch the game through the plate-glass window. A pub table stood to one side, where Ayden sat, staring at the court below.

Winter let her hand drift across the back of the couch as she eased closer to Ayden. "Easy. This is where I would have gone. How did you get in?"

"I don't know. The doors were unlocked. Why were the doors unlocked? What's happening to me?"

"You mean they were already unlocked?"

"I don't know. But every door I wanted to go through just opened." Ayden turned back to the window.

"We can't stay here, Ayden. We need to get you back someplace safe. We can talk about it then."

"Who's that?" asked Ayden as she pointed toward the glass.

Winter took the last steps to join her at the table and leaned forward to see. A dark-clad man stood in one of the stadium gateways directly across from them. Winter's heart raced. She grabbed Ayden's arm and tugged toward the floor. "Very slowly, drop down out of sight."

They slid down with their backs to the side wall and the window just to their left. The large glass didn't quite leave enough wall underneath to hide them completely, but with them sitting on the floor only someone in the top half of the stadium would even have a chance.

"What's going on?" Ayden asked.

Winter fished out her cellphone and called Agent Erickson, lifting up a little to try and get another glimpse of the man, but the stadium floor was far too low to see at that angle.

"Erickson," he answered.

"This is Butterfly, I've found Mimic."

"Mimic?" whispered Ayden. "What's that supposed to mean?"

"Good," said Erickson. *"Where are you? I'll have a team meet you there."*

"We're in the basketball stadium. There's someone already here."

Silence on the other end.

"What's he saying?" asked Ayden.

"Are you wearing your bracelet?" asked Erickson.

"Yeah, why?" said Winter.

"Listen to me very carefully. We don't have someone in the stadium at this time. I've activated the tracking device in your bracelet and I'm sending the location to the team at Tishbe. Stay where you are."

"If this person isn't with you, then who are they?"

"I don't know. Are you someplace you can hide?"

Winter wiped the beads of sweat from her forehead and pushed up high enough to peer over the edge to the stadium gate. "He's gone."

"*As in left the building?*"

"As in I don't know where he is. I can't see him anymore."

"*Secure yourselves. Hide and stay quiet. The team is on the way. When the building is secure, I'll call you with instructions. Got it?*"

"Yeah, okay."

Erickson hung up and Winter lowered her phone. She crawled across the room and made sure the door to the booth was locked, then crawled back to sit with Ayden by the window, where they could watch the door between the legs of the table and chairs.

"What do we do?" asked Ayden.

"We wait," said Winter. "Until Erickson's team gets here."

"But who was that?"

Winter shrugged. "I'm not sure. But when you disappeared, Erickson called and said there had been some movement. I thought you had been taken."

Ayden furrowed her eyebrows. "You mean, those people are looking for me right now?"

"Yeah."

"And that man was probably one of them?" A hint of panic colored her voice.

"Probably."

Ayden rubbed her hands down her pants legs and looked at the floor. "I'm sorry. I shouldn't have run away like that. I just needed some space to think, away from Agent Nanny. I needed to be away from everything for a little while."

"I understand," said Winter. "I spent most of my high school years trying to get away and think through everything. And sometimes I feel like the reason I did some of the things I did was because no one would give me enough space to get my thinking done. Everybody kept wanting me to talk, and I didn't want to talk."

"Sometimes talking helps," said Ayden.

Winter shrugged. "Maybe." She wanted to say more, she didn't really agree with the talking, but she turned to gaze at the door and let the silence thicken.

Eventually, Ayden continued. "Everything in my life is upside down."

Winter bit her lip to stay quiet. Did she really want to do this now? She would rather just keep quiet.

Ayden took a deep breath as if steeling herself. "I used to be so sure about things, and so...dogmatic at being agnostic. I didn't want anyone's beliefs. I figured people had the right to believe whatever they wanted, so long as they didn't try to force it on me. I never thought any of it was real, just a bunch of religious superstition. And then last spring...last week you told me it was all real...that God is real. And I saw it for myself. I've been trying to find another rational explanation, but I can't."

"That's because there isn't one."

"And that's another thing. As much as I wanted to hate you when I met you and even though we've never really spent much time together, you're already the closest friend I have. I was a real jerk in high school. It was a small school and I was smarter than everyone else, never missing a chance to prove it to them. I took summer classes to graduate a year early. By my last year no one would speak to me. My old friends hated me. I was completely alone. The reason I took a year off before going to college was because I was too depressed to think about school. I came here hoping things would be different, but at the same time expecting it to be exactly the same. The more I looked for excuses to push people away, the more they kept their distance on their own. Except for you."

"What about me?"

"You're almost always a jerk to everyone around you, but you still manage to inspire people," said Ayden with a half-smile.

Winter smirked. "I'm not sure I'd go that far. I'm not exactly a role model."

Ayden laughed. "No, I guess not. But when people look at you they see someone who's not afraid of what other people think and who's not afraid to just be herself. You were a jerk to me, but I couldn't hate you or push you away for it. All I could do was admire you for just being yourself and for not letting other people define you. You know exactly who you are."

"I'm not sure who I am counts for much. If you knew more about me, you wouldn't be so nice."

Ayden peered at the floor. "But you know who you are. I don't even know that anymore. Who am I, Winter?"

"Wow. Straight to the hard questions, huh?"

Ayden peeked at her and sighed.

Winter studied the door, trying to listen for any sound in the hall while she spoke. "The problem with people asking who they are is that they only ask because they refuse to be what they're supposed to be already."

"And what am I supposed to be?"

"You were created for a purpose. You've seen for yourself God is real, and now it's time to accept that he created you." Winter turned back to face Ayden. "Who you are is not defined by you or anybody else. It's built within how you are created."

"So what's my purpose?"

Winter shrugged and twisted a little to face her better. "Ayden, you're not asking the wrong questions. You're asking the wrong person."

"Are you suggesting I ask God?"

"Why not?"

Ayden turned back to her hands. "I…I don't know."

"Look at it this way. If I'm wrong about God, what have you got to lose? But if I'm right, you have everything to gain. Not much of a risk really. It seems that to get the answers you're looking for, it'd be worth it."

"I'll think about it."

Winter folded her arms. "I don't mind helping you talk through this, if that's what you need…even though I'm not much of a feelings talker. But sometimes…"

A gunshot outside made them both jump, the reverberation so intense and rumbling like thunder through the whole corridor, it was impossible to know how far away it started. A second after the shot, a door banged open, much more faint than the shot, but much too close to be more than a few doors away. Winter reached for her ankle and pulled out her gun.

"Where'd you get that?" Ayden whispered.

"Shh!"

Another shot. Another door banged open.

"He must have seen us in the window," whispered Winter. "He's checking all the booths."

"We have to get out of here. What are we going to do?"

Another shot. Another slam. Booted footsteps paced through the next room over.

"Quickly, follow me," said Winter. She stood and jogged across the room to the door, pointing at the restroom next to it. "You hide in there. I'll take care of him."

Ayden slipped into the restroom and pulled the door gently closed. Winter put her gun up next to her cheek and eased into the corner behind the door, taking long slow breaths and trying to listen beyond the pounding of her heart.

The footsteps came back to the hall and approached their booth. Winter held her breath. A gunshot ripped through the door latch, filling the booth with a sharp boom. Winter braced a foot sideways in front of her, anticipating the door bursting open. With a loud bang, it flew open and slammed against her foot, bouncing back a little, and then steadied by the person in the hall.

The barrel of a gun appeared first, and slowly the arms and body of the man came into view. Winter lowered her gun from her cheek and took aim, hesitating to let him pass fully into view.

"Stop right there," she said and pushed the door away.

The man halted and scowled over his shoulder. He lowered his gun and turned with a smirk. Black stubble peppered a gaunt face, and he eyed her down with the confidence of a wolf.

Winter's finger itched over the trigger. "Back up toward the window."

"No." He smiled

"Do it! I'll shoot!" Her voice trembled far too much to be convincing, and Winter knew it.

The man shook his head. "No you won't. You're not a killer. You don't have the guts. I can see it in your face." He started raising his gun toward her. "A helpless little girl like you and your even more helpless friend…"

Something large and white slammed into the man's head, cracking in two and shattering on the ground. The man crumpled.

"I am NOT helpless!" shouted Ayden, leaning toward him with the jagged edge of the porcelain toilet lid still clutched in her white-knuckled hands.

"Ayden!" said Winter. Blood spread on the floor beneath the man's head, mixing with the broken fragments of the porcelain. He could have been dead, but Winter didn't care to check.

Ayden sneered at her. "Next time, pull the damn trigger!" She bent down and picked up the man's gun, dropped the magazine to check the rounds, slammed it back into place, flicked the action, checked the chamber, and held it next to her cheek, with the smooth practiced motions of a well-trained marksman. "Let's get out of here."

Winter, eyes wide and mouth hanging open, followed Ayden into the hall as Ayden performed a perfect tactical sweep of the corridor before running for the nearest set of stairs down. She leaned against the wall out of sight of the stairs and began slowly to peer around.

"No," said Winter, running to catch up. "We can't leave."

"Yes, we can," Ayden hissed.

"No. Erickson's team knows we're here. They're coming. And

we don't know how many more of them might be waiting outside. We need to stay where the team can find us." Winter looked around for an idea and her blood ran cold when she spotted the little girl standing by a fire exit door. The girl lifted a finger to her lips and then pointed up.

"Who is that?" asked Ayden.

Winter's breath caught and she spun to Ayden. "You really can see her, can't you?"

Ayden nodded at Winter. "The little girl?" She squinted back. "She's gone."

"What?" Winter turned back to the fire exit door but saw no one there. "Come on. There must be another set of stairs behind that door. We have to go up."

She sprinted over and eased it open, Ayden jumping in and doing another tactical sweep. They ran on their toes up two floors, Winter with her gun pointed constantly up, and Ayden doing quick sweeps around each corner.

"Now what?" asked Ayden as they exited onto the top floor into a small unfinished hallway.

"We keep moving." Winter turned and ran down the hall. Where did the girl go?

"Here." Ayden pointed to a little alcove that might have been an unfinished storage closet. "We can hear well enough if anyone is following us, so we won't be trapped. It's dark enough they'd probably miss us."

"Good idea."

They slipped into the alcove with their backs against the wall and waited, the silence below nothing more than a false sense of calm. The minutes crept by, and Winter wondered if anything else were going to happen. Suddenly, her phone buzzed in her pocket. She pulled it out, almost dropping the gun in the process. "Hello?"

"The team is there. Where are you?"

"Top floor. The guy found us in the booth. He's probably still there, unconscious or dead. Box 350."

A pause on the other end. *"They're securing that now. Then they'll come for you. It's a team of four, plain clothes. I need a code phrase, something unique right now, that I'll pass on to the team. That way you'll know there's no way they could be faking."*

"A code phrase?"

"Hurry."

"Um…" she glanced at Ayden. "The little girl disappears at the door."

"The little girl disappears at the door?"

"Yes."

"Good. When you see our agent, you identify yourself by saying, 'the little girl.' The agent will answer with the full code phrase. Wait for those specific words. No change. 'The little girl disappears at the door,' but they won't say it unless you start it. Understand? Once they give you the safe phrase they'll identify you both by codename, and give you my regards with my codename. If they fail to do any of those things, shoot. Do not hesitate. Understood?"

Winter swallowed. Could she? "Okay," she said. He hung up and she shoved the phone back in her pocket. "They're on their way."

Ayden nodded.

More minutes crept by, and Winter strained to hear anything. What was taking so long? Maybe a team of four took a while to secure a building this size…if they could secure it in the first place. Maybe they were waiting for more help. Every once in a while, they heard a shuffling from the floors below, but no one ever came up the stairs.

After more than fifteen minutes, shouting and rapid gunfire echoed below, muffled by the distance.

"What's happening?" asked Ayden.

"I don't know. But be ready. Follow my lead. Whoever comes up those stairs may not be the right people."

"But how will we know? They could pass us here. If it's the FBI, we can't hide."

"Then we confront them," said Winter. "If we get the code

phrase, great. If not, we shoot."

Ayden frowned but nodded.

Silence followed for several minutes again. Finally, they heard slow footsteps padding through the hall, coming from further around the building where Winter thought there might have been more stairs. An older man in a t-shirt crept by, eyes darting into every shadow and crevice. As he spotted them in the shadows, they wasted no more time raising their guns and stepping out into the light.

He swung to face them, his own gun darting from one to the other. "Drop your weapons!" he demanded.

Winter shook her head. How long did they wait before shooting? He could pull his own trigger any moment now. "Identify yourself!" she shouted, her finger itching. From the corner of her eye she could see the steady calm of Ayden as she faced the man down. The man saw it too and his unsure gun rested to aim at Ayden.

The man stepped closer and steadied himself. "I said, drop your weapons!"

Winter heard Ayden click off the safety. "I can take him," she whispered.

Winter's heart pounded and her finger twitched. Why didn't he give the code phrase? "Who are you?" she screamed. Then she remembered...she had to start it. "The little girl!"

The man's face softened, but his gun never wavered. "The little girl," he said, "disappears at the door." He hesitated and then lowered his weapon. "Butterfly. Mimic. Alpha Echo sends his regards."

Winter released the breath she had been holding and nearly sagged to the floor.

11

Erickson stood behind the table, hands planted on the surface, and red face boring holes through Winter and Ayden on the other side. He inhaled long and deep, like billows preparing to stoke a fire.

"What were you thinking? Both of you? I don't believe you realize the seriousness of your actions. I have one agent critically injured because of your disobedience!"

He jabbed a finger in their direction and Winter winced as if jabbed in the heart.

Erickson shifted his eyes to her. "You were told to stay with Kaci! You left our most important witness exposed, without protection, without notifying me or anyone else. You left her vulnerable in the untrained hands of civilians, and you disobeyed a direct order from your superior. What do you have to say?" He watched her expectantly.

Winter shoved away her momentary lapse of guilt and stuck out her chin. "Ayden would have been dead if not for me."

"That's not the way I heard it. It seems Ayden has been holding out on us. According to the agent that found you, she was standing him down like a mercenary." He turned to Ayden, hand dropping back to the table. "Well?"

Ayden stared daggers at him, an angrier version of Winter's defiance. "I learned," she spat.

"I can assume we have your family history to thank for that. And what else did you learn from them? What have you not told us?"

Ayden didn't answer.

"Well, perhaps you'll tell me this." The finger came back up and jabbed toward her. "Why in God's name did you think it acceptable to remove your tracking device and disappear? None of this would have happened if you'd have stayed put. I wouldn't have an agent injured and Winter wouldn't have taken off on her own. We may have even been able to capture some of them, but in our hurry to find you they all escaped…even the one you say you knocked out. The events of tonight can be laid at your feet! We can't put an end to this, we can't protect you, unless you follow direction!"

"I can protect myself!" said Ayden, staring Erickson in the eyes.

"I DON'T CARE!" Erickson thundered. His face trembled for a moment as electricity crackled through the room. Then he visibly took hold of his composure, sighed, and looked down at the table, taking slow calming breaths. "If you two can't make this work, then I'm taking the whole lot of you and putting you in protective custody. Is that understood?" He looked back up. "You have to get on board with the plan. If we're going to stop Xaphan, then I need you to do your parts."

"It seems to me," said Ayden, "if you would just advertise that Kaci's the one and wait for him to come, it'd be the perfect ambush."

Erickson slammed his hand on the table. "We can't do that," he said through clenched teeth.

"Why not? What's so special about her? She's just another person Xaphan wants to murder, just like me and just like Winter. But you have no problem putting us in the line of fire. Why are you protecting her so much?"

Erickson took another deep breath. He spoke with ice in his voice. "Yes, he wants to kill both of you, but he's been after Kaci almost her entire life. We don't know what started it or why it's persisted, and until we figure those things out then we do everything we can to protect her. As long as she's Xaphan's priority, she's ours. And even if we did reveal her identity, Xaphan would kill both of you just to make sure we weren't lying. You're not getting out of this. So, what's it going to take to get you under control?"

"I'm not helpless, so stop treating me like I am," Ayden sneered.

Erickson clenched his jaw and nodded. "Fine. You're not helpless. Would it help if we loosened the reins on you a little? No more looking over your shoulder, but still within a couple hundred yards of backup. If I give you that much, then you have to agree no more leaving your tracking bracelet behind, no more hiding, and to call me directly if you suspect anything. Whether you can handle yourself or not is irrelevant. If you want a little more leeway, then I expect more obedience. Agreed?"

Ayden nodded.

Erickson turned to Winter. "And you?"

"I can do more, I can find Xaphan," said Winter. "Give me a chance."

"No. I can't allow that, sorry. Not the way you want. You leave Xaphan to us. I need you to be the first line of defense for Kaci and Ayden both. Do your prophetess thing and be there to keep them safe when we can't. To that extent I am grateful for what you did tonight. You got to Ayden first, and that's the sort of thing I want you to keep doing. If you have a hunch, or whatever you call it, and that hunch has something to do with those two, then I will let you follow it a thousand miles away. But don't ever do anything like that again without giving me a chance to cover Kaci. I don't care if the president calls you for help and sends a private jet, you don't go anywhere until I've sent someone to watch Kaci. Agreed?"

Winter nodded.

He flicked his eyes from Winter to Ayden. "Get it together. Both of you. Dismissed."

Winter spun and led the way out of the apartment, the pressure of Erickson's stare upon her back. She wanted to stomp all the way to her car, but she would not give Ayden the satisfaction of seeing her ruffled. Her jaw ached from constant grinding, and despite herself she slammed the car door.

"Listen," said Ayden, as they headed back to Tishbe. "We don't get much time alone like this, so there are some things I want to ask."

"Fine. Whatever." Winter suppressed a sneer at how calm Ayden sounded.

"Who is the little girl? I've seen her twice already, and both times you acted surprised."

Winter glanced at her, Erickson suddenly forgotten. "You really can see her?"

"Yes. Who is she?"

"I'm not sure. She won't tell me. But up until now, I've been the only who can see her. She shows up sometimes to guide me. I'm not certain why. I just thought it was one of the prophetess things. But you can see her too, so I'm not so sure anymore."

Ayden huffed. "Is she real?"

"What do you think?"

"What's happening to me? I don't understand why I can see someone only you can. I don't understand how I got into that stupid coliseum. It's like I was supposed to go there…" Ayden put her head to her hands and grunted. "I'm just so confused right now."

"It sounds like some of the same things that happened to me are beginning to happen to you too. Trust me. It's real," said Winter. "It's all real, whether you want it to be or not. You're confused because you don't want to let it be real to you."

"Fine. I give up. How do I let it be real?"

"Do you really want to know?"

"Yes," said Ayden. "Whatever you did to make sense of it, tell me."

Winter checked the clock on her dash. Two in the morning. She peered ahead and saw the lights at the gates of Tishbe coming up and the CLC building just outside the gate. "Let's pull in here and talk. Maybe your nanny won't get too upset."

Winter and Ayden walked together into the Union the next week for lunch on Monday. Winter scanned the crowds for her friends, and spotted Summer almost immediately. As Ayden stood in line for lunch, Winter went over to speak with Summer.

"Hey," Winter said.

Summer shuffled her straw in her drink, but didn't look up. "Hey."

Winter sat down. "You don't look so good. What's going on?"

Summer shrugged, but her eyes darted to the other side of the room. Winter followed and saw Davis sitting alone.

"Okay," said Winter. "Spill it. You two have been acting weird lately. Is something wrong?"

"I don't want to talk about it." Summer lifted her eyes and sneered at Winter. Then she stood to leave.

Ayden approached with her tray. "Hey, where's she going?"

Winter stared back at Davis. "I don't know, but I'm going to find out."

She stomped over to his table and sat. Ayden followed.

"Spill it," Winter said. "What's wrong with Summer?"

Davis sighed. "It's complicated."

"I can handle complicated."

Davis sighed again. "Since last spring…we've both been…"

"Been what? Stop stalling."

"I don't know. She's not the same. She refuses to talk to anyone.

She doesn't even talk to me anymore. I see her whispering on the phone to someone, and she won't tell me who."

Winter looked around, trying to locate Summer, but Summer had disappeared into the growing lunch crowd. "What do you think is happening?"

Davis shrugged. "I don't know. But I can't get that day out of my head either."

Peter and Kaci came to the table with their food. "What's up?" asked Peter.

"Winter, are you not eating?" asked Kaci.

Ayden snorted. "She's too busy running her mouth."

Winter shot Ayden a glare, which Ayden promptly returned.

"Do you want me to go get it?" asked Kaci.

"Um, sure. If you don't mind. Hold on." Winter fished out her ID card and passed it to Kaci. Kaci took it and returned to the lunch line.

"So what's so important you can't be bothered to get your own food?" asked Peter as he sat.

"Summer's acting weird."

Peter stiffened. "How so?"

"She's moping around and won't talk to anyone. Not even Davis."

Peter looked from Winter to Davis and back again. "I'm sure it's just shock. Maybe she just needs some time and space."

Winter narrowed her eyes, trying to read his. Again she saw something in them he wasn't telling. "What do you know?"

Peter shook his head. "Nothing. No more than you."

"So you've noticed too?"

"Of course. Couldn't help it the other night. After you left she barely spoke to anyone." Peter matched her gaze, refusing to flinch, his eyes defiant.

After a brief moment, he attended his food and didn't look back at her directly. Peter was hiding something, just like Summer. Winter was certain.

Winter glared back at Davis. He briefly met her eyes before looking back down. She saw more in his eyes, too. She turned back to Peter and then again to Davis. They were different things. Both of them afraid to speak, but hiding entirely different things from her. What was going on? How did Summer fit in?

Winter scanned the Union again, hoping maybe Summer had just relocated, but Summer was truly gone, probably back to her dorm. She frowned at Ayden, and Ayden just raised her eyebrow.

"Where's Nadeen?" Winter asked.

Ayden shrugged. "Around, I suppose." She pursed her lips. "Why would I know where my roommate is at all times?"

Kaci returned with a tray of food and set it in front of Winter.

"Hope a burger is okay," said Kaci.

"Yeah, it's fine. Thank you. Um, I need to go to the restroom." Winter stood and motioned to Ayden with her eyes.

"Yeah, me too," said Ayden with a half-hearted grunt. "Wait up."

As they left the crowds and entered the hallway leading to the restrooms, Winter leaned close to Ayden and whispered. "They're hiding something."

"Of course they are, you idiot."

Winter stopped and faced her. "You knew?"

"I think a better question is, how did it take you so long to see it? I noticed something wasn't right the first week of school. All three of them. Davis, Summer, and Peter."

Winter shoved her in the shoulder. "And you didn't say anything?"

"Shh!" Ayden turned to walk toward the restrooms. "If it was dangerous, I would have. And if it was dangerous they would have done something by now. I thought you trusted them?"

"I do." Winter folded her arms. Did she?

"So stop worrying about it. I'm sure it's nothing. Let them have their little secrets, and when it's important they'll tell you. Some things are just hard to express until you're ready. Or maybe you'll do the prophetess thing and find out anyway."

Winter ground her teeth. "You're right. Fine. I'll drop it. But if you hear anything, tell me."

Ayden shrugged. "Whatever."

Winter glared at her and turned to stomp back to the table.

"So, you're not really going to the restroom then?" Ayden asked to her back.

Winter grunted, half wanting to turn back around and punch her. The other half wanting to beat Davis, Summer, and Peter senseless. Then Kaci looked up and smiled at her. Winter took a deep breath, smiled, and sat down to eat her lunch.

Kaci was the priority.

12

Four Years Ago

For the first time since moving to Trenton Hills, Winter discovered a way to keep her anger at bay, to bury it deep within with the rest of her pain. But more significant than that, she found a way to allow a little happiness to creep to the surface. She didn't have to be so numb all the time. She didn't have to suppress everything at once. And right now, the one thought that brought her a little measure of happiness was trying to get out of that place. Her grades were perfect so far…perfect enough that both Claire and Stacy came to her for help on occasions.

The three of them had become somewhat of an awkward group again, with Winter the nucleus. Stacy and Claire had little in common anymore, save for their friendship with Winter and a shared past. Having the two of them at peace, for a change, made it easier to maintain Winter's new complacency.

As the last week of October approached, Winter noticed Claire making sideways glances at Stacy during lunch. Stacy prattled about the research report she had been assigned, while Claire kept her lips tight as if she had something important to say but didn't dare so long as Stacy was around. Winter just nodded at Stacy, allowing her to sustain the conversation on her own, and watched Claire patiently. When Stacy finally left with the rest of her class, Claire leaned over the table, just as Winter had expected her to.

"I want to invite you to something," Claire said.

"Not another witch thing is it?"

"Well, yeah. But that's not the point."

"I thought I wasn't allowed."

Claire shook her head. "I talked to Madam Morial. You were only asked to leave that one time because you surprised them. They didn't know what to expect. She said you can come now."

"What's going on?"

"Halloween. It's our Samhain celebration."

"What's that?" asked Winter.

"It's sort of a new year for Wiccans. It's one of the more powerful nights. Many who come will do readings for the next year. It's also a time to celebrate life and to say goodbye to those we've lost."

"Oh." Winter looked at the table.

"I know it's hard," Claire said as she grabbed Winter's hand. "But you have to do this. You have to say goodbye."

Winter nodded. "I know," she whispered.

"It's a completely safe environment, and you'll be around friends of mine who understand you and who know how to help you let go. And then after the celebration, there will be chocolate. Lots of chocolate."

Winter smiled and looked up. "What about Stacy?"

Claire shook her head. "She won't understand. I respect her beliefs, but this isn't something Christianity approves of. And I know you're not interested in any of my beliefs either, I respect you too…but, that's not what this is about. I just want you to have some fun and find a little closure somehow."

"And if it's too much for me?"

"Then I'll take you home. No questions asked. Okay?"

"Okay. I'll do it."

Claire grinned and stood, grabbing her tray. "Great. I'll pick you up about five-thirty."

"Sure," Winter said as Claire left. She took a deep breath. She could do this. She needed to do this.

Winter waited in the living room Halloween evening, sitting in the chair closest to the door and impatiently watching TV with her dad, her purse sitting in her lap. Five-thirty had just come and gone, and she wondered what was taking Claire so long. She wasn't really all that late, but still…if she had to spend another evening avoiding her dad…

A horn blew outside and Winter jumped out of the seat. Steve glanced at her and took another swig of the beer in his hand.

"That's her, Dad. I've gotta go." She shouldered her purse and ran for the door, hoping he wouldn't come up with an excuse to stop her.

"Winter," Steve said.

Winter huffed and paused with her hand on the knob. She peered over her shoulder, clearing her face to impassivity. "Yeah?"

"I'm glad you're getting out again. Be careful. And don't do anything stupid."

Winter rolled her eyes as he turned back to the TV, and then rushed out the door before he could say anything else.

Claire's car hummed at the curb. As Winter ran down the sidewalk, Claire leaned over and popped up the lock on the passenger side. Winter jumped in, shoved her seatbelt on, and faced Claire. "Okay, where are we going?"

"There's a bonfire back behind Madam Morial's house." Claire put the car into gear and Winter's street began to rush by.

"Not back in the forest?"

Claire chuckled. "No. There's a chance it might rain, so Madam Morial wanted to have an inside option." She looked at Winter. "Are you okay?"

Winter nodded. "Yeah. I'm just...um, a little excited about this."

"Really?"

"Really. Thanks for inviting me. And there's something I need to tell you..."

"No, there's something I need to say first," said Claire.

"I'm sorry," both girls said at once, and then filled the car with laughter.

Claire recovered first and continued. "I'm sorry for the way I acted last year. I got too caught up in myself and in my Wiccan friends. It's just for the first time I had a real sense of who I was. I felt like I belonged. For a little while there I resented you for not seeing how important these changes were to me and for not joining me in them. Deep down I knew it was selfish of me and that you just needed me to be a friend, and I wasn't there for you. I'm sorry."

"Thank you," said Winter. "That really means a lot. And I'm sorry for pretty much the same reason. I let all my confusion get in the way of being a friend."

"It's okay. You have plenty of reasons to be confused. But you seem different now. What happened?"

Winter shrugged. "Just something Stacy said. She really put things in perspective for me and showed me how other people were hurting around me. She said I went into grief shock, and she was right. So, no matter how much it kills me on the inside, it's not fair to my friends."

"Well, I'm glad you're really back. But for the record, don't keep all the junk hidden inside."

"That's what Stacy said. I won't anymore. I promise."

"Good," said Claire.

Madam Morial's house was an old wood-frame farmhouse with a wrap-around porch. It sat hidden behind trees several hundred yards off the rural paved road, invisible to most passers-by. It was already dark when they pulled up, and the light from the bonfire made an orange halo around the house.

Claire led her to the backyard, where at least two dozen men and women of all ages were talking, playing, and roasting marshmallows in the fire. The oldest of these, including Madam Morial, sat around a patio table on a large deck extending from the house. As they approached the table, Madam Morial stood and smiled.

"Hello, Claire. I see you brought Winter. That is very good." She turned to Winter with a nod of her head. "You are most welcome."

"Thank you," said Winter in a small voice.

Madam Morial waved her hand. "Make yourself at home. We have plenty of hotdogs to roast, chips, sodas, and candy."

"Thanks," said Claire. "Come on, Winter. Let's go eat."

The food table stood to one side of a concrete path bordering a carefully manicured flower bed. As they filled small plates with snacks, four girls crossed the yard to them.

"Hi, Claire," said the one in front.

"Hey." Claire tapped Winter's arm. "Winter, these are my sisters. This is Shannon, Madam Morial's daughter." She gestured the one who had spoken. "And this is Melissa, Kathrine, and Mary. They've all been a part of this their entire lives. Their parents are probably here somewhere."

"Hi," said Winter.

They each returned Winter a smile and greeting.

"We're all over there," said Shannon pointing toward the other side of the fire to a large group of teens sitting on the ground in front of a pergola filled with deck chairs, where more adults were sitting.

"Sure," said Claire. "We'll join you in a moment."

After they finished getting snacks, Winter followed Claire to the far side of the bonfire. Shannon waved them to sit beside her, a big grin on her face.

"Winter this is…" Shannon began, pointing to another new face beside them.

"She's not going to remember all of these names," said Claire. "She'll figure it out."

"Fine," said Shannon. "If anyone wants to talk to Winter, make sure you introduce yourself."

Everyone said their names at once.

Shannon laughed. "Idiots."

Winter wasn't sure what to think as she looked around at the faces of the group, some shadowed and some with sharp orange lines from the fire's glow. But a smile crept into the corners of her mouth.

A guy leaned close from Winter's left, and for the first time she realized she was actually sitting next to someone she didn't know.

"I'm Michael," he said. "I'm Shannon's brother."

"Hi," Winter said and then shoved the hotdog into her mouth.

"Never mind him," said Shannon. "He's just a flirt."

Michael tossed a marshmallow at Shannon and hit her in the face. Winter snorted.

As the evening drew on and the fire simmered down to embers, one by one people finished eating. Winter watched as everyone formed a circle around the fire. Tiki torches came to life outside the circle of people, supplementing the light.

"What's going on?" she asked Claire.

"Well, we've had our time of fellowship. So now we're going to have our time of remembrance. Then we'll have a time to look ahead.

And at the end will be the celebration. That's where the dancing and chocolate comes in."

"Dancing? You didn't say anything about dancing."

Claire laughed. "You don't have to. It's just for fun, really."

Madam Morial approached from the house, carrying a small table. She brought it just before the fire and set it as close as possible to the embers. "As I prepare the altar for tonight's ritual, take this time to reflect on those you wish to remember."

Everyone started whispering together, and pulling out photographs.

Claire leaned toward Winter. "Did you bring what I told you?"

Winter nodded and dug into her bag. She pulled out two pictures. "You're not going to make me burn these, are you?"

Claire shook her head. "No. But if you think that's something you need to do to let go…"

"No. I want to keep them."

Claire nodded.

Winter held both photographs side by side. The one in her right hand a larger copy of the photo in the locket dangling around her neck. Winter and her mom together on Winter's fourteenth birthday. Their arms wrapped around each other, cheeks pressed together as they smiled for the camera.

The one in her left hand was the bent prom photo of her and Ryan. Slicked-back hair and gleaming tux, hand gently resting on her waist. She held his hand beneath an arch of blue balloons and flowers.

She didn't know which one punched the bigger hole in her heart, but the pain of it burst out. She shifted the pictures into one hand and covered her mouth.

Claire rubbed her back. "Do you want to talk about them?"

Winter opened her mouth and a sob escaped. "It just hurts…"

Madam Morial was chanting something and lighting candles, ignoring Winter. Something had been added to the embers and a smell of mint, nutmeg, and apple wafted through the air. Winter wiped her eyes and peeked around. She wasn't the only one mourning. Somehow that made things worse and better at the same time.

Madam Morial raised her hands and everyone quieted, those crying still sniffing occasionally. "Samhain is here," she said. "The winter approaches, and the summer dies. It is a time of transitions. A time of death and of dying. And tonight we remember those who have lived and died before us, those who have crossed through the veil."

"I don't think I can do this," Winter whispered to Claire.

"It'll be okay. You need to do this."

Winter bit her lip and stared at the ground.

"Tonight is the night when the gateway between our world and the spirit world is thinnest," said Madam Morial. "Tonight we call out to those who have gone before us. Tonight we honor our loved ones."

Winter shifted, sliding her feet beneath her and eyeing the house. Claire grabbed her hand and tugged down.

"Spirits, we call to you and welcome you to join us for this night."

"I can't," whispered Winter.

"Yes, you can," said Claire.

Winter stood. "No. I can't," she said loudly and shoved the photos back into her bag.

Madam Morial stopped and watched her. Winter cast around and found everyone watching. She crossed her arms and glared at Claire. "You said you would take me home."

Claire sighed heavily and stood. "I'm sorry, Madam Morial. I'll be back soon." Madam Morial simply nodded in return.

As soon as they were beyond the torchlight, Winter heard Madam Morial begin again, and almost ran around the house and back to the car. She waited at the passenger side for Claire to catch up.

As they were about to climb into the car, Shannon and Michael came jogging around the house. "Wait up," called Michael.

"We have to go," said Claire, a slight edge of disappointment in her voice.

Shannon and Michael stopped at the hood of the car. "I know. It's okay," said Shannon. "We just wanted to say something. Winter…"

Winter looked up from the side mirror she had been staring at.

"So it was too much tonight. Big deal. Not everyone's into the ritual stuff. I get it," said Shannon. "We hope you don't pin it on us."

"We want you to come hang out," said Michael. "Just as a regular person. Whatever makes you feel comfortable."

"Why would you want to do that?" asked Winter, shuffling her feet.

Shannon shrugged. "Because Claire's our friend, and you're Claire's friend."

"Give them a chance," said Claire over the top of the car. "Please? No more rituals. I promise. Just normal stuff. You need to get out more and you know it."

Winter sighed and nodded.

"I'll be back as soon as I take Winter home," Claire said.

Shannon nodded. "We'll talk later. I have some fun ideas."

"Are you ready, Winter?" Claire asked as Shannon and Michael walked away.

Winter grabbed the handle and jumped in, trying desperately not to make any more eye contact.

13

Present Day

Winter's phone chirped. She rolled over and slammed her hand at it thinking it was the alarm. It chirped again. Winter lifted her head to glance at the clock. Two in the morning. She sighed and picked up her phone. The caller ID said "unknown," but Winter knew who it probably was.

"What?" she moaned when she answered.

"It's Erickson."

"I know."

He hesitated. *"How did you know?"*

"Easy," she said as she rolled onto her back. "No other idiot would call me this late."

"Oh." Winter thought she heard a muffled laugh. *"Listen,"* he said. *"I need you to come over here."*

"Now?"

"Yes."

"But it's the middle of the night," she said.

"I know. Our job requires us to work at any hour. We need you now. We

have something that's just come down and it can't wait until morning. Your particular…skills might give us something we need to take immediate action."

Winter sat up and took a deep calming breath. "Fine. I'll be there in a few minutes." She hung up.

After lying motionless for a moment, the still calming sensation of sleep washed over her. She wanted so badly just to not care, but then panic flooded through and she sat up on the edge of the bed with her head in her hands. With a weary grunt, she stood to get dressed.

The temperate autumn weather had dropped seemingly overnight. Winter pulled her hoodie tighter to her body as she approached the apartment that was the FBI field office. She climbed the stairs and knocked on the door, briefly glancing up at the little black lipstick-sized camera pointing down at her from a corner of the stairwell.

Agent Golbeck, fully dressed as if he were ready to leave that moment, opened the door and gestured for her to enter. Winter walked in, noticing how dirty the apartment had become. Empty coffee cups and drink cans littered the floor, and an overflowing trash can made a nice pile of garbage just beside the kitchen.

"What, the FBI can't spring for a maid?"

Golbeck chuckled. "We have a vacuum."

"I think it's time to use it."

Agent Erickson looked up from the table and waved her over, his face grim and obviously not in the mood for her sarcasm.

"What's all this about?" asked Winter. "I shouldn't be here for long. Kaci doesn't sleep well all the time. If she wakes up and sees I'm gone, she'll know something's up."

"If she finds out, she finds out. I think she'll understand us calling you over here, just don't give her any details."

"But who's watching out for her right now?"

"The undercover agents across from you have been awakened and notified. Give us a little more credit. You're not the only one assigned to her."

Winter crossed her arms and sat across from Erickson. "Listen, before we start, I need you do something for me."

"What is it?" asked Erickson.

"My friends, Summer, Davis, and Peter…I think they're keeping something from me."

"And you think it might be important?"

Winter shrugged. "They've never acted like this before. Just look into it, will you? Just in case."

Agent Erickson nodded as Agent Golbeck took the chair to her right, in front of a red folder. Erickson turned to him expectantly, so Winter turned too.

"Are we ready?" asked Golbeck. "Late yesterday evening, October 31, about four hours ago, three girls about your age were found murdered."

"What does that have to do with me?" asked Winter.

"We want you to look at the photos and see if you can identify the girls."

Winter stiffened. "Why me?"

"Because two of them were from Trenton Hills."

Winter looked at Agent Erickson. "Trenton Hills? Who were they? Where were they killed?"

"Two of them had identification, but we wanted to verify it through you and see if you knew the third. They were murdered in a rural area about two hours away. Will you look?"

Winter reached out for the folder, but Agent Golbeck pulled it away. "I don't think you understand. These are photographs of the crime scene. They are very graphic. Can you handle that?"

Winter took a deep breath. "I think so. But I have to know who they are."

Agent Golbeck opened the folder and slid one eight by ten photograph in front of her. It was a close-up of the face of a girl. The eyes still open, the skin pale gray. A black trickle of dried blood covered her upper lip from her nose.

He slid another photograph. Another girl. Eyes clenched, skin blanched, mouth open. A deep gash carved across her throat. Winter grimaced. If she had anything in her stomach, it would be turning. As it was, she wasn't hungry any longer.

He slid a third photograph. Another girl. Eyes open, staring blankly into the lens of the camera. A pair of scissors protruding from the side of her neck. The word "Culsu" carved into her forehead.

Winter covered her mouth and looked away. Agent Golbeck scooped up the photographs.

"Do you recognize them?" asked Agent Erickson.

"Give me a minute." Winter stood and wrapped her arms around herself. She walked into the living room area, taking deep breaths, trying not to let the images of Kaci in the tower join the images of the photographs. A wave of nausea gurgled through her stomach, but with a still moment of concentrating, she kept the lurching of her insides at bay. Dry heaving in front of trained FBI agents wasn't exactly her style.

"You're wrong," she said as she turned. "All of them are from Trenton Hills."

"All of them?" asked Golbeck. "Are you sure?"

Winter nodded.

"So you do recognize them?" asked Erickson.

Winter nodded again. "The first one was Melissa. The second was Kathrine. And the last was Mary. I don't know their last names…I didn't know them well." Winter eased back over to the chair and sat again.

"How do you know them?" asked Golbeck.

"I used to hang out with some Wiccans, with a friend of mine.

They were with us occasionally."

"All three of them?"

Winter nodded.

"So there's a connection between them," said Golbeck.

"But worse than that," said Erickson. "They have a connection to Winter."

"Can you tell us anything else?" asked Golbeck.

Winter took a deep breath. "The name on Mary's head. I know it too."

"A name?" Golbeck started writing. "What does it mean?"

"I'm not sure," said Winter. "But just before..." She took another deep breath. "Another friend of mine said that name just before she died. She was involved in some dark magic stuff. I think it was an invoked spirit."

Erickson nodded. "So what you're saying is, we have three dead Wiccans, and the possible murderer has a connection to dark magic."

Winter nodded. "Looks like it."

Erickson looked at Golbeck. "Skotos."

"Skotos?" asked Winter. "What would they have to do with people from my hometown?"

Erickson shook his head. "Not just people from your hometown, but people you knew. If we're dealing with dark Wiccans targeting people from your past, the most logical culprit has to be Skotos."

"Are you saying they died because of me?"

Golbeck shrugged. "We don't know. But we need to track down every possible lead to make sure it's not someone trying to get to you through other people."

"Do you know where they were staying?" asked Winter.

Erickson shook his head. "Melissa and Kathrine had Trenton Hills identification, the third...Mary...had nothing. We'll start there, along with your identification of the third, and maybe we can get a positive ID and find some relatives. After that we can work the process and track their movements some. Whether or not that'll lead to a definite place of residence nearby, I don't know. In any case, it could take some time." Erickson leaned forward. "Is there anything else you could tell us about these Wiccans you used to hang out with?"

Winter clenched her eyes. "Yeah. There's someone missing."

"What do you mean missing?" asked Golbeck.

"Shannon. She was one of them. The four of them were inseparable. Shannon was Madam Morial's daughter, the priestess of the coven. If someone were after them, they would have killed Shannon too. You don't think Shannon could have done it?"

Erickson stared at her. "What do you think?"

Winter glanced at the photographs still in Golbeck's hand. And for the first time that year, a spark of fear ignited within. "I...I don't know."

14

Winter drove her BMW through the streets of Cherithville to return to her apartment. Her mind's eye swam with the images of the three dead girls. The word Culsu pulsed in her ears. Suddenly she could see Alison clearly as she wandered into prom her second year of high school, hair in disarray and makeup streaked. Alison had found Claire immediately and began yelling, looking for Phillip...

Winter walked through the crowd to Claire and Alison, Ryan following and refusing to relinquish her hand.

"Ali, what's going on?" she asked.

Alison turned to face her. Her chin quivered. Her voice dropped. "Where's Phillip?"

"He's not here. What happened to you?"

Alison's eyes widened with confusion. She clutched the sides of her head and looked at the ceiling. "I...I don't know." She started to cry. "Culsu."

"Culsu?" Claire took a small step toward Ali and stretched out a calming hand. "Ali, what have you been doing?"

The word Culsu carved into Mary's forehead...

Alison looked around, seeming to notice the other couples for the first time. She blinked and focused on Winter.

"Where am I?" Alison asked.

"This is prom," said Winter. "Why are you here?"

"I don't remember."

Claire stepped closer to Alison and gave Winter a frightened, knowing look. "Ali," she said quietly, "what spells have you been trying?"

Alison screamed. "I don't remember. What's happening to me? Where's Phillip?"

"Have you been invoking spirits?"

Alison's face suddenly twisted. She bared her teeth and hissed. "Leave Culsu alone!" She shoved Claire backward, and then her face shifted again, softening with wide-eyed confusion. "Oh, no..." she moaned. "Phillip..."

"Do you know where he is?" asked Winter.

"I don't know...I don't..."

Alison lifted a trembling arm, and for the first time Winter saw that she clenched something in her fist. Alison held her hand out and slowly opened her fingers. A bloody pair of scissors fell to the floor.

"Where is Phillip?" asked Claire.

Alison's face changed again, wrinkling with pursed lips and narrowed eyes. "He's dead," she growled.

Scissors embedded in the side of Mary's neck...

"SHUT UP!" Alison roared. She put her hands over her ears and whimpered. "Culsu won't shut up..."

A cold shudder drizzled down Winter's back. Something flickered in the darkness of the passenger seat. She gazed over and found nothing there.

Winter took a deep breath to calm her heartbeat and laughed at herself for jumping at shadows. But despite the clamminess outside, she reached to the console and turned on the heat.

Was there really a connection between Winter and these murders? Was someone hunting down her past? And Alison…what had Alison gotten herself involved with?

What was Culsu?

Winter made another turn.

Wait. Another turn?

She looked around in panic at the street she was on. She didn't recognize anything. She had been driving by instinct, which could only mean the premonition had taken over without her fully realizing it. The panic ebbed away. She was on the right path. Her muscles already knew the motions, and she allowed herself to be guided through the dark neighborhoods.

Both the quality and the quantity of the houses dwindled. The road narrowed. Winter soon found herself outside of the Cherithville city limits and in what appeared to be a bad part of town. She passed by a couple of seedy characters sitting on the steps of their homes, smoking. Oddly neither of them looked at the gleaming BMW driving through the street. The only other creatures awake enough to mark her passing were dogs, and even they didn't acknowledge her with so much as a lifted head. Winter rolled through the neighborhood seemingly invisible.

She turned onto the dirt parking area of a one-story brick duplex that looked as if it had been built in the 1960's. The parking area was empty except for Winter, and all the windows of the apartment were dark. Winter opened the car door and stood, with one foot still in the car, peering around into the shadows and toward the nearest houses and duplex apartments. No one was visible. Winter stepped all the way out, locked her car, and gently closed the door.

She looked at the two apartment doors and drifted instinctively to the one on the left. The door opened easily for her and clicked locked when she closed it, without her having to do anything. Winter reached for the light switch, but thought better of it. Instead, she reached down to her ankle and pulled out her gun. With the gun extended, Winter paced through the living and dining area, and into the kitchen. No one there. She panned the gun around and faced the short hall. The nearest door stood half open. She nudged it with her foot and peered in. An empty bathroom. Winter rolled her feet further down the hall to the next door. With the gun pointed at the crack and one hand on the handle, she turned it and eased it open.

A bedroom. Empty. No bed, only a pile of blankets and sheets tousled together into one corner. She crept down to the last door and eased it open the same way. Another empty bedroom. A queen-sized bed stood in the middle of the floor, bedding in disarray. Laundry covered the floor. Another door inside the bedroom and to the right stood slightly ajar. Winter eased to it and pushed it open. Another empty bathroom.

Winter took a deep relaxing breath and returned the gun to her ankle holster. What was she doing here? Who lived here? Did God actually lead her to break into someone's home? There had to be something important here. But Winter knew she needed to be quick.

She checked that the blinds and curtains were closed in the bedroom before turning on the light. The room was messier than she could see in the dark, as if someone had already ransacked it. Every drawer in the dresser hung open, with the contents littered on the floor below. Winter checked each drawer and kicked through the pile, then she dropped down and peeked under the bed. Nothing stood out to her as important. She stood and went to the two bi-fold doors of the closet, one closed but the other jammed open and off its tracks. Inside Winter found plenty of clothes still hanging, mostly black just like Winter's own closet. Shoes littered the floor; most were some form of high-top or knee-high boot. Packing boxes lined the shelf above the hanging clothes and a couple more boxes sat stacked in the corner on the floor. Winter knelt and grabbed the first box, yanking open the intertwined flaps. She found nothing inside but a bunch of random junk: old cell phone chargers, pens and pencils, notepads, television cables. She set that box aside and looked back at the remaining boxes, trying to decide which to randomly pick next.

A small decorated box, no bigger than a shoebox, caught her attention. It was wedged between the wall and a much larger box, and Winter had to do a little rearranging before she could wrestle it free. She took it to the bed and opened it, finding exactly what she expected from a decorated shoebox...old photos. Winter grabbed a handful and started shuffling through them.

Immediately she almost threw them back into the box out of shock. The people in the photos were all people she knew. Shannon. Melissa. Kathrine. Mary. Winter fumbled through them quickly, not pausing long enough to focus on their faces for fear Agent Erickson's photos would surface in her mind.

There was Claire.

Winter put a hand to her mouth and studied the photo of her old high school friend. Though it surprised her to see Claire's face after so long, she should have expected Claire to show up in photos of the other girls.

She had to take a deep breath to steady herself before going on, clearing her mind of horrific memories she had buried long ago, things she would rather not relive. But the next picture destroyed all her calm and she almost screamed, this time tossing the photos across the bed before she could get herself back under control.

She eased back to the offending photo and picked it up again. It was a photo of Winter, standing with arms tantalizingly tight around Shannon's brother Michael. She remembered that picture.

Winter snatched up the scattered photos and shoved them back into the box, slamming the cover in place. Whose apartment was this? Winter scanned the room for clues. She had to know. She rushed over to the nightstand and yanked open the drawers. Nothing. Just papers and more random junk. She scanned the floor again, hoping maybe she would see something identifying amidst the piles of laundry. All she could tell was the room belonged to a girl, young, judging by the clothing styles, and a little larger than Winter. But there had to be something in here with a name. Or maybe somewhere in the rest of the apartment.

Winter ran back into the living area, ignoring caution and turning on the light. She saw what she needed immediately, sitting on the arm of the couch. A purse.

Winter grabbed it and popped it open. She dug around until she found a little wallet she knew should contain an ID. After flicking apart the latch, she finally found her answer.

Mary Hamel. The one who didn't have identification. The one with Culsu carved into her forehead and scissors shoved into her neck.

Keys rattled in the lock. Winter spun around, scanning the room for a place to hide. No, she would have to face whoever it was anyway. She reached down, retrieved her gun, and leveled it at the door, easing into the hall so the person wouldn't immediately see her.

Winter heard the person step in. "Hello?" a young woman's voice called out. The door closed. "Is someone here?"

Winter took a deep breath and stepped out of the hall to face her.

The young woman's eyes widened and her jaw dropped. "Winter?"

Winter's heart drummed and the gun faltered. "Shannon?"

15

Four Years Ago

Winter rode in the car with Claire again the next weekend. Her stomach flittered and she chewed the sides of her cheeks as she gazed out the window. Hanging out with Claire again, witchcraft, a boy...Too much intersecting at once forced images of Ryan and her mom to bob to the surface almost faster than she could shove them back below.

She glanced over at Claire. "I'm really not sure about this."

"I promise, no magic stuff, no remembering, just a fun time, okay? Before the evening is over, you'll be laughing and having a great time. You and I both need it."

"Is everything okay?" Winter asked, seizing upon the opportunity to shift the focus off of her. "You've been saying things like that a lot lately."

Claire shrugged. "My dad...well, he's been drinking a lot."

Winter turned away, not daring to push any further. She knew exactly what Claire meant. She was glad her own dad wasn't like that. It was the one thing she could be thankful for.

"Who's going to be there?" Winter asked.

"Just Shannon, Melissa, Kathrine, and Mary, I think. Those four are pretty tight. Michael, of course…it's his apartment. And he'll probably have a few of his own friends over."

"So, is this like a party? Alison took me to some parties. I didn't particularly like it."

Claire shook her head. "No, not like that. Well, it might be a little bit like a party. But it's just for a few friends. We're just hanging out having fun, that's all."

Claire turned on a street lined with carbon-copied duplexes. Three buildings down, several cars crowded the street on both sides. Claire pulled in behind one and they both got out. No thunderous music greeted them from the curb. No drinking teens waited on the porch. As Claire knocked on the door, Winter wondered if they were even at the right place.

Shannon answered with a smile on her face and a beer in her hand. "Hey guys, come on in."

Winter followed Claire inside. The apartment seemed more spacious on the inside than it did from outside. Shannon's brother Michael and three of his friends sat on the couch and on the floor, playing a video game. Michael gazed her way briefly and smiled, then went back to the game. Winter peered at the TV and saw a four-way split screen, each containing its own bobbing gun floating through the ruins of some building. Loud gunfire erupted from the TV speakers, and one of the guys shouted, "Yes!" Another grunted in frustration.

"Claire, Winter…this is Will, Trey, and Matt," said Shannon.

All three of them offered a simultaneous, uninterested, and un-looked-up-for, "Hey."

Shannon rolled her eyes. "As I'm sure neither of you are interested in the latest edition of Band of Commandos, you can join the girls over here at the table." Shannon pulled a fifth chair over to the table and Claire and Winter joined Shannon, Melissa, Kathrine, and Mary.

"So, Winter, you go to Trenton Hills with Claire, right?" asked Mary.

Winter nodded. "Yeah."

"What year are you?"

"A junior, same as Claire."

Mary nodded. "Kathrine and I are seniors at Charles Academy. Shannon graduated last year. She's at Parkway Community College. And Melissa is a junior like you, at North Trenton."

"What about Michael and the others?" asked Winter.

Shannon snorted. "Michael graduated high school a few years ago and went to work at Taco Sam's."

"That's right," said Michael over the rapid gunfire and the roaring of the other three. "Not interested in spending the rest of my life in school."

"So you'd rather make tacos the rest of your life?" asked Shannon.

Michael didn't respond and made a good show of being focused on the game.

Shannon shook her head. "He wants to be an artist. I keep telling him that Parkway has an awesome graphic design department and he could get a great job doing that, but he thinks it'll taint his creativity. He's actually very talented." She pointed to a painting on the wall, a photo-realistic girl from behind, with long feathery blonde hair and white wings dragging the ground behind her. "That's one of his."

"Wow," said Claire. "I didn't know. He really is good."

"Yeah, well," said Shannon. "He's wasting it on Mexican food."

All the girls laughed except for Winter. She allowed herself a smile, but kept her arms crossed.

The evening wore on without much change. The girls continued their small talk, every once in a while trying to draw Winter into the conversation. Winter spent most of her time just listening or occasionally shifting in her seat so she could watch the guys play their games.

When dusk began to settle, Shannon turned to her brother. "Okay, it's time to eat. You going to cook or what?"

"Yeah, hold on." He fiddled with his controller. "I'm dropping out, guys."

Michael went into the kitchen, followed by Kathrine. They shared a quick kiss and then Michael turned to a table-top grill while Kathrine pulled a bowl out of the refrigerator.

"How do you like your burger, Winter?" Michael asked.

"Um…with cheese?"

"Well-done it is," he said.

Winter eyed them as they prepped the food, bumping shoulder to shoulder and smiling at each other. The muscles in her jaw ached from the clenching and she tried to turn back to the on-going conversation, but just couldn't seem to look away…as if it should be her there, not Kathrine. And not with Michael, with Ryan. Well, maybe Michael. That thought sent a shock through her heart and she jerked her eyes away immediately.

"Are you okay?" asked Mary.

Winter turned back to the other girls. All three of them had stopped talking to watch her. All Winter could do was stare back, no words forming to explain how she felt or her odd behavior. Sizzling erupted from the kitchen. Winter peered back at Michael and Kathrine for a brief moment.

"I need some air," she said as she stood. Winter tightened her arms closer against her chest and walked toward the door, painfully aware everyone in the apartment watched her.

Outside, the street lamps cast a sterile white light on the neglected pavement. A cool breeze crawled through the air, nipping against Winter's face. She pulled her jacket a little tighter and sat on the concrete edge of the alcoved entrance. She could hear voices from within the apartment, no doubt Claire catching up everyone who didn't already know about Winter's story.

When the door opened and Michael came out, Winter's suspicions were confirmed.

"Can I sit too?" he asked.

Winter shrugged.

"Beer?" He sat and passed an open can to her while taking a swig of his own can.

Winter eyed the can a moment, not entirely sure she wanted it. Then again, maybe it would help. She lifted it to her lips and let the yeasty liquid slide down her throat.

"Look," Michael said, "we really don't know each other very well, but I have no bias, I don't know the people you do, and that makes me perfect."

"I don't want to talk."

"I didn't say you had to."

Winter huffed. "Why does everyone want me to talk about it? All I want to do is forget. Can you help me do that?" She turned to look at him. "If I can get these memories out of my head, then I'll be fine."

"Keep drinking. That's a start."

Winter took another long drink, alcohol plunging into her otherwise empty stomach.

"Was it something we did?" Michael asked. "I mean, I know we didn't do anything. But we did something to trigger those memories. Am I right?"

Winter stared at the wide mouth of the can.

"What was it?"

Winter shrugged. "It's stupid." She flicked her eyes to him and found him watching, expecting an answer. She sighed. "It's just, seeing you and Kathrine together…"

Michael nodded. "You don't have to say anything else."

"I'm sorry. I want to have a good time." She put her hands to her head, beer can pressed to her cheek. "If I could just burn him out of my head…" The reality of what came out of her mouth slapped her in the face. The memories of the car and the fire filled her mind's eye.

She dropped the can and buried her face in her hands to hide the sudden weeping. Her body trembled, her eyes stung, the air passed in and out of her lungs like cold jelly, the embarrassment of not controlling herself…

She heard him snatch up the can from the concrete. She heard him stand and open the door. She heard him softly call to Claire.

Claire's touch pressed against Winter's back. "Winter, do we need to go?"

"No!" Winter flared up, angry at herself. "I'm tired of feeling like this. I'm tired of crying. I'm tired of remembering. I want to stay. I just can't get it out of my head!" The deep guttural cry of her frustration echoed around the neighborhood of duplexes. Nearby curtains parted, eyes peering at them from across the street.

Claire tugged at Winter's arm. "Come on, then. Let's go back inside."

"I think I have something that might help," said Michael. "Bring her to the couch."

Inside, the living area was empty now. Trey and Matt stood near the table and Will was in the kitchen helping with the food. Thankfully, none of the guys or girls were paying Winter any attention. Winter suspected they were just trying to be nice and discreet, and the pit of her stomach sank further at being a disappointing mess to everybody. Even her dad.

Claire and Michael walked with Winter to the couch. Claire sat beside her while Michael placed Winter's beer on the coffee table and then sauntered off down the hall. Winter picked up the beer and sucked in another long swallow, thankful not much had been wasted on the concrete.

Michael returned, holding what looked like a fat, short cigarette. A pungent smell, almost skunk-like wafted into the room with him. "Here, try this," he said, handing her the already smoking roll.

"You're giving me weed?" asked Winter.

"Are you sure that's a good idea?" asked Shannon from the table.

"It's perfectly legal in some places," he said.

"Just say no!" jeered Will with a snicker.

"Shut up," said Michael.

"I don't know about this." Winter turned to Claire.

Claire shrugged. "I don't know. Maybe it'll help."

"I know it'll help," said Michael. "A little toke always makes me feel better when I'm down."

"Michael," said Shannon. "If it starts going bad, make her stop. You don't want to make things worse."

"Don't worry, sis." Michael motioned the joint closer to Winter.

Winter reached out slowly and took it from him. "You really think this will help?"

"It'll make you relax and it'll make your problems feel unimportant. And when that happens, we'll make sure you have something fun to focus on. Tonight, you're going to have a good night. No more crying. No more remembering."

Winter nodded. She put the joint gently against her lips and inhaled. The smoke scorched her throat and settled like fire in her lungs. Winter raised her other hand to her mouth and coughed.

While she coughed, Michael took the joint from her and put it to his lips. "Claire, want a hit?"

He passed it to Claire, who did the same. Claire passed it back to Winter. Winter toked on it again, this time prepared for the burning sensation and accomplished far less coughing.

"Good," said Michael. "You two enjoy that. I'll go check on the burgers."

Winter and Claire passed the joint back and forth. With each hit, Winter's muscles loosened more and more. Her thinking became liquid and compressed. Time lost sync.

They watched a movie that sent her and Claire into fits of giggles. Why was it funny? What were they watching anyway? She couldn't remember...She remembered the food...lots of food. Awesome food. She remembered beer. She remembered more marijuana. Michael did something stupid. What was it again? And then she remembered waking up.

Present Day

Shannon's face pinched and reddened. "What are you doing here?" she shouted. "After what you did to me and my family? How dare you show your face again!"

Winter tried to control the trembling in her arms. She took a deep breath and steadied the gun, backing up a step. "What happened to them? Did you kill them? Don't come any closer!" she shouted as Shannon began to step forward.

Shannon's face darkened even more. "Kill who? What are you talking about? Why are you in my apartment?"

"Just stay right there!" Winter took one hand away from the gun and reached into her pocket for her phone. She fumbled through her recent contacts, found Agent Erickson and pushed the call button. Then she tossed the phone onto the nearby couch and steadied the gun again. "Mary…and Kathrine and Melissa. What did you do?"

Shannon's mouth opened. Her face softened. "W…what?"

"They're dead, Shannon. And you're the only one still alive. What did you do? Answer me!"

"Dead?" Shannon's jaw tightened. "That's why you're here. You killed them and you're going to kill me too? Then you're going to blame everything on me! What's wrong with you?"

"I'm not going to kill you. That's ridiculous. I'm not going to kill anybody."

"Yeah right. I know what you've done, remember?"

Ice tore through Winter's veins. Shannon's words ripped all the strength from her body. She couldn't hold the gun up any longer, much less keep it steady. Her arms sagged and fell, and so did Winter. She managed to sidestep enough to land sitting on the couch beside her phone.

"I'm calling the cops," said Shannon, reaching into her purse.

"Don't bother," Winter said. "I already did." She looked up into Shannon's condemning, hate-filled eyes. "You have to believe me when I say what happened was an accident."

Shannon crossed her arms and glared.

"Well, if you won't believe me, then at least believe this. I was asked to identify three murder victims earlier tonight. Melissa, Kathrine, and Mary. So either you did it or you're next."

Shannon sank into a chair, the red in her face draining white. The anger in her eyes turned to shock. "How?"

"Stabbed, I think. With scissors."

"Scissors?" Shannon let her head rest into the palms of her hands. "Oh no. Culsu."

Winter straightened, half lifting the gun again. "That's right. How did you know?"

Shannon looked up into Winter's eyes. "You know I would never, right?"

Winter tensed.

"Listen," Shannon continued. "There are all kinds of spirits in the world. I know you never really went for the spiritual side of Wicca, but we believe in many, many spirits who govern the world."

"Actually," said Winter. "I'm a Christian now."

Shannon tilted her head. "Oh. Well, that's different. But never mind that. Maybe it'll help you understand what I'm trying to say. You see there are good familiar spirits and there are bad spirits. We believe all the religions of the world are tuned to different groups of these spirits. Does that make sense? That's why certain religions prefer certain gods. We believe all gods are part of a pantheon of spirits. I know it's not a Christian belief…so just try to think of it as angels and demons, if it helps you."

"What does this have to do with Culsu?"

"Culsu is the name of a very ancient spirit, from Etruscan beliefs. Culsu was malicious, a demon, who is said to watch over the doors to the underworld. Culsu had the image of a snake, meaning she's cunning and willing to wait for the perfect strike. She just doesn't act impulsively, she manipulates things, hides in the shadows, and takes her time. Scissors were one of her symbols. With them she would cut the lifelines of her victims, striking at the perfect moment to cut their lives short and bring her victims to the doorway of her underworld."

"So, what is this evil spirit doing here?"

"Alison, I think. That's when it first showed up. It plagued Alison, it plagued Claire and Michael, too. And it plagued me. You don't know what my mom and I had to go through to get it to leave me alone." Shannon held up her arms and pulled back the sleeves to reveal ugly scars across her wrists. "I did that. With scissors, just to stop the voices Culsu whispered in my head."

Winter leaned forward, suddenly conscious of her own scissor-inflicted, almost invisible scar line across her wrist. And seeing again the jagged gash in Claire's wrist, and the bloody scissors falling from her hand.

"I'm…sorry," Winter whispered.

"Yeah, well…"

"I…I…didn't know about Michael…"

"If you had, would it have changed anything?"

"It was an accident."

"Was it?"

Winter bit her lip but refused to look away. "Does this have anything to do with Skotos? What do you know about them?"

Shannon broke eye contact and pushed her sleeves back down. "Yes. It has everything to do with Skotos. Every Wiccan knows who Skotos is...they call themselves dark Wiccans, but what they do really has nothing to do with what we believe. They're more closely related to Satanists than anything else. They have a twisted interpretation of the three-fold rule. For every three dark deeds done, they could receive a desire. The darker the deeds, the deeper the desire. They mess with dark spirits that should be left alone."

Shannon tucked a strand of hair behind her ear and continued. "Not very many people know this, but when Alison was kicked out of our coven, she went to Skotos. I don't know what they did to her...I've heard horror stories about their induction ceremonies. She was probably tortured and raped repeatedly, and they wouldn't have stopped until she recited the most horrible incantations and called upon the most evil spirits to deliver her from what they were doing. It would have destroyed her and enslaved her under the thumb of the Skotos priests. And she probably would have become haunted by the spirits she called upon. That's part of their process...to drive the new inductees mad and to break them into submission."

"So, you think Alison called on Culsu?"

Shannon nodded. "She must have. We know she went to Skotos, and we know the Culsu spirit came back with her. After Alison died, the spirit stayed. It wasn't until a couple years ago, after I used the scissors on myself, my mom began to think something was wrong. When I kind of went crazy and tried to kill her with those same scissors, she finally figured it out. She gathered some of her priest and priestess friends to bind the spirit and cast it away from us. We put the pieces together with Claire and Michael afterward."

"How are you so sure about them?"

"Like I said, scissors are the symbol. I know you saw them both with scissors too."

Winter nodded, biting her lip to keep from revealing her own issue with scissors. Had it plagued her too? "Are you sure you're free?" Winter asked.

Shannon leaned forward, clasping her hands in her lap, and pleaded with her eyes. "Winter, I didn't kill them. You have to believe me."

Winter closed her eyes and shook her head slowly, trying to shake away the recurring images, but Shannon took it wrong.

"I know it wasn't really your fault…I know. But don't expect us to be friends again." Shannon's face tightened. "Can we just agree to believe each other?"

Winter nodded. "Okay, I believe you."

"Will you put the gun away?"

Winter nodded again and returned her gun to the ankle holster. "What do you think this spirit wants?"

Shannon shrugged. "I don't know. Maybe it's angry with my mom. Maybe there's something else. What should I do? If Melissa, Kathrine, and Mary…"

Shannon inhaled with the sound of scratching on a chalkboard and dropped her face into her hands. Her body trembled. A few seconds later, the room filled with the sound of her wailing.

Winter bit her lip and looked away. Emotions raw…body exhausted. It wouldn't be long before her fragile veneer cracked, too.

Red and blue lights flashed through the curtains. Winter stood to peek outside. "They're here."

Shannon looked up and rubbed her face with the heels of her hands. "Who?"

"The FBI."

"You called the FBI?" Shannon shrieked and leapt to her feet.

Winter ignored her and went to the door, opening it slowly. Bright lights pierced her eyes. "It's okay," she said to the light.

The light went out. Agent Erickson and Agent Golbeck jogged

to her, holstering their weapons.

"What's going on?" Erickson asked.

Winter stepped back into the apartment and motioned to Shannon. "I found her. This is Shannon. She has a lot to tell you."

17

The next Friday evening, Winter stepped into the Union and scanned the tables. Erickson was waiting for her in a corner. She took a deep breath and went to him.

"Are you sure it's safe to meet in public like this?" she asked as she sat.

"Yes. Anyone we may want to avoid already knows we're working together. So long as no one's close enough to hear, we're fine."

"Well? Did you do what I asked?"

Erickson nodded and slid a manila folder across the table. "All the specifics are there."

"Tell me. I'll read later."

Erickson shook his head. "There's nothing significant. We checked phone records, recent purchases, and even had all of them followed for a couple of days. If any of them are hiding something, it'll take a lot longer to find it. There's nothing on the surface, and I doubt they'd be covering their tracks this well."

Winter nodded. "Are you sure you didn't find anything?

Anything at all?"

Erickson sighed. "Peter has a cousin in the private security sector. They've been phoning lately. But unless you want to read into cousins talking, that's it."

Winter huffed and crossed her arms. "And Summer?"

"Like I said, nothing."

"Davis?"

"Same. Everything is in that folder. Winter, what is it you suspect your friends are doing? Why are you so paranoid suddenly?"

Winter shrugged. "I don't know. Things just seem off. I can't get a handle on what's going on behind the scenes this time. Ayden thinks so too."

"I thought you had abilities to help with that."

"That's just it, my abilities aren't being reliable about this. I can't...see...when it comes to these three. I feel blind."

"Well, that's no reason to be paranoid of your friends."

"But you even said not to trust them."

"That doesn't mean they're not trustworthy," he said. "It just means don't take chances. And keeping them out of the loop is the best way to protect them."

"So, do you think I should just drop it?"

"I'm not going to tell you what to do in your personal life, but you need to get more focused on the task and stop worrying so much about friends who are just friends. Okay?"

Winter nodded. "Okay."

"Good. Then you need to know there's been another murder. Same MO...scissors, and the word Culsu carved into his forehead. A twenty-six-year-old male named Logan Salvina. We've confirmed he was a part of Skotos."

Winter's eyes widened. "Logan?"

"Did you know him?"

She shook her head. "Not really. But I saw him last year. He was one of the ones looking for San...for Tulip. Along with a girl who goes to school here. At least, I think she does. I haven't seen her this year."

"What's her name?"

"Sophie…I'm not sure about her last name. She was in my dorm first year. A really spiteful girl. She got involved with the AFRC, and I'm pretty sure she has something to do with Skotos, too. I think she tried to warn me about the attack last spring."

He nodded and jotted the name down. "We'll look for her. She may be in danger too. If you see her, contact me immediately."

Winter nodded.

"One more thing, we've discovered one of the girls murdered last week was also involved with Skotos. Melissa."

"Really? Melissa?" Winter's eyes widened. "She was the quiet one…"

"It's always the quiet ones, isn't it? There's a pattern emerging here, though. Whoever is behind these murders is targeting members or former members of Skotos, including anyone closely associated with them. That's the theory we're working right now. We think Xaphan is hunting down all those responsible for failing to find Sandy last year and killing them and those closest to them as an example."

Winter stiffened and nodded. "Right. What do you want me to do?"

"Nothing. Just be aware. You have your assignment. Whatever you do, don't draw attention to yourself. We're getting close to him, so don't get in the way."

"I can help."

"No. Keep her safe. That's your job."

"You need my help! I can find him…I'm the only one who can."

"You need to protect her!"

Winter folder her arms and stared at Erickson, refusing to flinch. "Fine. Whatever. I need to talk to Shannon."

"Shannon? I'm not so sure that's a good idea. She's in protective custody."

"I need to talk to her. She had this picture of a friend. I need to ask her about it."

"Do you think this friend is in danger too?"

"No."

Agent Erickson studied her for a moment. Then he pulled a pad and pen out of his pocket. "I'm not sure what you expect to learn or what you want to accomplish from all this, but call this number." He slid a scrap of paper to her. "Give the agent who answers your full name and codename. Then ask for Sage. I'll call ahead and tell them to expect you." He put the pad and pen back in his pocket and stood.

"Thank you," Winter said as she stood with him.

"Just be careful and stay low."

Winter nodded. "I will."

As Erickson left for the back entrance, Winter walked toward the Union doors nearest the side parking lot. She fished out her cell phone and tapped in the number Erickson had given her. By the time she reached the parking lot, the phone had already rung ten times with no answer. She grunted, shoved the phone back into her pocket with one hand and with the other retrieved her car keys.

A motion near the adjacent building caught her eye as she approached her car. She paused and peered into the darkness, deepened by the stark shadow cut by the nearby streetlight against the corner of the building. A figure stepped nearer the light, but not enough to make out the face. A hand beckoned and then retreated back into the shadows.

Winter hesitated only a moment and then concentrated on the reassuring pressure of the gun against her ankle. She put the keys back into her pocket, glanced around the lot to make sure no one else watched, and casually walked toward the dark corner.

Someone in a hooded jacket stood in the darkest part of the shadows several feet back between the buildings and under the branches of a decorative tree in the flower bed.

"Who are you? What do you want?" asked Winter.

"Shh…" The female voice matched the delicate shape of the shadow. The woman beckoned Winter closer.

Winter slowly stepped into the dark shadows, and blinked rapidly to help her pupils adjust.

"Who are you?" Winter asked again with a whisper.

The figure's head turned as if scanning all directions, then with trembling hands the hood was lowered.

"Sophie?" Winter asked.

Sophie nodded.

"What are you doing here?"

"I had to come. I had to tell you something. It's after me next."

"What's after you?"

"Something horrible. And it's coming for her."

"What do you mean?" asked Winter.

"Xaphan knows what you're doing," said Sophie. "He knows Ayden's not the real Sandy. He knows you still have her hidden, and he's sent something to find her. It's coming."

"I don't care what it is," Winter said. "I'm ready."

"There's nothing you can do to stop it."

"Don't tell me what I can't do!"

"Winter," said Sophie. "It's not human."

Winter paused. Her heart surging. "I don't understand. What is it?"

Sophie wagged her head. "I don't know. It's more than a spirit. It's a demon. A demon in human form."

"Like the man in the silver and black mask," said Winter.

"Maybe. We called him the Eater, because he said he delighted in eating souls. But this thing is different, I think. They call it the Acolyte. They say it is the right hand of Hell. No one even knows what it looks like because everyone who's seen it is dead. The Eater was a part of Skotos, but I have no idea where the Acolyte comes from. All I know is it's wiping out Skotos. And when it's done, it's coming for you and Sandy."

"Why did you come to warn me?"

"Because they made me do some horrible things, Winter. Things I never really wanted to do, but I was forced to. I had no choice. I'm so sorry. I wish I had never gotten involved with them. Now I'm next and if I can do this one thing to stop him I will. Xaphan is angry at Skotos for failing. There are only a few of us left, and I don't know how long before the Acolyte finds me."

"Only a few left?" Winter asked. "But I've only heard of two...Melissa and Logan."

Sophie shook her head. "Only heard of two. And that's only because it couldn't destroy the bodies before they were found. Most of us don't have much family or friends to speak of. No missing reports will be filed. No one will miss us. No one cares...It wouldn't matter anyway. Look what it did to all of Melissa's friends...just for knowing her."

"Not all of them," said Winter. "The FBI are protecting one. And they can protect you too. Let me help."

"You think they can protect me?" Sophie's voice raked and she shook her head. "No one can stop this thing. You have to run. And you have to keep running. That's all anyone can do. That's all I can do, too. And Melissa's friend? No offense, but FBI protection is probably the worst place she could be. She's probably already dead."

Winter held her breath. "How do you know?"

"I told you. This thing is not human. It's only a matter of time before the Acolyte finds Sandy." Sophie flipped the hood back over her face and started backing away. "Take Sandy and run. Never stop running." She turned and ran into the darkness between the buildings.

Four Years Ago

Winter furrowed her brow during the Geometry quiz, trying to remember the formula for determining the length of the hypotenuse given the opposite angle and one adjacent side. When it finally clicked, she jotted it to the side of her paper and began punching the appropriate numbers into her calculator.

All A's so far in the class, no way Winter would drop this quiz. As she moved on to the next problem, her mind wandered a little. A flicker of memory stirred and she quickly shoved it down. Then she thought of Michael's solution to her remembering problem, and her body lurched with the ache to try it again. Winter shook it all away, concentrating on the one thing she was sure of…that she wanted to get out of this place…and renewed her concentration to ace the quiz.

The bell to change classes blared through the speaker. Metal bells rang in the hall. Winter looked at the wall clock, as did the rest of the class. As did the teacher. The bell stopped momentarily and then started again. A second later it paused again before staying on continuously.

"Okay, that's the fire alarm," said Mrs. Lockett.

"Is there a fire?" someone yelled out.

The teacher shook her head and stood, her face tightened with surprised annoyance as if she had once thought she knew the limits of human idiocy until proven wrong just now.

"How in the world should I know?" She crossed over to the door, gradebook in hand. "It's probably a drill. Everyone line up. I know you're not in grade school any longer, but it's important we do this in an orderly fashion so we can more easily take roll once we get to the football field. We want to do this right, so they don't make us have another drill next week. Leave everything at your desk."

Winter dutifully stood in line right behind Stacy. Stacy looked over her shoulder and raised her eyebrows, as if to say "this should be fun." They snaked out toward the nearest exit. Other classes were doing the same, and soon multiple lines become one long line of the student body, each class separated by a teacher. As they came to the stadium, the line began to file into the bleachers and split into rows according to classes. As the students sat, the teachers went down the line, roll in hand, checking to make sure every student was accounted for. After Mrs. Lockett finished, she sat at the end of the row and waited like everyone else. And as all the teachers completed their duties and sat, the murmur of conversation and speculation spread through the student body.

"Do you think it's really a fire?" asked Stacy.

Winter shrugged. "Probably not. Just a drill, like the teacher said." Winter craned her neck to look around the bleachers, trying to spot Claire. Instead, she spotted a boy she had never seen before, tall, with reddish blond hair.

"Who's that?" Winter asked.

"Who, the new boy?" Stacy asked. "I think his name is Chad something-or-other. He's in my Spanish class. Cute, isn't he?"

Winter shrugged. "I guess."

"Want me to introduce you?"

"What? No. I was just wondering who he was."

"Come on. Why not? He seems really nice."

"Drop it, Stacy. I'm not interested. At all."

"Fine. Whatever," said Stacy. "Listen, my youth group is having a little get together at my house this Saturday. Why don't you come?"

Winter frowned. How could she say no again without hurting Stacy's feelings? "I'll think about it."

Stacy nodded. "I know what that means. Look, if you don't want to come, just say so."

"It's not that I don't want to come, it's that I'm just not sure about being around your Christian friends."

"Well, they were good enough for you to hang around during prom." Stacy covered her mouth. "I'm sorry. I didn't mean it like that."

Winter gazed at the bleacher floor between her feet. The familiar stab pierced through her chest again. She wished Michael were there to help. Stacy put a hand on Winter's shoulder and Winter shrugged her off.

"I'm sorry. What I meant to say is my friends aren't that bad. They're not going to try to convert you or anything. It'll just be a fun time to hang out in a way that's healthy. No alcohol or anything, just people who enjoy being around each other. I thought maybe it would be fun for you, too."

Winter shook her head. "They'll ask me questions."

"No, they won't. I'll make sure of that. Don't worry about them, come for me. When was the last time we did anything together? It's been way too long. Why don't you come over Friday the night before, just you and me. And then you can decide Saturday if you want to stay for the thing that night. If not, I'll bring you home. Deal?"

"I'll think about it." Winter glanced up to see Stacy look away and her face fall a little.

"Yeah…okay. Just let me know," Stacy said, all enthusiasm gone. "Just tell me one thing—why Claire and not me? You're quick enough to go hang out with her and her friends. Why won't you give me and my friends a chance?"

"I don't know…"

"Because I know what kind of people Claire hangs out with outside of school, and they're all into some crazy stuff. Stuff you don't need to get involved with. And I'm not talking about the witchcraft, I'm talking about drugs. You haven't gotten involved in that, have you?"

It was as if Stacy had punched her in the stomach. She closed her eyes and chewed the inside of her cheeks.

"You have! I can't believe this. No wonder you don't talk to me anymore or want to do anything with me…"

"It's not that…"

"Then what is it? You're going to destroy yourself, is that what you want? Maybe it is, but there's a better way."

"I don't have a choice."

"Lie! You do have a choice. You always have a choice. Whatever you're trying to run from or ignore needs to be dealt with, not covered over with alcohol or drugs, no matter what Claire's friends are telling you. If you don't deal with it, bad things are going to happen. You need to choose right now whether you want to actually fight for life or to keep running from it."

"But Claire…"

"Claire's just like you. She's been living in hell her entire life. And rather than face it and do something about it the right way, she buries it inside. One day it's all going to burst out and it'll be the end of Claire. You two need an intervention. You need someone to slap you in the face and tell you to snap out of it."

Winter jutted out her jaw and stood to move. When she did, the principal picked up a bullhorn and called out, "Claire Parker."

Winter froze. She cast around until she spotted Claire moving toward the bottom of the bleachers, her face pale and white…scared. Winter stared back down to the principal. A deputy stood at his side.

Winter eased back into her seat beside Stacy, butterflies pounding her stomach muscles to get out.

"Oh my God," said Stacy.

"What's going on?" asked Winter.

"It wasn't just a fire drill. They brought the drug dog."

Winter's eyes widened. She watched Claire be led away by the principal and the deputy, and then turned back to Stacy. Stacy seemed just as shocked as Winter.

For the first time Winter allowed herself to think maybe Stacy was right. Maybe she could find a better way. Maybe she did have a choice after all.

But Michael's way was just so much fun…

19

Present Day

Winter watched Sophie melt into the inky shadows and then spun back to the parking lot, her heart hammering against her ribs. She had to choose right then to either fight or run.

Shannon.

Winter had run too much in her life. Today she would fight.

She yanked out her cellphone and dialed the number again as she ran back to her car. No answer. She tossed it onto the passenger seat as she twisted the key and the black BMW roared awake. Winter closed her eyes, took a deep breath, knowing without any kind of supernatural help she could never reach Shannon in time. But the premonitions had almost disappeared that year, except for one blind guiding that helped her find Shannon just the other night. And those dreams about Claire, but dreams would do her no good right now.

She tried to will a premonition into being, the sweet ecstasy of information flooding her mind, downloading in real-time, and unfolding every action and reaction around her before they even happened. Still nothing.

Frustrated, she mumbled, "Please help…" Still, nothing came to show what to do next.

Winter cursed loudly, flung the car into gear, and floored the gas, hoping somehow that blind guiding would take her to Shannon again. As the tires chirped exiting the parking lot, Winter snatched up her phone again, stealing glances at it trying to find Agent Erickson's number. She took her eyes away from the road for half a moment, and jerked back up when she felt the car go off the road. She cursed again and tugged the wheel. Finally, she managed to get Erickson's number and put the phone against her ear.

Erickson answered after the second ring. *"Yes?"*

"Shannon's in trouble," she said.

"What? Are you sure?"

"Yes. I'm going there now."

"You stay with Kaci. Let me check with our agents stationed with Shannon…"

"They're probably already dead too," said Winter.

He paused. *"What do you know?"*

"A little more than you this time. I'm not sure it'll help, but get as much firepower sent to her location as you possibly can. Now!" She checked the dash clock…ten till eight. Summer and Davis were coming over soon. Winter sighed, knowing she'd have to make excuses again…to lie. "Give me Shannon's address."

"You said you were already heading there."

"Yes, but I can get there faster if I have the address. Either way, I'm the best hope she has, so just give it to me!"

Erickson paused. *"359 Basil Street. It's south of town."*

Winter hung up, slammed on the brakes, and swung into a parking lot. "Come on…come on…" she muttered as she tapped the address into her navigation system. Then she floored the gas again.

Thankfully, she wasn't all that far away from the location. She might actually beat the FBI there. The BMW soared through the streets as Winter deftly guided it around slower vehicles. She followed the audible guiding of the navigation system into a part of town she'd never seen before. After only a few minutes she arrived at the address, an obscure gravel road that led deep into the forest. At the end of the drive was a large facility, razor-wire fence wrapping the perimeter.

And a broken and twisted gate, ripped from the hinges. A guard lay dead by the road.

Winter pulled her car behind the guard house and got out, retrieving the gun from her ankle. She sprinted through the open gate toward the compound, hoping the premonition might still kick in soon and make sense out of everything. She reached the door, twisted the knob, and pulled. Gun extended, she cleared the entryway before stepping into the small sterile corridor. Fluorescent lights buzzed overhead. Doors opened to either side, but Winter knew the door she needed was at the end of the hall. The stairwell. Shannon would be on the second floor. Was that the premonition talking?

She ran down the hall, not bothering to look in any of the rooms…knowing she'd most likely find more dead bodies lying in each of them. As she opened the stair door, sounds floated down to her.

Screams.

Winter bit her lip. No solid premonition. No backup. She fought the urge to just run away and wait for Erickson. Instead, she took a deep calming breath.

"I can do this," she whispered.

The screams rose higher, panicked, torturous. Winter rolled her feet on each step, watching the landing above past the barrel of her gun, and then watching the exit door as it came into view, propped open by another dead guard. She eased past the dead guard into another hallway, similar to the one below, but shorter and more dimly lit.

One closed door drew her like an unholy magnet. As she approached it, a strange sensation washed through her mind. What little clarity she had, with her training and basic intuition apart from a full premonition, began to erode into a kind of numbness. Everything she thought she knew halted at that door. Beyond the door waited…nothing. Only emptiness. It was as if a mental wall had been erected that prevented her from thinking or feeling or even imagining anything beyond that door. It was a void in the fabric of existence.

With each step closer, her thought processes diminished, her ability to reason ground to a halt, until finally she stood before the door…not knowing what to do, what would happen next, and only barely registering how she got there.

The screams came from within the void beyond the door. One last shred of instinct told Winter she had to help the one screaming. She remembered Shannon. With pure muscle memory, her mind not fully registering why she was doing it, she reached out and tried to turn the knob.

Locked.

The screams pierced the fog of her mind a little more, and she looked around the hall for anything that might help. Another door just further down the hall stood barely cracked. She could see a darkness through the crack that clawed at the light of the hall, swirling as if alive, and she knew the two doors opened into the same room.

Winter eased to the next door and put a hand on the surface. As she pressed gently, the door swung into a wall of darkness, disappearing within. It was darkness unlike anything Winter had ever seen. Not just the absence of light, but the embodiment of hate and despair, writhing to drag more souls into its eternal agony. It was breathing, pulsing at the entrance, tugging at Winter's flesh, begging her to step inside.

Shannon was in there. Still screaming.

I can do this.

Winter swung the door fully open, unable to see beyond the wall of evil. Instinctively, she held her breath, extended the gun forward, and then stepped in. The moment she entered the darkness, all of reality changed, as if the darkness had transported Winter to some malevolent nest that couldn't possibly exist in the real world. It was like walking through compressed hate that wanted to smother and crush her from the inside out.

Winter whimpered, and with what little breath she had in her lungs she whispered, "God help me."

The darkness reacted to the cry, pushing her back, trying to expel her into the hall. She pushed forward, knowing Shannon was nearby. Every sluggish movement dragged through the thickness like slow motion. She couldn't see. She couldn't move. Her lungs burned from lack of oxygen, and she reflexively opened her mouth to inhale. But the air had no life, if it could even be called air. She couldn't breathe, she couldn't think. Winter's heart thundered. Her knees weakened. She had to get to Shannon. Winter was the only one who could save her. Ignoring the life draining from her body, from each individual cell, siphoned out by the evil darkness, she fought, pushing inch by inch toward the screams.

You can't stop this. It's not human. Never stop running, said the voice of Sophie in her head. Now Winter understood. If she made it out alive, she would take Kaci and run.

Winter sensed, rather than saw or heard, something move above her, falling toward her. She screamed and raised her gun toward the ceiling, firing a single shot. As the thunder compressed her ears, the darkness compressed her chest, forcing the remaining air out with a painful gasp. As the gunshot dissipated into silence, the darkness fell like vanishing ash, leaving behind the earthly light of the fluorescent bulbs above.

Shannon lay just ahead, stretched out on a dining table, ropes binding her to the surface. She rolled her head to face Winter, eyes widened and skin pasty white.

"Winter," she sobbed. "Get me out of here! Help me! Hurry, before she comes back!"

Winter ran to her side, scanning for a way to release her. Shannon's skin bore small slashes everywhere, minuscule droplets of blood tracing varicose paths across her flesh. The word Culsu had been carved into Shannon's forehead, the blood running into her eyes and down her cheeks, mixing with the blood oozing from her nose.

Winter checked the knots, but they were too tight. She dug her fingernails into them anyway, hoping maybe she could pull them apart in time.

"Hurry!" said Shannon.

"I'm trying."

Footsteps echoed through the hall, just outside the door.

"Oh gods," said Shannon. "She's back. Listen to me, Winter. She's not really alive. Ask my mom! It's in the book!"

"What?"

The doorknob of the first door twisted and the door began to swing. Winter fell to the ground and slid beneath the table. And as she did, the darkness engulfed the room again, choking out all breath and hope. It pressed against Winter, ripping her heart. Laughing at her.

Shannon screamed again, and as she screamed the mocking darkness thickened. The shadowy outlines of feet appeared next to Winter. The table began to gyrate as Shannon convulsed under the intensity of her panic.

Metal slid against metal. Winter knew the sound…scissors opening and closing. A thunk, like a butcher slamming a knife into meat, and a groan interrupted Shannon's continuous scream. Then the scream reached another octave, and the table rattled against the floor. Another thunk, and the scream morphed into a gurgling moan, the table lurching with a rhythmic throb. Something started pouring onto the floor. She put her hands over her mouth to keep herself silent…to stop herself from vomiting.

Another thunk.

All went still.

All went silent.

The feet moved away back toward the door. The darkness vanished again. Winter peered toward the door, through the legs of the table, through the dripping of blood, just in time to see a female figure with blonde hair pull it shut.

For a moment she thought she recognized the woman. Winter shook her head. It couldn't be…

She slid out from under the table, carefully avoiding the growing pool of blood, and forced herself to look at Shannon. Blood saturated every inch of her chest, running liberally off the table. Scissors protruded from her neck, embedded halfway up the blades. The briefest flutter of an eyelid was the last movement Shannon made.

Winter backed away. Hands over her mouth, taking deep breaths to hold the sick at bay. Anger and adrenaline surged through her too. She looked at the gun in her hand and squeezed her jaw. Tight. *I can do this…*

Winter ran through the door and back to the stairs. She took the stairs three at a time and burst through the bottom door just in time to see a flash of blonde hair exit the building. Winter readied the gun and ran through the hall. She wouldn't let this thing get away. She wouldn't give it the slightest opportunity to find Kaci.

No premonition. No backup. No clue what this thing was. Winter was going to pull the trigger this time. She was going to put a bullet in the Acolyte.

With her free hand she twisted the doorknob; with her shoulder she shoved it open. She swung the gun forward, clenching the handle with both hands, fixing the bead on the back of the blonde head now only twenty feet away. She readied her stance. Flicked off the safety…

The woman stopped and turned. Massive burn scars covered the right side of her face, as if the skin had melted over the bone. Where an ear should have been, nothing more than a knotted lump of flesh clung to her skull. Where the cheek should have been, a stringy patchwork of discolored skin and sinew left a small hole revealing the teeth within. The eye flesh hung, resting almost directly on the cheekbone. No hair grew on that side, only charred scars.

The other side of her face was perfect. And Winter recognized her.

"Alison?"

"Are you going to kill me again, Winter?" Alison asked, her eyes suddenly glowing red.

Winter's arms trembled and the gun sank away from the mark.

Alison smiled, turned her back to Winter, and walked away.

Winter could only fall to her knees and weep.

20

By the time Agent Erickson finally showed up with less than adequate backup, Alison was long gone. The entire encounter at the safe house had lasted only minutes, and Winter hadn't moved from where she'd fallen to her knees. As Erickson's men secured the building, both Erickson and Golbeck escorted her back to the cars. They tried to question her, but the shock still numbed her ability to think clearly. Once they had squeezed as much information out of her as she could give, they told her to go home.

As she drove back into the busier parts of town, life teemed everywhere, unaware of the horrors that had occurred that night. Unaware that at any moment they could suffer the same fate with that thing still out there. What was it? Could it really be Alison?

It was nearly nine as she pulled into the parking lot of her apartment. The lights were on beyond the balcony door. She imagined Peter and Kaci, Summer and Davis, all laughing...maybe playing a board game....maybe watching a movie. She knew she was welcome, but...

But they didn't know how she felt. Seeing Alison tonight brought back a flood of memories she had tried to suppress. Now thinking about the two couples beyond the window, a wave of what-ifs joined the guilt. What would life be like today if Ryan were still alive? Would Winter have come to Tishbe? Would she have met her new friends? Would she be happy like them? Would she and Ryan have been the third couple there tonight?

Winter pulled the keys out of the ignition—she was expected inside and if she waited too long they would start calling. Perhaps she could claim illness and retreat to her room to save herself the awkwardness of being a fifth wheel. She took a deep breath and climbed out of the car, trudging up the sidewalk and stairs, and finally standing downcast before the door.

The old tricks of taking her emotions and shoving them down, hiding them behind a wall of stone, beckoned her. She obeyed and plastered a smile upon her face, letting that smile creep into her eyes because it was the eyes that made the trick convincing.

She twisted the knob and stepped in, but she found no laughter, no board game, no movie, and no Summer. Someone she didn't know sat next to Davis at the table with Peter and Kaci. He had reddish-brown hair, soft eyes, and the smile of someone who had been forced into an uncomfortable situation.

"Sorry I'm late," said Winter. "Where's Summer?"

"Kind of a long story," said Kaci.

"Well, not that long," said Davis. "We broke up. She says she doesn't feel welcome around the rest of us anymore."

"That's ridiculous." Winter stood over them, half wanting to sit and talk about Summer, half wanting to flee to her room and lock the door. "Who are you?" she asked the strange guy.

"Oh, I'm sorry," said Peter. "This is my cousin Graham. Graham Hughes. I invited him tonight so we would have a sixth…I had a game I wanted to play that required teams. Didn't expect Summer not to show."

"Hi, Graham," said Winter, remembering the FBI folder she had left in the car and wondering if she should go get it. She felt more than a little bit foolish for questioning Peter at all now that his cousin sat in the room.

Graham smiled and nodded. "Hi."

"Where have you been?" asked Peter.

Winter sighed. "Sorry. I had some…homework to do. Look, I'm really tired and lunch didn't settle well with me. So I think I'll go shower and turn in. Besides, with me here now it messes up your teams." She turned to leave.

"Winter, are you okay?" asked Kaci.

Winter nodded. "Yeah, I'm fine." Winter left before Kaci could question her further.

After a quick shower, Winter hid in her room. She lay awake for a long time, listening to the others trying to have fun. They eventually gave it up around ten-thirty and all three of the guys left. Winter could hear Kaci banging around in the kitchen, probably cleaning. When the noise stopped, a soft knock rapped at her door.

"Yeah?" asked Winter.

The door cracked open. "Do you need to talk?"

Winter shrugged.

"What happened tonight? Don't keep things from me, I don't care what Erickson says. If there's something going on I want to know about it."

Winter rolled over to face her. "I'm not sure I know how to talk about it. I saw something tonight…" Tears stung at her eyes. "I've seen some horrible things, but nothing like this." She sat up and put her head in her hands. She opened her mouth, but couldn't find the words to describe the churning of her insides. Instead, she said, "I'm sorry. I'm being stupid. It's nothing."

Kaci sat next to her and rubbed her back. "You know that's not going to work on me. So just tell me. I'm not sure I can help. But you don't have to keep it bottled up."

"I know." Winter clenched her eyes and pushed away Shannon's screams in her head. "But there's something else much more important than me."

"Don't say that…"

"They know Ayden's not the one."

Kaci's eyes widened. "What?"

"I don't think they know about you, but they know we're hiding you. That the FBI would outright put us in the same apartment probably hasn't even occurred to them, so at least all our tricks have been doing something."

"That's good I guess. Did you tell Erickson?"

Winter nodded.

"But that isn't what's upset you, is it?"

Winter shook her head and bit her lip. "They've sent this monster to find you. It's been killing all the members of Skotos, simply because they failed last year. I saw it tonight. I practically watched it murder someone I knew from high school." She caught a sob in her throat before it escaped and choked it down.

"What? Someone you knew?"

"Yeah. A friend I met through Claire."

"I don't understand," said Kaci. "You said a monster killed her? What did it look like?"

"Remember the wreck I told you about?"

Kaci nodded. "How could I forget? I've never seen you cry so much."

Winter took a deep breath and continued, careful not to let the memories of the wreck swirl with the images of Shannon. "Well, Alison, the girl who…you know…"

"I know."

"Well, this thing, whatever it is…was her."

"Like, Alison was alive?"

"I don't know. But it was her. When she came into prom before the wreck, Alison had changed. Something was terribly wrong with her. What if it started then? What if this thing possessed her and kept her alive?"

"If she's possessed, would she still be Alison?"

"I don't know. But I saw her alive. She was there. Right in front of me." Winter trembled. She turned to look Kaci in the eyes, not bothering to stop the shaking in her voice this time. "How can she be alive? I watched her burn."

Kaci shook her head, face paling like the moonlight outside. "Are you sure it was her?"

"It was her, Kaci. I ran into Sophie tonight, too. Outside the Union. She tried to warn me. She called Alison the Acolyte. She called her the Right Hand of Hell."

Kaci watched her for a long time. "Are we safe here?"

"It doesn't know about you yet," Winter said, staring back at the floor. "But I'm afraid it's only a matter of time."

"What should we do?"

Winter shrugged. "I don't know."

The central hall of Trenton Hills High School stretched out before her. Winter stood in the middle, looking from one direction to the next, not sure how she got there. Nothing had changed. Even the bulletin boards were exactly as she remembered. A chill crept through the air, more than just the normal chill of a drafty hallway. This chill dug deeper, alive, hungry.

"Hello?" she called to the empty hall.

Nothing but empty reverb returned.

Winter walked forward toward the intersection of the wing where she had taken most of her senior classes, hoping to find something to trigger the vision's message. Yes. This is a vision, she said to herself.

"Hello?" she called with a little more confidence.

This time she heard a locker rattling, the sound coming from the hall she already approached. Winter pivoted the corner at a run and slid to a paralyzed stop.

Claire stood near the end of the hall in front of an open locker. "Claire?"

Claire pulled some books out and held them to her chest.

Winter blinked.

Then Claire stood right in front of her. She smiled warmly.

Winter took a step back. "What are you doing here?"

Winter blinked and Claire was gone. A door slammed. Winter spun running for the exit. She hit the pushbar and flung the door open, but Claire was already at the school gates. Walking.

"Claire, wait!"

Blink.

Winter stood on the corner of a busy intersection in Trenton Hills, muscles clenched to sprint after Claire. She jumped back as cars buzzed by. Winter turned, searching for Claire in the crowd of pedestrians.

There. Just at the end of the block across the street. Still walking. Winter shoved through the crowd and ran to her, jumping through traffic as drivers leaned on their horns. As Winter caught her up, Claire never turned, but steadily continued forward. Winter reached out to grab Claire's shoulder.

Blink.

The highway Winter drove to reach Cherithville. Cars flew past, sending waves of air pummeling against her. Winter took an instinctive step back and off the highway shoulder into the grass. She looked around again and found Claire several yards down the side of the highway. Still walking. Winter ran after her again.

"Claire! Talk to me. What's going on?" She reached for Claire's shoulder...

Blink.

Hoole Boulevard. The old oak trees swaying in the breeze, casting cool shadows not allowed on the much busier highway. Claire was just ahead, this time running. Winter rushed after her, taxing her muscles for more speed. The more Winter pushed to catch up, the more her legs responded like syrup and the further away Claire became. Winter heaved to a stop, frustrated, and stared after Claire. Claire's image flickered, and suddenly she reappeared further down the road.

Blink.

Winter stood at the intersection turning toward her apartment complex from Hoole Boulevard. Claire was only feet away now, but running again. Winter sprinted after her, through the roads of the apartments, always just behind, never catching up. With a flicker, Claire disappeared completely.

Winter rounded the next building and found Claire standing halfway down the street. Staring up. Winter followed her gaze and realized Claire watched Winter's and Kaci's apartment. This is where the dream was supposed to end, but this time Claire pointed and turned to Winter with a smile.

Blink.

Claire stood on the balcony, peering into the apartment.

"No!" cried Winter, sprinting toward the apartment stairs.

Blink.

Winter was inside now. And so was Claire, standing just in front of the glass door.

"What are you doing here?" Winter asked. "What does this mean?"

Claire tilted her head and gave her that warm smile again. "It means…I'm here."

"I don't understand."

"I'm here."

"But you can't be!"

"I'm here."

Winter sat up on her bed and put a hand to her forehead. It wasn't the first time she'd had that dream, but it was the most vivid. And the first time she had actually managed to follow Claire all the way to the apartment. What did Claire have to do with anything? What did it mean? Did it have something to do with Shannon? Or Alison? Winter glanced at the clock - 10 am, Saturday morning.

She swung her feet out of bed and searched for something to wear. Out of habit she picked out a mostly black t-shirt and black pants. Out of new habit, she strapped the gun to her ankle. She sighed as she brushed her hair, looking at the golden-brown roots beginning to show. Then she took a deep breath to shake the recurring dream out of her head and left the room.

Laughter floated down the hall.

Winter huffed. "Is Peter back already?"

"Oh, she's up," said Kaci from the living room.

Winter exited the hall into the living room. And froze, her insides instantly turning to ice.

Claire smiled warmly up at her from the couch.

"NO!" Winter shouted. She reached down for her ankle and yanked out the gun, leveling it at Claire.

"Winter!" Kaci yelled as she stood and backed away out of the line of fire.

"Get away from her, Kaci! Now!"

Claire jumped up and stretched her arms out to either side. "Just calm down, Winter."

"No! You can't be here! Kaci, back away!"

"What's going on?" asked Kaci.

"It's not Claire! Who are you?" Winter screamed.

"It's really me," said Claire.

"Winter, put the gun down!" said Kaci.

"No! It's not you, it's impossible. It can't be you. You can't be here!"

"I'm really here." Claire took a careful step forward, eyes wide.

"Why can't she be here?" Kaci stretched a calming hand toward Winter.

Winter bit her lip, heart fluttering, suddenly unsure and confused. "Because I saw her die!" She shook the gun at Claire. "I saw YOU die!"

"Winter, it's really me," said Claire. "Please, just put the gun down and let me explain."

Kaci stepped to Winter's side and put a hand on her back. "Put the gun down, Winter."

"I'm still alive," said Claire.

Winter trembled. The gun wavered and she let it fall. The trembling in her arms and legs surged into her core and up into her face. Her chin quivered and she felt the telling sting of tears in her sinuses.

"It's okay," said Kaci as she took the gun from Winter's hands.

Winter sank to the ground, sobbing into her palms. Kaci and Claire knelt down with her, both of them reaching out to gently touch Winter's arms.

Winter looked at Claire through the kaleidoscope of tears and sobbed. "But I saw you die…"

21

Four Years Ago

It was two weeks before Winter saw Claire again. Winter called the first three days, but Claire never answered her cellphone, and after the third day the line had been disconnected. Winter thought about going over to Claire's house, but she didn't want to ask her dad or Stacy for a ride.

When Claire finally did return to school, Winter almost didn't recognize her. Her clothes were normal and her hair had been colored back to its original shade. When Winter saw her from across the hall, she ran through the crowd to catch her, but with one glance at Winter, Claire ducked into her classroom.

Winter finally cornered her at lunch, plopping down at the table with Claire and staring at her full-on. "What happened to you?"

Claire wouldn't meet her eyes. "I don't want to talk about it."

"At least tell me something. You're always telling me I need to talk, so now it's your turn."

"At first I was expelled. Then the court worked out a probation with the school. Now I'm back."

"That's it? But you've changed…"

"Part of the probation."

"And you're okay with that?" Winter asked.

Claire finally looked up. "Can we talk about something else?"

Winter shrugged. "Yeah sure. Well, things basically sucked without you around."

"Hey!" said Stacy as she joined them. "I resent that. If you don't be careful, I'll tell Claire about Chad." She looked at Claire. "I'm glad you're back."

"Thanks. Who's Chad?"

"No one," Winter said, glaring at Stacy. "Stacy's being stupid."

"He's new," said Stacy. "Only been here a few weeks."

"I'm not interested," said Winter.

Stacy shrugged. "Well, I think he's cute. Your loss."

"So, can you do anything at all?" Winter asked Claire. "Can you come over?"

Claire pursed her lips. "No. I have to stay home."

Winter exchanged a look with Stacy. Both of them knew exactly how much weight that one statement contained.

"Was your dad mad?" asked Stacy.

"What do you think?" Claire pushed her tray of food away. She grabbed her bag and stood. "I need to go to the restroom."

As Claire walked out of the cafeteria, Winter turned back to Stacy. "Do you think there's anything we can do?"

Stacy shrugged. "Maybe it's time one of us actually called someone."

"But Claire would hate us for that."

"Better her hate one of us than keep living like this."

Winter looked away. "I don't think I could do that to her. I mean…I don't think I could do that to myself. I don't want Claire to hate me. And you know if someone found out, then she'd probably have to leave or something."

Stacy shook her head. "Stop being so selfish, Winter. This isn't about you. And if you won't be the friend she needs to call someone, then maybe I will."

Winter's mouth hung open. "I'm not selfish."

"You're one of the most selfish people I know." Stacy flashed her a teasing smile. "Even now, you're trying to make this conversation about you. You try to make everything about you. All this moping around, pretending you've got the worst life on the planet, meanwhile it revolves around you. It's getting a little old."

Stacy's words sliced all the way through Winter's shell. Her suppressed emotions bubbled up again, and the edge of the knife she walked between control and chaos thinned.

"Why are you being so mean?"

A twitch at the corner of Stacy's smile and a tightening of her eyes told Winter it had not been teasing at all. "For the same reason I'm going to call someone about Claire. I'm your friend. And it's about time someone said it. You need help. And so does Claire. If I'm going to be any kind of friend to either of you, then I need to do something about it."

Winter shook her head. "I'm fine. I don't need any help. I can handle this on my own."

"Whatever it is you think you can do on your own, you can't. You need help. You've always needed help because you've never been able to do it alone. It's time you realized that. You're at your worst when you're at your most alone."

Winter peered at the wall. Was Stacy right? Did she need help? She had tried that once…with *his* dad. She couldn't go back, not to him.

"I don't have a choice," Winter said.

"You always have a choice. Just like Claire. Your choices make up who you are, and right now you're a sad selfish girl who can't seem to find happiness even though she's surrounded by people who love her."

"Stop it!"

Stacy held up her hands. "Fine. But I'm not sorry. It's time you heard it." Stacy picked up her tray and left, crossing the room to another table to sit with someone else.

Winter took a deep breath. Selfish? Stacy was an idiot. She had no idea what Winter had been through. She couldn't possibly understand underneath her perfect life and her perfect Christian friends.

Winter watched the exit to the cafeteria, wondering if Claire would come back since her class was still there. Finally, she gave up waiting and went to find her. No one seemed to be in the bathroom, so Winter bent over and peered under the stall doors to see if Claire was hiding.

Under the last stall she finally found Claire, sitting on the floor in the corner beside the toilet, where she couldn't easily be seen. Blood covered her clothes and pooled on the tile floor, trickling toward the nearby drain.

"Claire!" Winter screamed. She flung herself on the floor and slid under the door. "Help! Someone help!"

Winter knelt over Claire, and Claire blinked at her with dim eyes, her skin pale as porcelain. Winter started to grab her wrist to pull her out, but stopped when she saw the huge gash gurgling blood to the surface. Claire's hand flopped open and a large pair of bloody sewing scissors fell to the floor.

"Help!" Winter slid the stall lock open and kicked the door wide. Not knowing anything else to do, she tugged at the toilet paper until she had a large wad. Then she shoved it onto Claire's wrist.

"Just leave me," moaned Claire. "Go away…"

"Help!" Winter shouted again.

Someone came in.

"Help!"

"Oh my God!" a girl said over Winter's shoulder.

Winter flicked her head around to look at her. "Go! Get help! Now!"

The girl ran out screaming.

Winter looked back at Claire. "Someone's coming."

"No…"

"Yes. You can't leave me. We need each other."

A tear rolled down Claire's cheek. "Let me die. Please…"

"I can't."

More people came in. "Move," said a deep voice.

Winter backed out of the way, as two teachers took over.

22

"How? How are you still alive?" Winter asked as she tried to choke down the tears.

"Come on, Winter," said Kaci. "Let's sit down." Kaci stood and pulled Winter to her feet. They eased to the table and sat, Claire taking the seat opposite Winter.

Winter couldn't stop staring at Claire. It was her. She was really alive. Winter squeezed her jaw tight. A cold electricity burned just beneath her skin.

Claire held her hands together on the table and looked down at them, letting her reddish brown hair swing forward. "Let me try to explain. What you think you saw…"

"I saw you die," Winter spat.

Claire glanced up and nodded. "I know. But I wasn't dead. I don't remember much. All I know is after you ran away, Michael found me. He took me to Madam Morial. When I was able to talk again, I told her everything. She started giving me all kinds of herbs and stuff, nursing me back to health and somehow fixing my problem. And while I was still sick, she arranged a fake funeral with the ashes of a goat. Even invited my parents. She kept me alive in secret, but to the world I really was dead. It was the plan, remember? You helped me make it."

Winter lurched to her feet and lunged her fist at Claire. Her foot slipped and the punch flew wild. Claire jerked back, eyes wide.

"Winter!" screamed Kaci.

"You were alive! And you never told me!" Winter ran around the table, pulling her fist back again. Before Claire could stand, Winter slammed her knuckles into Claire's jaw, sending Claire sprawling to the ground. Winter flung the chair out of the way, straddled Claire, and pulled her fist back again. But before Winter could swing, Kaci grabbed Winter's elbows from behind and yanked her back.

"Let me go!"

"Stop it, Winter!"

"No!"

Claire scrambled backward, holding one hand to the side of her face, until her back pressed against the wall.

Kaci twisted around until she was in front of Winter and placed a hand on Winter's chest. "Just listen to her!"

"You don't understand, Kaci! She was alive this whole time and she never told me? I've been living with the guilt of that night for four years!"

"I know," Kaci said in a much more soothing tone. "But just listen to her."

Winter bit her lip and nodded. She turned her back on Claire and sat again, turning her chair to face toward the kitchen instead of Claire. She heard Claire scrambling to her feet.

"I wanted to tell you," Claire said. "Really. You have to believe me. They said if I wanted a new life then everything…everyone…from my old life had to believe I was dead. I am SO sorry, Winter. But I just couldn't go back. You know what kind of monster my father was."

"No letter? No email? No phone call? I would have kept your secret, Claire. You know that. How could you do this to me?" Winter turned her head and glared at Claire.

Claire finally sank back into the chair and put her face in her hands. "I know. I'm sorry. I'm so, so sorry." Claire's voice trembled from within her palms.

Winter took a deep breath, trying to discharge the electricity. "What are you doing here?"

Claire looked up and wiped the tears from her cheeks, the left bearing the bright red impression of Winter's fist. "I don't go by Claire Parker now. My last name is Nelson. Madam Morial put me in touch with some people who could help me get a new ID without raising any red flags. Claire Parker really is dead. I've been working odd jobs all over the state for the past four years or so, mostly waitressing. I moved to Cherithville this summer and got a job at a diner just outside of town. Last week I saw you coming out of the grocery store and I followed you here. It took me a whole week to find the courage to face you."

"But why? Why come to me now?"

"I wanted to a long time ago," said Claire. "But when I was ready, when I thought I could face you again, you had already gone off to college. And I didn't dare go home and ask a bunch of questions to find out where. I don't do social media or anything…it's too risky."

"So what do you want?"

Claire shrugged. "A friend again. You have no idea what it's like never being able to have friends."

"You have no idea what it's like when they keep dying."

"That's not fair," Claire said. "Look at you now. You've got so many new friends. Kaci was telling me a little, and it seems you've really done it. You found whatever it was you were looking for." She broke eye contact and looked away. "But I've been running this whole time. If ever I feel like someone suspects I'm not who I claim or they start asking too many questions about my past, I run. I drop everything and start over where people don't know me. I haven't had a friend in a very long time."

"Do you honestly think we could just pick up where we left off?" asked Winter. "Things are different now. You've been dead for almost four years. I can't just…" Winter turned away and bit her lip.

"I know," said Claire. "Believe me, I understand. I don't expect you to forgive me. But I had to try."

"Well, you tried," Winter sneered.

Claire sighed.

"Look, Claire," said Kaci as she slid her cellphone in front of Claire. "Put your number in my phone. Give her some space and some time to process this."

Claire forced a smile. "That's Winter. Space and time." She picked up the phone and started tapping.

"Let me talk to her. I'll call you, okay?"

Claire nodded and handed back the phone.

"It won't make any difference," said Winter.

"Stop it," Kaci told her. "Claire, it was nice to meet you."

Claire stood. "You, too. Bye, Winter."

Winter looked toward the wall, waiting for the sound of the door to close. When Claire had left, she eyed Kaci venomously.

Kaci jutted out her jaw from her already flushed face. "What's wrong with you? I thought this is what you wanted. That's what you've been dreaming about, remember?"

Winter shook her head. "No. It's not the same. You don't understand."

"I think I understand perfectly," said Kaci. "Your best friend from high school shows up to apologize, and all you want to do is go on living like she's dead. Well she's not. She's alive and she's back. She came here trying to make things right. What kind of person are you, anyway?"

Winter turned away. "You don't understand."

"Then explain it to me."

Winter pointed to the door and leaned toward Kaci, the electricity boiling back up to the surface. "She left me alone, just like everyone else! She abandoned me! My life has been one horror show after another. I keep losing everyone. But Claire? Claire left me on purpose!"

"She felt like she had no choice," said Kaci. "And now she's trying to put everything right. Why won't you let her? Why won't you forgive her?"

Winter clenched her teeth. "No. She always had a choice. Everyone has a choice." Winter stood and grabbed her car keys. "I need some time to think. I'll be back in a little while."

23

"*Claire Parker died in the spring almost four years ago. Claire Nelson applied for a driver's license a couple months later. Employment records indicate a broken string of restaurant jobs all across the state, finally landing here in Cherithville this past summer at Roger's Diner outside of town. I have had an agent tail her to work and to her apartment, and nothing seemed out of the ordinary. Her story checks out.*"

"Are you sure?" asked Winter as she sat on the edge of her bed with her door locked.

"*Yes,*" said Erickson. "*And if this Alison is our suspect for murdering Skotos and Claire has a history there, then Claire may be in just as much danger as the other girls. As much as I thought you were being paranoid again when you called, I'm glad you brought her to my attention.*"

"Are you going to protect her then?"

"*In this case,*" said Erickson, "*I think it best to watch her indirectly. She's new to the situation and unaware of what's happening. Revealing your involvement with the FBI might not be the best idea. We certainly don't want her to know anything about Kaci or Ayden. For now, we'll monitor her communications and I'll assign a team to watch her. If Alison comes after her, we'll have someone nearby to intercept."*

"But you put Shannon in a safe house."

"We were already looking for her and she had a direct connection with the previous victims. This is different."

Winter heaved a deep sigh. "I guess you're right. But Shannon wasn't safe with you, how do you hope to protect Claire indirectly?"

"My agents are briefed and more prepared now. We'll keep her safe. Don't worry."

"Are you sure? What about Sophie? Have you even found her yet?"

"Not yet. But if she's part of Skotos, there's a chance she's already dead."

"She tried to help us," Winter said.

"I know. We're doing our best."

Winter pursed her lips. "Yeah, okay. Thanks." She pressed *end* on her phone and stared at it, a twinge of guilt fluttering inside of her for not doing more the night Sophie showed up. But there was nothing she could do for her now.

Claire was the real reason she had called. She had been thinking and praying about Claire for the past three days, hoping Erickson would come back with holes in Claire's story or at least something she could use as an excuse to keep avoiding Claire.

But everything was exactly as Claire had said. Winter couldn't deny she desperately wanted her old friend back in her life, to feel something a little more substantial emotionally, a little more concrete than the spiritual whirlwind of her new faith. To be free from the guilt of what happened to Claire took a mountain of weight from her shoulders.

Winter had to admit she had no reason not to give Claire the benefit of the doubt. Giving her another chance might not be easy, but Winter wanted to at least try.

Having made up her mind, she went into the living room to find Kaci.

"Do you still have Claire's number?" she asked.

Kaci smiled and pointed to the table. "Of course I do. It's right there in my phone."

Claire was already sitting in a corner booth the next Saturday, waiting at the Raven for Winter. Winter loosened her coat and tugged her black stocking hat straight as she crossed the room. It was mid-afternoon and so cold outside that few people were there eating...just like Winter hoped.

Claire watched her approach but didn't speak until Winter had settled down and ordered a basket of nachos.

"This is a nice place," Claire said as the waitress walked away. "Not just the restaurant. I mean the school. I drove through campus on the way here."

"My mom went to school here." Winter scanned the Raven for anyone who might be watching. "I'm sorry about the way I reacted last time."

"You pulled a gun on me."

Winter closed her eyes and grinned. "I know. I'm sorry. There have been some strange things happening around here, and well...self-defense and all..."

Claire smiled. "It's okay. I forgive you. What are you even doing with a gun, anyway? I didn't know you knew how to use one."

Winter shrugged. "I learned. Got a concealed carry permit. My dad gave me the gun," she lied.

"I see. Well, I'm just glad you called. I was really hoping you'd come around. I know it was a shock..."

"Claire, you've been dead to me for almost four years."

"I know..."

Winter took a deep breath. "And you never contacted me. Why would you do that? Do you realize how that made me feel?"

"I'm sorry. I really am. At first I didn't want you to know I was alive because I was afraid you would call the police and my dad would find out, and I would be forced to go back home. I couldn't handle that. I couldn't go back home. And when I was better, Madam Morial hooked me up with some friends of hers out of town who could help me start over, to get a new identity, a place to live, and a job. They said the most important part of the process was leaving everything and everyone behind, never to make contact, never to go back, and to forget like my previous life had ever happened. I wanted so bad to get away I did everything they told me." Claire's gaze fell to the table. "I realize now that was a mistake. Maybe not for all the other stuff, but leaving you behind was the wrong thing to do. You probably would have come with me. I mean, we talked about it, didn't we? And I left you behind. So I understand if you hate me for it."

Winter sighed. "I don't hate you, Claire. I've had some time to think. Maybe you did do the right thing, I don't know. I probably would have come with you, but it wouldn't have been right. I'm sorry I overreacted when I saw you."

"You? Overreact?"

"Shut up." Winter smiled. "So where do we start, then?"

Claire shrugged. "I don't know. I just want you to be a part of my life again. We're in the same town now…I thought it would be nice. Like I said, I don't get many friends, and having someone from my old life feels really freeing, you know?"

"I do know. I'm glad you contacted me. I'm still hurt…"

"I don't blame you."

"…and it may take me some time, but I want to try."

"That's more than I expected, really. I knew before I knocked on your door this was a long shot."

Winter frowned and nodded. "I've always been a long shot, I guess."

Claire bit her lip, pausing as the waitress brought the snack. When they were alone again, Claire spoke with a much lighter tone. "So, how is everyone back home?"

Winter crunched on a chip. "Stacy's fine. She went to college two states away and she's never home anymore. We email occasionally. Studying pre-med. She wants to be a pediatrician."

"Wow. Go Stacy. What about everyone else?"

Winter frowned again, wondering how much detail she should tell Claire and what Erickson might say if she told Claire anything at all. In the end, she decided Claire needed to know more than Erickson would probably allow. "Actually, there's something you need to know."

"Is something wrong?" asked Claire.

"Yeah. Shannon, Michael, Mary, Kathrine, Melissa…" Winter hesitated and met Claire's gaze. "There's no easy way to tell you this. They're all dead."

Claire's eyes popped open and her jaw fell. For a moment her mouth worked without sound. "What? H…how?"

"How is actually the big problem. It was Alison."

Claire flung her head back and forth. "No. That's impossible. She's dead."

"I thought you were dead, remember?"

"That's different. Alison is really dead. The coven went to her grandparents to get permission to bury her. She may have gone off the deep end, but we still took care of her as if she was one of us. Madam Morial got what was left of her and we had a Wiccan burial ceremony. There is absolutely no way she's alive. I was there. I was part of the circle that laid her in the ground."

"But I saw her alive the other night. Her face was half burned, but it was her, I'm sure of it. Just after she killed Shannon. I thought I was going to stop her, but when I saw it was Alison…"

Claire's eyes flicked back and forth between both of Winter's. "Even if she was alive, why would she be killing everyone we know?"

"What do you know about Skotos?"

Claire sighed and her shoulders sank. "Not Skotos…"

"So you've heard of them? Melissa was one."

Claire shook her head vigorously. "No…that's not true. It can't be."

"And Shannon said Alison was too. The people we know aren't the only ones Alison has killed. She's killing everyone involved with Skotos and anyone connected to them."

"But Alison's still dead. This doesn't make sense."

"Shannon talked about the spirit Culsu. There's a connection between Culsu and Alison. Alison was already mixed up with that spirit before she died. I think maybe, it kept her alive, or resurrected her, or possessed her, or something. Is that possible?"

Claire shook her head, mouth hanging open. "I don't know."

"Right before Shannon died, she said Alison's not really alive. So maybe that's exactly what happened. Maybe it is Alison, but she's no longer completely human…someone else said that to me too. Called it the Acolyte."

"Maybe you're looking at it wrong," said Claire.

"What do you mean?"

"This Acolyte creature. Maybe it's just something making you think you're seeing Alison."

Winter thought about it for a moment and nodded. "That kind of makes sense. Shannon said her mom could prove Alison was dead, to check the book. Do you know what she was talking about? Maybe that could clear this up."

Claire shrugged. "Probably Madam Morial's logbook, where she keeps all the records."

"How would that help?"

"I'm not sure it would help. It's just a log of important ceremonies, so it'll have all the information about Alison's burial. All it would do is give you the same information I gave."

Winter looked away. "Oh."

"Winter, you don't think she'll come for me, do you?"

Winter picked up another chip. "I don't know."

Claire wrinkled her face. "What should I do? I don't want to move again."

"I don't think it'll come to that. I think this thing's after something different. I don't think you're involved. But you're welcome to crash at my apartment if you don't feel safe. Would that help?"

"It might. I'll think about it." Claire checked the time on her phone. "Listen…I've got to get to work, my boss is a real jerk if I'm late. Thanks for calling me and for the snack. I'm glad we could patch things up."

Winter smiled and stood as Claire stood. "Me too. And listen, you know where I live, so if you ever feel unsafe, just show up."

Claire nodded and leaned in to give Winter a hug. "I will."

24

The next week, Winter lurked around the Meadow and the Union for any sign of Summer. Summer wouldn't return her texts or calls, and Winter had resorted to physical stalking to find her. If she could make an effort to put things right with Claire, then she could do the same with Summer. But by the end of the week Summer was still nowhere to be found.

Winter went instead directly to Summer's dorm, something she probably should have done already, and pounded her fist on the door. After seconds of silence, Summer's door finally cracked open and her wide eyes peered back at Winter.

"What?" Summer asked.

"We need to talk. Can I come in?"

For a moment, Winter thought Summer might say no. But then Summer backed away and let the door open completely. Winter stepped in, took in the pink disarrayed room, most uncharacteristic of Summer, and then plopped down on the bed.

"What's going on?" Winter asked.

Summer crossed her arms and sat in a chair, staring at the wall just over Winter's shoulder. "Nothing."

"Don't lie, Summer. You're a terrible liar. Something's going on, it has been all year, and you know you can't hide it from me. You haven't been the same since last spring, so spill it."

Summer shrugged.

"I'm not leaving until you talk."

Summer finally looked at her. "I'm not the one who changed. All of you are moving on with other friends. You've got Ayden now…"

"How do I have Ayden?"

"…Kaci has Peter."

"And you had Davis. But you dumped him. Why?"

"It's just not the same. He doesn't act right anymore."

Winter shook her head. "And he says the same thing about you. You're not telling me something, so stop beating around the bush and get to the point. This isn't about any of us, is it? You just made that up. What's really going on, Summer? Tell me."

Summer gazed at the floor. "Do you really think I could experience something like that and be the same?"

Winter shook her head harder. "Wrong answer. That's not it either. This has nothing to do with what happened last spring, does it? You want me to think it's some kind of PTSD, but it's not. It's guilt, as if this whole thing were your fault."

Summer shot her eyes back to Winter and then quickly away.

Winter leaned forward. "So just tell me. Whatever it is, I can help."

"No," said Summer. "You can't help with this, so just drop it. Everyone's better off if I'm not around."

"That's not true. Why would you think it's your fault? It wasn't."

Summer glanced up, her eyes red and her cheeks flushed. "Yes it was. Just go, please. Leave. I've caused enough problems like it is, I don't want to hurt you too."

"Summer…"

"Just go." Summer stared at the wall and stuck out her jaw.

"Fine. Be a selfish snob." Winter jumped to her feet and pointed her finger in Summer's face. "But I will find out." She turned and stomped out into the hall.

Just before leaving, Winter heard Summer sobbing behind her. Summer really did believe she was at fault for last spring. But why? Winter sighed and pulled the door closed, shutting out Summer.

Thanksgiving came, along with the cafeteria's annual promised turkey sandwich. Winter and Kaci invited everybody over to their apartment for an actual traditional meal. It was a cheerless gathering with Peter and Kaci trying to tip-toe their relationship around a depressed Davis. Winter and Claire tried to catch up on the past four years, probing for new common ground despite their very different lives, but the conversation was awkward at best. Everyone eventually gave it up and left shortly after lunch, except for Peter who would move in and live on the couch if Winter and Kaci would let him. But out of everyone, Peter alone didn't seem surprised at Summer's absence. Winter watched him, wondering what he knew, but unable to find an organic way to approach the subject without Kaci around.

Finals came with the customary cramming sessions and late night coffee binges. With the floundering attitudes in her social circle, Winter was excited to be going home for a few days just for some solitude and maybe even a chance to spend some time with Stacy, someone who definitely wouldn't hide things from her.

Since all indications pointed to the fact Xaphan had yet to discover where Kaci or Ayden lived away from school, the FBI relented to everyone going home as normal for Christmas break, though they would be overseen by local field officers. Winter gave her dad a story about using vacation time away from work, which also provided her the convenient excuse to return back to

Cherithville after only a week.

Once finals were completed and all other school-related obligations fulfilled, Winter and Kaci settled their plans to go home. As they stood in the living room two days before Winter's birthday, they hugged.

"One week," Kaci said.

Winter smiled. "Just one week. You can handle that, right?"

"Of course I can handle a week away from you."

"I wasn't talking about me."

Kaci blushed.

"You know," said Winter. "Maybe it's time you took him home and made things parent-approved official."

Kaci laughed. "Maybe. But not this week." She opened the door and walked out. "Day after Christmas, right?"

"Right. See you then."

Winter watched Kaci leave from the balcony door, giving her one last wave before Kaci began backing out. Once Kaci had gone, Winter knocked on the door across the landing for the agents assigned to watch them constantly.

"She's gone," Winter told the agent who answered.

He nodded. "We saw. Erickson's already been notified. There's an agent tailing her."

"And I'm about to leave too, by the way. You want me to lock our door?"

"Thank you." The agent backed away and started closing the door.

"Just checking in," Winter yelled into the shrinking crack. "Like I was told to do." The door clicked closed and Winter spun back to retrieve her luggage. "Jerks," she mumbled.

The drive home was just as boring as usual. Winter kept herself entertained with loud music and with trying to lose the FBI tail she spotted easily on the highway. At least she thought it was the tail, but every hour or so the car she thought was following would turn off and another would take its place. Winter figured they were taking turns.

As Winter pulled onto the street of her dad's house, the newest car she thought might be the tail pulled into an apartment complex two blocks down. She shook her head and put the FBI out of mind, focusing instead on the jitters in her stomach over seeing her dad for the first time in months. She pulled in beside his work truck, and by the time she climbed out of the car he was there beside her.

He wrapped his arms around her before she could even turn to face him properly.

"I missed you," Steve said.

"Ditto." She pulled away. With the key remote she popped the trunk. "What are you doing home?"

"I took off to meet you, of course. I'll get that," Steve said as he jogged to the back of the car. He reached in and hoisted out Winter's duffel bag. "How's school?"

"Fine," Winter said. "I don't have my grades yet this term, but I think I did all right."

"And the job?"

Winter shrugged, thankful she didn't have to lie. "Stressful sometimes."

He chuckled. "I should have made you get a job a long time ago, even if it does mean you have to take shorter vacations to home. But I'm glad you did it on your own. Come on, let's get you inside." He hefted the bag onto his shoulder and led the way to the door. "How are your friends?" he asked over his shoulder.

"Fine, mostly. Kaci and Peter are dating, and I think they're pretty serious too."

Steve opened the door for her. "What about your old roommate?"

"Well, Summer and Davis were dating, but they're being stupid. They broke up, probably because they won't talk about whatever the problem is. I think it'll work out if they stop being stubborn."

"Everyone's dating, huh?"

Winter nodded.

"And are you okay with that?"

She shrugged. "Yeah, I guess. I'm okay, Dad." But inside, her stomach churned.

Steve dropped the duffel bag onto the couch. "I've got dinner cooking. It should be ready in a little bit."

"Okay." Winter took up the duffel bag, an unexpected wave of loneliness hollowing her out. "I think I'll go to my room and lay down. I've been working late and everything...Just a short nap."

Steve laughed. "And an early bedtime too?"

She smiled. "Probably."

As she climbed the stairs and Steve disappeared into the kitchen, she let the fake smile disappear. Why did he have to ask her that question? Why was she being so stupid? She was okay with everything, wasn't she?

Inside her room, she locked the door and dropped the duffel bag onto the dark blue carpet. She knelt on the floor of her closet and began digging around under the junk for a small green shoe box. Inside, she riffled through old papers and photos until she came to the one crumpled prom photo etched permanently on her heart. She took it to her bed and lay down with it.

Everyone's dating, huh? And are you okay with that?

He had no idea how much that question hurt.

25

Four Years Ago

"Mrs. Crabtree?" came the voice over the school intercom the next day as Winter worked through her Science classwork.

"Yes?" answered Winter's teacher.

"Would you please have Winter come to the counselor's office?"

Mrs. Crabtree nodded to Winter. Winter took the cue and began packing her things. "She's on the way," said Mrs. Crabtree.

As Winter walked through the deserted hallway, she ran through a short list of possible reasons the counselor would want to talk to her, and settled on the suspicion it had something to do with Claire. The counselor's door was open. On the wall next to the open door was a small plaque reading, "Linda Gibbs." Winter knocked on the frame before stepping in.

"You wanted to see me?"

"Yes," said Mrs. Gibbs, an older lady, with short salt-and-pepper hair and half-moon glasses. She turned away from the paperwork on the table behind her desk and swiveled to face Winter. "Have a seat."

Winter placed her backpack beside the chair as she sat.

Mrs. Gibbs tapped her forefingers in front of her face.

"Is Claire okay?" asked Winter.

Mrs. Gibbs nodded. "You probably saved her life. She'll be fine. It's my understanding the hospital kept her overnight and will send her home pending a social services review."

"Social services?"

"After being arrested for drugs and then attempting suicide, are you surprised?"

Winter stared at the floor. "I guess not."

"That's actually the reason I called you here. You're one of Claire's closest friends here at the school. Has she mentioned anything out of the ordinary?"

"What do you mean?"

"Is she afraid to go home?" asked Mrs. Gibbs.

Winter shrugged. "I don't know."

"Have you ever been to her home?"

"No."

"Why not?"

"Because…" Winter crossed her arms and legs. "Because…my dad lets us do more, so we just always go to my place."

"Does she ever talk about her parents?"

"No," Winter said quickly.

"Has she been behaving oddly?"

"No."

"Does she ever try to cover up bruises?"

"No."

Mrs. Gibbs took a deep breath. "Winter, why don't you want to answer?"

"Why are you interrogating me? I don't know what you want me to say, but Claire's my friend. I'm not going to do anything to hurt her."

"You do realize if you know something and don't report it, that *is* hurting her."

"There's nothing wrong with her. Maybe she just got mixed up with the wrong friends or something."

Mrs. Gibbs frowned. "You know these friends?"

Winter pursed her lips together.

"Is there anyone else I can talk to who might know more?"

Winter narrowed her eyes, bobbing her foot up and down.

Mrs. Gibbs sighed. "I hope you know what you're doing. Think about what I said. If Claire needs help, as her friend you should want to get her that help. You might save her life again."

"Can I go now?"

Mrs. Gibbs watched her for a moment before nodding and turning back to her paperwork.

During Christmas break, Claire spent much of her time at Winter's house, and Winter was glad to give her a retreat. Mrs. Gibbs was right...she did need to help Claire more. But she would not turn her in. Claire never talked about the drug bust or the suicide attempt, and remembering her own desperate attempt to slit her wrists last year, Winter didn't care to ask. She was, however, surprised Claire had been allowed the freedom to come over so much. Maybe social services knocking on the door and asking questions scared her father. Maybe Claire threatened to turn him in. Claire didn't explain and Winter had no desire to ask those questions either. Steve was surprisingly accommodating, considering Claire's record and past influence on Winter. That made Winter more than suspicious social services had called him too.

The day before Winter's birthday, Claire knocked on the door early that morning.

"Hey!" Claire said as she bounced into the room.

"You're a little too chipper for this time of day," Winter said.

"What gives?"

Claire smiled. "Nothing. Just glad to be out of the house for a couple of days."

"A couple of days?"

Steve came out of the kitchen, a mug of coffee in his hand. "I arranged for her to stay over a couple nights."

"So…I get to spend your entire seventeenth birthday with you. We can go out and do what we want…"

"Well, not anything you want," said Steve.

Claire ignored him. "And then I get to crash with you again that night."

Winter glanced at her dad and smiled. "Sounds like fun," she said to Claire.

The rest of the day, they hung out at the house watching movies and playing video games. Claire never lost the over-excitement and Winter suspected Claire was overcompensating for something, but again she didn't dare ask.

The next day, Steve made pancakes for both of them, complete with a number 17 birthday candle.

"I hope you don't mind me working today," he said as she finished up her third pancake.

"No, I don't mind," she said. "Thanks for breakfast."

Steve handed her a purple envelope. "Here. Happy birthday."

Winter paused with the envelope in her hand, thinking about last year. She looked her dad in the eyes. The sadness there told her he was thinking the same thing.

"It's nothing special," he said.

She opened it and discovered a gift card worth $150, and grinned. "Thanks. This is perfect."

"Where are you two going today?" he asked.

"We're going to meet some friends at the mall," Claire said. "Maybe see a movie or something. Not sure yet."

Steve stood and grabbed his coat. "Well, not too late. Let me know when you think you'll be home. And no parties."

Winter rolled her eyes as he walked out. She craned her neck around to watch him leave. Then she turned back to Claire "Okay, so what have you really got planned?"

Claire shrugged. "The mall, maybe a movie…and then hanging out at Michael's."

The mischievous grin on Claire's face told Winter everything she needed to know. And Winter knew an equally mischievous grin crept onto her own face.

Christmas Eve, Winter woke up to a silent house. At first she thought her dad was gone somewhere, but she found him sitting alone at the table, staring at the wooden surface. A surge of panic spread through her, thinking maybe he had found out about the other night.

"Dad, is something wrong?"

He looked up at her, eyes sad and face soft. "It's your grandmother. I haven't told you, but she hasn't been doing well. Ever since my dad died last spring, she's been sort of self-destructing with depression and not eating. Her health has been deteriorating." He shrugged. "The doctor says it's fairly common that when one spouse dies the other follows."

"What are you saying? Did she die?"

He shook his head. "Not yet. I got a call late last night that she was taken to the hospital. I went down there in the middle of the night while you were sleeping, didn't want to wake you. Just got back an hour ago. Anyway…it doesn't look good. The doctors can't really pinpoint what's wrong with her other than she just doesn't want to live anymore." His voice failed and he looked back at the table.

Winter studied him, wondering what she should say. Or if she should say anything. Or if she should even feel anything. Feeling nothing and thinking of nothing to say, she turned and went to the cabinet for a bowl of cereal.

"I know you didn't know her that well," Steve said. "But maybe you'll come down and see her before she dies."

Winter set the cereal box down before pulling it open, wanting to turn back to him and shout no. But at the same time trying to restrain herself and search for a better response. After all, he'd been good to her lately, and she had been…well, she didn't want him to find out.

"Will you?" he asked.

"Dad…I don't know. Do I have to?" Winter busied herself with finishing her bowl.

"It would mean a lot to me."

"Why? What's the big deal anyway? So she's dying. People die. Why get so upset about it?"

Steve scowled at her, his face turning red. "That was uncalled for. I thought maybe you'd be a little more sensitive…considering."

"Considering what?"

"Considering this is my mother about to die, and you've already been through that. I love my mother same as you."

"Stop it."

Steve stood. "You're not the only one who loses people. You're not the only one who hurts. My mother's about to die and I thought maybe this time you'd be a little sympathetic."

"Stop it!" Winter slammed the full bowl of cereal to the floor. "I'm not going to see your stupid mother!"

Winter ran out of the room and up the stairs. She threw on the first pair of jeans and the first shirt she found lying on the floor, grabbed her coat and then went back down. Steve was standing at the kitchen door watching. She glared once at him, and then left the house, slamming the door behind her, expecting him to shout, but heard nothing.

At first she jogged down the street to the corner and turned. She did this several times to make sure Steve couldn't find her quickly. Then she slowed down, took stock of her location, and began the long trek to a destination she logged in the back of her mind but wouldn't admit to herself consciously. It took her almost three hours to get there, and with each car that passed her heart fluttered expecting her dad to arrive. But he didn't. Winter arrived at the gates of the cemetery unhindered.

It had been almost two years, but she still remembered everything. She remembered exactly how to get there. She remembered exactly where the grave was. In just a couple of minutes, Winter found herself at her mother's grave for the first time since the funeral.

Her mom's smiling face looked back at her, lacquered to the granite surface. Her name etched just above it - Marie Abigail Maessen. Below the picture was the Bible verse John 16:22, *"So you have sorrow now, but I will see you again; then you will rejoice, and no one can rob you of that joy."*

Winter covered her face with her hands and fell to her knees. The shell containing all her pent-up emotions cracked and everything spilled out. Her whole body shuddered and she could barely see the tombstone through the kaleidoscope of her tears. A sound filled her ears, and it took a moment for her brain to admit it was the sound of her own wailing.

She had no idea how long she spent in that state, only that her head became thick from the pressure, her throat began to ache and the wailing eventually subsided. Tingling began to spread through her legs, little prickles that soon died away into numbness, and she wished her whole body would just numb in the same way. If she could, she would lie there and die too.

As the flood of emotional pain trickled away into something almost bearable, Winter wiped the tears out of her eyes and gazed again at her mom's picture. Within moments, a fresh wave crashed upon her, filling her head with dry tears, bursting forth in silent sobs from her open mouth, body jerking with each one.

An arm wrapped around her back. Someone knelt beside her. She wiped the moisture away long enough to see her dad, red-faced, and tear-stricken just like her.

He handed her a bundle of roses. She took them and cradled them a moment, then slowly set them into the vase. She leaned against him, and let him pull her tight.

"I'm sorry," she croaked.

He squeezed her and kissed the top of her head. "It's okay."

They stayed there, silent for a long time, both crying, both trembling, until neither had any tears left to shed and the evening shadows grew long. And then without a word, they stood to leave.

Together.

Present Day

Despite having little to do, the time flew by. Before she knew it, it was her birthday. Steve surprised her with a home-cooked breakfast and even took another day off from work to hang out with her. Rather than a full-sized cake, he baked her twenty-one cupcakes and grinned when he presented them to her mid-morning.

"Twenty-one," he said. "You're a legal adult now."

"Dad…"

"Now you can drink beer."

"Ha, ha. I've had enough of that stuff for a lifetime, I think. Don't care for any more."

Steve shrugged. "Well, at least you know you can buy it."

"Whatever." Winter took one of the cupcakes and bit in.

Steve handed her a card. "You know how it is. When I'm not buying you cars…"

Winter opened the card and found a prepaid gift card. She laughed. "Always the best gift. Thanks, Dad."

"And if you're willing, I'd like to take you out for lunch. We can go to the mall, or wherever it is you shop nowadays. I'll even follow you around and suggest things."

Winter snorted through her laughing. "Sounds like fun."

On Christmas day, after the exchanging of gifts and the annual Christmas pizza, Winter took the roses out of the refrigerator and drove her car to the cemetery. Part of her hoped to run into Daniel again, but she didn't recognize any of the other people making Christmas visits.

Winter knelt onto the cold ground and placed the roses in the vase.

Time really did make things easier. She thought her heart would ache again or a tirade of confessions would come out like it had in the past. But Winter found herself content just to sit there, staring at her mother's picture, and remembering the good times they had together. Each year the pain weakened and the joy grew stronger.

Winter sighed and stood. She glanced over to Ryan's tombstone a little ways away. A sudden, sharp pain stabbed through her heart. She knew one day she would have to face the memory of him like she had her mom, but not this year. Somehow dealing with Ryan's death was taking longer and brought more pain than she thought possible. Her mom had been a part of her heart, but she had given the entire thing to him. Such a stupid thing for a sixteen-year-old to do, and it would take more emotional strength than she had even now at twenty-one to fully repair the damage. Not this year. She turned and trudged back to her car.

As she sat down and turned the ignition, she scanned the cemetery again for Daniel. Suddenly a thought occurred to her…was Alison's grave here? *She's not really alive. Check the book*, Shannon had said. Claire said Madam Morial would have logged when and where

Alison was buried. Was it here? Could she find it? The book would know, and Madam Morial had the book.

Winter put her car into gear and left, hoping she could remember the way to the Moon and Willow. Being Christmas, the Wiccan store was likely to be closed, but Winter hoped a little of her prophetic ability might kick in and help her get inside. Within minutes, she found the small street where the Wiccan shop was located.

She expected it to be deserted, but found it filled with the flashing lights of police cars, several of them unmarked. Winter stopped well back and pulled to the side. What was going on?

She got out and fished around until she had her FBI identification handy in the pocket of her black trench coat. She straightened the stocking hat on her head, and brushed her hair behind her ears. Then she set her jaw and walked briskly forward.

An officer near the perimeter had been watching her since she parked. As she approached he stepped forward. "I'm sorry, Miss. You can't go any further."

Winter took a deep breath and pulled out her ID, trying to make her voice sound confident. "FBI, who's in charge?"

The officer looked at the ID intently and then frowned. "A little young to be FBI, aren't you?"

Winter bored into him with her eyes. "Maybe looks can be deceiving. Are you going to hold me up or answer the question?"

He nodded over his shoulder. "Detective Martin. He's inside."

Winter didn't wait for any further permission and strolled past him.

By inside, the officer meant the Moon and Willow. The front door stood open and a couple more officers guarded the entrance. For the first time, Winter noticed the ambulance facing the opposite end of the street from which she entered.

Winter flashed her ID to the new officers and identified herself again. They scrutinized it and let her pass. Once inside, the thick smell of sandalwood almost overwhelmed her like it had the last time she had been there five years ago with Alison. The place looked exactly as she remembered, wooden floors and wooden shelves along the walls. Wooden gondolas made neat rows, but this time no candles flickered from the counters.

Two plain-clothes agents with badges on lanyards stood near the register counter, talking. The thin one with sparse reddish hair looked at Winter and asked, "Who are you? How did you get in here?"

Winter flashed the badge. "FBI. What's going on?"

The thin man swore. "You're joking? You're just a kid." He snatched the ID from her and studied it. "You know, impersonating an officer is a federal crime."

Winter shot him the same glare she had given the officer outside. "Excuse me? I'm not impersonating. Would you like me to call my superior? Are you Detective Martin?"

"I am," he said as he handed her back the ID. "Agent Maessen. How old are you exactly?"

Winter's train of thought momentarily crashed. No one had ever called her that before. "Twenty-one. Old enough to carry the badge. Old enough to go undercover." She hoped that last little tidbit would shut them up about her age.

"Why are you here?" Detective Martin asked. "If you think I'm giving you jurisdiction over me, then think again."

Winter shook her head. "No. I was just on my way to question the owner of this shop."

"Well, you're too late," he said. "She's dead. Murdered."

"What? Show me."

Detective Martin frowned and his head wagged a little. "Are you sure about this, kid?"

"Agent Maessen," Winter snapped.

"Fine. Follow me."

He led Winter through the shop, past the glass beaded curtain, and into a back storage room, where two men in white coats knelt over a body. They looked up when Detective Martin approached and backed away, giving Winter a clear view.

Madam Morial lay dead on her back, blood saturating her chest and gelling on the floor. A pair of scissors stood straight up, embedded in her heart. The word Culsu was carved into her forehead.

"Oh, no," said Winter. She shoved her hand into her pocket to get her phone.

"What?" asked Detective Martin. "What do you know?"

The phone rang against Winter's ear twice before Agent Erickson picked up. *"Erickson."*

"It's me, Winter."

"What's wrong?"

"There's been another. Scissors. Culsu. Everything's exactly the same."

"Where?"

"In Trenton Hills. Thirteen Shade Street. It's Shannon's mother."

"Are you by yourself?"

"No. I was coming for a different reason. The local police were already here."

"Okay. Give the phone to the officer in charge."

Winter held her phone out to Detective Martin. "My supervisor. He wants to talk with you."

Detective Martin mumbled something and took the phone. "Hello... Detective Martin... Yeah..." Long silence. Suddenly Detective Martin cut his eyes to Winter with surprise and anger. He stared at her while Winter could still hear the faint mumbling of Agent Erickson from where she stood. "Understood, sir." He handed the phone back to Winter and she put it back to her ear.

"Yeah?" she asked. Detective Martin was still staring at her.

"You're in charge until I get there." Winter's heart fluttered. *"I'm taking a helicopter shortly. I shouldn't be more than a couple of hours. We have agents in Trenton Hills who will come to assist you. I'll call them as soon as I hang up."*

"Are you sure?" But Erickson had already hung up.

Winter put the phone back in her pocket as Detective Martin turned to the men kneeling over the body.

"Gentlemen, we're done here. I've just found out this is out of our hands, and is part of an ongoing federal investigation."

The men stood and stepped away from Madam Morial.

Detective Martin turned to Winter. "We've been given instructions to comply with this young lady until her superior arrives. Apparently, she's an FBI expert in the occult."

Everyone in the room watched her. Winter's mind spun, trying to figure out what to do. But she had been trained for this…trained a little.

"Okay," she said. "So until additional FBI arrive we need to leave the scene as untouched as possible."

Detective Martin grinned and snorted. He crossed his arms, watching her with amusement.

Winter's blood boiled and she eyed him down. His grin slid away.

"There's a book I need. A book of records, specifically burial records, though that may not be the only records in the book. Find it."

Detective Martin huffed. "You heard her. We're looking for a record book. Gloves on, people."

After ten minutes of searching two FBI agents arrived. The officers at the door directed them to Winter.

"Agent Maessen?" one of them asked.

She nodded. "I need you to go to the victim's home and look for a record book of some kind. It'll have burial records in it."

They nodded and left again.

Winter and the police officers scoured every book in the shop, every book in the storage room, and every book in the office. They couldn't find the record book.

Erickson arrived two hours later with a team, swooping in and running every regular police officer out. She told Erickson all about the record book, and he ordered his men to go through the entire store again, while the FBI forensics team processed the body. She hung around while they cataloged everything, hoping they might discover some secret location Winter and the others overlooked. But they had no better luck than she did.

Erickson's phone rang, and when he hung up he came to Winter. "That was the local agents. Good idea sending them to the victim's home. I've sent some others to help them secure and process any evidence that might be there. They said they couldn't find the book either."

Winter sighed. "Then whoever killed Madam Morial must have taken it."

"Maybe. But we can check out the lead anyway."

Winter nodded. "We have to find it."

As Erickson started barking more orders, Winter looked past him to the pale body of Madam Morial. "What are you doing, Alison?" she said softly.

27

Despite Winter's protests, Agent Erickson made Winter return to Cherithville the next day and assured her his people would do everything possible to make sure the book hadn't been overlooked. Winter packed that night and in the early morning, day after Christmas, she hugged her dad goodbye and began the long drive back to her apartment.

As she drove, her mind wandered, often taking her so far away from the wheel of her car that she would cover several miles without remembering it. So much was hitting her at the same time, she couldn't get a firm grasp on what to do. Where were the premonitions? It seemed this year she was forced to do more on her own than she had in the past. It was both frightening and liberating, to know how much she was capable of without having to rely on God all the time.

But she could use the premonitions now. Davis, Summer, and even Peter were keeping something from her, and she had to find out what. She wanted to trust them, to bring them into what was going on, but Agent Gains' final words to her kept echoing in her mind...Trust no one.

And what about Claire? The idea of having her best friend back gave her a thrill. But things had changed. Once she could trust Claire with anything. But now that Claire had spent so long hiding from her? Now that Winter knew she'd deliberately left her behind? Her misgivings about Claire aside, Claire might be in terrible danger. Alison would come after her next, Winter was almost certain. So Winter added Claire to the list of people to protect, a list infested with lies, full of people Winter no longer knew if she could trust.

Then there was Alison...the Alison who wasn't really alive. Alison the Acolyte. Who was murdering her way through every member of Skotos, their families, friends, and everyone from Winter and Claire's past.

At that thought a moment of panic seized her. Stacy. She fumbled with her phone until she had dialed Stacy's number. It rang a couple of times in her ear before Stacy answered.

"Hello?"

"Stacy? It's Winter."

"Winter! Hey, long time no talk. How was your break?"

"Not bad. I just wanted to call and check on you before I made it back to school. I'm on the road now, so I don't really need to talk long I guess."

"Everything's fine. Just about to head into work. I'm planning on going home spring break, what about you? Maybe we could get together or something."

"Yeah, maybe we can. Are you sure everything's fine?"

"Why wouldn't it be? Is something wrong?"

"Maybe..."

"What's going on?"

Winter took a deep breath, wondering how much she should tell Stacy. Of all the people in the world, except maybe her dad, Winter knew she could fully trust Stacy. Stacy would keep secrets if Winter asked.

She took another deep breath and went for it. "Claire's alive."

"What? Are you serious? I thought she…"

"Yeah. Me too. But she's back. Apparently it was all a fake so she could start over away from her dad."

"Well, I guess I can't blame her. Still, I wish she'd told someone."

"Same here."

"But that's a good thing, right? Is that what's wrong? How are you doing with this? Are you okay?"

"I'm fine. I mean, I wasn't at first. I'm angry with her…so angry. But I'm trying. She's not why I wanted to call, though."

"Then what is it?"

"Well…there have been some murders. People Claire and I used to hang out with."

"The witches?"

"Yeah. I just wanted to make sure you're safe…just in case. If the murderer is just after the Wiccans then that's one thing. But if it has something to do with me and Claire…"

"What in the world have you gotten yourself into now? Why would anyone be killing people you know? What's going on?"

"Umm…" Winter bit her lip. "I don't know. Claire and I weren't exactly saints, you know?"

"Have you called the police?"

"Of course, Stacy. I'm not an idiot. It's all being taken care of. I'm fine, really. Claire's fine. I just wanted to give you a heads up, that's all."

"You think I might be in danger?"

"Well, I don't know. Just be safe, okay? If you see anything out of place, call the police."

"Don't worry, I will."

"Speaking of police, let me go so I don't get pulled over for swerving all over the road."

Stacy laughed. *"Sure. Call me later so we can talk more, okay? I want to hear more about Claire."*

"I will." Winter hung up and shook her head. How was she supposed to protect Stacy too?

The rest of Christmas break went by uneventfully, except for Kaci talking constantly on the phone with Peter. Winter kind of wished she actually did have a real job just to pass the time.

Erickson called her with bad news. They thoroughly cataloged everything in Madam Morial's shop and home with no trace of any kind of a record book containing burial information. Winter knew without it she couldn't get to the bottom of what Alison was up to.

Still no dream or premonition to help.

The day before classes began, Ayden called to check in, and then Peter arrived. He spent less than an hour at his dorm before coming over. As Kaci and Peter snuggled on the couch watching a movie, Winter studied him from the corner of her eye, wondering just how much she could trust him…and just how much Kaci had told him already.

"Peter," Winter said, deciding to probe a little during a lull in the action.

"Yeah?"

"Have you talked to Davis lately?"

Peter shook his head. "Not since before Christmas. He wasn't back when I got to the dorm. He'll probably be in later tonight. Why?"

"Do you think he's hiding something?"

Peter frowned and just looked at her.

"You do, don't you?" asked Winter.

Peter sighed. "Yeah. But I don't think it's anything big. Considering all that happened last spring, both of them are pretty shaken up. That's probably all there is to it."

"Are you sure that's it?"

"Yeah, pretty much."

"Well, maybe you're right about Davis. But Summer's hiding something else."

Peter turned back to the TV.

"Do you know?" Winter leaned forward.

"No."

Winter glared at him, but he wouldn't look back at her. What was he up to? What did he know?

"I wish you two would be quiet," said Kaci. "I, at least, am trying to watch a movie. If you want to talk, go out on the balcony."

Winter stood and checked the time. "I'm going to go find him. Kaci, are you good here?"

She waved a hand of dismissal. "I'm fine. Go."

Winter glared again at Peter, hoping whatever he was up to, maybe at least Kaci would be safe for a little while. She gathered her coat, hat, and keys from the other room and left for campus.

Winter didn't bother calling Davis until she was in the parking lot of Edwards Hall and had spotted Davis's car. Even then all she told him was that she wanted to talk, putting just enough edge to her voice to make him believe she would burst into his room if he didn't show. She might just. One way or another, Winter wanted answers.

She waited for him in a secluded corner away from the lounge television watchers, and arranged two chairs to face each other. It didn't take long before Davis emerged, red-faced and staring at the floor, looking like he would rather be anywhere but around Winter. He shuffled toward her and sagged into the chair.

Winter leaned forward, eyes firmed. "Spill it."

His gaze darted all around the carpet and the wall behind her, but he wouldn't look at her directly. He wouldn't answer. His face just grew more red.

"Don't make me beat it out of you. I want to know what's wrong, and I want to know now. I'm not letting you keep this secret any longer."

He still didn't speak.

"What is it? Are you working for him now? Blackmail?"

He shook his head.

"Are you in love with me?"

He snickered that time. "No."

"Kaci?"

"No."

"Then what's your issue? Look at me!"

He lifted his face and met her eyes.

Winter focused on his pupils, trying to sink into his memories like she could do last year, to dive into some kind of vision from his past. But nothing happened. She sighed, more frustrated with herself than Davis now.

"Tell me everything," she snapped with such ferocity Davis jumped.

"Last spring..." He clamped his mouth shut.

"Yeah, I know. I was there but I'm not pouting about it. You and Summer are starting to sound like babies. Keep going."

"I was running to the Union trying to find you, and there were all these people lying around bleeding to death. When I got there you came out...and then he came out. He was going to shoot you so I..."

"You attacked him. I saw. That was a very brave thing to do."

"Was it? I thought he was going to kill me."

"We thought he did. What happened? You never told us how you escaped."

"I was lying on the ground. He had his gun, standing over me. And he congratulated me. He said well done. Why would he do that? Did I help him? Was it my fault Ayden was captured? I just can't get that out of my head."

"Is that all?"

Davis gazed at the floor again.

Winter laughed and slouched back into the chair. Davis looked up at her, stunned.

"I thought it was something more serious," she said.

"It's not funny. I'm really confused and messed up over it."

She pushed herself back up. "Sorry. I know it's not funny. But that guy was insane, you realize that, right?"

Davis nodded.

"I'm not even sure he was completely human."

"But why would he say *well done*? He should have killed me like everyone else. All those people dying in the Meadow and in the Union, and I'm still alive. I'm the one who actually tried to do something, and I'm the one who lived." His chin began to quiver.

"Maybe that's why he said what he did. Maybe that's why he let you live. This sicko didn't have to kill anyone. But if someone got in his way…Look, everyone else was running. You're the only one who had the guts to stand up to him. I think in some sick way in that monster's eyes, you did something honorable. Maybe that's why he let you live."

"But it's not fair that I'm alive."

"Don't say that. God kept you safe…albeit in a very strange way. But your actions were rewarded. What you did saved my life, don't forget that."

Davis pursed his lips. "So you don't think I helped him?"

She shook her head. "No. I don't think you did at all. You stood up to him, and he recognized the bravery in that. So he let you live. That's why he said well done."

Davis took a long deep breath. "Maybe you're right."

"And don't feel guilty for living. You had no control over that."

Davis nodded.

"Feel better?"

"A little. I need to process it. But I hadn't thought of it that way before. I just thought I'd made this huge mistake."

"You didn't make a mistake at all," Winter said. "And I need the old Davis back. I need the old team back."

"I'll try," he said. "Thanks for not giving up on me, and making me talk. It helped."

She smiled. "That's what I'm good at."

Four Years Ago

Winter lay on her bed after school, crying to herself and clenching the prom picture of her and Ryan. Earlier that day, the school had made its first announcements about the upcoming prom, and Winter had struggled the rest of the day to keep the turmoil from boiling out.

Now alone in the house, behind the locked door of her bedroom, everything ruptured to the surface. She reveled in the pain this time, hoping that if the intensity were strong enough, it might stop her beating heart.

The doorbell rang. Winter sat up and grabbed a tissue from her nightstand, shoving the picture beneath her pillow. She ran into her bathroom and checked the mirror. Her black mascara had run and she wet her hand to rub away the streaks.

The doorbell rang again, followed by loud knocks. Winter rushed downstairs and peered through the peephole.

Claire.

Winter unlocked the door and pulled it open.

"Hey," Winter said and stood out of the way so Claire could

enter.

"I wanted to check on you," Claire said.

"Check on me…why?"

"Because you were very quiet all day. Even when I tried talking to you, you didn't seem to hear. I thought maybe something was wrong."

Winter bit her lip. "Um…I'm fine. Nothing's wrong."

Claire tilted her head. "You're lying to me. I'm the queen of faking things so you can't hide from me. Besides, your make-up's all messed up and your eyes are puffy."

Winter rubbed beneath her eyes where the mascara had run. "It's just allergies." She moved to the couch and sat.

Claire sat next to her. "No, it's not. It's about Ryan, isn't it? I heard them make the announcement about prom."

Winter leaned forward and put her face in her hands. She wanted to make another denial, but sobs bubbled out instead.

Claire put a hand on her back. "Look…it's okay."

"I just don't understand…" Winter croaked. "I loved him. Why did he have to die?"

"I don't know."

"And why did I get to live? Why is it everyone dies around me, but I live? Why do I have to be the one to suffer? Why can't I just die, too?"

"It's not your fault."

Winter lifted her head to face her. "Yes it is. It's all my fault. I'm the one who was driving the car."

"Yeah, but Alison…"

"I'm the one who took Alison to Madam Morial's. I'm the one who told her all about the magic stuff, about the love spell. I helped her become what she was."

Claire shook her head. "You couldn't have known."

"But I still did it. If I had kept my mouth shut, Alison wouldn't have turned on you and she wouldn't have messed with dark magic."

"She hated me already. I think she would have gone down that path anyway, whether you helped or not."

"But I did help. Don't you get that? If it had been someone else helping, then she wouldn't have made me drive the car and Ryan would be alive. It would have been someone else's problem. But now...Ryan is dead and it's all my fault!" Winter collapsed against her hands again.

"No, it's not."

"I killed him, Claire."

"No, you didn't."

"Yes, I did!" Winter shouted into Claire's face.

Claire's eyes glistened and she looked away. "Then what about me? What about my dad? What about your mom?"

"Leave my mom out of this."

"Just listen to me." Claire turned back to her. "I'm the one who wanted to get into magic in the first place, remember? If it wasn't for that, Alison would have never done what she did, she would have never come to you for help in the first place. And Ryan would be alive. Both of them would be alive. So if it's anyone's fault it's mine."

Winter stared at her, anger rising up. She opened her mouth...

"I'm not finished," Claire said, turning her whole body to face Winter better. "But why did I do that? It was because of my dad and your mom."

"Are you blaming them now?"

"No. Because their issues weren't their fault either, really. My dad is the way he is because of his parents. Your mom was sick and she had no control over that...maybe it was genetics, maybe it was something she ate...I don't know. And then we can go back further, to find someone else to blame." Claire leaned forward. "Don't you see? We can what-if these sorts of things forever, trying to find the source of blame, but it's never good enough. There's always something or someone else. But the truth is we are not in control of our destiny. Destiny is written around us, defined by what people do and the universe's reaction to it. It's not just about us, it's about everybody, karma weaving the threads of our lives together in ways we have no control over."

Winter snorted. "I've heard the same sort of things before…from Stacy. Different words, same point. All your religions are the same. All pointless really…because karma or God, it doesn't matter….the universe hates me."

"Well, for what it's worth, I've never been impressed with Stacy's god. It's stupid to think a god who is supposed to love everyone would let someone like you suffer so much."

"Well, your religion isn't much better."

"It is. There's a different way. There are spirits who help and spirits who can hurt. When troubling spirits come after us…like the ones screwing up your life…calling upon a friendly spirit can help. I realized this just a few weeks ago. I didn't think I had anything worth living for and I wanted to end it. While I was in the hospital Madam Morial came and explained a dark spirit was surrounding me. She helped me call upon a friendly spirit…and it's made all the difference in the world. I actually feel happy now. And Stacy's god can't do that."

"You've been calling on spirits? Isn't that what Alison did before she went crazy?"

"Sort of, yeah. But she didn't know what she was doing. She called up a very evil spirit and didn't know how to get rid of it. I had help. I'm not an idiot."

Winter shook her head. "Just sounds like superstition to me."

"Just give it a try, maybe you'll change your mind."

"You want me to call upon a spirit?"

"Maybe."

"No, thanks." Winter wiped her nose with the palm of her hand.

"Well, you need to do something to get yourself moving forward again, even if you don't want my help. Maybe you should go to prom again this year. Face it and get past it."

"With who? No one would ask me."

"Then you ask someone."

Winter snorted with derision. "Even if I did, I doubt they'd say yes. Besides, who would I ask?"

Claire smiled. "What about the new boy, Chad? I saw you looking at him the other day at lunch, despite your insistence that you're not interested."

Winter turned away, feeling her cheeks blush. "Maybe."

"That's it," said Claire. "That's the answer. You can face this head-on by going to prom with Chad."

"I don't know…"

"Listen, you don't have to love this Chad, okay? But you can still move forward. So ask him."

Winter took a deep breath. "I'll think about it."

Claire clapped her hands together. "Good. Now that that's settled, let's go do something fun. Are you up for the mall?"

Winter shrugged. "Sure. Anything to get out of here."

Claire stood and held out her hand. "Then let's get out of here."

29

Present Day

She was fleeing Egypt, that much she knew for certain. A staff in her hand and sandals on her feet, she trudged up the low rising hill of desert rock. At the apex, the warm breeze blew her hair wild, carrying the sweet, tangy smell of salt water, as she looked down upon the sea blocking the path. The sun hung low on the horizon behind her, casting her shadow almost to the gently pulsating water along the rocky shore.

This isn't good, she thought. *How will we get away now?*

She turned to look back at the masses who followed, knowing they clung to a mere thread of hope. At the front of the faceless crowd were people Winter knew. Kaci. Peter. Summer. Davis. Ayden. Her dad. Kaci's parents. Stacy. Even Agent Erickson and Agent Golbeck. As she watched her friends, the rest of the crowd began to evaporate, leaving behind only those she cared about. They watched her in despair, each carrying the shadow of hope, desperately wanting a way to escape but not daring to believe it could be possible.

Winter lifted her eyes to the desert stretching beyond them. A black cloud roiled in the distance, obscuring the horizon like a wall of ink, blocking out the sun which only moments ago warmed their backs. As it churned toward them, the desert floor splintered, breaking away and being consumed in the insatiable appetite of the evil cloud. It was coming for all of them, to kill and destroy.

The Acolyte.

Winter turned back to the water and knew what she had to do. She lifted the staff with both hands and ran. Down the slope she flew, carried by the momentum of gravity, almost losing her balance before the end. She pushed herself even faster when she reached flat ground. As she charged the water's edge, it pulled away, retreating as if afraid. But Winter was faster. She chased the water far into its bed as it bent around her like a giant horseshoe, until she caught the fleeing sea.

As her feet hit the water, the water paused, frozen in that moment of time, ripples in mid crest and spray hanging like dust in the air. Winter hesitated and looked behind. Her loved ones stood just within reach, watching with fear-stricken faces. And beyond them on the ridge where they had just stood came the blackness, spilling over like a heavy mist, frothing as it crashed to the flat ground.

Winter spun away and took another step into the water. She swung the staff high overhead and plunged the end down. As soon as the wood touched the surface of the sea, the water fled from it as if blasted by a cannon of air. As the water flew away, it piled upon itself, building two walls to either side of Winter and her friends. In just moments every drop of moisture had cleared the ground, laying a dry path out before her to the other side of the sea. To safety.

Sitting on the ground just feet in front of her was a book.

The dream pulled away, dragging colors and shapes into an invisible point on the horizon, as if the fabric of reality had been pinched from the back side and yanked through a pinhole. She reached out to pick up the book, but it too swirled into the vortex. Where reality had been peeled back, blinding light took its place, the light of pure untainted existence. She clenched her eyes against the intensity. The light transformed into an angry red, yet still purely white; an infrared Winter could feel as heat, burning, punishing, tearing at the hardness in her heart, the stronghold where she protected the most intimate elements of her identity. It roared over her in that furious rumble she had heard and felt from God, now crashing full force upon her, crushing, stealing her breath, demolishing security.

A brief shockwave against her body told her things had changed. She dared to open her eyes, blinking, heart pounding against a lingering fear, and found nothing more than her room. She took a deep breath and tried to still the rhythm of her heart and checked her clock. Only minutes remained before her alarm would go off, so she jumped up to claim the shower.

At least the dreams hadn't stopped, even if the premonitions were gone completely. Maybe she could actually make sense of this one. It might lead to the book, which she assumed was the journal they had been looking for. But that light...

After the shower, she found Kaci already dressed and eating a bowl of cereal.

"Good morning," Kaci said.

Winter huffed. "Morning."

As Winter mindlessly went through the motions of pouring cereal and sitting down to eat, she couldn't get the dream and the book out of her mind. Distantly, she was aware Kaci tried to have some sort of conversation with her. Winter just watched Kaci and nodded, randomly reforming Kaci's words into questions in hopes Kaci wouldn't notice her inattention.

By the time they got into Winter's car to go to campus, Kaci had finally picked up on Winter's mood and kept mostly to herself. They parked behind the Union and walked around to the front where they would make the ritualistic secret exchange of handlers.

But instead of walking down the sidewalk as usual to fall in behind Ayden, Winter stopped and waited, watching Kaci, Nadeen,

208 | Keven Newsome

and Ayden walk away.

She had to do something about that book. It had to be done today, before Alison caught up to her. Winter turned to go back to her car.

"Hey!" said Ayden, jogging up beside her and falling into step. "What are you doing?"

"Sorry. I've got to go somewhere."

"Where?"

"I don't know."

"For what?"

"I don't know."

"Then what in the world are you doing?"

"Going back to my car."

"Is this one of those prophetess things?"

Winter paused, suddenly realizing that nagging feeling at the back of her mind was indeed the premonition, though more subtle and less urgent, tainted with that infrared heat she didn't understand and chose to keep ignoring. After all this time of having little to go on, finally she was getting a something to tell her what to do next.

Winter nodded. "I guess it is."

"I thought you weren't having those anymore."

"Kind of. The dreams have never stopped. But this sort of thing has been rare this year. I can't control it. When I want it, it never comes. It's only showed up a couple of times when I wasn't expecting it. It must be important right now, though. I'm sorry. I really have to go."

"I'm coming."

"No, you can't. You need to stay here."

"With who? You're the one who's supposed to be shadowing me. So I'm coming with you."

"No," said Winter. "It may be too dangerous."

"I really don't care. There's a reason I can see that little girl and a reason I sometimes know things I'm not supposed to, and I want to find out why."

Winter glared at her. "Fine. But you have to follow my instructions, got it?"

"Sure, whatever."

Winter unlocked her car and climbed in. Ayden jumped into the passenger side, bright-eyed and eager.

"Okay, now what?" Ayden asked.

Winter shrugged and cranked the car. "I guess we start driving."

"Where?"

"I don't know."

"I thought you could, like, see things in the future."

Winter grunted as she pulled out of the parking lot. "Not always. It doesn't really work like that."

"Then how does it work?"

Winter shrugged. "I get impressions, images, of what to do next mostly. I have dreams or hear voices. Sometimes I know things before they happen. It's all kind of random. I guess it's a little different every time and depends on the situation."

"And now?"

"I don't know. I think I know the moment…but nothing beyond. Like…" She turned onto Hoole Boulevard. "…I know I need to drive this way, but I don't know why. I can't feel anything else. Actually…" Winter frowned. "It may have just gone away."

"So now what"

Winter shrugged. "I guess we just keep driving until something else happens."

Ayden crossed her arms and peered out of the windshield. "I've been thinking about that little girl. Do you know who she is?"

"I've told you I don't."

Ayden huffed. "I'm not sure I believe you. But you are the only one who can see her?"

"Except for you."

"Right…and do you know why? Let's get on the highway."

Winter glanced at her and then back to the road. The intersection with the highway was approaching and Winter turned. Once she reached highway speed, she turned back to Ayden.

"I have a suspicion," Winter said.

"What?"

"Maybe you're coming down with the same thing I have."

"A prophet?"

"Prophetess. Yeah, maybe."

Ayden shook her head. "I don't know. I mean, I gave in to being a Christian and all, but I don't know about this prophecy stuff."

Winter shrugged. "Well, maybe I'm wrong."

They drove for a couple of hours and Winter wondered if they might be going all the way to Trenton Hills. Within minutes of that thought, in a lengthy stretch of highway where trees marched for several miles on either side of the road, an exit approached leading to a rural community which the sign said was still another fifty miles away.

Ayden sat up and studied the exit. "If I were going to hide something, I bet this would be a good place."

Winter nodded and turned. At the intersection at the end of the ramp, Winter looked both ways. "What do you think?"

Ayden shook her head. "I don't know. Away from the town?"

"Right," said Winter, and turned toward the middle of nowhere.

"So, do you know yet?" Ayden asked.

"No. I actually don't know what's going on."

"You don't even know what we're looking for?"

"I think it's the book from Madam Morial's shop."

"The one Shannon spoke about?" Ayden asked.

"Yeah. It might be in water or something."

"Great..."

The turn into the wilderness didn't last long. As a bridge approached, Ayden pointed and said, "Look, water. Let's check here."

Winter nodded and pulled onto to the side of the road. As the car settled into place and Winter put it in park, she looked at Ayden and shrugged. "I guess now we go on foot."

"Is it always like this?" asked Ayden.

"Not always."

Winter got out and stood at the front of her car to button her coat, looking down upon the creek below, crusted with ice along the edges and small enough in some places to possibly jump to the far bank.

"Look, there's a path," said Winter, pointing a little further to the right.

"No," said Ayden, peering across the road. "If someone's going to hide something, it's not on the path. We need to go over there." Without waiting for Winter, Ayden ran across the road.

Winter grunted and followed. On the other side, no paths led through the overgrown brush, spindly and stiff from the cold. They pushed through, slowly and trying to keep the limbs from slapping them in the face. Thankfully, the brush didn't last long and it opened up into a larger stand of trees where they could walk comfortably. The creek gurgled to their right, rushing down to the bridge.

Just a little way upstream, the trees opened all the way to the water's edge. The bank was soft with cold moss, dropping off in a straight ledge into a deep pool of the creek, at least thirty feet wide. Here the water collected almost stagnantly and waited its turn to pass through the more narrow and faster exit downstream. Ice clung to the edges of the pool and in places crystalline water floated along the middle.

"Now what?" asked Ayden.

Winter studied the dark water, without any more nudges since getting into her car, and still not sure they were at the right place at all. So what was she supposed to do? What did a random pool of water have to do with anything?

"You do know what to do next, don't you?"

"I'm thinking," said Winter. She played back the morning, retracing the path of coming here, and looking for some clue. She never received any insight, any vision, any foreknowledge, any premonitions except for that brief moment on campus.

"Wait," said Winter. "This whole thing was triggered by a dream I had last night."

"A dream?"

"Well...maybe. At least I think they're connected. I could be wrong."

"So, what do think you have to do?"

Winter took a deep breath and let the dream replay itself in her mind's eye. She had stepped into the water. She had struck it with her staff.

"I don't have a staff," she said.

"A staff? What in the world do you need a staff for?"

As she thought about the staff, she realized she was fondling her locket...something she often did when she was deep in thought. It gave her an idea. She reached to the back of her neck and unclasped the locket, holding the chain tightly in her hand so the locket dangled a couple of inches.

"Well, here goes."

"Here goes what?"

"If the water is over my head, be ready to help me out."

"WHAT?"

Winter held her arms up at her sides, closed her eyes, and took a long step forward over the water. The rush of cold seized her muscles tight and expelled all the air from her lungs. She held her breath, waiting for the iciness to wash completely over her, but it stopped just beneath her waist as her feet hit the mushy ground. Winter let her mouth fall open and she gasped, holding both arms tensely out so they wouldn't touch the surface. She peeked over her shoulder at Ayden, already shivering to her core and now wishing she had taken off her coat and left her phone on the bank.

Ayden grinned. "You…are an expert level idiot. I don't suppose you brought a change of clothes did you?"

"Sh…sh…shut…t…t…up…"

Winter slowly pivoted back to face the center of the pool. She brought her locket around in front of her, jingling in her twitching hand, and prayed this would work, that this was what she was supposed to do. That she wasn't just a very wet, very cold idiot.

She lowered the locket down toward the surface, and the dream replayed itself right in front of her eyes. The water rushed away from the locket as if blasted by air, sucking into giant walls on either side of her. The sound of the splitting water roared through the glen like the rustle of a collapsing tree.

In moments, the ground was uncovered and the moisture vacuumed from the mud. Winter felt her clothes drying as the water sucked out. When every drop of moisture had joined the walls of water, Winter clasped the locket back around her neck, took a deep sighing breath, and turned back to look at Ayden.

Ayden's eyes bulged like bouncy balls. "What the…"

Winter turned away with a smirk and let Ayden's string of expletives roll off her back. That's when she saw the book.

A brown leather-bound book, no bigger than a day planner, lay in the middle of the dry path between the walls of water. Winter walked on the dry ground and bent down to pick it up. She looked at it only a moment, sparing a brief thought to recognize it too was dry, before rushing back to the bank.

As she reached out to Ayden, the infrared heat suddenly blazed down upon her back. She sensed the condemning pressure and knew she had to hurry.

"Help me," she almost shouted.

Ayden rushed forward and grabbed Winter's hand. As Winter planted a foot on the high bank and climbed back up, the water sloshed back into place, grabbing her right leg from the knee down as she swung up.

"Had enough fun?" asked Ayden.

"Shut up. I'm still cold." Winter swore and tried to wring out the frigid water from her right leg.

"Is that it?" asked Ayden.

"I think so."

"What is it doing way out here?"

Winter shrugged. "I guess whoever took it must have ditched it here."

"Well, that's dumb. Why didn't they just burn it?"

"I don't know. Maybe they couldn't." Winter cracked it open and thumbed through the pages. Everything was there. Births, naming ceremonies, induction ceremonies, expulsion ceremonies, deaths, burials. She peered closely at the dates and flipped forward to when Alison would have died. After scanning a moment, she found it.

"Here." She pointed out the entry to Ayden.

"That's her? The one that's been killing everyone?"

"Yeah." Winter shoved her hand into her pocket and took out her phone. Dry. Thank God. She pointed it at the book and snapped a picture. Then she flipped another page and found the entry for Claire. She snapped another picture.

"Why did you do that?"

"Because I'm going to have to give this to Agent Erickson. And I just needed to see those names for myself."

Ayden nodded. "Now what?"

"Well..." Winter sighed. "I guess we go back."

When they returned to the car, Winter immediately called Agent Erickson while Ayden thumbed through the logbook.

"Winter," he answered. *"Where are you? I've been calling for hours and you haven't answered. Ayden's missing. We have people out searching for both of you. Your tracking bracelet says you and Ayden are near each other in the middle of nowhere about two hours away. Are you in trouble? Is Ayden with you?"*

"Yeah, I'm fine. There's nothing to worry about…just something we had to do. We're headed back now." She pulled the phone a little away from her mouth and turned to Ayden. "Did your phone ring?"

Ayden shook her head.

"What were you thinking?" Erickson barked in her ear. *"Your priority is to protect Kaci, not Ayden, even if you shadow Ayden during the day."*

"I know, but I had this dream…"

"I don't care if the Almighty came down and presented you with a handwritten letter, Kaci's life is at stake and you act like it doesn't matter. Maybe I made a mistake giving you this assignment."

"No! I'm sorry. I've got the book."

Silence for a moment. *"The one you were looking for in Trenton Hills?"*

"Yes."

"Bring it to me. We'll talk then. Come straight to the field office. Bring Ayden with you...she could probably stand to hear this too." He hung up.

"Well?" asked Ayden.

Winter pursed her lips. "I think we're in a little trouble."

"Trouble? Why? For leaving the school? He's not our dad."

"Well, we've already been warned once, remember? And it's a little more complicated this time."

Ayden stared at her. "What are you not telling me?"

Winter sighed. "You'll probably find out soon enough." She put the car into gear and turned back toward the highway. "Erickson is kind of my supervising officer."

"Your supervising officer. You mean..."

"I'm kind of an agent too."

Ayden flopped back against the headrest, put a hand to her forehead, and cursed. Then she smiled. "Sucks to be you."

Ayden continued to thumb through the book the entire drive back, and even though Winter blasted past the posted speed limit, Ayden never looked up and didn't bother speaking. Within a half hour of driving, two sedans filed in behind Winter, and Winter's heart sank knowing Erickson had called for a grand escort back to Cherithville. Once in Cherithville, Winter drove straight to the apartment serving as the FBI field office, and as she pulled into the parking lot, the following sedans broke away and drove in separate directions.

Several of the neighborhood people were out walking the sidewalks, cleaning cars, or doing other random outside chores. Most of them watched her as she parked, most of them probably agents themselves.

Agent Golbeck opened the door for them expectantly as they walked up the sidewalk. He glared so hard as they entered, Winter couldn't help but look at the floor. Inside, Erickson sat at the table, hands folded together and a sternness to his face that chilled the butterflies in her stomach.

"Sit down, both of you."

They obeyed and Winter gently placed the book on the table.

Agent Erickson picked it up and flipped through a few pages. Then he handed it to Agent Golbeck, who walked to a back room with it in hand.

"We'll look through that carefully." He tapped his index fingers together. "You two are beginning to be a problem."

"What do I have to do with anything?" Ayden asked.

"You have the same stubborn rebellious attitude she does and a knack for wanting to show it off." He narrowed his eyes. "This is the second time you've disappeared, Ayden, though this time you at least didn't leave behind your tracker. And both times I found you with her." He turned to Winter. "And this is the third time you have run off and left Kaci behind, and the two times before this you were directly told by me to stay with her and to let us handle the situation. Of course you didn't listen, putting me in the awkward position of either backing you up or letting you run recklessly into danger alone. Not to mention you waltzing into a local police investigation during Christmas and practically taking it over without authorization from me. I had no choice but to back you up then either. And what do you do? Take every resource available to look for a book instead of the killer.

"Now you've both just disappeared without notifying me, and that makes me very unhappy. But at least you found your little book. Did you find what you were looking for? What was it? Oh yes…just a line entry about the death of the person this new killer is impersonating. Did you really think she was still alive? Have you any idea how sophisticated disguises and masks could be? Xaphan has your life story and apparently he's learned exactly how to push your buttons. All he has to do is dredge up the right memories and the right emotions, impersonate the right people, and you shut down like a wind-up toy. If that's all it takes to neutralize you, what good are you really?"

Winter turned her face to the table, guilt stomping on her chest, feeling like a complete moron. Of course Erickson was right. Of course Alison was nothing more than an impostor. It was the only thing that made real sense.

"It's hard enough trying to capture this incredibly intelligent, incredibly violent sociopath, who obviously has very lucrative resources, without you two chasing ghost stories and jumping at shadows." Erickson took a deep breath and continued. "The only advantage we have right now is we know they know Ayden isn't the right person. But they don't know we know that."

Ayden snickered.

Erickson fixed her with a firm glare. "This isn't funny. Your life is one of the ones in jeopardy. The only reason you're still alive is that we are continuing the ruse. They think we're not paying attention to their continued search, but we are. We are closer than ever to locating Xaphan and putting an end to this. Our agents have been able to infiltrate his network and trace the lines of communication and the flow of resources, as well as plant false trails pointing away from Kaci. Meanwhile you two must continue the original plan or they'll know something has changed on our end. Once that happens, the chess match changes and we lose the advantage. Everything is going smoothly except for you two. If you keep going solo, if you keep stepping outside the parameters of the operation, you could put everyone in jeopardy…the undercover agents, Kaci, your parents, and yourselves."

He paused for a long time…long enough Winter looked up. Erickson's eyes darted from her to Ayden.

"I want both of you to look at me and listen closely," he said. "If either of you screw up again, I'm canceling the whole operation. You and your families will disappear into protective custody. We'll lose years of progress and digress back to a reactionary strategy to Xaphan's occasional slip-up. You'll live in fear, always looking over your shoulders, and there will be nothing we can do to warn you if he's found you out. Is that what you want?"

Winter shook her head. Erickson watched her until Winter mumbled, "No, sir." Then he scowled at Ayden until she did the same.

"One toe, ladies. That's all you get. Now go."

Winter dropped off Ayden at the dorm room into the irate hands of Nadeen. As Winter arrived back at the apartment, Claire drove up in a faded old compact car and parked next to her.

"Hey," said Claire as she popped out. "That's your car? Nice."

"Hey," Winter said as she closed her door. "What are you doing here?"

"Well, that's friendly. I had some time before work. I thought I'd drop in to see you. Are you busy?"

Winter shook her head and smiled. "No, it's fine. Sorry. Stressful day. Come on in."

Winter led them into the apartment. Upon opening the door, Kaci and Peter jumped away from each other on the couch, both faces flushed and Kaci's hair a little tousled.

"Sorry," Winter said and stepped in. Claire followed her through the door, taking one look at them and snickering.

Peter and Kaci stood.

"No, it's okay," said Kaci. "Peter's got an afternoon class. He needs to be going." She grinned and shoved him in the shoulder.

"Fine," Peter said. He leaned down to kiss her on the lips, but she turned away and he landed on her cheek.

Peter sighed and walked toward the door. "I'll see you later then."

Winter and Claire stepped out of his way. Peter grinned at them and heat rose into Winter's cheeks. She glanced away as he passed and found Claire watching her.

"Hey, Claire," said Kaci. "Would you like something to drink?"

"No thanks."

"Peter and I are going out for dinner after his class. You two are welcome to join us."

"I can't," said Claire. "I've got to work."

"Winter?"

"I…I don't know. Maybe. I don't want to be the oddball on your date."

Kaci chuckled. "Call someone, then. Anyone. We don't care. Maybe Ayden or Davis. Or Peter could call his cousin Graham."

Winter's eyes widened. "You're not setting me up on a double date."

Kaci laughed. "Okay, whatever. Just let me know. I'm going to go shower." She left for her room.

Winter plopped down on the couch and sighed, covering her face with her hands.

"I take it you haven't told him?" asked Claire.

"Told who what?"

"Told Peter you're in love with him."

Winter's chest filled with ice. She sat up to see if Kaci had come out of her room yet. "I'm not in love with him, are you insane?"

"Liar. You've probably been nursing this for a while, haven't you? It's all over your face. And if I can see it, so can they. At least they could, if they weren't making out so much. I bet you loved walking in on that."

Those words punched her in the stomach. Winter groaned and sagged back into the couch. "You think they know?"

Claire shrugged. "Well, you are better than average about hiding things, and I can read you better than most. So probably not. Do you actually love him? Or is it just some empathetic jealousy?"

Winter shrugged. "I don't know. Kaci's happy. And he only has eyes for her. I don't want…"

"…to hurt them. I know," said Claire.

"But it's nothing. I'll get over it."

"How long have you been trying to get over it?"

Winter sighed. "It started last year."

"Listen," said Claire. "You're special and unique, and I've always known you deserve something great in your life. Everything has always sucked for you, and I think you've gotten so used to it you're not willing to fight anymore for something good."

"Kaci's my friend. If I do anything I'll hurt her. I can't do that. She's the best friend I've had since…since you left. And I'd never do anything to hurt you either."

"Well, if I was involved with someone and that person was meant for you, I'd do nothing but hurt my own karma by standing in the way. I might be upset for a little while, but doing the right thing would bring more happiness to everyone in the end."

"I don't know."

"I'm sure Kaci would say the same thing I just did…only, being Christian she'd probably use different words."

"Yeah. Us Christians don't usually use the word karma."

"Destiny…fate…what is it you Christians like to say?"

Winter smirked. "Calling, I think."

"That's it! Maybe it's your calling to be with Peter. Maybe it's his calling to be with you. And Kaci wouldn't stand in the way of that, because she has her own, right? Her relationship with Peter is standing in the way of everyone getting their true *calling*."

"I don't know," said Winter. "I think things may be the way they're supposed to be right now. Maybe this is right."

"You miserable and never getting to love someone properly for the rest of your life? I don't think so."

"Well, what should I do then?"

Claire shrugged. "Just talk to Peter. Tell him how you feel. Then see what happens."

31

Four Years Ago

Christmas break was over. The new semester at Trenton Hills High School had begun. Winter renewed her passion to be rid of school by excelling and doing whatever it took to graduate and find a way out of that town. Claire found her old stoicism again, rarely smiling and rarely volunteering any sort of conversation.

With slightly different class schedules this term, Claire and Winter no longer shared lunch. In fact, Winter didn't share lunch with anyone she really knew. She sat at the end of the table where several other outcasts from her class sat, eating in silence until the end of lunch period. The only time Winter saw Stacy was if they crossed paths before and after school. The only time Winter saw Claire was if they happened to reach their neighboring lockers at the same time or they were required to report to homeroom on that particular day.

Two weeks into the new semester, Winter rushed back to her locker between third and fourth periods to switch out books. Claire was already there, closing her locker door and turning to join the crowd surging to class.

"Hey, Claire," Winter called.

Claire paused and turned to her.

"Are you doing anything this weekend?"

Claire shrugged.

"I thought maybe you'd like to come over. We haven't really done anything since Christmas."

Claire shook her head. "I can't. My dad won't let me."

"What do you mean you can't? You came over during Christmas. That doesn't make sense."

"I lied. I lied to you and I lied to your dad just so I could get away from home. I didn't tell my dad where I was going. I just left."

Winter caught her breath. She could only imagine what Claire's dad would have thought about her running off like that. "So you can't go anywhere?"

Claire's eyes narrowed to slits. "What do you think? I got busted for drugs. I tried to kill myself. I'm lucky he lets me out of his sight at all."

Winter bit her lip. "Do you want to talk about it?"

"No." Claire closed her eyes and took a deep breath. "I'm fine." When she opened her eyes a smile came with it. "As long as I don't think about it, right? Just another year or so until I turn eighteen, then I can drop out of school and leave." She grinned. "Maybe you could come with me."

The crowd in the hall began to thin. Winter cast around. "Um, I think we should probably go to class before we're late."

Pounding feet came around the corner. Winter turned to see Chad running to class. He gazed their way, caught Winter's eye, and smiled. Winter smiled back and wondered if this might be the best chance to stop him and take Claire's advice.

"I guess you're right," said Claire. She turned and stepped into the middle of the hall…right in front of Chad.

The collision sent Claire's face slamming into the floor. She slid a couple of feet and her books slid even further. Chad yelped and crumpled on top of her, twisting so his feet flew into the air.

For a moment, silence filled the hall. Then Claire came off the floor, face crimson and twisted by all the pent-up rage buried within. She filled the hall with deafening swears, sending everyone still in the hall scurrying away.

Chad scrambled to his feet, pale and holding his hands up. "I...I'm s...sorry. I'm s...sorry!"

Claire seemed to grow with fury. A glimmer of fear passed through Winter and she took an involuntary step back to press against the lockers. She had never seen Claire like this. The only other time she had witnessed this much ferocity from one of her friends was last year when Alison showed up at prom.

"You're going to die for that!" Claire yelled.

"No!" Chad shouted. "I'm s...sorry! I di...didn't mean to!"

Claire shoved her hand into her backpack, which somehow she still held. When she pulled her hand back out, she held a black-handled pair of scissors. She dropped the backpack and shifted the scissors to hold them like a knife.

"No! I'm sorry!"

"Claire, stop it!" Winter shouted.

Claire took a step toward Chad and raised the scissors. Winter did the only thing she knew to do. She dropped her books and stepped between Claire and Chad.

"No, Claire!"

Claire was already swinging. The scissors came down, aimed for Chad, but now descending on Winter. At the last moment, Claire's face changed. The twisting dissolved and recognition flashed behind her eyes. She loudly sucked in air and tried to stop the descent of her arm, but she had too much momentum.

Winter flung up her arms to deflect the blow. The scissors struck against Winter's long sleeve, the tip barely pricking through and jabbing her arm.

Claire ripped them away as quickly as she could. "Winter…I…"

"You're crazy!" screamed Chad, looking from Claire to Winter with the same frightened look for them both. Then he ran the other way yelling. "Help!"

Winter clenched her arm. "What's wrong with you? Are you insane? Do you realize what you just did?"

"I don't know what happened. It all just…"

"You've ruined everything! I hate you!"

Winter slid her sleeve up. A small trickle of blood oozed out from the wound. Nothing a band-aid couldn't cover. She ground her teeth and let all of her own anger and pain swell to the surface, unleashing it upon Claire with everything she could project onto her face. Before she could unleash any of it from her mouth, Chad returned.

"There," he said from behind Winter.

"What's going on here?" a deep voice asked.

Claire's eyes flicked over Winter's shoulder. "Nothing, Principal Montgomery."

"That's not what I've been told."

"She tried to stab me with those scissors," said Chad.

Winter glared deep into Claire's eyes, knowing her face was more red than the blood dripping from her arm.

"Ask the other girl, she saw," said Chad.

"Is this what happened?" asked Principal Montgomery, stepping to Winter's side and eying her and the scissors on the floor.

Winter tightened her eyes further at Claire, letting her jaw jut out just a little more. Then she shoved her sleeve back over the cut and turned. "It was an accident. He ran into Claire and everything scattered. When she picked up the scissors he got the wrong idea."

"That's a lie!"

Winter shrugged and plastered a smirk on her face. "Like you said, I saw the whole thing."

The principal studied her, unblinking for a moment. "Very well." He looked at Claire. "Miss Parker, you know you're not supposed to even have scissors like that on campus. Please collect your things and come with me so we can talk." He pulled a small notepad from his pocket and scribbled, handing a note each to Winter and Chad as Claire shoved her things back into her backpack. "Miss Maessen, Mr. Camp…report to class."

As Claire followed the principal, she glanced over her shoulder at Winter, big-eyed and apologetic. Winter threw the last of the hate she had stored up into glaring back.

After they turned the corner, Winter slid the sleeve up again. She fished in her purse for a band-aid and gently laid it over the cut. Chad watched her, as if he wanted to argue. Winter opened her mouth, hoping to smooth things over, but his face paled and he fled to his own class. Alone now in the hall, Winter sighed, grabbed her things, and went to class too.

The other girl. He didn't even know her name.

32

Present Day

Over the next couple of months, Winter took great care to behave exactly as Erickson had instructed. Each morning Winter and Kaci rendezvoused with Nadeen and Ayden, clandestinely swapping handlers for the duration of the school day. As the claws of winter began to scrape away under the persistent pressure of spring, there had still been no changes of instruction from Erickson. The only evidence Winter had that the investigation still progressed was Erickson's occasional call for a report. No more murders had happened since Madam Morial. All was quiet, and Alison seemed to have disappeared just as quickly as she had appeared.

In mid-March, as Winter walked with Ayden between classes—Ayden once again interrogating Winter about the gift of prophecy—Davis spotted them from across the Meadow and ran up to walk beside Winter.

"Can I help you?" Winter asked.

He shook his head. "I just wanted to see if you've talked with Summer again."

"Not since last week. And nothing's changed since the last time you asked me two days ago. Why don't you try to talk to her yourself? Maybe persistence will pay off."

He shook his head again. "I've been trying, but she still won't talk. She won't even answer my calls anymore. Maybe you could at least get her to talk with me?"

"I'll try."

Davis eyed her. "You don't think her issue is important, do you?"

"Everyone's issues are important. Some are just more dramatic than others, but that doesn't make them less important, especially to them."

"You know what I mean," said Davis. "Do you think maybe she's…"

"No. I don't think Summer has anything to do with Xaphan."

He nodded and his shoulders relaxed. "That's good, I guess. I thought maybe…you know…maybe it was something else. Not me."

"It's not you." Winter smiled at him. "Look, do you remember how long it took Kaci to get even a little bit back to normal? Summer's always been more fragile than Kaci, and last year messed her up pretty bad. Just give her some more time."

"I guess you're right. But…are you sure?"

Ayden grunted. "My God, shut up! When did you become such a crybaby?"

Davis stared at her, shocked.

"If you love Summer, quit making excuses and go get her. She's hurting, you idiot. Stop feeling sorry for yourself, man up, and go save your princess."

Davis looked away, staring into the distance. "Yeah. Okay." Suddenly his eyes grew bright. "Right. Do you think she'll come to Peter's big cookout this weekend?"

"I know he's tried to invite her," said Winter. "But maybe if you don't give her a choice…"

He grinned. "I've got some ideas."

"About time," said Ayden.

"One more thing," said Davis. "I know I've been out of it and I let last spring get to me. But I think I'm ready to help. I know you and Ayden are still trying to stop Xaphan, so what can I do?"

Winter exchanged a look with Ayden. "I'm sorry," Winter said. "This time you really can't."

"Why?"

"Because the FBI are calling the shots," said Ayden. "And that's all we can tell you."

Winter nodded. "But just because you can't be involved officially in what's going on behind the scenes this year, doesn't mean you have to stay away from us. Mostly, we just hang out anyway. The FBI are doing all the work. So you're welcome to come over anytime you want…really."

Davis smiled again. "Thanks."

Peter's much anticipated weekend cookout had been planned for weeks, Peter doing an inordinate amount of work to make sure everyone was free to be there. All Winter and Kaci had to do was agree to host it and he promised to take care of the rest.

Saturday morning, Peter and his cousin Graham arrived just after nine o'clock. Winter eyed Graham closely, wondering why all of a sudden Peter was bringing someone new to the group. She made a mental note to corner Kaci about this, since Kaci didn't seem at all surprised by Graham's presence. Did Graham have something to do with Peter's secret? Was he dangerous?

Davis showed up not long after, without Summer.

"I thought you weren't going to take no for an answer?" Winter asked.

Davis shrugged, but he wore a timid smile. "I tried. She wouldn't talk long with me."

"Well, I called her a couple of days ago," said Kaci, tugging at the scarf around her neck. "I think maybe she's starting to come around. She almost seemed like her old self again. She promised to come, so here's hoping." Kaci gave Davis a warm smile.

Winter smiled at him too. "I'm sure she'll be here then. Good luck."

Near eleven, Peter, Graham, and Davis relocated to the pavilion in a courtyard behind their apartment building, where the backs of four buildings connected to make a small grassy square. Peter had already brought a grill, a cooler, and several bags of groceries out there, and wouldn't let the girls know what he intended on cooking.

Winter and Kaci watched them through the window from the kitchen table as they had a snack.

"He's up to something," said Kaci. "Are those steaks?"

Winter squinted. "Maybe."

Someone knocked on the door, and Kaci went to answer.

"Summer!" Kaci announced.

"Hey," said Summer, smiling and face to the floor as she stepped inside.

Winter jumped up and wrapped her arms around her. "I'm glad you came." Then she shoved Summer in the shoulder, almost knocking her back onto the couch. "Stop avoiding me."

Summer blushed. "Sorry. I'll try to do better. It's just…"

"You don't have to explain," said Kaci, scowling at Winter and pulling Summer toward the table. "We understand. But you really need to talk to Davis."

Summer nodded and sat, glancing out of the window at Davis and tucking a strand of hair behind her ear. "I will. I promise. I really miss him, actually. Do you think he's seeing anyone else?"

Winter laughed and took her seat again. "Are you kidding? The boy mopes around like a kid who lost his favorite dog. Not that I'm calling you a dog. But you're way out of Davis's league and he knows it. He's an idiot over you, and that's not changing anytime soon."

Summer bit her lip and her ears turned pink. "I'm not out of his league. And I'm the one that's been an idiot."

"Go talk to him then," said Kaci with a grin. "I'm sure everything will be just fine."

Another knock on the door and Winter wrinkled her eyebrows at Kaci.

Kaci shrugged. "I don't know."

Winter went to open the door this time and found Claire waiting outside.

"Hi," said Claire.

"Hey."

"Your friend Peter called. I hope that's okay."

"Yeah, it's fine. Come in." Winter stood out of the way to let Claire through. "Summer, this is Claire, a friend of mine from high school."

"Hi," said Summer with a smile.

Claire returned the smile. "Hey."

"Sit down," said Kaci. "We were just chatting while the boys are down cooking the food."

"You don't think we should join them, do you?" asked Summer.

"Nah," said Winter. "Let them beat their chests and do manly things. We'll go down when it's time to eat."

"I don't know," said Summer. "Peter sounded like he had some plans."

"Like what?" asked Kaci with an uplifted eyebrow.

Summer shrugged.

At that moment, Kaci's phone rang. "Speaking of…" She lifted it to her ear. "Hey…yeah sure…okay…we're coming." She hung up. "Peter says we need to come down. Looks like we won't have to wait much longer to find out what he's up to."

As they went out the front door, down the steps, and made the turn toward the back of the building, the wind shifted and wafted the smell of the grill over them.

"Something smells good," said Claire. "What are they cooking?"

Kaci shrugged. "He wouldn't tell me. I just assumed hamburgers or something, but it kinda looked like steaks from the windows."

"That certainly smells too good to be hamburgers," said Claire.

"Ladies!" said Peter, lifting his arms out, a set of grilling tongs in one hand. "About time. The steaks are almost ready and the last of our guests will be here shortly."

"Steaks?" asked Kaci.

"More guests?" asked Winter. "Who else is coming?"

Peter grinned and turned back to the grill.

Kaci walked over to him. "What's going on? Tell me." She jabbed him in the ribs, but he just laughed.

Two folding tables had been shoved together and Davis was covering them with red fabric tablecloths. Without saying anything to him, Summer went over and started helping. After covering the tables, they set out folding chairs. Everyone but Peter began to take seats, Summer sitting next to Davis and grabbing his hand. She smiled at him and his face turned crimson.

"Can we talk later?" she asked.

Davis nodded and Summer laid her head on his shoulder. Winter caught his eyes and he grinned.

Kaci took a seat next to Graham and probed him about the mystery guests. Claire sat down next to Winter.

"Your friends are really nice," Claire said.

"I know."

"You must be happy."

Winter nodded. "Look, you can hang out with us anytime. I know they may not be your type of people, but they really are great to be around."

"I believe you. It's been a long time since I've had friends I could be myself with."

"You can be yourself here."

Claire looked away. "I don't know. I mean…these are your friends, not mine. And I assume they're Christian just like you?"

Winter smiled. "Just relax."

"Hey!" called Peter. "Looks like our last guests are here! Just in time for the food. Figures."

"Mom? Dad?" yelled Kaci.

Winter turned to see Chris and Beverly strolling hand in hand toward the pavilion. Kaci ran to them and embraced them both at the same time.

"Peter," said Winter glancing over her shoulder to him still standing over the grill. Peter grinned at her. "You know I don't like secrets." He winked and went back to work.

Beverly came to Winter first, hugging her tight, and Chris did the same a moment after. They both found seats at the table next to Kaci.

Winter turned back to watch Peter, who was now placing steaks, grilled ears of corn, and large chunks of potato onto a platter. Graham must have had an unspoken cue because he immediately began filling glasses with ice and placing them around the table…real glass tumblers, not plastic. Pitchers of water and lemonade were set out. Davis, seemingly in on the secret now, set several candles on the table and lit them. Then Davis and Graham put out glass plates and real silverware in front of each person. Peter divided the food between two platters and placed one in the center of each of the two tables.

"Peter, this is really nice. What's going on? Is everything okay?" asked Kaci.

"This is all wrong," Peter said. "Everyone stand up."

Everyone did as instructed and watched Peter.

"Now, Kaci, you sit here." He tapped the chair at the head of the table. "Mr. and Mrs. Williams next to her on this side and I'll sit on the other. Graham next to me. Winter, why don't you sit next to Kaci's parents. Claire join her. And Davis and Summer over here by Graham."

Everyone rearranged according to his instructions, with a lot of bemused chuckles. When they had settled, Peter stood behind his chair and looked over everyone as they gazed back at him.

"Now," he said. "Before we give thanks, there's something I want to say."

Kaci's face paled. "Are you okay?"

He smiled at her. "I'm fine, Kaci. In fact I'm more than fine. I know this isn't exactly a fancy dinner or anything terribly romantic, but these are the people who love you…your friends and family. And I know the people here are more important to you than anything superficial or anything temporary."

"What's going on?"

Peter's chin quivered. "I love you. I've loved you for a long time, longer than you know, from the first time you sat down in my CLC small group as a freshman. I've watched you, wishing after you, too afraid to speak about how I really feel. And I drove Winter crazy last year with it." He grabbed Kaci's hand, a tear dropping down his cheek. "I love you, and I don't intend to let you go now I have you. In fact, if you let me I will spend the rest of my life proving to you just how much I love you."

In one fluid motion, Peter knelt on one knee and drew his hand out of his pocket, to present an open ring box. Kaci's mouth fell open and her eyes began to scrunch.

Winter chanced a look around the table. Summer had her entire face covered with both hands, except for her eyes which were red and glistening. Davis and Graham both grinned like idiots. Beside her, Beverly was already sobbing. She couldn't see Chris well, but his arm squeezed Beverly tight against him. When she looked back to Kaci, tears covered her red face and she was already nodding.

"Kaci," Peter said. "Will you marry me?"

Kaci's nodding became more pronounced and enthusiastic. "Yes," she croaked and flung herself around him.

Winter chanced a look at Claire sitting next to her.

Claire just stared with narrow eyes. "You never told him," she said softly.

Guilt and hopelessness washed through Winter when she knew she should be rejoicing for her best friend. As a tear rolled down her cheek, she hoped everyone else at the table would take it for joy, but one more look at Claire told Winter at least one person knew the truth.

33

"Can you believe it?" Kaci asked that night after everyone had left. She held her hand out to look at the ring. "A year ago I would never have thought this possible. But he actually loves me."

Winter faked a smile. "I'm really happy for you." She turned back to the TV, trying to act normal.

Why did she care so much? Why did this one thing gouge her inside? Peter and Kaci. Davis and Summer. Memories of dancing with Ryan, kissing him beneath the colored lights, holding his hand. Everything ended well for everyone but her. Why couldn't she be happy for once?

Winter crossed her arms and legs, struggling to keep her face composed.

"Are you okay?" Kaci asked. "Is something wrong?"

"I'm fine. It's just been a long day."

"You're not jealous, are you?"

Winter shook her head, probably too fast to be believable. "No. Why would I be jealous?"

"Because everyone's dating but you."

"Not everyone. Claire and Ayden aren't. I don't think. Guess I'm not sure. Never asked them."

Kaci grinned. "You know, when you get something stuck in your head you really are a blind stubborn idiot."

Winter scrunched her eyes at Kaci. "Excuse me?"

Kaci laughed. "You're so wrapped up in what other people are doing and sulking that you don't have the same thing, to notice what's right in front of you."

"What do you mean?"

"Graham. You haven't wondered why he's been coming over with Peter? He wants to ask you out, he's just too frightened of you."

"What? Really? No."

"Why? Isn't that what you want?"

"No…it's…" Winter grunted. "I don't know. Wait, why is he frightened of me?"

"Are you kidding? Everyone's frightened of you when they first meet you. Do you realize you haven't even talked to him? You just pass over him and move on, like he's not even there. He's actually sweet, you know. Even though they're cousins, he's still one of Peter's best friends."

"I've talked to him. I mean, I asked him his name the first time I saw him."

"No, you didn't. You demanded his name. Poor guy."

Winter allowed herself a smile. "I suppose I could do better."

"Yes, you could. Next time he comes over you should talk to him."

Winter shook her head. "I'm not sure I want a relationship. Well, I do…but I don't. I don't know. I'm really confused about it. Yes…I am jealous. I want what you have. But there's only one person I want it with and he's…"

Kaci's face softened. "I know. And I think Peter told Graham about it. Just talk to him a little. No one's forcing you to do anything you don't want."

Taken, Winter finished the thought her head, took a deep breath and smiled at Kaci, glad at the interruption and Kaci assuming she meant Ryan. "I really am happy for you. Have you talked about when the wedding will be?"

Kaci shrugged. "We talked about late in the summer, maybe August."

"Wow, that's quick."

"I know. I just don't want to wait very long, you know? With things being the way they are…"

"Have you told him everything yet?" Winter asked.

"No." Kaci shook her head. "Not everything. I want to talk with Agent Erickson first. But I'm sure things will be fine."

Winter pursed her lips, not sure they would be. She didn't want to say anything to Kaci, but Peter was still hiding something. And it wasn't proposing to Kaci or setting up Winter with Graham. She needed to get the truth out of him soon, before things went horribly wrong.

The next evening, Winter and the others sat in the Union, studying for the final mid-terms. Ayden sat next to her, with her feet propped up on the square coffee table in the middle. Peter and Kaci nestled closely together across from them, and Summer and Davis sat together on a couch to the right, both with their noses in books.

All around the Union, students filled available seats or sat along the walls in groups, all doing the same thing. A lull of voices filled the room, with the backdrop of more jovial and louder conversations oozing in from the dining area.

"How's your roommate?" Winter asked Ayden after wrestling with a particularly difficult vocab word.

Ayden snorted and looked up from her tablet. "Not a roommate.

She barely stays in the room, but she's always within fifty feet of me when you're not around. Who knows where she is now…probably out sharpening her knives."

Winter laughed and looked over at Kaci and Peter calling out questions to each other. She watched them for a moment, fidgeting with her locket. Had Kaci told him who she really was yet? It was only a matter of time. Winter knew she might not get a better chance to corner Peter than now.

"Peter," Winter said. "Can I talk to you?"

He glanced to her, a glimmer flashing through his eyes that Winter thought was suspicion. "Sure. What do you need?"

Winter cast around at everybody, all eyes watching her. Maybe it was just her own paranoia, but she had to be sure. "Um…Sorry, but can we talk in private?"

Peter hesitated and looked at Kaci. Kaci shrugged. "Yeah. Okay," he said as he stood, suspicion flashing through his eyes again.

Winter led him through the exit and into the chilly darkness. She sat on the wing wall of the steps, beneath the white light illuminating the entrance into the union, and motioned with her eyes for him to sit beside her.

"What's going on?" he asked as he eased down.

"That's what I wanted to ask you. What's going on?" Winter looked around to make sure no one else was within hearing distance.

He smiled. "Just studying…"

"No." Winter narrowed her eyes. "What's really going on? What aren't you telling me?"

"Nothing. You know everything."

"That's a lie. You're hiding something, I know it."

Peter frowned at her. "Whatever it is you think you know is wrong."

"How can I trust you when I know you're hiding something? You're going to marry Kaci…but do you remember what I told you last year? If you hurt her, you'll have me to deal with."

Peter shook his head. "The last thing I want is to see her hurt. You can trust me, really."

"Then what are you keeping from me?"

Peter leaned closer to her, eyes wide with sincerity. "Trust me."

"I can't!" she shouted, and then looked around again. A couple of students walking by stopped to stare at her. "Take a picture!" she yelled at them, and then turned back to Peter as the students ran off. "I can't just let you put her in danger, do you understand? She's my responsibility…"

"Not anymore," he interrupted. "Her safety is now mine to deal with, whether you like it or not. What you think I'm hiding from you is merely my efforts to keep her safe, understand?"

"I can't just assume she's safe. And I can't just assume I can trust you. I need to know and the fact you won't tell me what's going on makes me doubt you even more."

Peter tilted his head. "Why so paranoid? Maybe there's more going on with you than you've told me." He watched her, silent accusations leaping from his eyes.

How much did he know about the truth of her waning abilities? Of her jealousy? How much did he guess? Winter pursed her lips.

"So you're keeping things from me, too," he said with a smile. "Then that makes us even. Look, you can believe me when I say we both have Kaci's best interest at heart. I'll agree to trust you if you'll agree to trust me."

Winter bit her lip, her heart suddenly fluttering and distracting her from what she needed to say. His smile melted her on the inside like lava pouring down her throat. The torture of it was almost unbearable and she had the impulse to do exactly what Claire told her to do. She wanted to admit her feelings, to tell him she loved him. More than that, she wanted to grab his face and kiss him.

Winter looked away and squeezed her eyes shut. "Fine."

Peter patted her arm. "Thank you."

She nodded without looking back up, waiting several minutes

after he had left to take control of herself again.

Finally, she went back inside and resumed her place beside Ayden. Peter smiled up at her as she sat.

"Is everything okay, Winter?" Kaci asked.

"Everything's fine," she said. "I just needed to ask Peter something…"

Peter's eyes suddenly flicked over to Summer and Davis.

Winter followed his eyes. Summer stared at the ground, face pale white, as if she had been caught doing something or at least suspected she had been caught. Winter clenched her jaw and looked back to Peter.

Peter watched Winter now with the same firm sincerity in his eyes. Winter glared back at the pale-faced Summer.

He knew. He knew what was wrong with Summer. That's what he was hiding. It was more than Summer merely freaking out about being kidnapped last year. Summer was in trouble. That's why she had been avoiding Winter all year. That's why she broke ties with all of her friends. Now she feared Winter had finally discovered the truth…she thought that's what Winter and Peter were talking about. It all made sense now. But what did it have to do with Kaci? Winter looked back at Peter.

Trust me, he said with his eyes, firming them around the corners now he realized Winter was putting things together.

"Stop being dramatic and help me study," said Ayden. "If you three don't stop shouting at each other, you're going to give me a headache."

Everyone turned to look at Ayden, even Summer.

Ayden just shrugged. "If everyone would just talk to each other…" she mumbled without looking up from her tablet. "I'm just saying…"

"What are you talking about? Who's shouting?" Kaci asked.

Ayden huffed and looked up. "Like in the movies? Everything goes wrong because stupid people won't get over themselves and tell one another the truth?"

Winter's mouth fell open.

"I don't understand," said Kaci.

Winter's phone rang. She rushed to answer, almost dropping the phone in the process, hoping the moment would pass before the phone call was over. "Hello?"

"Winter, help me!" Claire shouted into Winter's ear. Winter jumped out of her seat, notebook tumbling to the floor, all eyes on her now instead of Ayden.

"What's going on?"

Screams in the background. Claire whimpered. *"She's here. Alison. She's at the diner."* A pause and Claire's voice came further away from the phone. *"Oh god!"*

"Claire!"

Explosions. More screaming. Claire sobbing and breathing heavy as if she were running.

"Claire!"

The phone went dead.

34

Four Years Ago

The phone rang again.

"Dad!" Winter called from the couch, and immediately remembered he was working late. She grunted with resentment at having to get up and miss the next segment of the show she watched. But it might be her dad calling and heaven forbid she not answer.

She snatched the cordless from the wall in the kitchen and stepped back into the living room where she could still see the TV.

"Hello?"

"Winter…" It was Claire, a shaking in her voice.

"Claire? What's wrong?" asked Winter, the TV show now forgotten.

Claire whimpered. *"I'm scared."*

"Why? What's happening."

"He's drunk again." Screams in the background. A man yelling and a woman howling out in pain. *"Mom! Leave her alone!"* More yelling. Winter heard a string of vulgarity through the phone…things a father should never say to his daughter.

"Claire…what do you want me to do? Do you want me to call someone?"

"No," she said. Scuffling. Panting. A door slammed. *"I locked myself in my room. Can I come over for the night?"*

"Yeah, sure, whatever. Just get out of there."

"Thank you."

Winter heard pounding through the phone. Claire whimpered again. A muffled voice shouting, *"Open this door and give me that phone!"*

All Winter could do was hold her breath. Was this actually happening?

The pounding grew heavier. The loud boom of splintering wood, followed by a scream from Claire. Bumping that might have been the phone dropping. Sharp claps that might have been Claire being hit.

"Claire!" Winter shouted into the phone.

More cursing. More vulgarity. More flesh striking flesh. Claire's screams slowed into moans and sobs. Her dad's voice softened into a sick, seductive croon. Claire's sobbing became a defeated whimper…

Winter hung up the phone, shaking all over, staring at the innocent handset, like she had just severed a connection to hell.

Winter paced the room for the next hour, holding the phone and begging it to ring again. She wanted to call the police, or her dad, or somebody…but Claire had always been so insistent no one be called. Winter couldn't understand why. She couldn't understand how Claire's dad could do those…things…to his own daughter. She didn't dare try to call Claire because she didn't want to be the reason it started up again. So she waited and paced, wondering if Claire was all right. Wondering if she were even alive.

After another ten minutes, Winter had just about made up her mind to call the police and then the doorbell rang. Without hesitating Winter ran to it and flung it open. Claire shuffled in, eyes on the ground, dried crusty blood at the corners of her mouth, left eye swollen almost shut.

"Are you okay? I've been worried to death."

"I'm fine." Claire headed for the stairs. "I ran out as soon as I could. He doesn't know where I am, so don't tell your dad I'm here, okay?"

"Yeah, sure," said Winter. "He's still at work. He'll be back soon, but he doesn't come to my room much. It'll be fine."

Claire began to climb the stairs. Slowly.

"Are you sure you're okay? Should I call someone?" Winter bit her lip, hoping she hadn't gone too far.

Claire paused and glanced over her shoulder, chin quivering. "If you call, he will kill me. Don't you understand? He'll kill me and my mom. And he might even kill you, too."

Winter nodded quickly. "Okay. I understand."

Claire turned back away and started ascending again. "Do you mind if I take a shower in your bathroom?"

"Of course not."

"Thank you."

Winter followed Claire upstairs and Claire went straight to the shower with her duffel bag and locked the door. Winter sat on her bed and waited, staring at the bathroom door and listening to Claire softly cry the entire time the shower was running. Thirty minutes into the shower, Winter heard her dad come home. He came up the stairs and Winter held her breath, not wanting to get up and betray someone else running the shower. He paused at her door and then went back downstairs.

After forty-five minutes, Claire finally turned off the water. Moments later she came out, hair hanging wet and wearing long-sleeve pajamas.

"My dad's here," Winter whispered. She rushed into the

bathroom and rubbed the fog from the mirror to look at herself. She ran back into her room, ripped off her clothes and threw on her pajamas. Then she went back to the bathroom, splashed some water on her face, and slapped her cheeks a few times.

"What are you doing?" Claire asked.

"I have to go talk to him," Winter said, tossing her hair forward and wrapping it in a towel. "He thinks it was me in the shower." She rushed to her bedroom door. "I'll be right back. Do you need anything?"

"Maybe something to eat."

Winter nodded and left. She could hear her dad messing around in the kitchen.

"Hey dad," she said rounding the corner.

"Hey."

"Long day at work?"

He watched her for a moment. "Yeah."

Winter opened the pantry. "Mind if I take a snack to my room?"

"Since when do you ask permission to do that?"

Winter bit her lip and shrugged.

"Yeah, sure. Knock yourself out."

She grabbed a box of crackers and the jar of peanut butter, pulled a butter knife from the drawer, and then went to the fridge. She reached for a soda, then checked to see if he was watching, and grabbed two.

Turning her back to him, she said, "Good night."

"Night," he said.

Back upstairs, Winter locked the door and brought the snacks to her bed where Claire waited. Winter jumped up on the bed, cross-legged, and turned on the TV on her dresser. She raised the volume until it was loud enough to cover them talking.

"Eat," Winter said.

Claire sighed. "Now that I see it, I'm not sure I want it just yet."

"That's okay. When you're hungry it's here." Winter watched her, trying to think of some way she could help.

Claire just stared at the floor.

"Do you want to talk?" asked Winter.

Claire shrugged. "There's not much to talk about."

"Sometimes it helps. At least that's what all of you have been telling me, remember?" Winter tried to smile.

"I just wish…" Claire pursed her lips and sighed.

"Wish what?"

"I just wish things were different. I wish…that I had a different life. Either that or no life at all."

"Don't say that," said Winter. "You only have a little bit longer, and then you could probably drop out of school and leave."

"I'm not sure my life would be any better. You just don't understand…"

"I'm trying. And I probably understand more than anyone else. My dad doesn't…you know…but at least everyone you love is still alive."

Claire looked at her and nodded. "Sorry. I must look like a mess."

"No. You look like you need a friend. You've been there for me plenty of times. I might suck at this, but I'm trying here."

Claire smiled. "I know." She sighed and turned back to the floor. "Have you ever wondered what's the point?"

"The point of what?"

"Everything. The point of life. Why do we have to go through so much when it would just be better to kill ourselves? Don't we eventually end up dead anyway? Why not just get it over with…"

Winter shook her head. "Don't go there. Do you dare go there again. You don't really want to kill yourself."

"No. But I don't want to live the life I have anymore."

"What about your coven? What about your friendly spirits? Don't they help? You keep trying to convince me you've found the right answers."

Claire laughed. "I don't have any of the answers. Nothing I've tried helps. It all just happens again and I end up in the same place. How am I supposed to do this? What's the point? Why can't I just give up and be done with it?"

"But your life doesn't have to stay this way. You still have a choice," said Winter. "You can be whatever you want to be. Don't let your dad control you any longer. Stand up to him. Report him. He either kills you and you're right where you're talking about going anyway, or he doesn't and you're free."

"No."

"Then do something. Take your life back and make something out of it that you like."

"What are you suggesting?"

Winter shrugged. "I don't know. Run away. Fake your death. Anything. Get a new name and start over."

Claire studied her, eyes flicking over Winter's face with renewed energy. "Do you really think I could?"

"You'll be seventeen in a month. Of course you can."

"But where would I go? What would I do? Where would I live?"

Winter shook her head. "I don't know. But we can figure it out. Together. Let's make a plan. Tonight."

Claire smiled and nodded.

35

Present Day

Winter lowered the phone and gaped at it, mind reeling. Should she call Erickson? Should she go herself? She looked up at the others, everyone on their feet and watching her.

"What's happening?" asked Ayden.

Winter pivoted toward her and then turned her head to look back at Peter. His arm held Kaci close to him, protecting her just by sheer instinct. She looked back at Ayden. "It's Claire. Um...I've got to go help her." Panic surged at the thought of what might be happening that very moment. "I've got to go now." She looked back at Peter.

"Don't worry," he said pulling Kaci a little tighter. "I've got this."

Winter nodded and then she turned to run. She didn't think about anything else other than getting to her car and getting to Claire. She yanked her keys out and unlocked the car just before she reached the door. Only when she saw the spiky red hair pass her by and rush to the passenger side did Winter realize Ayden had followed.

"What are you doing?" Winter yelled over the top of the car.

Ayden already had the door open and was climbing in. "You

don't have time to argue, so just go."

Winter grunted and sat behind the wheel. She shoved the car into gear and floored the accelerator. As the tires chirped on the pavement, Winter stole a glance at Ayden. "You know we're both going to get it for this."

"I don't care. Got your gun?"

"Of course."

"Good. Me too. Faster."

"You have a gun?"

"Do you really want to do that now?"

Winter huffed and concentrated on the road.

The diner Claire worked at was on the opposite side of Cherithville. Winter silently prayed for some kind of supernatural guidance this time, but once again nothing came. At least they never met any patrol cars in their mad race through town, and if they did she could always flash her badge. But if Winter hadn't already known where to go there wouldn't have been any chance of getting to Claire on time.

In ten minutes they arrived. Winter wasn't sure what she had expected, but what was waiting for them was nothing short of a bomb explosion. The entire diner was a collapsed inferno. All the cars in the parking lot were smaller bonfires around the larger mother-blaze, all freshly lit.

Winter and Ayden eased out, guns over the doors. Winter scanned the angry shadows for any sign of movement. Small shadows between them and the building were the perfect size and shape for bodies.

"We need to find Claire," said Winter.

"We need to look for survivors," said Ayden.

Winter clenched her teeth. "We do both. Come on."

Winter ran around the door and rushed to the first shadow on the ground, a young lady wearing a diner uniform. Dead. Blood saturated the ground beneath her. Culsu carved into her forehead.

She went to the next body. Same thing. But not Claire. Winter looked for Ayden and saw her moving from one body to another.

"Anything?" Winter asked.

"No," said Ayden.

Winter gazed around the parking lot and back to the blazing diner. "Claire!" she yelled.

Something knocked nearby, followed quickly by panicked banging and muffled screams.

"Over here!" yelled Ayden as she ran toward a car.

"Claire's car," said Winter. The interior burned bright, but the fire had not yet spread to the exterior parts of the car.

"The trunk," said Ayden.

They both ran to the back of the car where someone kicked and screamed from within.

Winter reached for the lip of the trunk and tugged. "How do we get in?"

"We need something, what do you have in your car?"

Winter ran back for the tire iron and, upon returning, shoved it under the lip of Claire's trunk.

The fire blazed, the sound like a flapping parachute. Winter held her breath as the memories crashed down. The screams from within grew…a tire exploded.

Winter fell back. Alison screaming in the night. Ryan lying dead in the backseat. "I…" Winter covered her face.

Ayden grunted and grabbed the tire iron, leaning into it to bend the fiberglass. She repositioned it against the locking mechanism and banged the curved end with her hand. Ayden cursed and shook her hand, then banged it again.

"Help me!" Ayden yelled at Winter.

Winter shook herself back to reality and reached for the iron, pressing her weight in with Ayden's.

The trunk popped open.

Claire tried to roll out immediately, hands bound and mouth

covered with duct tape. The back of the seat smoldered and rolled black smoke into the trunk. Claire hit the ground and Winter and Ayden heaved her away from the car. As they rounded the back of Winter's car, Claire's car blew up.

Sirens wailed in the distance.

"Winter, we're not supposed to be here," said Ayden. "We have to go."

"Okay." Winter hoisted the nearly unconscious Claire to her feet. "Sit in the back with Claire and get the tape off."

Winter and Ayden helped Claire into the back seat. Ayden climbed in with her as Winter ran back around to the wheel. Winter put the car into gear and floored it. They pulled onto the main highway, just in time to see a fleet of emergency vehicles round the bend and turn toward the diner. Ayden finally pulled the tape from Claire's wrists and Claire handled the tape over her mouth herself, gasping and coughing, becoming more lucid with each deep breath.

"How?" is all Claire could say, voice trembling.

"Are you okay?" asked Winter.

"Oh my god...everyone at the diner..." Claire covered her face with her hands and whimpered. "They're dead, aren't they?"

"Yes," said Winter.

After moments of silent crying, Claire looked up and rubbed her eyes. "I can't believe it...Alison's really alive. And my friends..."

"There's nothing we can do," said Ayden. "At least you're safe. Did you see what happened?"

"No. We had just closed up. I was sweeping when everything went dark. But it wasn't just light...I don't know, it's hard to describe. It was more like a fog. A pitch black fog. And I swear the fog was alive. It was choking me."

Winter nodded. "I know what you're talking about. I've seen it."

"You've seen it?"

"Once. The night Shannon died. Then what happened?"

"Screams. That's all I remember. I crawled on the floor until I reached the door. Then I called you and ran as fast as I could. When I looked behind me, Alison was there. Winter…she wasn't even walking. She was just floating toward me, her eyes red. I've never seen anything like it, not even with the coven."

"It's an imposter, Claire. It's not really Alison. Alison is dead."

"I don't know," said Claire. "Now that I've seen her…the way she looked at me…the hate. It was just like prom night. Maybe you were right to begin with. Maybe it's her spirit, or even her whole body, fused with Culsu. Maybe they are one now."

"How?" asked Winter.

"I'm not sure. I'd have to ask Madam Morial. But, that *was* Alison. I'm sure of it."

"Madam Morial is dead too."

"Oh god," said Claire. "She's killing everyone, isn't she? She's erasing everyone I know, and she's not going to stop until she gets me too, is she?"

Winter let the question hang in the air, knowing the truth wouldn't help and that a lie would be obvious. Everyone in the car already knew the answer anyway. "What happened after you called?" Winter asked.

"I was on the phone with you when Alison grabbed me. She taped me up, shoved me in the trunk, and almost immediately you opened it again. How did you get here so fast?"

"What do you mean?" Winter asked. "It took us a good ten minutes or more driving as fast as I could."

"No, it couldn't have been more than a couple of minutes," said Claire. "I'm sure of it. Otherwise I'd be dead. She set the car on fire. If it had taken you as long as you said, I would have suffocated."

"That's impossible," said Winter, glancing into the rear-view mirror at Ayden.

"What time did you leave?" asked Claire.

Winter shrugged. "I don't know."

"Eleven fourteen," said Ayden. "I checked." Her voice trailed off. "Look at the clock, Winter."

Winter checked the dash clock. 11:18. "No. That's impossible."

"Were you at the school? How did you do that?" asked Claire.

"I...I don't know."

"Must be another super power," said Ayden.

"Super power?" asked Claire.

"It's not super powers," said Winter.

Ayden snickered. "No wonder we didn't see any cops and we didn't have any trouble with traffic. Have you done that before?"

"Maybe. I don't know. I was the first one to Shannon too."

"What's going on?" asked Claire.

"She's a prophetess," said Ayden.

Claire sat silent for a moment. "You mean, you can see the future?"

"Sometimes," said Winter.

"Usually she just does these weird random things," said Ayden. "Like apparently she can make time stand still if she wants."

"I can't make time stand still!" Winter bit her lip, more confused than she'd been all year. With all the silence and lack of premonition, how could she be stopping time and not knowing it? How could any of this make sense? As far as she was concerned, she hadn't done anything at all. Had she?

"Well, this is great! You can help me," said Claire. "You can protect me, right? Alison was always scared of you. She didn't understand what the bubble was around you, but now I know...it's a gift. And it can save us from her."

Winter frowned. What would Erickson say if he found out she'd taken on another ward? "I'm not sure I can...I mean, I can but...Listen, it doesn't work like that, okay?"

"You don't have to do anything. Just let me stay with you...you said I could if I thought I wasn't safe. Well, I'm not safe. And if Alison comes looking for both of us...which I'm sure she will...then you can stop her."

"She's right," said Ayden. "You're probably the only person who can."

"I don't know…"

"Well, what am I supposed to do?" asked Claire. "I can't go back to work. I can't go back to my apartment. And my car just blew up."

"I didn't say you couldn't stay with me. You can. Stay as long as you want."

"And if Alison comes looking for me?

Winter sighed. "I'll deal with her. I promise."

Winter dropped off Ayden at the dorms and returned to her apartment with Claire. As they pulled into the parking lot, Agent Erickson called.

"Winter, there's been another incident."

"I know. Claire was at work when it happened. She's with me now."

"Is she okay?"

"She's fine."

"Who is that?" asked Claire.

Winter covered the receiver. "I'll explain later."

"I believe with this incident, what happened in Trenton Hills, and what you told me about the person you saw doing this, your friend Claire is in real danger."

"We think so too. Claire saw her tonight. I told Claire she could stay with me until we figure it out. I hope that's okay."

"Good idea. Give me her current address and I'll make sure her things are brought over."

Winter covered the receiver again. "What's your address?"

Claire gave it to her and Winter relayed it to Erickson. Then he hung up.

"What's going on?" Claire asked.

Winter finally turned off the car and pulled the keys from the ignition. "I've been helping the FBI track down Alison."

"You're kidding me...really? The FBI?"

Winter grinned and nodded.

"Wow. When I first saw you I thought you hadn't changed at all. But now...everything's different, isn't it?"

"Yeah. Very different. Listen, they're going to bring you some things from your apartment."

"Are you sure you don't mind me staying with you?"

"Not at all. Besides, where else are you going to go? It'll be like old times. Come on." Winter opened the door and got out. "Kaci's probably home by now." She glanced around the parking lot. "In fact, there's Peter's car." She looked back at Claire and Claire was frowning at her. Winter glared. "Don't start..."

Claire shrugged. "I wasn't saying a thing. It's your loss."

Winter grunted and walked away. "Listen," she said turning back to Claire at the bottom of the stairs. "They can't know the truth. So just follow my lead, okay?"

"Sure."

The second they walked into the apartment, Kaci rushed at them and flung her arms around Claire.

"Are you all right?" asked Kaci.

"Yeah, I'm fine," said Claire. "Thanks to Winter. She's apparently pretty awesome."

"Yes she is," said Peter, a grim smile on his face.

Winter looked away from him, hoping the heat in her face didn't show. Kaci offered Claire something to drink, and when Winter heard Kaci and Peter walk into the kitchen, she finally lifted her eyes. Claire watched her, a twinkle in her eyes Winter almost slapped away.

"What happened?" asked Kaci, bringing Claire a glass of water. They all moved into the living area and sat.

"It was…um, an accident…" said Winter.

"A fire," said Claire.

"…at the diner," said Winter. "She lost her car too."

"Wow. Sounds like a serious fire," said Peter, his eyes bright…analyzing.

"What about everyone else?" asked Kaci.

Claire stared at the floor. "Not everyone made it."

"Um," said Winter. "Claire needs to stay with us for a little while. To sort things out. I hope you don't mind."

Kaci shook her head. "Not at all. I've got some extra sheets and stuff. She can have the couch tonight until we figure something else out."

"Thank you, so much," said Claire.

"How did your car catch on fire?" asked Peter.

Winter blinked at him and his accusatory eyes. She couldn't think of anything…

"Sparks, I guess," said Claire.

"Sparks," Peter repeated.

Kaci punched his thigh. "The important thing is you're okay. It must have been terrifying. You can hang out with us as long as you need."

"I should be going," said Peter. "Good night." He leaned over to kiss Kaci…a kiss that seemed intentionally short.

"Good night," said Kaci.

"I'm glad you're okay," he said to Claire.

"Thanks."

"Winter," he said, suspicion oozing from his voice so strongly Winter thought Kaci might get up and hit him again. "You can fill me in later."

The bottom of Winter's stomach gave way and all she could do was nod, the blood rising in her face again.

After he left, Kaci stood. "Sorry about that. He's been really protective since we got engaged. He just doesn't know you yet, Claire.

There's nothing personal."

"It's fine. I understand," said Claire

"Thanks. I'll get you some things." Kaci disappeared into her room.

Claire leaned toward Winter. "My dad was protective like that," she said softly.

"You don't know the whole story. It's not like that at all."

"Are you sure?"

"Of course. Peter's super sweet and romantic. He'd never do anything to hurt her. It's just…" Winter paused, wondering how much of the past two years she could trust Claire with. Trusting her with her own secrets was one thing. But Kaci's?

"What?" Claire asked.

Winter frowned. "Nothing."

Claire shrugged. "I'm sure you know him best. Sounds like he's a really awesome guy, if you're right."

"He is…"

"Then maybe you really should…"

"Drop it," Winter snapped as Kaci emerged.

Kaci returned with a pillow and a set of sheets. "I'm going to turn in, hope nobody minds." She placed the sheets on the couch and went back to her room. "Claire, I'm glad you're okay. Good night, you two."

As Kaci left, Claire watched Winter again.

"What?" Winter hissed.

"Nothing."

"If you have something to say to me, spit it out."

Claire pinched her lips together before speaking. "You have all these abilities, prophecy and whatever, you do all these courageous things with the FBI, but you're really still just a coward."

Winter crossed her arms. "Well, what am I supposed to do? They're engaged."

"Have your feelings changed?"

Winter looked away.

"If you see the future and everything, maybe you feel this way because it's supposed to be this way. What if this is your gift's way of telling you what to do?"

"I don't know."

"Did you think your gift is only to help others? Maybe there's a little something in it to help you be happy too."

Winter put her forehead in her hands. "Maybe…"

"It's your calling, Winter."

Winter grunted.

"Do you love him?"

Winter shook her head in her hands and didn't answer.

Claire leaned closer. "Do. You. Love. Him?"

Winter trembled, images of Ryan passing through her mind, one by one being replaced with images of Peter. And the more she saw Peter, the stronger her heart pounded.

"Yes or no, Winter. Answer me."

Winter took a deep breath and wiped a solitary tear from her check. "Yes."

"Then you have to tell him."

Winter sighed. "Okay."

Winter sat curled up beneath a blanket early that Saturday morning watching cartoons from the couch. But she wasn't paying much attention to them. She had dreamed about Peter last night in such a way she blushed to think about it, but couldn't *stop* thinking about it.

Could Claire be right? Could her feelings for Peter be a nudge from her gift of prophecy? Could there actually be a chance God was finally trying to give her something good?

She glanced at the dining table where Kaci and Claire were chatting, and smiled to see they had found enough in common to laugh together and get along. It was nice to see her old best friend at the same table with her new best friend, as if Winter's whole life suddenly made a little more sense.

Winter didn't want to hurt Kaci at all…she had threatened Peter over and over again about doing that. But what if in the long run keeping silent about this was the wrong thing to do? Would allowing this marriage to go through be a mistake for everyone? In the end, would not speaking up cause Kaci more heartache later?

What about Peter's secret? He obviously knew something about Summer, but what if he had more? What if…Winter's heart fluttered. What if it was the other way around? What if Summer knew Peter's secret? Could it be he had feelings for her too and that he didn't want to hurt Kaci either? That maybe Summer found out and that's the secret? But then why would he propose? Maybe because he didn't think Winter would ever share his feelings…

She heard a knock on the door. Winter knew it was Peter, so she didn't bother. Kaci jogged over and let him in.

"Hey, everybody," he said. "Good morning."

While the others greeted him, Winter folded her arms and stared at the TV, mostly to avoid seeing the kiss she knew was coming.

"Something wrong with her?" Peter asked.

"You know her," said Kaci.

Claire chuckled as Peter and Kaci joined her back at the table.

"Right…" said Peter.

"I can hear you," Winter growled, looking up to glare at them.

Claire laughed again and went into the kitchen. "Anyone else want a soda?"

"I'll take one," said Peter.

The conversation at the table struck back up and Winter tuned it out again. After a few minutes, Claire came to sit by Winter on the couch.

"Are you okay?" she asked.

"Yeah."

Claire handed her an open can of soda. "Here. Maybe a little caffeine will help."

Winter took it and sipped. "Thanks." She stole a glance at Peter. He was looking at her again, though trying not to be obvious about it. Was that a blush?

Claire leaned closer. "You need to talk to him."

"I know. I'm just not sure I can. Not now. Definitely not with Kaci around."

"I'll tell you what..." Claire smiled. "If I find a way to get you two alone, will you talk?"

Winter sighed.

"Relax. I know this is the right thing. You wouldn't feel this way unless it was meant to be. And I'm sure his response will surprise you."

"I don't know if I want him to respond that way."

"Why not? You deserve it. You're awesome and beautiful and gifted, and it's time something good came of it for a change."

Winter turned back to the TV. "Fine. Whatever. I'll talk to him. But that's all. Okay?"

Claire grinned. "Perfect. Just leave the rest to me." She stood to go back to the table and then turned to Winter. "And...try to loosen up."

Winter smirked.

"Winter's not feeling well," said Claire as she approached the table.

"Well, no wonder," said Peter.

"What's wrong, Winter?" asked Kaci.

Winter opened her mouth, but Claire spoke for her. "Migraine. And nausea."

"Do you need any medicine?" asked Kaci.

"I'll get something in a bit. I just need to sit," said Winter, biting her lip.

"That means I need you to do me a favor, Kaci," said Claire.

"Sure, what?"

"Well, Winter was going to take me to the store so I could pick up some things. And now she's not up to driving. Do you think you could take me?"

Kaci sat up and looked at Peter then at Winter. "Um, yeah. I guess. Peter...you want to come with?"

"Well..." said Claire. "I kinda need some...girl things."

"Say no more," said Peter. "I'm out."

"When do you want to go?" asked Kaci.

"We were going to go this morning, but we can wait until later if you want."

"No...I'm not doing anything. We can go. Just let me get my things."

"Thank you, so much," said Claire, glancing back at Winter and winking.

Kaci went to her room and came back with her purse around her shoulder and car keys in her hand. "Sorry, Peter. I'll call you when we're done and you can come back over, okay?"

"Yeah, sure." Peter stood and drained the rest of his soda.

"Winter, do you need anything?" asked Kaci.

Winter shook her head. "I'll be okay."

"Just send me a text if you do."

As Peter followed Kaci toward the door, Claire stood behind them making urgent faces at Winter and pointing at Peter.

Winter's heart fluttered, a flush of dizziness surged through her mind, and she sat up. "Um, Peter."

Peter paused and Claire rushed passed him to join Kaci outside.

"Can I ask you something?"

"Yeah." He leaned out the door. "I'll call you," he shouted to Kaci. Then he stepped back in and closed the door. "What's up?" He came toward her and teetered a little, catching himself on the couch arm. "Sorry, suddenly a little dizzy," he said as he sat.

Winter smiled, relaxed and confident. Peter smiled back at her in a way that told her Claire had been right…he did feel the same way. Her head buzzed with the possibilities, ringing in her ears like static. The pounding of her heart brought a giddy sense of spinning. Surely Kaci would understand…

He chuckled, smile widening. "You don't look like you feel bad. You look really…nice."

"You think I look nice?"

"Yeah. Why not?"

"That's what I wanted to talk to you about anyway." Winter laughed and the warmth of it spread through her body, settling in her muscles, and bringing with it a sudden drowsiness. Winter pushed it away, no longer scared to tell Peter exactly how she felt…almost excited about it. She scooted closer to him until her knee touched his, and placed a hand on his thigh.

Peter blinked slowly and he grinned. "I'm pretty sure you should be doing that…" He laughed and his head lolled backward. "I'm sorry. My brain is kind of fuzzy for some reason. You probably shouuldn't…"

"Peter, I love you." She burst out laughing uncontrollably. "Sorry. I didn't mean to say that yet."

"Yet?" He joined her hysterics and they laid their heads back on to the cushions of the couch.

Winter let her hand slide up his thigh, but he didn't seem to notice.

"You're pretty," he said, running his hand over her shoulder to her back.

Winter leaned toward him as he tugged her, and she wrapped her leg around his.

Something pinged in the back of her mind, some kind of warning, lost in the static and the fuzz of her elation. A flicker of judgment told her something wasn't right but she couldn't stop. Her head spun, her eyes drooped. She didn't care anymore. This felt good. It felt right.

She leaned close to him, placing her lips on his. He didn't resist. He caught her up in his arms, drinking as deeply from her kiss as she did from his. It invigorated her and she shifted her hips over him and placed herself perfectly on his lap, letting the passion take over. Letting time blur. Letting the moments swirl together. Letting their bodies do what bodies were supposed to do.

Something clicked in the peripheral of her hearing, but she didn't care. It was just more background fuzz, just another dizzy artifact of her ecstasy.

"Peter!" a voice shouted. At least the tone was harsh, but it sounded distant, as if coming from a tunnel.

Winter tried to pick up her head from Peter's lips, finding it heavier than she remembered, and almost falling back onto the couch. She turned toward the muffled voice, and saw a blurred figure who might have been Kaci standing at the door, hands over her mouth.

"What are you doing?" another distant shout.

What was she doing? Winter couldn't remember. She grinned at the boy she was sitting on. He looked so much like Ryan with his shirt off. When did he take his shirt off? She looked down at herself and her own bare chest.

Laughing, she glanced back at the girl by the door. The world speckled and Winter fell to the floor, still laughing, and slid her hands over her naked torso, down to her hips to see if she were still wearing pants. She let out a pouty mewl that she was and that the strange girl at the door had interrupted them. Sighing, Winter decided she really did need a nap.

As she closed her eyes, she heard the same interrupting voice from far away say, "Go to hell, Winter." Then a door slammed.

37

Four Years Ago

Winter closed her locker at the end of the day and turned toward the buses. Stacy jogged up to her, bright-eyed, before Winter could leave.

"I'm having some friends over this weekend. Want to come?"

Winter shuffled her feet and shrugged. "Maybe. What do you have in mind?"

"I don't know," said Stacy. "It's just been so long since I've done anything fun. Maybe we'll watch movies or something."

"Who all will be there?"

"Don't know that either. You're the first one I've asked." Stacy smiled. "Claire can come too, if she wants."

Winter grimaced. "I'm not sure she can. Her dad isn't letting her do much, you know."

"But didn't she go to your place last weekend?"

Winter gazed down and let her hair swing in front of her face. "Well…what he doesn't know…"

"Winter!" Stacy's eyes widened. "Don't encourage her to do

things to make it worse."

"I don't," said Winter. "She does it herself. I just give her a safe place to stay. What's wrong with that?"

Stacy crossed her arms. "Still. I'm not sure I like it. I'm not sure I like any of it."

"Neither do I, but what can we do?"

Stacy glanced toward the exit. "You're going to miss your bus."

"Give me a ride?" Winter asked.

Stacy nodded and turned. Winter fell into step beside her.

"I'm worried about Claire, again," Stacy said. "She hasn't been the same since she came back. I think her other friends are really messing her up."

"Her friends aren't all that bad," said Winter. "I think they're trying to help her like we are."

"But they're the ones who got her into the drugs in the first place," said Stacy.

"Maybe. But I'm sure it wasn't their intention."

"You're not still…"

"No," Winter lied.

Stacy nodded. "Well, I just don't know. I wish she'd talk to me. If she's sneaking out to see you, maybe she really will come to my place this weekend. Will you convince her?"

"I'll try," said Winter. "But I'm not sure she'll want your Jesus stuff."

Stacy sighed. "I know. I'm just worried everything's going to crash together and something bad is going to happen."

"Believe me, Claire won't let it get that far."

Stacy tilted her head and looked at Winter. "What do you mean? She's not going to do something stupid is she?"

"Trust me, it's nothing stupid."

"What's going on?"

"Nothing. Just drop it, okay?"

Stacy's face reddened. At that moment, Chad rounded the far

corner and Stacy's face lit up.

Chad didn't notice Winter at all as he approached Stacy. They smiled at each other and Winter had to clear her throat.

"Oh, sorry. Chad, do you know Winter?"

For the first time, he noticed Winter and looked as if he might run away. But he regained his composure and smiled, though the smile failed to touch his eyes. "Yeah. We've met once." He turned back to Stacy. "I've gotta run. I'll call you later. Okay?"

"Sure," Stacy said. As Chad walked away, Stacy watched him with doe eyes.

Winter crossed her arms. "What was that?"

Stacy turned back to her. "What do you mean?"

Winter nodded toward Chad. "That. What was that?"

"Oh, um...he asked me to prom." Stacy grinned. "Isn't it great?"

"He asked you to prom? How'd that happen?"

Stacy frowned. "We have a class together, remember? We've been sitting next to each other since he got here."

"And you've been flirting with him the whole time."

"Maybe. What does it matter to you, anyway? I thought you said you weren't interested."

"I'm not!" Winter's words came out louder than she meant, so she took a deep breath and tried again. "I'm not. Do whatever you want. I don't care."

"Are you jealous?"

"No."

"Because I hope you know if I had any idea..."

"Any idea?" Winter sneered. "Any idea? Since when have you ever had any idea what I'm feeling?"

"Winter, don't start this again."

"I'm not starting anything! You started it! Maybe I *did* want to go to prom with him, did you think of that?"

Stacy shook her head. "But you said..."

Winter spun away. "Just forget it okay. I've got to go."

"But the buses…" Stacy reached out to her. "Come on. I'll still give you a ride."

Winter shrugged her off. "You know what? I think I just want to be alone. I'll walk."

Present Day

Winter blinked against the light, a psychedelic erotic dream clawing for a place in her memory, but sucked away by consciousness. By the time she could fully open her eyes, it was gone, just beyond reach.

A chill swept over her body and Winter looked down at herself, panicking when she realized she lay on the floor topless and pants unbuttoned. She bolted upright and found the black lump that was her t-shirt, clutching it against her chest, and scanning the room for anyone else. But she was alone.

"Kaci?" she called out with no answer, hastily slipping the shirt over her head.

Kaci. A relic from her dream broke through, something about Kaci being angry. Kaci leaving and slamming the door. With that sketch of a memory, something about Peter came through.

"Oh, God!" she said out loud. "What did I do? What happened?"

She searched for her phone and found it tossed onto the floor near the balcony door. She crawled to it and called Kaci.

No answer.

By now, more fuzzy relics were surfacing. She remembered why she was topless, and guilt numbed her from toe to head. *It can't be true. I would never…What's going on?*

Winter wiped the tears from her cheek and tried to call Kaci again. Nothing. She ran to her room to redress properly and to retrieve her car keys. On her way out of the door she called Summer. Only Summer's voice mail answered.

"Summer, it's me. Something's happened and I'm not sure what. I don't remember anything. Kaci's gone…I think I did something. Oh, God…I need to find her. I'm coming over."

She ran down to her car and made the impulse decision to call Peter. Maybe he could tell her whether or not what she thought she remembered was true. He didn't answer either.

When she finally made it to Boon Hall, Winter ran into the lobby and found Summer just inside waiting.

"Where is she?" Winter asked.

Summer crossed her arms and frowned. "She doesn't want to talk to you."

"I need to explain. I need to fix this. Something isn't right."

"Winter…no. Even if you could explain, you need to leave her alone right now."

"But I'm not even sure what happened! I don't remember!"

"Do you want to know what happened? You tried to have sex with Peter right in front of her."

Winter scrunched up her face, the guilty tears surging out of her eyes again. She put both hands on her head. "Oh, God…what's going on? Where's Peter? Why can't I remember?"

Summer shook her head. "I don't know. He keeps calling too."

"Let me talk to her. At least let me talk to her on the phone."

Summer sighed. "I'm sorry. You need to go." She turned and walked away, leaving Winter trembling by the door.

When Summer had gone, and people in the lobby began to watch

Winter and whisper, Winter shuffled outside, holding herself tight. She drifted toward the heart of campus, leaving her car behind, trying to conjure up more details from her elusive memories, trying to figure out exactly what happened and why. The worst of it all was the part of her that remembered enjoying what happened...and that part didn't regret anything. It filled her with more guilt, which only strengthened the dormant defiance that liked it. Finally, as she neared the Ancient, the weight of the guilt folded her inside, breaking the defiance, and snapping the fight within like a rubber band. She pulled out her phone and called Davis.

At least he answered. *"What?"*

Winter sniffled. "Have you talked to Peter?"

A moment of silence on the other end. *"Yeah."*

"Can I talk to him?" Her chin quivered and a sob escaped from her mouth. She collapsed on a bench beneath the Ancient.

"He's not here."

"Do you know where he is?"

Another moment of silence. *"No."*

"Can I talk to you then? In person? At the Ancient?"

Silence from the other end.

"Please, Davis? I'm not sure what's happening. I just need to talk to someone."

Davis sighed. *"Fine."* He hung up.

Winter leaned forward, elbows on knees and her face in her hands. She waited, like a puddle waits for more rain, feeling like the whole of existence wanted nothing more than to dry her up.

She didn't know how long he took getting there, but she finally saw him coming in her peripheral vision. She sat up and waited for him to sit, not daring to look at him, almost holding her breath trying to stop herself from more crying. He sat next to her, but noticeably a little further away than normal.

"I can see on your face it's true," he said.

Winter sniffed. "What did Peter tell you?"

"That you came on to him pretty strong…and that he didn't resist. He seemed pretty confused about it. He couldn't remember a lot of the details. But he said he woke up on your couch, with you topless on the floor asleep. He got out as quick as he could and came to me."

Winter shook her head. "This isn't right. I would never…he would never." She threw her hands in the air and looked at Davis. "I need to talk to him."

"No," he said. "He's really confused and all things considered I don't think it would be a good idea for you to see him."

"But it's not my fault! I need to fix this."

Davis frowned. "It happened. Maybe you shouldn't try to pass blame or fix it. Maybe you should admit it and apologize."

"But I didn't do it on purpose!"

"Really? What were you trying to do then?"

"I was…" She put her head in her palms. "Oh, God…I was going to tell him I had feelings for him."

"You have what?"

She looked at him, pleading with her eyes. "It's not what it sounds like. What if I feel this way for a reason? What if it's part of my prophecy? Shouldn't I tell him?"

Davis recoiled and twisted his face. "Are you serious? They were engaged! How could you possibly think it would be okay to tell your best friend's fiancé you're in love with him?"

"I don't know! But what if God made me feel this way for a reason…"

"Screw the what if," Davis said as he stood. "When are you going to realize this gift, this ability, has nothing to do with YOU? It's not your power and it never has been!"

"Davis, it's not like that…"

"I hope you got what you wanted." He spun and walked away.

"Davis!" she called. "I messed up, okay? Don't leave me, please! I need your help! I can fix this!"

Davis continued walking away as if he hadn't heard her.

Winter grabbed the hair on both sides of her head and screamed, the shriek bouncing from the buildings and turning the heads of the people walking through the Meadow.

Davis paused, but still didn't turn.

Winter pulled her feet onto the bench and lay her head on her knees. The new life she had built for herself, her entire happiness, was disintegrating around her, crumbling like ash. And she didn't even understand why. Her body shook and she moaned into her knees. She tried to replay the events of that morning in her mind, but the memories of it slipped away like wet ice. She could remember bits of it, but only as if they were a part of a dream, and completely shocked she might have done them for real. It couldn't be true. It wasn't true. Maybe this was the dream…the nightmare…and she'd wake up and find everything exactly like it should be.

She shook her head. "It's not real…It's not real…"

The afternoon grew long and the shadows even longer as she sat there, unwilling to move. She never looked up and the only footsteps approaching the Ancient always went the long way around. At some point the sun dipped beneath the low boughs of the Ancient and the warm rays washed over her. Still she didn't move and she didn't look up. Where would she go even if she wanted to?

More footsteps approached, but these didn't avoid her, they came straight to her bench.

"Winter, what's going on?" asked Ayden.

Winter glanced up, blinking against the late afternoon sun. "I don't know," she croaked.

Ayden's face softened and she sat. "I heard some stuff…from Summer. I've been calling all over looking for you."

Winter shook her head, her face scrunching again. "I don't know what's happening…"

"Why don't you tell me what you remember."

Winter let her knees fall back down. She clutched her hands

together and stared at them, letting all the snatches of dream-like memory spill out of her mouth, being painfully honest about the more embarrassing details. When she finished, she looked at Ayden hoping to see understanding, but finding anger just like everyone else.

"And you thought it was okay to do that?" Ayden asked.

Winter shrugged. "I thought maybe I should at least tell Peter how I felt...that maybe I feel this way for a reason."

Ayden shook her head. "But that's not what you did."

"It's not my fault. I would never do that! I don't know what happened. I...just..."

"What? You just couldn't control yourself?"

"Exactly. That's exactly what happened. I completely lost control..." Winter's voice raked, and for the first time she heard the hoarseness come out. "It wasn't like I was giving in to my feelings or anything, it was like something took over my body. My mind went crazy and my body just did what it wanted. I don't understand what happened..." She leaned into her hands and covered her face. "I would never act that way. Ever."

"Has it ever happened before?"

Winter sighed. "The closest I've ever come to feeling like that was after smoking a lovely."

"You mean, like weed and PCP mixed? Dude, I knew you used to be messed up, but wow."

Winter glanced at her and found the anger had disappeared. Ayden's brow furrowed intently at Winter.

"What? I did drugs, so what?"

"No. Not that," said Ayden. "Just say what you said again. And listen to yourself this time."

"The closest I've ever come to feeling like that was..." Winter covered her mouth with both hands. "Oh my God...I was drugged?"

Ayden nodded. "Maybe you were drugged."

"And Peter?"

"Probably drugged too. Some sort of date rape drug, it sounds like. And strong too. You're both lucky to be alive."

Winter's mouth hung open. "But how? Who? I don't understand."

Ayden lifted her eyebrows. "It's obvious. Xaphan got to you again. He knows where you live now. Maybe he sent that Acolyte thing…Alison."

"But why would she drug me? That doesn't make sense. She's killed everyone else."

"Yeah, *everyone else*." Ayden leaned in. "*You* are not everyone else. She needs you alive because you can bring her to Sandy. She probably followed Claire to find you."

"And Peter?"

"Do you think she cares about anyone else? She'd probably take out the whole apartment to get to you. Peter just got caught in the crossfire. It could have been any of them."

Winter shook her head and laid her face in her hands.

Ayden gently touched her on the shoulder. "Kaci's not safe around you anymore."

Fire rose into Winter's cheeks. She stuck out her chin and stood. "I have to talk to her. I have to make her listen. If Peter and I were both drugged, then this wasn't my fault."

Ayden rose beside her. "I don't think you should. Maybe her being angry will keep her away. Maybe you should leave her alone, and let her keep moving around. Take the hit…for Kaci's safety."

Winter spun on her, anger coursing through and cauterizing every ounce of the guilt and shame. "I will NOT let that monster tear my life apart! I'm the victim here, and I'm going to fix this! So back off!"

Ayden took a step backward, holding up her hands as Winter pulled out her cellphone to call Agent Erickson.

"Winter, what have you done?" he shouted.

Winter scrunched her eyes. "I don't remember. Everything's so fuzzy. But what you've heard is only part of the truth. I can explain."

Erickson snorted. *"I don't care if you can explain. I knew you had a past, but I didn't realize you were this much of a liability."*

"Just give me a second to explain. It wasn't my fault. I was drugged. Peter and I both were. Ayden thinks it was some kind of date rape drug. You have to know I would never do something like that to them. It was Xaphan. He did this."

"Can you prove that?"

"Not yet, but I will. I promise. Give me a chance and I can fix this. I'll get the proof."

"Even if you are telling the truth, we have a much bigger issue at stake."

"What do you mean?"

"It means truth or not, you're still a major liability to this operation. The apartment's been compromised and you've been compromised. He's trying to use you to get to Kaci. If you really were drugged and he had captured you in that state, you would have told him everything. I can't let that happen."

"No," pleaded Winter. "This is a mistake. Let me talk to Kaci. Let me make everything right. We can reset in another apartment. I'm sorry, please let me fix this. I can do it. I have to try."

"NO!" Erickson's voice echoed momentarily in her ear. He took a deep breath. *"You're finished. You've ruined everything. You can't fix this and you never will be able to fix this. It was a mistake to get you involved. And as of right now, you're out…out of the mission and out of the FBI. Until we figure out what's going on Kaci will be relocated. Someone will be by later to pick up her things. We're too invested in the operation right now to put her into complete protection and, in doing so, revealing her true identity. So we'll reset the operation without you. And I suggest you don't seek out Kaci. Don't even talk to her. Don't do anything that might lead them to her, understand? Kaci is out of your life."*

Winter's chin quivered, a chill crawling over her skin. She turned to look at Ayden, who was watching her. "What about Ayden? Peter? Summer? Davis? What about my friends? My life?"

"Make your own life from here on out, but it won't be this one. I don't care about Summer and Davis, they were never a part of this. But Ayden is, and since

278 | Keven Newsome

the engagement so is Peter. I don't want you around them either. Don't talk to them or call them. Don't even look at them on the street."

"But…"

"And Winter, if you even so much as sneeze in their direction, I'll have you arrested. You're done. Understood?"

Winter nodded even though she knew he couldn't see. A tear rolled down her cheek as Erickson hung up.

"Well?" asked Ayden.

Winter blinked at her, mouth hanging open in wordless protest. She slowly slid the phone back into her pocket. "I have to go," she said as she turned away.

Winter crashed onto her bed as soon as she reached the apartment, lying face down with a tissue in one hand and a fist made out of the other. After a couple of hours she heard the front door open and a moment later Claire spoke from the bedroom door.

"What happened to you?"

Winter sniffed. "I don't know. Kaci's not coming back. All my friends hate me now." The bed sagged at the edge as Claire sat.

"She was pretty freaked out. She couldn't drive. Made me take her to Summer's," said Claire.

"Did you see?"

"No. I was in the car. Kaci had forgotten something. I don't even remember what. Guess it's not important anymore."

Winter took a deep breath and her chest shuddered. She twisted and sat up next to Claire. "It's not my fault. It's not Peter's fault. I think we were drugged."

"How?"

Winter shrugged. "I don't know. The only thing I had was the soda you gave me."

Claire covered her mouth. "I gave one to Peter too."

"Yeah, but you had one and nothing happened."

Claire shook her head. "I changed my mind and had water. Do you think it was in the soda?"

"Had to be. Where did you get them?"

"I didn't. They were already here. I thought you bought them."

Winter huffed and closed her eyes with a defeated grimace. "We don't buy that kind of soda."

Claire's eyes widened. "Oh my god! How did they get there? What if we had all had them? Do you think…"

Winter nodded. "Alison. I don't know how. But she knows we're both here."

"Then we're not safe, are we?"

"Would we be safe anywhere?"

"What about your FBI friends?"

Winter snickered. "I've sort of been fired."

Claire bit her lip. "I'm sorry." She paused and leaned forward to try to catch Winter's eyes. "What are you going to do?"

"I don't know. There's nothing really left for me here. I thought about just going home."

"Quitting school?"

"Yeah…"

Claire frowned and shook her head. "Are you sure you want to do that?"

"I don't know," said Winter. "I'm not sure of anything right now."

"Well, you've come this far…you should at least try to finish out the year."

"Maybe. I'd have to get a job."

Claire laughed. "Jobs aren't that bad, you know. Maybe it would do you good to have a real one anyway. It may not be as glamorous as the FBI…but it pays the bills." Claire bumped her shoulder against

Winter. "And for the record," said Claire, "not all your friends hate you."

Winter smiled. "Thank you."

The next day, Agent Erickson called and asked Winter and Claire to leave the apartment so Kaci could come by and get her things. Winter agreed and left the remaining sodas on the table for Erickson to get analyzed. They went to the store and when they returned, Kaci's room had been emptied.

Winter looked at the empty space and clenched her teeth. "Well, I guess it's your room now, if you want it," she told Claire.

"I don't suppose this place is any safer than my old apartment. As long as you're with me I'm as safe as it gets," Claire said. "I'll let my landlord know, and maybe we can go get the rest of my stuff soon."

"Right," said Winter. "We'll go this afternoon."

A few hours later, they arrived at Claire's tiny dilapidated apartment to find it ransacked. Furniture stuffing covered the floor like fluffy snow. Shattered dishes littered the floor like over-sized confetti. Claire swore and ran back to the bedroom. Winter followed. The bed had been slashed like the furniture and all Claire's clothes ripped from the dresser and torn out of the closet.

"Well, there goes my deposit," Claire said.

"Is all this furniture yours?"

"No. This was a furnished apartment. All I really have are my clothes and some dishes. We should be able to get most of it in your car."

Looking around the trashed apartment, Winter felt the blood rising in her face. That wall of defiance rose within her again. "I have to find her and stop her," she said through barred teeth.

"You will."

Winter almost growled. "I have to find Alison now. I can't let her destroy my life or yours anymore. This needs to end."

"How can you do that? What about me?"

Winter screamed. "Don't you see? She's taken everything!" Winter stepped up to the bedroom wall and punched it, denting the drywall and sending a sharp pain through her knuckles.

"Winter, calm down…"

"No! We find her right now! I have the power to put an end to this! I need to make her suffer for what she's done! She took Ryan and all my new friends…No more!"

Claire backed away. "You're scaring me…"

"Let's go. We'll get your things later. Alison is out there right now." Winter reached down and pulled the gun from her ankle. "And this time, I WILL pull the trigger!"

"No." Claire shook her head. "I don't want to go. It's not right."

"I don't care if it's right or not, it's time someone did something about her. And I'm the only one who can. I'm the only one with the power to stop her."

Claire took a slow step toward her. "Don't do this. Not now. I'm not going with you…so please don't leave me here alone."

"I have to, Claire. I'm the only one who can."

"But why now?"

"If I wait she may do something else. She may take you, or my dad, or somebody else." Winter's body trembled, her chin quivered, and she could hear her voice shaking. "I can't let that happen."

Claire lifted a hand and stepped close enough to touch Winter's arm. "Fine. But not today. Not like this. You need to have a plan, remember? Remember the plan we made four years ago? You're the one who wouldn't let me go without one. And I'm not letting you go today without one. Got it? We'll make a plan. Together."

Winter bit her lip and nodded.

"Now will you please put the gun away?"

Winter holstered it back against her ankle.

"Why do you still even have that thing, anyway?" Claire asked.

Winter shrugged. "I don't know. Habit? I thought they'd ask for it back, but they didn't."

"Maybe you should put it someplace safe. Lock it up, so you won't be tempted like this again."

Winter sagged and nodded. "Yeah. Sure."

Despite spending all evening getting Claire settled in and then sitting around talking about how to find Alison, nothing they could come up with was safe enough to try. Without backup, any attempt to find Alison would put Winter in danger from others who might be with Alison. It made Winter even more angry, and she wanted to run for her car regardless of the dangers. They finally decided for now the best they could do was wait for Alison to show herself, and Winter spent the rest of the evening pacing the apartment and watching out of the windows. More than once, Winter shouted at Claire about the inadequacy of the plan, and Claire would simply talk her down again.

One week later, Winter sat at the table, staring at her cell phone sitting just in front of her, her back to the living room. She heard Claire come in behind her from job hunting and drop her things on the couch.

"I've been thinking," Winter said.

Claire rounded the table and sat across from her.

Winter looked up at her. "We can't stay here. It doesn't matter if we get jobs, Alison will find us there too. She already knows where we live...so it's only a matter of time before she comes back."

"But you'll stop her," said Claire. "That was the plan."

"I know. But I don't want to be out of control. Right now, we're just waiting on her. I want to be somewhere we can dictate things

284 | Keven Newsome

and control how I find Alison."

Claire nodded. "Okay. So what do you want to do?"

"I don't know yet, but I know we can't stay in Cherithville. Maybe we can draw her away from everyone here, someplace new. But I can't go without talking to Peter and Kaci."

"Are you sure that's a good idea?"

"I have to try. They're my friends and I can't leave with things unsaid. If there's anything I can do to get my friends back, I have to try. I have to make them understand what really happened."

"I'm sure they know," said Claire. "I'm sure your FBI friends told them already."

The knot inside Winter leaped into her throat. "Then why haven't they called me?"

"I don't know."

"Do you think they just don't want to talk to me anymore?"

"Winter...I think you know as well as I do, they might not."

Winter pounded the table with her fist. "I can't!" She put her head in her hands.

After a moment of silence, Claire said gently, "Can't what?"

"I can't let this happen." The knot was unraveling, fraying her inside out. "They're my friends. I can't let them go...Please, God..."

"You may not have a choice."

"I'll do anything." She looked down at her phone. "Anything."

"Calling won't help," said Claire.

"They won't answer. I've been calling all morning. Kaci's number has been changed."

"Then there's nothing you can do."

Winter shook her head. "There's always something I can do. I will do anything. I can use my power to find her. I can go knock on her door and explain." Winter stood. "She'll forgive me, I know...if only she knew the truth. The reason she hasn't called is because she doesn't know. I have to talk to her."

"Sit back down, Winter."

"I'll find Peter too…I know what dorm he's in. I'll sneak in and make sure he talks to me, and I'll let him know it wasn't my fault."

"Winter…think about it. Doing that won't help."

"I have to." Winter ran to her room for her keys. When she came back out, Claire was standing in front of the door.

"You can't do this," said Claire.

"Get out of my way!" Winter narrowed her eyes and glared, fists squeezed tight.

Claire sighed. "Why don't you go talk to your FBI friends…see if they told them the truth. And if they have, then you'll have your answer, right? You won't be embarrassing yourself by showing up when they don't want to see you. But if they haven't, then I'll help you find them. How does that sound?"

Winter's stomach lurched at the thought and she sat on the couch, as if she had been punched, letting reality fall back into place. "I can't. I'll be arrested."

"What? Why? You just said…"

"I'm not really allowed around them anymore." She covered her face with her hands. "I just don't know what to do anymore. I need to talk to them…but I can't."

"That's not fair. Why would they ban you from your friends? Unless…" Claire sat beside her, wide eyes staring into nothingness. "Unless they really did tell them the truth, and your friends don't want you around anymore. Which means…oh, Winter, I'm sorry. I didn't realize."

Winter nodded, allowing her eyes to tear up and the fight inside to cower. "You're right. I'm still the freak. I always have been, and it hasn't changed. I guess it was only a matter of time before they learned the real truth about me."

Claire gently rubbed her back. "At least you still have me. We'll figure this out. And when we do, we'll run away together like we always wanted to."

Winter smiled weakly, but felt more alone than ever.

40

Four Years Ago

Spring break finally arrived, and with its coming the first steps in their plan to find Claire a new life activated. Late Saturday evening, the day after school let out, Winter paced her room wondering if Claire would have the courage to go through with things, only half paying attention to the movie on the television, slightly louder than normal to mask any sounds or conversation she and Claire might make later. Except for the ambiance of the TV, no lights lit up the room. Winter's dad had long gone to sleep, so she didn't dare leave her room and risk alerting him to something unusual. Claire was supposed to come to the window anyway.

It was near one in the morning and Claire should have been there by midnight. Winter glanced again out of the open window, wondering what was taking Claire so long and if anything had gone wrong. What if Claire's dad found out about the plan? What if he saw her packing? What if he caught her sneaking out? What if someone on the street alerted the police? What if she had been arrested already?

Winter chewed the tips of her fingers and peered out the window again. This time she saw movement just beyond the street light, and held her breath. A moment later Claire ran into view and crossed to the dark shadows beneath Winter's window. Winter exhaled with a long sigh.

She rushed back to her bed and dug out the small rope she had stashed beneath it. She tied one end to a bedpost, just for extra safety, and tossed the other end out of the window. Then she grabbed the rope tightly and wrapped it around her hands.

Winter stuck her head out of the window and watched as Claire tied the end of the rope to her duffel bag. Claire grabbed the rope firmly between her hands and turned to the brick wall.

"Ready?" she whispered.

Winter nodded, placed one foot against the windowsill and leaned back against Claire's weight. As the rope tightened around Winter's hands, pinching her skin, she eyed the point where the rope dived out of the window as it strained and jittered. Winter could hear Claire huffing, and once thought she heard Claire slip. It took longer than she thought it should for Claire to reach the window, but eventually both hands reached in to grab the window ledge. Winter dropped the rope to help Claire inside.

"We did it," Claire panted, sitting beneath the window.

Winter rubbed the red lines around her hands and smiled. "Yeah, we did it. I snuck some snacks in if you want something. Do you think anyone saw us?"

"No. Let's get my bag up."

They both stood and grabbed the rope, slowly reeling it back into the room until the duffel bag appeared at the window. When they finally hauled it in, Winter closed the window, pulled the curtains tight, and they both sat again with their backs against the bed.

"I've got it all figured out," said Winter. "My dad never comes in my room while I'm asleep. He never really comes in my room at all, unless there's a good reason…and even then he usually knocks."

"Lucky you," mumbled Claire.

"But he has been known to peek in on me before he goes to work. I figured if you sleep on this side of the bed, close enough to the wall, then even if he did peek in he wouldn't see you in the morning. Once he goes to work, we'll have the whole house to ourselves until he comes home. We can hide easy enough in here. I spend most of my time in my room anyway."

"It'll be fine," said Claire. "At least until it's time for the next step. Have you made up your mind yet?"

Winter shrugged. "I keep going back and forth. We'll talk about it tomorrow."

The next day, Steve left for work, as usual, without checking in on Winter, and the girls hung out watching movies in the living room. No one called or came by looking for Claire, as expected, and the day passed without any complications. When Steve arrived home from work, Claire sequestered herself back in Winter's room. Winter was careful to keep the extra dishes clean, and if Steve noticed Winter doing housework without complaint, he didn't say anything.

The second day started the same, but as they sat before the television again, they heard a knock on the door. Winter's eyes widened as she turned to Claire. Claire nimbly sprinted up the stairs to lock herself in Winter's bathroom like they had planned. They had been expecting someone to come looking for Claire, and they needed to establish Winter's ignorance of Claire's disappearance before they could proceed with their plans. Behind the door could be Claire's parents or the police...they had planned responses for both.

Winter ran her fingers through her hair and rushed to the door after Claire had vanished. She squinted through the peep-hole and saw a female police officer standing outside. Winter slid the locks back and cracked the door open just enough to stand in the gap.

"Yes?"

"Are you Winter Maessen?"

"Yeah. What's going on?"

"Are you friends with Claire Parker?"

"I am. Is everything okay?"

The officer shifted in her stance. "Claire was reported missing this morning by her parents. Have you seen her?"

Winter went through the rehearsed reaction. She put her hand over her mouth. "Oh my God. No, I haven't. Do you think she's okay?"

"Would you mind if I had a look around?"

"Um…I don't think that's a good idea without my dad home. Why would you want to look in my house anyway?"

"We were told you are Claire's best friend, correct?"

Winter nodded.

"We just need to be certain she's not here."

"Well, I promise you, she's not here. If you don't believe me, feel free to come back when my dad's home. He's usually here by six."

"Of course. Well, if you see her, be sure to call the police, okay?"

"Yeah, sure. I hope you find her. I can't imagine her being out there on her own."

The officer peered at Winter. "She didn't say anything to you about leaving, did she?"

"No. Not at all. I just assumed…I'll call right away if I see her. I promise."

The officer nodded. "Make sure you do." She turned away and Winter eased the door closed.

After locking the door back, Winter rushed upstairs to let Claire know it was all clear. They immediately began prepping for the police to return. All traces of Claire's presence was cleaned or packed back into her duffel bag, and the duffel bag placed in the bottom of a garbage bag full of stuffed animals Winter kept on the top shelf of her closet.

As soon as Steve arrived home, Winter went down to tell him about the police visit and about Claire missing, so he wouldn't be surprised if the police came back. Then she watched the street from her window, and at six-thirty, saw a police cruiser approaching.

"They're back," Winter said.

"Come on," said Claire. "We need to hurry."

In Winter's bathroom, they had cleared all the bottles and cleaning supplies out of the cabinet of the vanity. Claire crawled in and squeezed into the tiny space behind the drawers, drawing her knees up to get her feet out of the middle. Winter stacked towels against her and gave her one to cover the rest of herself. Then she shoved all the bottles back in.

Winter ran out of her room, turning out the lights. She took a long moment at the top of the stairs to catch her breath, listening to the conversation below between her dad and what sounded like two officers this time.

"Is someone here?" Winter called.

"It's the police again," Steve called back. "Why don't you come down?"

Winter descended, plastering a concerned look on her face. The moment she saw the police, she asked, "Have you found her yet?"

Steve frowned at Winter. "You don't know anything about this, do you?"

Winter shook her head. "Do you think I would keep something like this from you?"

"Well, regardless...they've asked if they could look around."

"Whatever, Dad. She's not here."

Steve shrugged to the officers. "I'll show you around."

Winter shadowed them through the house, cautiously optimistic seeing they weren't being so thorough as to open cabinets. Winter's room was last, and after walking in and glancing around, poking their heads into the closet and the bathroom, they turned back to Steve and Winter, still standing in the middle of Winter's room.

"Thank you for your time and cooperation. If you hear anything from her, please call us."

"We will," said Steve.

"Will you call us too?" asked Winter. "If you find her?"

The lady officer who had come that morning nodded. "If I'm allowed to, I'll drop by personally and let you know what we've found."

"Thank you," said Winter.

Steve led them all back downstairs and the officers left.

"I hope she's all right," Steve said to Winter as Winter was turning to go back upstairs.

"Me too," she said without looking at him.

Back at her bedroom door, she paused, listening for Steve downstairs to make sure he wasn't following, then she went in and locked the door. Winter pulled all the stuff out of the vanity and helped Claire out. Claire emerged with a wry grin.

"Well, first hurdle done," said Claire as she stood and stretched. "Now we just wait for Michael to tell us they've questioned the coven."

"Yep," said Winter. "Now we wait."

41

Present Day

Winter lugged her suitcase into the living area. Claire sat on the couch with the TV blaring, and eyeing her sideways.

"Are you sure you won't come with me for spring break?" Winter asked.

Claire shook her head. "I left Trenton Hills a long time ago, and I don't intend to ever go back."

"But it might not be safe to stay."

"I'd rather take my chances here. Why don't you just call your dad and stay with me?"

Winter shrugged. "I need this. I just need to get away from here for a few days and clear my head…make some decisions."

"I'm afraid you won't come back," said Claire.

Winter laughed. "I have to. Most of my stuff is still here. Besides…I've moved on from Trenton Hills too. Other than my dad, there's nothing really left for me there. I thought this place could be home, but now…" She sighed. "We've waited a long time for this, haven't we?"

Claire grinned. "Our own apartment together. New lives. A fresh start."

"I'll only be gone a few days. When I get back, we'll finally run away and start someplace else. Just us. If something happens while I'm gone..."

"I'll call you, don't worry," said Claire. "I think I'll be fine. Nothing has happened in a couple of weeks anyway. Besides, I think your FBI friends have been keeping an eye on us, you know? Using us as bait. Alison's not showing up anytime soon."

"I know. Just...don't take any chances, okay?"

Claire smiled. "I promise."

As Winter drove home, she didn't bother with the radio. She let her mind wander back into the events of the past weeks, trying to puzzle out how everything went wrong and trying to find a way to justify her indignation. By the time she arrived in Trenton Hills, it was clear to her that even if she hadn't been drugged her intentions were wrong. The drugs only amplified what she really felt inside.

Winter dragged her suitcase into the house, her face to the floor and dragging her heart just as heavily as the suitcase.

"Hey, sweetheart," said Steve as she walked in. "Welcome home."

"Hey, Dad." She turned and trudged up the stairs, the suitcase banging on each step.

"Are you okay?"

"I'm fine. Just tired. I'm going to go lie down."

"Well, dinner will be ready in an hour. I have a roast in the crockpot."

"Thanks. But I'm not really hungry. I ate on the road," she lied.

"Oh, okay," came his deflated response. "Well, it'll make good sandwiches tomorrow, anyway."

Winter didn't respond. She ambled into her room, locked the door, and collapsed into a weepy mess on her bed, almost more ashamed of crying yet again than she was of what she'd done. Almost.

The next day she tried to call Stacy, but had no answer. Instead, she spent all morning alone, sitting in her pajamas on the sofa, watching game shows and soap operas while her dad was at work.

Maybe starting over with Claire was the best idea. A new town, a new home, a new life. A chance to find new friends. A chance to find someone who might actually love her. Being back home made her heart ache for Ryan. Why could she not let go? Why was it so difficult to escape this constant life of misery? Was she permanently damaged? Chronically unlovable?

If she had any chance to get to Kaci and explain...But what would she say? The truth of Winter's intentions would hurt Kaci more than what Winter actually did. Winter did like Peter...from the very beginning. But he only ever saw Kaci.

It wasn't fair.

Agent Erickson was right. She was a liability to the whole team. Kaci and Peter were safe now, away from Winter, away from her compromising emotions and her inability to control herself. Maybe Winter had done the job God wanted her to do with Kaci already and it was time to move on to something else...maybe protecting Claire from Alison. Maybe that's what God wanted her to do next. If he wanted her to do anything.

As she finished lunch, someone knocked on the door. Winter trudged to it and eased it open. Ayden stood outside, brow wrinkled and jaw slack, as if she were simultaneously confident about what she was doing and surprised she was actually doing it.

Winter let the door pivot open as she turned back into the living room. "What are you doing here?" she asked with her back to Ayden.

"I came to see you. Somehow, I just knew where you lived."

"You're not supposed to be here. I'm not supposed to even look at you. Erickson will arrest me."

"Screw Erickson," said Ayden.

"He'll track you."

"Left the bracelet on campus," said Ayden as she closed the door. "Listen, we've got bigger problems. I need your help."

"I can't help." Winter collapsed onto the couch. "Didn't you hear me?"

Ayden sat in the armchair and leaned forward. "I don't care. I need your help. Even if it's just for today."

"What is it then?" Winter turned off the TV, folded her arms, and faced her.

"I had a dream."

Winter closed her eyes and sighed. "Of course you did. It all makes even more sense now. You're replacing me."

"I'm not replacing you."

"Yes, you are. You've been having all of these experiences and I haven't. They stopped a long time ago. I didn't tell anyone and I didn't notice at first. But all the things I thought I'd done this year happened with you around. It's been you all year. You're the new prophetess, apparently. You have been for a while now." Winter huffed and looked at the wall. "Even God fired me."

Ayden pursed her lips. "I don't know if God fired you or not, but I had a dream and only you can help me figure out what it means."

"Fine, what is it?"

"It's about that book."

"I gave Erickson the book. Why don't you go talk to him?"

Ayden shook her head. "No. It has to be you. Erickson's sort of in…def-con mode."

Winter paused to take a deep breath. "The book didn't really tell us anything. All it did was confirm what Shannon said…that Alison was supposed to be dead. The coven buried what was left of her body…or at least they thought they did."

"Wait…" said Ayden. "Did you say buried? I thought she died in a car fire."

"She did…well, I thought she did. Maybe she survived. I don't know."

"Did Shannon tell you she was buried?"

Winter shrugged. "No. Claire did, I think. What does it matter?"

Ayden furrowed her brows and stared at the floor. "Because I very clearly saw in my dream the page in the book with Alison's name. And the page was on fire."

"So? That's how she died. Easy."

"That's not all," said Ayden. "I also saw the page with Claire's name. And that page was in a hole in the ground, being covered by dirt."

Winter tilted her head. "What are you getting at?"

"You told me the coven faked Claire's death. What did they do?"

"Claire said they cremated a goat or something, and passed the ashes off as hers."

"And do you think she was telling the truth?"

Winter sat forward. "I guess. She could have gotten the details wrong…it's no big deal. She was practically in a coma at the time, so she wouldn't have seen what happened herself."

Ayden stood and started pacing, one hand on her chin and the other hand holding her elbow. "In my dream…Alison's page burned and Claire's page buried. But according to Claire, Alison was buried and she was cremated. Right? It's backward. Something doesn't add up…I can feel it. If only we had that stupid book. "

Winter stood and pulled her phone out of her pocket. "Look. I took pictures, remember?"

Ayden stepped to her side as Winter navigated to her photos and pulled up the first picture.

"Look," Winter said.

Ayden almost yanked the phone from her hand. "That can't be right."

The first picture showed the listing for Alison. "Alison Young.

Buried in the Old Circle Cemetery." Winter flicked to the next picture. "Claire Parker. Cremated. Ashes spread at the banks of the Trenton River. See, it's just like Claire said."

Ayden shook her head, blinking. "Something isn't right here."

Winter shrugged. "Even if you're right about Alison, they could have taken her ashes and buried them instead of scattering them. It would amount to the same thing. And Claire was so out of it, she wouldn't have really known what they did. But it doesn't make sense for them to have buried Claire like you think...how could they fake that with her parents there? Maybe they took those goat ashes and buried them too. The coven could have done the same thing for both of them."

"No," said Ayden. "Look at the entry at the top. That person was cremated and ashes buried. It says so...they would have noted the difference."

"Maybe you got something wrong, then. Maybe your dream meant something else. You misinterpreted."

"I didn't misinterpret! If you don't believe me, fine. But my dream has something to do with this and I'm going to find out with or without you!"

"What do you suggest?"

Fire pulsed through Ayden's eyes. "I don't know. But first we have to find that cemetery."

42

Winter scrolled through the search screen on her phone. "There's no Old Circle Cemetery showing up."

"Call the courthouse," said Ayden.

Winter nodded and searched for the Trenton Hills courthouse. The first person who answered transferred her, and after several minutes of waiting someone finally picked up from the tax assessor's office. "Could you give me the address for the Old Circle Cemetery?" Winter asked. She moved the phone away from her head and looked at Ayden. "She's looking it up." A moment later, the lady came back and Winter hastily scribbled the address on a piece of paper. Winter ended the call and turned to Ayden. "Got it. The GPS in my car should be able to get us pretty close."

"Good. Let's go then. Get dressed."

"Wait, Ayden. What do you plan to do when we get there?"

Ayden shrugged. "I don't know. Alison has been killing people and we need to know once and for all if she's really dead."

"How?"

"No clue. Maybe I'll figure it out when we get there."

Winter ran upstairs and changed, then led the way to the garage. As Winter raised the garage door, Ayden started searching the room.

"Pop the trunk," she said.

"Why?"

Ayden ran to the corner of the garage and snatched up a shovel.

"Are you insane?" asked Winter. "We're not digging up a grave."

"Just in case," Ayden said. "Pop the trunk."

Winter opened the trunk and Ayden tossed in the shovel. Then they both got into the car and set off. As Winter drove toward the highway, Ayden punched in the address into the GPS. The navigation system led them to the outskirts of town and onto a gravel road.

"I think I'm remembering now," said Winter. "I knew I'd been to this cemetery before, I just couldn't remember how to get there."

"You have?"

"Yes."

"From your tone, I gather you don't want to talk about it?"

"No."

After driving down the gravel road for a while longer, the road widened enough to accommodate several parked cars just before a bridge. To the right a trail snaked into the forest.

"That's the way to the circle," said Winter. "I came with Claire for her induction ceremony. They didn't let me stay. The coven had a place where they did important ceremonies and stuff back there somewhere…a circle of willows, I think."

"Well, the cemetery is on the other side," said Ayden pointing to the left.

"I know," Winter said, turning.

A sign stood by the road on that side, with Old Circle Cemetery written on it. Beyond was a large cleared area, scattered with old trees and even older headstones. The further in from the road, the newer the headstones became.

"You remember this place?" Ayden asked.

Winter nodded. "Sort of. I had…other things on my mind."

"Well, this is it," said Ayden as she took off toward the cemetery.

Winter followed. "You know, we could still be arrested for this. They can track both of our phones. They'll know you're with me."

"Good. Maybe they'll show up and start listening for once. But we should probably hurry anyway."

As they passed by the oldest part of the cemetery, Winter couldn't help but glance at some of the names and dates...many of them more than a hundred years old. As they neared the newer section, they slowed down and started scanning the names more thoroughly. Winter went one direction while Ayden went another. Secretly, Winter thought Ayden was overreacting, but she had to admit seeing Alison's grave would answer a lot of questions she'd had since she first saw Alison after Shannon was murdered.

Winter neared the ridge and gazed out over the river lazily crawling back toward the bridge. She wondered how many ashes had been scattered off the ledge. She wondered if this is where the coven stood when pouring out Claire's fake cremation. Did Claire's parents stand here too? But she thought of those things mostly to avoid other memories...memories of sitting here herself on the ledge, waiting...

"Over here!" Ayden called.

Winter turned and jogged through the cemetery to Ayden's side. The headstone Ayden had found looked new, rough and unpolished, but still clean and unfaded.

"Alison Young," read Winter. "That's her." Winter continued, reading the poem written in smaller letters beneath Alison's name:

"Do not stand at my grave and weep. I am not there; I do not sleep.

"I am a thousand winds that blow. I am the diamond glints on snow.

"I am the sunlight on ripened grain. I am the gentle autumn rain.

"When you awaken in the morning's hush I am the swift uplifting rush

"Of quiet birds in circled flight. I am the soft stars that shine at night.

"Do not stand at my grave and cry; I am not there; I did not die.

"By Mary Frye," Winter finished.

"What do you think it means?" asked Ayden.

"It's a poem. It probably means nothing."

"But what about that last line? What about what Shannon said? She's not really dead. Do you think it's a clue?"

"Shannon said she's not really alive. She said to check the book. The book brought us to this grave. Someone must have tried to get rid of the book to stop me from finding out the truth...to make me think Alison was alive. But this answers the question."

"No, it doesn't. There's a grave, but do we really know if Alison is in it?"

"Shannon. The book. Claire. This grave existing. It all points to Alison being dead, Ayden."

"And the poem?" asked Ayden. "I did not die…"

Winter shook her head. "Just a poem. Something to give mourners hope. I'm sorry, Ayden. But you're wrong about this."

"So who has been killing all those people?"

"My guess is someone possessed, like the man in the silver and black mask, pretending to be Alison to get to me, freak me out, I don't know."

"And Claire?" asked Ayden. "Why attack Claire?"

Winter shrugged. "Why target anyone from my past? Everyone killed were all people who know the truth about Alison's death and could lead me to this place...to find the truth."

Ayden nodded. "I guess that makes sense. As long as you thought she was really alive then you were less likely to have the emotional capacity to confront her."

"That's what Shannon was trying to tell me."

Winter stared at the solitary headstone, tracing the carving of Alison's name with her eyes, rereading the poem, allowing vestiges of memory from the wreck to creep into her mind's eyes, careful not to drift into the backseat. The corners of her eyes stung and she took her eyes away from the stone.

"But what if Alison really is alive?" asked Ayden. "What if Shannon was wrong?"

Winter shook her head. "Let it go, Ayden. It's not possible. I was there when she died. There's no way she could have survived. And Claire said she was here when they buried her."

They stood in silence, staring at the marker. The wind rustled the leaves overhead, sending a warm breeze over Winter's bare arms. She tried to reach inside for some sort of premonition, some kind of small voice to help her understand what to do with this information. But she found nothing there. Just silence from God and the sound of the shame of her own heart.

"Something's not right," said Ayden. "I can feel it."

Ayden's words punched through Winter, hammering into her soul the cold reality she was no longer God's chosen one. The new life she had worked so hard to build was gone and her old life had been forsaken long ago. Winter had nothing left except to start over again…maybe with Claire.

"The answer is right in front of us, you know," said Ayden.

"What?"

"The real truth about Alison…whether she's really dead or not, whether the Acolyte is her or somebody else. Maybe even why you've been targeted the way you have. All those answers are right in front of us." Ayden knelt to the ground and dug her fingers into the earth. "Nice and soft."

"What are you doing? She's dead, Ayden. Trust me."

Ayden stood, a look of awe and confusion on her face. "Whoa…talk about déjà vu." She spun and sprinted back to the car.

"Ayden?" Winter watched after her, lost and helpless…and a little jealous. She knew exactly what Ayden was feeling, and it was something she hadn't experienced in a long time.

Ayden returned with the shovel in hand, grinning. "I knew I

would need this."

"You can't just dig up her grave," said Winter.

"Yes I can. I'm supposed to. I know it. The answers we need are here."

"You need…" Winter bit her lip and stepped back as Ayden attacked the ground with the point of the shovel.

"We've come this far," said Ayden as she tossed the first shovel-full of dirt. "I'm not leaving until I have ALL the answers. Either Alison is here or this grave is empty, and I intend to find out which."

After half an hour, Winter relented to help Ayden dig. The soft ground made digging easy, though the handle still rubbed her palms raw. But after only a couple of hours they were so deep Winter expected to find the body at any moment.

"You know Wiccans don't use caskets, right?" asked Winter as Ayden shoveled another pile of dirt out of the hole.

Ayden paused and wiped sweat from her forehead with the back of a grimy hand. "So…are you saying I'm going to find a body in the dirt?"

Winter shook her head. "After five years…you'll only find a skeleton. Just be careful."

Ayden nodded and slid the shovel in much more gently. Moments later, she paused and looked up.

"Something hard," Ayden said. She knelt and dug in the dirt with her fingers. "This is it. I found bone. You were right. Alison is here. What should I do?"

"I don't know. Clear as much dirt away as you can so we can see."

Ayden nodded and threw the shovel out, digging into the dirt with her fingers. Winter jumped down to help. Ayden managed to clear away a hip bone covered in tattered black rags.

"Look," she said.

Winter studied the exposed bone for a moment, not exactly sure if it meant anything. Then the images of the wreck returned and something clicked. "That's not right."

"What do you mean?"

"I'm pretty sure Alison's hip was crushed in the wreck."

Ayden shook her head. "Are you sure? Because this isn't broken."

Winter's heart pounded and she turned back to the area she was clearing...the area nearest the head. "Help me!" she said, surprised by the panic in her voice.

Ayden squeezed beside her and with all four hands they began to clear away the dirt over where the head should be, piling where the stomach should be.

"There's something metallic here," said Ayden.

With another brush of dirt, Winter uncovered the forehead...dirty bone with scraggly vestiges of hair of an indeterminable color and an unmistakable crack from one temple to the middle. "Uncover it all," said Winter.

Ayden moved to the facial area and began helping her. Winter moved to the neck and dug out the metallic something Ayden had found.

As Winter pulled the object out, Ayden leaned back. "Done."

Winter brushed the dirt off the object, a necklace of some sort, and held it gently in her hand. It was a jade pendant, wrapped with silver bands.

"Oh my God..." Despite the warm air, the rush of adrenaline, and the sweat making her clothes cling to her body, Winter went suddenly cold. Her heart pounded so hard her vision speckled. "It can't be..."

"What? What's wrong?" asked Ayden.

Winter looked at the partially uncovered skull, with its clear crack from forehead to temple, imagining flesh and hair color...all the pieces of the puzzle beginning to fall into place. "No!"

"What?"

"No, no, no, no, NO!" Winter gaped at the jade pendant. "NO!" She dropped it and scrambled out of the pit.

Ayden followed. "Winter! What's wrong?"

Standing on the side of the grave, looking down on the cracked skull...the jade pendant around the neck, lying gleaming on the dirt...the unbroken hip bone. Winter trembled, not sure she could speak, mind reeling at what she was seeing.

Ayden grabbed her by both shoulders and shook her until Winter looked into her eyes, blinking. "Tell me!"

Winter's jaw quivered as she opened her mouth to speak. Her trembling arm pointed into the hole. Her voice no more than a rippling whisper. "That's not Alison...it's Claire."

43

Four Years Ago

Winter sat on her bed in the darkness of her room watching the outline of Claire by the window.

Claire sat still, peering down to the street below, careful to hide mostly behind the curtains. "That's the third police car I've seen. And I swear a black SUV has driven by five times...the same one." She turned to Winter. "I have to go soon. They'll come back looking for me. I won't be able to hide a second time."

"But Michael hasn't called yet. It's not safe."

"It doesn't matter. I can't wait on him anymore."

"He's the one who's supposed to connect you to people who can help. You can't do this without him," said Winter.

"I don't care. I'm not going back home and I can't risk getting caught here."

"Maybe it won't be so bad."

"So bad?" Claire said loudly as she leaned toward her.

"Shh!"

"You have no idea what I go through. I'm not going back. One way or another."

"What do you mean, one way or another?"

Claire turned back to the window. She didn't answer and Winter didn't push her. After a silent minute Claire said, "There goes that SUV again."

"So what do you want to do?" Winter asked. "How are you supposed to get out of here?"

"We'll have to time it. And hope we don't get caught."

Winter bit her lip and held her breath.

Claire turned back to her. "You're coming, right?"

"I don't know, Claire."

"Come on! I need you. I can't do this alone."

"But my dad..."

"Will be happy to be rid of you. And you know it. You don't like the school and your only other friend just stabbed you in the back. It could be perfect...you and me living together. So what do you really have here worth staying for?"

Winter gazed into the darkest shadows of her room. "I don't know. My dad and I don't really get along, but I still don't want to upset him."

"So? After a couple of years, when you're eighteen, you can get back in touch with him and patch things up. You're always saying how he never wanted you anyway. You'd probably be doing him a favor. Just think about it...me and you...our own apartment, maybe working at the same place. Maybe a diner or something. No parents bothering us, no school to worry about. Wouldn't that be perfect?"

Winter wrapped her arms together and rubbed her elbows. "Yeah, maybe. I've got to think about it, okay?"

Claire grunted. "Look, we don't have time to wait for you to work this out. So don't decide right now. Just come with me tonight. Maybe you don't come with me all the way, maybe you come back home after I've left...make the decision later. Deal?"

Winter clenched her jaw and nodded. Before she could let her mind change, she jumped up and flipped on her lamp. "I need to take a few things."

Claire pulled the curtains closed. "I'll help. What do you need?"

Winter took a small duffel bag from her closet and directed Claire to stuff it with some things. While Claire worked at Winter's dresser, Winter went into her bathroom, pulled her hair back, put studs in all her piercings, and wrapped her locket around her neck. She also made sure the little emergency cellphone her dad had given her was secure in her pocket.

She came back out and found Claire had almost over packed the bag.

"Leave enough room for the snacks," Winter said. "We might get hungry later."

"Right. See? I'm glad you're coming. I didn't even think about food." Claire shoved the chips and cookies Winter had stashed under her bed into both of their bags.

"I don't think we'll be able to take any more," Claire said. "Turn out the light."

Winter flipped out the lamp and Claire opened the curtains again. After watching for a few minutes, Claire lifted the window open.

"Get the rope," Claire said.

Winter retrieved the rope and tied it around the foot of her bed again. Claire wrapped the loose end through the handles of both of their bags. Winter crawled to Claire's side on the floor by the window and they both peered out. A police car rolled by. After it passed, they eased the bags out of the window and lowered them to the ground.

"You don't think they'll see the rope, do you?" asked Winter.

"Let's hope not. At least not until we're gone." Claire grabbed the rope and put a leg through the window.

"Hurry," said Winter.

Claire smiled as she lowered herself.

Winter looked up and down the street, head stuck out of the window. To her horror, the black SUV rounded the corner.

"Claire! Hurry!" Winter whispered as loud as she dared while pointing down the street.

Claire glanced toward the approaching SUV, and almost fell. Her weight tugged on the rope with a jerk, and Winter's bed slid across the floor. Winter swore and jumped back to make sure the bed was stable. When she felt the rope go slack, she ran back to the window. The SUV was near now, just about to make the final turn, bringing it within headlight sight of the house. Claire frantically tugged at the end of the rope, trying to untie the bags. Finally, they came loose. As Winter yanked the rope back into the window, Claire grabbed both bags and leaped behind a shrub bush. The last of the rope came in and Winter collapsed onto the floor…just as the SUV lights panned over the house.

When the lights had passed, Winter pushed up and peeked out the window. As the SUV drove away, she thrust her head back out to find Claire standing beneath the window again.

"Come on!" said Claire.

Winter tossed the rope back down and slipped through the window, praying the bed would hold still, and eased down as quick as she dared.

On the ground, Claire handed her the duffel bag. "We'll go that way." Claire pointed down the street to a crossroad. "They haven't been turning that direction. If we can get there, it'll be easier."

"But what about the rope?" asked Winter.

"There's nothing we can do about it. Let's go."

44

Present Day

"What?" shouted Ayden. "You're not making any sense. Claire is in Cherithville!"

"I know!" said Winter. She put both hands to either side of her head.

"She's your new roommate! You're running away with her in two days!"

"How do you know about..." Winter shook her head. "Never mind. But it definitely isn't Alison, so it has to be her. Alison burned, Claire buried. That's what *you* said!"

"Are you sure about that? Winter...are you sure that's Claire?"

"I don't know, okay? It was your stupid dream! Let me think." Winter sank to the ground.

Ayden shook her head and sat beside her. She pointed to the grave. "Either that isn't Claire..." She pointed in the general direction of Cherithville. "...or that isn't Claire."

"But that is Claire," said Winter with a nod to the grave.

"How can you be sure?"

"Because Claire stole that necklace the day she died, a whole year after Alison was burned alive. Does that body look burned to you?"

"Then who is in your apartment?"

"Oh my God..." whispered Winter. "She's not really alive..." Winter jumped back to her feet. "Ayden! She's not really alive. Shannon wasn't talking about Alison, she was talking about Claire!"

"But...how?"

"Don't you see? The book was changed...and so was the headstone! Look at it! It can't be five years old...it's too new. All of this just to make me believe Claire was really alive!"

"That means..."

Winter nodded and pointed toward Cherithville. "Claire is the Acolyte. She has been this whole time! God...I'm such an idiot!"

"But the book?" asked Ayden. "Why did they try to get rid of it?"

Winter wagged her head, more pieces falling into place. "The book was a setup. That's why it wasn't burned. She wanted me to find it, to have a trail to follow, to lead me here. And the stone was changed to give me a dead end instead of the truth."

"But why?"

"To keep me chasing ghost stories. To keep me out of the way. Oh God! Kaci!" Winter grabbed Ayden's arm and took off running. "We have to go...now! We have to get back to Cherithville!"

"But we can't just leave the grave open!" Ayden shouted behind her.

"Stay and fill it in if you want."

Ayden grunted and when Winter jumped into the car, Ayden jumped in too. Winter spun the tires in the gravel, slinging the car around, and jetting down the road.

"We can't just fly straight to Cherithville," said Ayden. "It's too far away. We need to think this through."

Winter nodded. "Call Erickson. Tell him what we found."

Ayden pulled out her phone and stuck it to her ear. "No answer."

"What do you mean no answer?"

Ayden twisted in her seat and shouted. "It means he didn't frickin' answer!"

"Try Kaci."

Ayden did. "No answer."

"Peter?"

A moment later... "No answer."

Winter slammed her palms against the steering wheel.

"Summer?"

Ayden put the phone back to her ear. "Summer? Hey, it's Ayden..."

"Give me that," said Winter, reaching her hand toward Ayden. Ayden handed over the phone. "Summer! Is everything okay?"

"Yeah, why wouldn't it be?"

"Something's happening right now, and I need your help."

"What's going on?"

Winter bit her lip. "This is going to sound strange, but you have to trust me okay?"

"Okay."

"Claire isn't really Claire. She's something else...I don't know...something looking for Sandy."

"What? Claire? I don't understand..."

"I don't have time to explain right now. I need you to trust me and warn Sandy."

"You mean Ayden? Isn't she with you?"

"Not Ayden. Ayden's a decoy."

"What?"

"I've been guarding the real Sandy all year. Listen, I can't get a hold of anyone else, so I need your help. You have to warn her and get her to safety. Got it?"

"Sure, I guess."

"And I need you to stay with her and be my eyes and ears, to call me if anything...anything...happens. Can you do that?"

"Okay..."

"And when you find her, get in a car and drive. I don't care where you go, but don't stop until I find you or Agent Erickson does."

"Okay..."

"Have you got all that?"

"I have it, Winter."

"Repeat it to me, please."

Summer sighed on the other end. *"Warn Sandy that Claire is the one after her, drive off with her until you or Erickson get there, call you if anything happens."*

"Right. Summer, right now you're the most important person in the world."

"Fine...but who is it? I can't very well do this until you tell me who."

Winter clenched her teeth. "I trust you, Summer. I always have. You should have been told a long time ago." Winter paused and looked at Ayden. "It's Kaci."

"Kaci? Really? All this time?"

"All this time. You have to find her, Summer. Ayden and I are coming as quickly as we can. But right now, Kaci's life is in your hands. Do you know where she is?"

"Yeah...I do. I'll go right now."

"Thank you." Winter hung up and handed the phone back to Ayden.

"Now what?" asked Ayden.

"Now we have to split up. We'll swing through town and get your car. I don't know which way Summer and Kaci will run, but you have to find Erickson and then find them."

"What about you?"

"It's time I faced Claire."

After Winter dropped Ayden at her car, she floored the throttle and left town. As she flew down the highway, deftly passing cars, she had the strangest sensation time was wrong, that she barreled through a hole in the universe where time didn't matter and everything she passed somehow existed outside of the stream. She kept checking the clock on her dash, but it never changed. Occasionally she would catch wisps of something like smoke or haze in the peripheral of her vision, something ghost-like racing with her in an impossible way.

It was the first time she'd had any kind of spiritual sensation in a long while, yet she still had no idea what it meant or how to control it. If she tried too hard to watch the ghost-like mist, that infrared heat would quickly stare back at her. So Winter resigned herself to ignore it and hoped it would do what she wanted when the time came.

As she slowed to exit the highway onto Hoole Boulevard, a journey which should have taken about five hours, Winter glanced back down at the clock and saw only five minutes had passed and her gas gauge had barely moved. Yet Winter's internal clock screamed. Even though she knew it couldn't have been all five hours…maybe one, she couldn't get a handle on the actual time passed. It all blurred together in a shadow of reality spinning her head with jet-lag. She just hoped Summer and Kaci had gotten out already and that Claire was still at the apartment.

She pulled into the parking lot, watching the balcony door for movement and wondering if Claire was still inside. With any luck, Winter could take control of the situation before the fake Claire realized Winter had figured out the truth. Before climbing out of the car, Winter pulled the gun from the glove compartment where she had shoved it after Erickson had fired her. She didn't bother with the holster and just held the gun to her side as she got out and walked up the sidewalk to the stairs, head down and quickly, hoping none of the neighbors noticed.

Winter stepped through the unlocked door and closed it, twisting the lock…not that it would do any good, but it might slow Claire down if she tried to escape. A shuffling in the back told Winter that Claire was in another room. A moment later, Claire emerged, face paled and hair unbrushed.

"You're not supposed to be here yet," she snarled, stepping into the living area. Panicked mumbling followed Claire out of the other room.

Winter raised the gun. "Is that Kaci?"

"Don't worry," Claire said, her voice back to its normal friendliness. She took a slow step closer. "Kaci's fine. Why are you back so soon? Why are you pointing a gun at me?"

"Stop!" Winter shouted.

Claire paused, extending her hands out to the sides. "Come on, Winter. Let's talk about this. Something has obviously upset you." She took another step.

"I know you're not Claire…I dug up the grave. Claire's dead. So who are you?"

Claire's eyes glowed red. "I can be whomever you like." The face melted like thin plaster and reformed, becoming the half-charred face of Alison. "Maybe you're not asking the right question."

Winter trembled. The gun shook and wavered from the mark.

The thing now wearing Alison's face stepped closer. "Ask it!"

Winter opened her mouth, her voice a whisper. "What are you?"

Alison laughed. "I am the Acolyte. I am the Right Hand of Hell."

It twitched its head to one side and the gun flew from Winter's hand, slamming against the far wall. Winter yelped, and spun back to face Alison. Winter reached deep for the premonition or any other ability she might use, to leverage the power she always relied on in situations like this.

Nothing happened.

The thing laughed again and stepped within arm's reach of Winter. Winter flung out with her fist, but Alison simply flicked a hand at Winter. Winter's arms flew to the walls on either side of the door, pinned tight.

"So defiant. So much temper. Do you really think you have the power to defeat me?" It stepped just in front of Winter and leaned in close. "Perhaps another face might calm you." The skin melted and morphed into Winter's mom.

"Stop it!" cried Winter. "Just stop it!"

"Are you not having fun, sweetheart?" the cooing voice of her mom whispered in her ear.

Winter clenched her eyes, and tried to suppress the sudden swirl of heartache that rushed in to join the cold terror clawing against her chest.

Claire's voice returned. "Aww...you're not much fun when you're scared."

Winter chanced a peek back at Claire and saw her walking away. She yanked against the invisible bonds, but they wouldn't budge. "Let me go!"

Claire turned, eyes glowing like embers again. "I wanted to thank you, by the way. I knew once I removed you from being important you'd eventually confide in someone. And I knew the weak link was Summer. Well done on the scavenger hunt, by the way. I never imagined you'd actually dig up the grave."

"What did you do to Summer?" Winter shouted.

"Oh, nothing. She told me everything I needed to know of her own free will. Called me immediately after you called her. She'd been waiting all year for that."

"You're lying!"

Claire stepped closer again. "What would you know about truth? You've been lying your whole life. Tell me, Miss Prophetess...have you told your precious friends what you did?"

Winter shivered. When she opened her mouth, no sound came out.

"What was that?" Claire said with a grin as she leaned even closer. "I didn't hear you."

"S…stop…" Tears ran down Winter's face, dripping from her chin.

"I take it they don't know do they? Winter Maessen…the Queen of Deception. Is there anything real about you? Your appearance, your emotions, your actions…even your faith. Such convincing lies even you believe them now. Shall I tell your friends the truth? Shall I tell them who you really are? What you've really done? I can begin with Kaci right now."

"No! Please…"

"Do you not want them to know you're a killer?"

"N…no…I didn't…"

"Slow and methodical. Savoring every stroke of the knife."

"It was an accident!"

Claire laughed. "We both know it wasn't an accident."

"I had to…I had no choice…"

"You always have a choice. And that makes you a murderer!"

Winter screamed. "No! I didn't! Let me go!" She jerked against the invisible bonds and kicked at Claire.

"Oh…you think that's me holding you, do you?" She raised her arms. "Look again!"

The room filled with the same smoke she had seen in the room with Shannon. It clawed at her skin, sucking the life from her lungs. Winter could still see Claire as the smoke swirled around her, living, breathing, and bowing to her. Winter looked back at her arms, smoke wrapped around each wrist.

"Look closer!"

The smoke around Winter's wrist took shape, filling invisible molds and defining itself as bony fingers. Winter followed the solidification of the smoke up a monstrous arm, to a grotesque black body, a sinister smile with jagged teeth and black eyes set too deep into a leathery skull.

Winter shrieked. Every cell in her body wanted to run. Cold fear filled her bones. She thrashed against the demonic hold, flicking her head to the other arm and finding another monster pinning her other wrist down. She convulsed to get away as the smoke in the room settled like ash into dozens of sneering demons, some laughing at her from the floor, some crawling across the ceiling, and some pawing at Claire as if she were their god. Beneath the flesh on Claire's body glowed the image of another monster like the others, yet so different by virtue of its dominant controlling stare Winter couldn't help but be drawn into its hell-filled eyes.

The Acolyte smiled and walked through her subjects to Winter, opening and closing a pair of scissors at her side. Winter quaked and whimpered, unable to breathe, unable to escape.

"Beg," said the Acolyte. With a flick of its hand, Winter fell to the ground, a demon's grip shoving her face to the floor.

Winter loosened her jaw and parted her stale lips. "P...please..." she croaked.

"Again." The Acolyte knelt and leaned into her face.

Winter closed her eyes and turned her head away from its sulfur breath. "P...p...please..."

The Acolyte flexed the scissors beneath Winter's nose. "Say my name."

"Culsu."

"Goodbye, Winter."

Winter braced for the stroke of the scissors.

Instead a blast of wind tore at Winter's clothes, swirling around her, pulling her hair, and ripping against her face. It began as if the door to hell had opened to swallow Winter whole, but it morphed into a frigid gale. She clenched her teeth, clenched her fists, and clenched her body, waiting for the inevitable death blow.

Then in the space of a single heartbeat, Winter noted several things. The wind stopped. The grip on the back of her head vanished. But the cold air lingered, and dim light pressed through her eyelids. Winter heard sounds, soft chirping and singing of birds, the rustle of a gentle breeze through the trees.

She opened her eyes, seeing nothing but green, and stood. Winter spun around in a glade of tall grass and wildflowers. She scanned the horizon, finding no road, no civilization, and only an endless march of dark forests in every direction. The sun hung low in the western sky, setting, even though it had only been near noon just a moment ago.

"No…"

She spun around again, pulled out her cellphone, and found no signal.

"No!"

Then the panic grabbed her worse than before. She sank to the unrecognizable land and lifted her face to the foreign sky. Winter screamed a scream that echoed through the dark forests around her, exiled where no human could possibly have heard it.

45

All concept of time abandoned Winter as she knelt on the ground. What her senses registered as sunset, her internal clock told her was early afternoon. But neither could tell her how long she stayed on her knees weeping, as darkness crept in with the setting of the sun.

Everything was gone…her friends, her dad, her home, her entire life. What Claire…Alison…Culsu…no, the Acolyte - had done, broke her to the heart of her deepest insecurities. Isolated from everything that insulated her soul from pain, Winter realized just how much she hated being alone. She had spent so much energy since her mom became sick to push everyone away, but it was all an act to surround herself with people who could give her the attention she craved. Isolation was never the point…it was acceptance, it was love, it was the opposite of loneliness. Now, she had none of that…no acceptance, no love, and she finally understood what it meant to be completely alone.

It broke her heart. Worse yet, her insides writhed with the toxicity of her hypocrisy. What kind of friend could be so selfish as to force them to meet her needs at the expense of their own? What kind of daughter could be so disrespectful as to deny him the joy and pride of a having a loving child? What kind of Christian follows God with an attitude only concerned with worshiping self? This filthy mirror standing before her brought Winter face to face with the truth of her existence, the complexity of her misery, the depth of her fraud, and the reality of the lie she called a life. The Acolyte was right. Winter was the Queen of Deception, and after so many years she had actually succeeded in deceiving herself.

Now the truth was revealed.

So she wept…past the setting of the sun. She moaned…throughout the twilight. And her body trembled…deep into the darkness. A part of her wanted to cry out to God, but kneeling exposed beneath the twinkling stars, Winter knew just how inadequate she was and just how insignificant her prayers would be. What right did someone so disgraceful have to call upon the maker of the universe? How could God even love her after all of this? How could a perfect God have ever loved her in the first place? She had said similar words in the past, but for the first time she actually felt them. Whenever she inclined her face toward heaven in an effort to explain herself, that angry infrared light tore through her.

It was the raw despair and weight of the heavenly accusation that eventually made Winter fall upon her side into the tall grass. It was the vacuum of hopelessness that curled her knees up tight.

The cool night air set in and a fog crept over the countryside. Winter tried to still her sobs, to sleep, and hope beyond hope she might wake to find this all a dream. But sleep would not come, her own internal clock simply refusing to comply. So she sat up again and gazed out upon the moonlit countryside, silvery and ethereal, and after an unrecognizable amount of time spent allowing her emotions free rein within, suddenly rational thought began to engage again.

Winter thought about her location, about the position of the sun, and her internal clock refusing to sleep. Provided Claire (she could not think of it as anything else so long as it wore Claire's face and used Claire's voice) had not done something with time and had only transported Winter to a new location, she knew it was impossible she could still be in North America. Her best guess would be Europe, and this intrigued her. She stood and searched the horizon for signs of civilization. It might be too late for Kaci and her other friends, but perhaps she could at least return home for her dad. She checked her cellphone, just in case she could call, but it was already dead.

Finding no definitive evidence of a town, Winter took a deep breath, picked a random direction, and started walking, making the best of her insomnia. At first her pace was slow, needing to step high over the grass, but as she neared the tree line, the grass thinned and she could walk more comfortably. The darkness closed in tightly beneath the canopy of the trees and Winter struggled to maintain a straight path. Several times she found herself slapped in the face by low-hanging branches and brambles growing tightly against larger host trees. Still she pressed forward, hands outstretched, following the moonlight that ran before her like a path of silver. As the night deepened, so did the cold. Winter alternated rubbing the chill from her arms and blocking branches clawing for her face.

She trudged forward for hours. The moon passed overhead, providing a wider blanket of illumination to help her walk just a little faster. The night noises were strange to her here, the crickets somewhat different, the tree frogs singing with foreign voices. She tried not to think about what exotic larger wildlife might be watching, or hunting, her, but on occasion she heard big somethings crashing through the forest, stopping as they neared Winter, and then turning to another direction or disappearing without another sound.

Winter had no idea how long she had been walking as she pushed through a line of especially thick brush and found herself on the edge of a brook. The gurgling water was a welcome sight and she knelt, plunging her face full into the cold liquid and drinking deeply. As she sat back up, wiping the water from her face, weariness overtook her finally, and if the time was near her normal bedtime back home, then dawn might be approaching soon here. She lay down by the edge of the brook and closed her eyes, hoping some measure of rest would come.

A hoarse croak woke her up after what seemed like only a moment. She blinked against the early morning light and sighed with unrequited sleep. The croak erupted from next to her again, this time a little more squawky than the first time. Winter turned to the sound and saw a gleaming raven standing by the brook, looking at her with a tilted head. She blinked at it and the raven tilted its head the other direction.

"Shoo," Winter said.

The bird squawked again and flew away.

Winter cupped her hand and leaned back to the water for another drink. It occurred to her that if she followed the brook she might eventually find a road, a house, or maybe even a town somewhere downstream. At any rate, it was the best plan she had. It didn't matter how tired she was, she had to find some kind of civilization while it was still daylight.

Another squawk at her side, and she turned to find the raven back. It dipped its head to a small apple it had brought, then squawked and flew away again. Winter squished her eyebrows together and picked up the apple, turning it over in her hand.

She lifted her head after the raven, but it was already gone. "Thank you?" she said uncertainly to the quiet forest treetops.

Winter's stomach awoke and she washed off the apple. It wasn't much to eat, but it was enough to give her the strength she needed to begin her walk that day, despite the lingering fatigue.

It didn't take long for her to figure out walking along the bank of the brook wasn't the best idea, so she pushed back through the brambles and followed the brook from a little distance. There she found a clearer path through the trees, always moving in the same general direction as the brook. If she suspected she had strayed too far from the water, Winter turned aside until she found it again.

She traveled this way through the forest for several hours, until about mid-morning when the sun finally rose high enough over the horizon for her to see it peeking through the tree trunks. The weariness grew steadily, blurring her thoughts, and dragging her feet through the leaves. It was all she could do to continue plodding one foot in front of the next, desperate to find some signs of life.

Just before noon, she stumbled upon what she had been hoping for...a road. It was the merest dirt and gravel road, but it was something. A little warmth spread through her chest, and Winter allowed herself the smallest of smiles.

The canopy of the forest wrapped over the top of it, branches almost touching each other from either side with outstretched leafy fingers. Winter studied one direction for a long time, then she turned to study the other direction. Either would bring her to something, but one might be sooner rather than later. She sighed a shuddering exhausted sigh which morphed into a yawn, then turned to her left to begin the next leg of her journey.

As she stepped forward, she heard a raven's squawk from behind her. Pausing and glancing back, she saw what might have been the same bird that had brought her the apple, now flying in the other direction. Without a second thought, Winter followed.

Four Years Ago

Winter and Claire walked most of the early morning hours, dodging any vehicle that approached by ducking behind bushes and parked cars.

"Claire, you know we can't keep doing this in the daytime," said Winter.

"Don't worry, I've got a plan for that. We just need to get to my grandmother's house. Then we'll have our own car."

A sinking feeling plunged into Winter's stomach. "You're going to steal your own grandmother's car?"

"Just borrow it to get to Michael's. Come on." Claire ducked behind a parked truck and Winter followed. A police cruiser rolled past.

They continued walking and hiding until the horizon glowed and the dew glistened on the lawns they passed, covering the asphalt in a thin layer of reflectiveness.

"I'm starving," said Winter.

"Don't worry, I'm sure we can have some breakfast at Michael's.

We're almost there. Look." Claire pointed down the street, but Winter couldn't tell where she was pointing.

When Claire began to jog, Winter followed. They ran past the next couple of houses until Claire stopped in front of an older mid-century house, covered in blue paint. A fifteen-year-old sedan sat in the drive.

"My Gran has always kept a spare key under the wheel well in one of those little magnetic boxes. After she locked herself out of the car several times, my mom made sure she had one."

Claire knelt down by the driver's side front wheel and stuck her hand inside. Winter could hear her scratching around

"Got it," Claire said. She pulled out a black box and held it outstretched in her hand. After sliding it open, she took out the spare key and grinned. "Let's go!"

"Won't she report it stolen? Won't they be looking for this car?"

"Yeah, but we'll be at Michael's before then and we'll ditch it somewhere. Don't worry, she'll get it back safe."

Claire put the key in the lock and turned it. As Claire threw her stuff into the back and sat down behind the wheel, Winter ran to the other side and did the same.

The car rumbled loudly on the quiet street when Claire turned the ignition. Winter scrutinized the house for any signs of life while Claire backed out of the drive, pointed the vehicle down the street, and floored the gas.

Winter sighed as they turned the first corner. "We did it."

"Yup! Now it's only a short drive to Michael's apartment."

Winter leaned forward. "It's not getting any brighter. I think it might rain."

"Can't be helped," said Claire.

Minutes later, the clouds gave up their reserves in a torrent, forcing Claire to slow down significantly.

Winter twisted in her seat and peered behind them, but the rain obscured everything.

"Look on the bright side," said Claire, as the wipers squeaked, one torn and leaving an uneven streak on the glass. "They'll have trouble looking for us in this. Just relax."

"I suppose," said Winter, fingering the locket around her neck.

The car sputtered.

"No!" shouted Claire.

"What's wrong?"

The car sputtered again with a lurch.

"Gran!" Claire huffed and put one hand to her forehead. "She's out of gas."

"You didn't check that?"

"No! I didn't check it. Come on!" Claire pounded her hands against the wheel as the car lurched again.

"We'll just stop and get some," said Winter as she peered through the sheets of rain for a nearby gas station. But they were surrounded by a neighborhood of widespread houses.

The car sputtered, lurched, and slowed down. With the next sputter, the engine died. Claire swore and spun the key in the ignition again. The starter whined, but nothing happened. As the car rolled to a stop, Claire looked at Winter and then looked out at the storm.

"Now what?" asked Winter.

Claire shrugged. "We're not that far from Michael's. We'll just have to walk the rest of the way."

"Not in this?"

Claire lifted her chin and leaned toward Winter, a curled fist pressing against the center console between them. "Do we have a choice? We can't stay in the car, the police will find us for sure."

"Won't they see us in the rain? I mean...we won't be able to see them coming fast enough to hide. We'll be caught either way."

"Do you suggest something then?" Claire clenched her jaw and narrowed her eyes.

Winter glanced at the river of water running down the street, then up to the sides of the road. Empty lots full of trees lined the right side, but across the road the outlines of houses emerged beyond the gray sheets of water.

"I think we'll be better off going to one of these houses. We'll just tell them our car ran out of gas…they won't know any different. We can try to call Michael again and get him to pick us up."

Claire looked around at the houses and took a deep breath, sagging a little back into her seat. "Okay. I think you're right. We'll do that. But we need to hurry."

Claire twisted and reached to the back seat, grabbed her bag, and pulled it into her lap. Winter did the same, already shivering with the anticipation of the sudden wet cold they were about to plunge into.

"Okay…" said Claire, voice trembling. "Okay. It's like pulling off a bandage, right?"

Winter nodded. "On the count of three. One…Two…Three…" She grabbed the handle, flung the door wide, and jumped into the rain…and was instantly drenched. The water saturated her clothes and obscured her vision, chilling her as if she had jumped into a bucket of ice. Winter spun to Claire, who was standing hunched over with her arms out from her body, mouth open, and looking like she had been slapped. Winter ran around the front of the car.

"Come on!" Winter shouted against the relentless droning of the rain.

She grabbed Claire's hand and darted across the road. Since they were already soaked, Winter passed the nearest houses to find one a little away from the dead car. She didn't wait or give Claire time to argue as she ran past three houses. Winter turned up the sidewalk of the fourth house, a small two-story home painted white and green. Little statues decorated a waterlogged lawn, like miniature monoliths rising from a lake. Several wind chimes sang on the porch by the breeze of the storm.

As they ran up onto the porch, the sudden cessation of the pelting rain sucked Winter's clothes against her skin like plastic wrap. She wiped her even blacker dripping hair from her face and knocked on the door.

47

Present Day

Hours crept by. Winter shuffled along the dirt road with no idea how far she had traveled or how long it'd been since she came to this foreign land. Her best guess, based on the extent of her weariness, hunger, and the screaming of her internal clock, was that it should be nearing sunrise back home. Which meant, with the exception of her nap in the forest, she had been awake almost twenty-four hours.

There seemed to be no end to the road and no civilization in sight. The forest fell away and the land became a series of sharp rolling hills dotted with scattered trees. In the distance, dark clouds slid through the sky, sending gray sheets of rain onto rocky hills, and the sweet smell of freshness wafted through the air. At the top of a hill in the road, she could make out rectangular fields far away, but still no homes. Seeing the jagged terrain between the road and those fields, Winter decided to remain on the easier path, hoping something would eventually appear.

The relentless sun beat down upon Winter's head, even if the cooler air kept her chilled. She tried to rub warmth into her bare arms, but lack of sleep and food slowed her movements. She fought the urge to collapse and wait to be found, but never gave in. Maybe something was just over the next hill…

Shortly after noon, the immediate land to either side of the road flattened and two plowed fields took advantage of the change. Winter heaved a deep breath and tried to speed up, knowing these fields were the signs she had been looking for. Beyond the lengthy fields, a grove of trees stood inside an elbow in the road. As Winter neared the grove, she could make out some form of structure within the shade. A little closer, and Winter could clearly see a house.

She stretched her tired arms toward the home, still trudging forward and almost stumbling into the yard. "Help…" she croaked.

That one word brought with it the weight of the turmoil within again. It reminded her of the lies she lived and the friends she had betrayed. It mocked her for trying to be something she wasn't. It was the deepest, most desperate cry of her soul, and it came out not to the house, but to anyone or anything in the universe who might listen. Her knees nearly buckled as her chest shuddered and her heart lamented through a sudden outburst of tears.

The last few feet to the wooden steps of the house, she dragged her feet through the dirt with no energy or will left to lift them even an inch. By the time she climbed onto the porch and collapsed onto all fours, a young man watched from the door. His disheveled black hair stood out to one side and his unshaven face masked a dark complexion beneath.

Winter wiped the tears from her face, sitting back onto her ankles, and reached out to him. "Can you help me?"

The man's eyes widened and he stiffened. He slammed the door and ran back inside shouting.

Winter peered after him and tried to stand, suddenly afraid he might return with a gun. After so much time trudging through the forest and along the road, she probably looked scarier than usual.

Everyone's frightened of you when they first meet you, she heard Kaci say.

Winter turned and considered returning to the road.

The door opened and the man stood there again, this time with a dark-haired young woman at his side. The woman's eyes widened in much the same way as the man's had. Then a thin smile crossed her face.

"Don't make her stand on the porch, Alin. Bring her in." The woman took a step toward Winter and reached out to her. "It's okay. My name is Mrs. Popescu. Please come in." She took Winter's hand and led her inside, past her husband. "Please forgive Mr. Popescu's rudeness."

"I'm sorry," said Mr. Popescu from behind Winter with a laugh. "I just didn't really think she would come."

Mrs. Popescu looked over her shoulder at him. "That's your problem. Not enough faith. Of course she would come."

"It's a miracle, Sylvia. If I had the kind of faith you're talking about, would it still be a miracle? Let miracles be miracles."

Mrs. Popescu shook her head. "You're full of nothing but nonsense. If you don't have the faith, the miracle may not come."

"But if you know it is coming, it is not a miracle."

"Never mind him," Mrs. Popescu said to Winter. "You look like you could use a bite to eat."

Winter pressed her lips together and nodded.

Mrs. Popescu led Winter to a table and motioned for her to sit.

"You're going to feed her first?" asked Mr. Popescu. "I thought she came to help us?"

"She can't help us if she's dead!"

"What do you mean, *help you*?" Winter asked.

"Never mind that right now. You need to eat." Mrs. Popescu placed a platter of bread on the table and a glass container of a whitish liquid Winter took for milk. She poured Winter a glass and then cut her some bread.

"This should get your strength back up. Don't be in a rush. Let us help you first."

Winter took a long drink from the glass. The white liquid was indeed some kind of milk, but far sweeter and thicker than she was used to. "I don't understand…" said Winter as she lowered it.

"We don't have time for this…" said Mr. Popescu.

Mrs. Popescu shook her head. "Ignore him, eat."

Winter took a large bite from the bread, firm and hardy, almost bagel-like. As soon as the milk and bread hit her stomach, her body awoke to a deep hunger aching within her abdomen. She attacked the bread again, more animalistic than she intended, washing each over-sized bite down with a long drought of the sweet milk.

Mr. and Mrs. Popescu watched her eat, both of them grinning, and Winter slowed down enough to feel awkward. She paused between bites and looked around. "Where am I?"

"You mean you don't know?" asked Mrs. Popescu.

"How could she not know?" said Mr. Popescu. "She was walking down the road through our country."

"Please," said Winter. "I really don't know."

"You're in Giurgiu County, about twenty kilometers north of Giurgiu," said Mrs Popescu.

Winter shook her head. "Where's that?"

Mrs. Popescu furrowed her brow. "In South-Muntenia."

Winter looked back and forth from them both. "I'm sorry. I still don't know."

Mr. Popescu threw up his hands. "She can't be as lost as that!"

Winter bit her lip to keep from yelling back, and just concentrated on his wife. "Listen, I know it doesn't make sense, but I really have no idea where I am or why I'm here. It's a long story…I sort of just appeared here. Please, am I in England?"

They both laughed. Mrs. Popescu shook her head and said, "My dear, you're in Romania."

Winter stiffened. "But…but you're speaking English!"

"No," said Mrs. Popescu. "You're speaking Romanian."

48

Winter leaned back and shook her head. "I'm not speaking Romanian! I'm speaking Romanian? How is that possible?"

"I do not know how it is possible," said Mrs. Popescu. "Do you think you're speaking English?"

Winter nodded, almost afraid to speak again.

Mr. Popescu's mouth hung open. "Another miracle…"

"How did…" Winter rolled her tongue around her mouth, wondering if she could notice it doing things differently the next time she spoke. It felt normal enough. "How did you know I was coming? And what do you mean I can help you?"

Mrs. Popescu caught her husband's eye and nodded. As he stood and ran out of the room, Mrs. Popescu clenched her hands together and stared at the table.

"Our son is sick. We don't know what is wrong with him. We've taken him to doctors in Giurgiu and a specialist in Bucharest, but no one can help. We don't know what to do. They sent him home, because according to their tests there's nothing wrong with him. Most days he seems fine and then others he doesn't wake up. He fell asleep two days ago and we haven't been able to wake him. We think he's dying."

"And you believe I can help?"

Mr. Popescu returned and handed his wife a piece of paper.

"Before our son fell asleep," she said. "He drew this."

She slid the paper to Winter, a drawing of an angel, with drooped wings dragging along the ground. The angel wore all black and had a girl's face, sad, with tears running down her cheeks. Below the drawing were some strange words Winter couldn't read.

"What does this say?" she asked.

Mrs. Popescu grinned a sad grin. "You speak flawless Romanian, but you cannot read it?" She looked at the drawing. "It says, 'My angel will save me.'"

A knot formed in Winter's throat. "You think this is me?"

"When I saw you walking up to the house," said Mr. Popescu. "I knew it was you. You're the weeping dark angel. You've come to save our son."

Winter shook her head. "But I'm not an angel and I can't save your son. I'm sorry. But I'm not who you think I am."

Mrs. Popescu reached across the table and grabbed Winter's hand. "Maybe you are not a real angel, but you've been sent here to help us. I know it. In here." She stabbed a finger into her own chest.

A tear rolled down Winter's cheek and she jerked her hand away. "If you knew me, you wouldn't let me near your son."

Mr. Popescu jabbed his finger on the drawing. "But this is you. He knew you would save him. God gave him this vision."

Winter shook her head again. "No...I can't do what you want. Maybe once I could, but not now. I'm not that person anymore. It's all gone."

"Of course you can't," said Mrs. Popescu. "But God can. And he'll do it through you. That's why you are here. That's why he sent you."

"I can't..."

"Please." Mrs. Popescu leaned toward her, wide eyes watering and chin quivering. She took Winter's hand back and squeezed. "He's dying. At least just come see him. You can do that, can't you?"

"But I'm no one," Winter croaked. "I can't give you what you want."

"It is not your gift we hope for." Mrs. Popescu stood, still clinging to Winter's hand and tugging. "Come."

Winter closed her eyes and nodded.

They led Winter through the house to an open door near the end of a hall. Toys stood organized against the walls, some homemade and most very old. In the middle of the room sat an old bed, on which a child no more than eight lay beneath a thin blanket. His pale face barely looked alive. His chest rose the merest fraction with each slow breath.

Mr. and Mrs. Popescu went to one side of the bed and knelt, hands clasped together as if preparing to pray. Winter stood on the opposite side, looking down upon the dark-haired boy, and her heart broke. She covered her mouth as she knelt, not sure what to say or what to do.

Mrs. Popescu fell weeping against her husband and he wrapped his arms gently around her. Winter watched them, letting her heart break further with theirs, forgetting her own problems for a moment, and hoping God would spare some miracle for this family.

Winter looked back down at the boy and shook her head. "I'm not sure what you're expecting of me..."

"Please," said Mr. Popescu with strained control as he stroked his wife's hair.

Winter glanced up at them both and then back to the child. "What is his name?"

"Rica," he said.

Winter studied Rica's ghostly face, like the day she knelt at her mother's deathbed, powerless to stop it. She bit her lip and trembled, remembering when she broke into Kaci's surgery room and prayed over her. Maybe that's all it took. Just prayer. And faith.

"Maybe I can pray for him," Winter said. "If he is healed, it is not my doing, but God's. If God does this healing it is not for my sake, but for your own faith's sake."

Mr. Popescu nodded.

Mrs. Popescu wiped her face and sat up. "Isn't that how it should be?"

"Maybe." Winter paused as she continued to watch the boy. "Yes. But it seems I've forgotten that along the way." She looked back at the couple. "Please...leave me alone with him."

They nodded and left, pulling the door closed behind them.

Winter reached beneath the blanket and grabbed Rica's clammy hand. Just the thought of praying hollowed her, parading her own frailty before her like a mirror again. It was pointless to hide from God, pointless to not face him with what she had become, pointless to keep running from that infrared light which burned more than a desert sun.

She tilted her head back and cried out to the ceiling with all the anguish building inside her since she first found herself in the wilderness. But before where she wanted to hide from God, this time she let her heart speak directly to him, to face the consequences. As her heart poured out in wordless confession, she saw clearly how deeply the stain of her pride ran, how she had let herself take credit for God's power, how she had viewed herself as superior to her friends, how she used her past suffering as a crutch for pity and attention, and how the very persona she wore every day as armor was nothing more than a denial and a refusal to accept the way God created her to be.

With the confession of her own inferiority and inadequacy came the weight of God's judgment, that infrared light searing her from the inside out.

She laid her head on the bed, the spiritual pressure too much to withstand. "I'm sorry," she moaned, the only words she could muster from her mouth.

Minutes ticked by, as the sorrow crept into every shadow of her heart, every hiding place of her mind, and every reserve of pride tucked away, the perfection of God demanding total surrender. When nothing of her being had been left from the searching of God and everything that defined her had been laid bare for his inspection, the weight and burning changed into gentle warmth, the accusation to forgiveness, the judgment into acceptance. All the pride and lies in her heart melted away, and though a part of her mourned their passing, the greater part of her heart embraced the new freedom and cleanliness. Three years ago she had given her heart to God, but now he had everything.

She lifted her head and gazed down at Rica, stilling her tears and her breathing. "Even if you hold my wrongs against me, do not punish this boy. I don't know why this family expects anything from me, but I know only you can do what needs to be done. These people believe in you and are trusting you. Don't let them down. Not now." Winter stood, squeezing the boy's hand, and kissed him on the forehead. "I pray God makes you well, Rica."

Rica's eyes fluttered and opened. Color rushed back into his cheeks, overfilling them into a blush. He blinked at her until his pupils focused.

And then he smiled.

Winter gasped and covered her mouth with her free hand.

"Are you my angel?" he whispered.

Winter shook her head and smoothed his hair. "No, sweetie. I'm not an angel."

"Did God send you here to save me?"

Winter sat on the edge of the bed and caught him up in her arms, sobbing. "I think I was sent here for you to save me."

49

Four Years Ago

Winter and Claire waited dripping on the porch, listening to the relentless drone of the rain upon the world around them and the distant rumble of thunder. Winter knocked again, more vigorously this time, and wiped more water from her face.

Someone pulled back the lacy curtain in the window of the door. An elderly face peered at them for a moment and then the door opened. "Can I help you?" asked the old man.

"Our car ran out of gas," said Winter. "We wondered if maybe we could stay here on your porch out of the rain until someone can come get us."

The man looked at them a long time and nodded. "You can't go back in this weather. You can stay dry here, I don't mind."

"Thank you," said Winter. "I promise we won't be here long. Just long enough for our friend to come get us."

The man smiled. "You're welcome, young lady." He gently closed the door.

Winter found the nearest chair and sat. She wrapped her arms around herself to try and hold out the growing cold. "Keep trying Michael until he answers," she told Claire.

Claire nodded and pulled her cell phone from her pocket.

The door opened back up. An elder lady, slightly hunched over, came out carrying two large towels. "Dears, you must be freezing. Here, take these. Dry off a little and wrap them around you to keep warm. Would you like something to eat?"

Claire grabbed a towel with her free hand and widened her eyes at Winter, shaking her head.

"Um…no thanks," said Winter.

"Are you sure? It's no trouble." She handed Winter the other towel.

Winter's stomach rumbled. "Well, maybe something small."

The woman smiled. "I'll be back in a moment."

As soon as the door closed, Claire stepped closer to Winter. "What are you doing?"

"Trying to act normal, not suspicious like you. Maybe you should be nice to them too so they don't think something is wrong and call the police."

Claire gasped and jerked her head to watch the door. "Do you think they would?"

"Probably not. Besides, I'm hungry. It won't hurt to eat something. Sit down before a cop drives by."

Claire looked to the street and quickly moved to the seat next to Winter, putting the phone up to her ear again.

Winter ran the towel through her hair and patted down her body. Then she put the towel over herself like a blanket, hoping to keep a little more body heat in.

"There's still no answer," said Claire, lowering the phone. "I don't know what's going on."

"Keep trying. He's the best chance we have."

The old lady came back out with a tray in her hands. She set the tray down on a little table between their two chairs. Seeing the two glasses of juice and a plate of toast made Winter's stomach rumble louder.

"Thank you," said Winter. She picked up a piece of toast and shoved the corner in her mouth.

The lady grabbed another chair and pulled it close. "So what are two young girls like you doing driving around this early in the morning in this kind of weather?"

Claire glared at Winter, jutting out her jaw and face turning red.

Winter bit her lip. "We're supposed to be meeting a friend to go...shopping."

"Is that who you're trying to call?"

"Yes."

Claire turned her glare back to the road and Winter followed her gaze. A police car drove by. They watched it roll up the street. The brake lights gleamed through the pouring rain. The car stopped...next to the car they had left behind.

Winter and Claire stared at each other. Winter's heart pounded and the little hairs on her neck prickled.

Claire put the phone down. "He's still not answering." Her voice squeaked near the end.

"What are we going to do?" Winter whispered.

Claire shook her head, flicked her eyes back to the stopped patrol car, and then turned to the lady. "Do you mind if I use your restroom?"

The lady smiled. "Sure, dear. Just follow me."

Claire motioned for Winter to follow. The lady closed the door behind them both, and waved for Claire to follow her deeper into the house. Winter waited by the door, where she could still hear the outside sounds.

Old photographs of children and grandchildren filled the walls of the front room. A floral couch and several chairs made a square around a glass table. The faint smell of mothballs reminded Winter of the car they had stolen from Claire's Gran.

Winter looked down to her feet at the puddle she was leaving on the wood floor. She smeared it with one foot and then turned to peer behind the curtain covering the door window. The patrol car had not yet moved.

Winter heard scuffling, and a whimper. She jerked back around. "Claire?"

"Winter, help me!" Claire yelled.

Winter ran through the room and around the corner into the hall. The first door she came to was a door to the kitchen. Claire's back was to her and when Winter rushed in, Claire glanced over her shoulder.

"Find something to tie them with," Claire said.

Winter peered around and saw the old couple sitting in chairs. The woman was wide-eyed and trembling, the man red-faced and jaw clenched. Claire brandished a large pair of scissors at them.

"Hurry," said Claire.

"What are you doing?"

"We can't leave them to tell the police when they come to the door."

"Stop this, Claire! It isn't right! They were helping us!"

"I don't care! I won't go back…I have to get away!"

"Take our car," said the old man. "Just leave us alone. We won't tell anyone you were here."

"Liar!" roared Claire.

"Stop it!" said Winter. "Put the scissors down. You don't want to hurt them."

"Are you going to help me or not?" Claire sneered over her shoulder.

Winter shook her head and backed away. When she was back in the hall, she ran for the door and plunged back into the rain.

50

It was mid-afternoon when she finally woke up. Mr. and Mrs. Popescu had let her sleep in their bedroom, while they fed and fawned over little Rica. She found the bathroom without disturbing them and went in to take stock of just how horrible she looked. All in all, it wasn't that bad. She hadn't been wearing much makeup and the mascara that had run from her eyes had mostly been rubbed away. Her hair was a mess, but manageable enough with just her fingers. Her clothes rubbed grimy against her skin, or maybe her skin rubbed grimy against her clothes, but either way it didn't affect her appearance much. Winter tugged at a lock of hair and looked a long time at the golden-brown roots showing through…and for the first time her impulse wasn't disgust.

Winter searched the room until she found something to tie her hair back. She scrubbed her face with a cloth until it hurt, being careful not to snag her nose ring or eyebrow ring. Then she took off her shirt to rub the sweat away from her neck and chest, and to clean around her belly ring. Finally, when she had cleaned up as best she could without a full-blown shower and change of clothes, Winter went back into the kitchen where she found Mrs. Popescu at work at the stove.

She smiled at Winter. "Thank you, again."

"You know it wasn't me."

"I know."

Winter glanced around at the otherwise empty room. "Where are Mr. Popescu and Rica?"

"Alin is out at the barn, milking the goats. Rica is playing outside. I'm watching him from the window." She peered out and smiled, then returned to the stove, casting a smile to Winter. "Please, call us Sylvia and Alin. You are family to us now. We would have you stay as long as you need. Forever, if you wish."

"I can't," said Winter. "I'm sorry."

Sylvia nodded.

"My friends need me. I know there's nothing I can really do, but I can't just abandon them. Maybe God will help me, maybe not. But I have to try."

Sylvia nodded again. "How will you get home?"

"I don't know. I don't even know how I got here. I suppose I'll just do the best I can…you know, find a city, try to get on a plane or something."

"Will you stay the night?"

"I can't," said Winter. "I'm still on my home time, so I'm wide awake right now. I'll need to go soon…preferably before it gets dark."

"Then you must at least eat before you go. I will see you full. There should be enough fuel in our car to get you to Bucharest."

Winter shook her head, a flicker of premonition telling her not to accept. "I can't ask you to do that. I came here by walking and I need to leave the same way. Who knows, maybe then I'll get home the same way I arrived."

"By miracle?"

"I suppose you could call it that."

Sylvia smiled and looked back out the window. "You never told us your name, angel."

"It's Winter...like the season."

She turned to Winter and stepped closer. "We will pray for you, Winter, as you prayed for us, that you will return home to your friends. And we will never forget you nor what God did the day you came. And whatever happens, know you will always have a home with us."

Warmth spread through Winter's chest and she smiled. "Thank you."

A half-hour later, Alin and Rica were both back inside and Sylvia was preparing the table for dinner. Rica jumped on and hung all over Winter, as if she were his newest toy. Winter tried to play with him as best she could, but he kept running just out of her reach. Alin watched with a grin on his face.

The plate Sylvia placed in front of Winter had a strange fried sausage thing on it beside a bed of reddish-brown rice stuff and a pile of light green and red leafy mush. Winter tested the sausage thing with her fork, not sure what to do with it.

"I'm sorry, but what is this? It's nothing like my food from home."

Alin chuckled and Sylvia smiled.

"It's a special meal for you," said Sylvia. "Traditional Romanian cuisine. Pork schnitzel filled with ham and cheese, rice and potatoes, and stewed cabbage and tomatoes."

"Okay," said Winter. "Those things I recognize."

Alin clasped his hands together and bowed his head. As Sylvia followed, so did Winter. "Glory to the Father and the Son and the

Holy Spirit; both now and ever, and unto the ages of ages. Amen."

"Amen," Sylvia echoed.

"Good appetite," said Alin and they began to eat. Winter followed the lead of her hosts and cut into the schnitzel first.

She enjoyed the meal far more than she expected, though the cabbage and tomatoes remained questionable. She forked around with it, and even tasted it a little so as not to offend her hosts, but left it mostly uneaten. Rica ate as if he'd never eaten before, and asked for more before Winter had made it halfway through the rice and potatoes. After the main meal, when Winter couldn't eat any more, having had second helpings of both the schnitzel and the rice with potatoes, and having to repeatedly insist she couldn't eat more, Sylvia brought out a glazed apple cake and served Winter a giant piece.

When the meal finally ended, Winter looked out of the window. "How much daylight do you suppose is left?"

"The days are long here, this time of year," said Alin. "If you start soon, you'll have about three more hours of daylight."

"Then I should probably start," Winter said as she stood. "Thank you for your hospitality and the meal."

Alin and Sylvia stood with her. "We'll see you out," Sylvia said.

She led Winter to the door and Winter stood on the front porch gazing out upon the late evening landscape. She eyed both directions, following the road with her eyes as far as she could.

"If you wish to go to Bucharest," said Alin, "you should return the way you came." He pointed off to the right. "It is a long journey, especially by foot. This road will lead you to other roads, which will eventually take you where you want to go. It is difficult to explain to someone unfamiliar with this country. But perhaps you'll come across someone who can give you a ride." He pointed to the left. "That way is a much shorter journey to Giurgiu, but you'll not find the kind of airport you need to return home. If you do not rest and continue into the dark, you can walk there without stopping. Perhaps you'll find connecting transportation to get you to Bucharest. If so, it'll be the quickest."

Winter looked both directions, considering Alin's advice, and more determined than ever to try to get home. She smiled and turned to him. "Giurgiu it is."

"Are you sure you wouldn't want us to take you?" asked Sylvia, a concerned furrow on her brow.

"I'm sure. I came here by walking, and I'm supposed to leave the same way."

"Then let us give you water to take," said Sylvia.

Winter's premonition flickered again and she shook her head. "I'm sorry. I have to leave exactly as I arrived." Winter stepped forward and wrapped her arms around Sylvia. "Thank you for everything. I'll never forget you."

Sylvia squeezed her back, but didn't say anything. When Winter released, Sylvia held her at arm's length and kissed her on both cheeks. Alin was there immediately to hug and kiss her too.

Finally, Winter knelt and hugged Rica. "Have some fun for me, okay?" she said.

Rica smiled. "Will you come back to see me?"

"I don't know. Maybe one day."

Rica nodded vigorously and kissed her quickly on both cheeks.

"You come into our lives and leave so quickly, angel. It doesn't seem right. Know you're always welcome here," said Sylvia as Winter stood.

"Thank you." Winter said, descending the steps. She peeked back over her shoulder and smiled at the Romanian family that had loved on her unconditionally, and sighed that she could not stay longer.

Winter set her face to the road, walking with long strides and forcing herself not to look back a second time.

The count of fields increased. She passed several other farms, garnering curious looks from the locals who watched her. She tried not to make prolonged eye contact, but felt the pressure of their stares upon her back until she had sufficiently passed by. Winter thought she was making good time, easily surpassing the distance she had traveled the day before in a fraction of the time.

As night fell, she had still not reached anything resembling civilization. Anytime a crossroads presented itself, Winter continued straight, hoping Alin had not neglected to tell her of any necessary turns. The number of people she saw outside working the farms dwindled to nothing with the fading of the sunlight. In return, all of the houses now glowed at the windows as vigilant sentinels of their farms. Winter wondered why she never saw any vehicles along the road, but guessed these farmers saw little value in traveling the way Americans did.

The last luminescence of the sun clung to the western horizon like glow-in-the-dark paint. As the blueness of the sky dissolved into pure black, stars filled the sky as if the sun had taken a brush and splattered its paint onto the canvas. The moon again hung low on the eastern horizon, a giant marble of white light sending Winter's ethereal shadow chasing after the departed sun.

Beneath this mysterious luster Winter continued forward in confidence, able to see almost as clearly as she could beneath the sun as the full moon climbed ever higher into the sky. Somewhere in the distance a wolf greeted the moon, but Winter only gave its presence a passing thought. Far away, a man-made glow pushed back against the dark, an indication Winter neared her destination.

For miles, other than the chattering of nighttime insects and the occasional howling of a lonely wolf, only the sound of her own footsteps kept her company. But as she gazed upon the glow of Giurgiu, larger heavy footsteps joined just behind her on the road. The slow methodical gait sounded more horse-like than human, and when the animal sighed into the cool air, Winter's suspicion was confirmed. She slowed and began to turn to it.

"Do not turn around," said a deep, commanding voice.

Winter held her breath and stopped. She pivoted back to Giurgiu, holding her hands up. "Who are you?"

"One who has been watching. You must continue walking, you have a very long way to travel."

Winter started walking again, and so did the mystery rider behind her.

"What do you want? I have nothing, so you're wasting your time."

"I want nothing from you but your ear. I come as a messenger from God, to give you a warning, to give you advice, and to speed you along your way."

Winter nibbled at her lip and she couldn't control the tremble in her voice. "Listen, I know I've been screwing up lately, but I've made my peace with God about it. Things are going to be different...I promise. Please don't hurt me."

The man laughed, a deep rumbling like thunder. "Take my warning, Prophetess. You are going into a battle which you cannot fight and cannot win. The enemy has strengthened itself. If you face this enemy with the flesh, you will be destroyed."

Winter swallowed hard. "Then what am I supposed to do?"

"This is my advice. Do not fall into the trap laid for you again. Do not be tempted to rely upon your own strength. You cannot face the legions prepared against you, but the Warriors of the Lord can. An army is being prepared for you to command. They will fight this battle."

"What? Are you insane? Are you talking about an angel army? You can't be serious." She moved to glance over her shoulder.

"Do not turn around!"

Winter took a deep breath and kept moving forward. "You've got the wrong person. I can't command an angel army. There's no way..."

The rumbling laughter washed over her again and Winter clamped her mouth shut. "You humans are amusing to watch...always reaching for things not yours, but never claiming what is already given. You have been given this authority and this task, Prophetess. Claim it, but be warned not to reach for things not yours."

Winter could do nothing but nod, like a scolded child.

"And now, to speed you along your way."

The footsteps of the horse disappeared. Winter spun around and found nothing behind her. She took several deep, calming breaths, peering into the moonlit darkness, waiting for the movement of some shadow to give her a hint of the rider's departure. But she saw nothing.

The engine of a car revved along the road, coming from Giurgiu. Winter turned back to the sound and saw headlights not far away, emerging from behind a stand of trees in a bend of the road. Winter stepped to the road's edge and prepared to flag down the driver, hoping this was the speeding along the way the rider spoke of, that maybe this was a ride directly to Bucharest.

When the lights washed over her, she waved her arms frantically. When the car was only a few feet away, she shouted at them to stop. The car slowed and halted. Winter shielded her eyes against the blinding light, trying to see what kind of vehicle lay beyond. She saw the shadow of a door open and with it the interior dome light came on.

Winter thought she recognized the faces within. She held her breath, not daring to believe her own eyes. A spiky red-haired girl rushed toward her from the open door and shoved her in the shoulder.

"Where have you been?" Ayden shouted. "We've been looking all over for you!" Then Ayden embraced Winter, squeezing her tight. "Thank God you're still alive."

51

Four Years Ago

Winter ran through the pouring rain until her lungs gave out, thankful the cop didn't see her. She leaned against her legs, letting the water stream from her face and trying to catch her breath. The storm didn't show any signs of letting up and Winter hadn't seen any vehicles yet on the neighborhood street. She peered through the hazy downpour, searching for some form of shelter where she could call her dad and forget this day ever happened. But she found nothing nearby short of knocking on another door…and she certainly didn't want to do that again. So Winter crossed her arms and started walking.

Minutes later, she heard the slow slushing of a car behind her. She bit her lip, hoping it wasn't the police, and tried to act as normal as possible for a teenage girl walking through a storm. The car pulled along the curb on Winter's side of the street and slowed.

"Get in!" Claire yelled from the window.

Winter turned to Claire, who sat behind the wheel of an old brown sedan she didn't recognize. "No!" she yelled back, her voice swallowed by the pounding rain. "You stole their car?"

"Come on, Winter! I'm sorry. But…you just don't understand. I have to get to Michael's apartment."

"This is getting out of control. I want to go home!"

"Fine. Just come with me to Michael's and we'll get him to take you home, okay? Just get in the car…please…"

Winter chewed the inside of her cheek, then ran around the front of the car, through water over her ankles, and jumped into the passenger seat. Water pooled beneath her on the leather seats and saturated the beige carpet. Winter gathered her hair into a ponytail, leaned over the floorboard, and squeezed as much water out of it as she could.

"We have to hurry," Claire said. "They'll have called the police by now."

"What's that?" Winter asked, pointing to a jade necklace wrapped in silver bands hanging around Claire's neck.

"It was here in the car. I thought it was cool."

Winter curled her lip. "You're stealing that?"

"I just stole a car, you think they care about a stupid necklace?"

Winter crossed her arms and looked away, leaning back into the seat. "Something is seriously wrong with you, right now."

"Well, don't worry. You'll be rid of me soon enough."

"They were trying to help us," said Winter. "And you threatened them. You threatened them with a pair of scissors. Why would you even do that?"

Claire shrugged. "I don't know what came over me. I just saw the scissors on the counter and I snapped."

"But why? You're not like that. What's going on? What's wrong?"

"You don't understand…"

"I'm trying to. But I'm not going to put up with that anymore. Do *you* understand?"

Claire sighed. "I know, I know. I'm sorry, okay? I just…I just have to get away so bad, you know? I'm not going to let anything stand in the way."

"And what if I'm in the way? You going to try and kill me too?"

"I didn't try to kill them! I was never going to kill them...it wasn't like that."

Winter clenched her teeth. "You didn't answer my question."

"Do you think I would hurt you? Really?"

"I don't know. What about when you tried to stab Chad? You hit me instead, remember? How do I really know you won't turn on me?"

Claire sagged a little in the seat. "I won't. I'm sorry. I promise...I won't hurt anyone else, ever again."

"Promise?"

"Yeah. No one else will be hurt on account of me...ever again."

Winter nodded and looked back out the window, the windshield wipers flapping to keep up with the rain. The street lights glimmered like kaleidoscopes. The cold water enticed gooseflesh onto her arms and legs.

"How much further to Michael's?"

"We're almost there," said Claire. "We'll drive by to make sure everything is okay and then ditch the car somewhere away from the apartment."

Winter tried to keep the pounding of her heart at bay as she watched the neighborhood pass by, anticipating police cars at every passing street. She recognized some of the buildings and knew they were getting close. Winter peered into the distance as best she could, hoping no police waited for them, but she could only make out the gate leading into Michael's apartment complex on the left. They wouldn't be able to see in until they were much closer.

"What do you think?" asked Winter.

Claire shrugged. "I don't know."

Claire slowed down as they came nearer to the apartments and both of them looked out to the side, through the fencing, and held their breath as they neared the place where they would clearly see

Michael's apartment. The corner of the building nearest the fence, the building which was only two away from Michael's in the same row, crept near. Claire nearly stopped the car just before the corner, then allowed the car to inch forward until they could see around.

Two police cars sat in front of Michael's apartment, spinning lights sending red and blue through the prism of rain.

Claire cursed and put the car into reverse. When they were far enough back that the police wouldn't see them, she did a U-turn and then turned onto the next cross street.

"What do we do now?" asked Winter.

"Shut up, I'm thinking."

"Without Michael you can't get away. They're looking for this car already…they know we're coming here. Claire, they're going to find us!"

"Shut up!"

Just then, another police car rounded a bend in the road, heading straight toward them.

52

Present Day

Ayden grabbed Winter's arm and tugged her to the car. "Come on, we don't have any time to waste."

"Is this your car? But how did you get here?" Winter asked. "I don't understand."

"I don't know what you're talking about or if they did something to you again, but we have to get back to Cherithville right now."

As Ayden led Winter to the front passenger side. Graham got out, gave her a smile and squeezed her hand. "Glad you're okay," he said.

As Graham opened the back door, leaving the front for Winter, Winter noticed movement in the backseat, making room for Graham.

"Who else is with you?" Winter asked over the top of the car.

Ayden firmed her lips. "Don't freak out, okay?"

"Don't freak out...what are you..." Winter leaned into the car and found Summer sitting in the back, wide-eyed, red-faced, and shrinking away from her into Davis's arms.

"You!" Winter shouted.

"I said don't freak out!"

"She can explain," said Graham as he sat beside Summer.

Winter flicked her eyes to Davis holding tight to Summer's hand and looking ready to defend her against anything.

Winter huffed. "Fine." She flopped into the seat as Ayden got back behind the wheel and floored the gas.

"First things first," said Ayden. "Where have you been?"

"You should know. You just found me."

"That doesn't tell me anything. Do you not know where you are? We're about five miles outside of Cherithville. Only God knows how we found you."

Winter scrunched up her forehead. "You mean I'm not in Romania?"

"Romania?" Ayden glanced at her with her jaw open. The three in the back started mumbling.

"Yeah…isn't that where we are? I was just there."

Ayden shook her head. "I don't know if you were really there or not…"

"I was! I swear…I wouldn't make something like that up."

"Then it doesn't matter. You're back now, we've found you, and now we've got to find Kaci."

Winter looked over her shoulder into the darkness of the back seat. "I want to know everything, Summer. You've been lying to me all year. What's going on?"

Summer sobbed in the shadows. Winter turned back to the front and took a deep breath to calm her anger.

"I'll explain," said Graham.

"Yeah," snapped Winter. "While we're at it, who the freak are you really? I'm guessing you're not Peter's cousin and you're not here by accident."

"I really am Peter's cousin and my name's really Graham. But you're right, I'm not here by accident. I have a master's degree in criminal justice and I own a private security firm upstate."

"You own a private security firm? But aren't you our age?"

"I'm thirty. I'm older than I look."

"So what are you doing here?" Winter asked.

"Last spring, Peter called with a problem. He needed my help." Graham paused for a moment. "Summer had confided in Peter. She had been threatened. Someone connected with Xaphan threatened to kill her family if she didn't turn over the real Sandy."

"What?" Winter spun in the seat. "Summer, is this true?"

Summer buried her face in Davis's shoulder.

"Why didn't you tell me?"

"She couldn't," said Graham. "That was part of the threat. If they thought she had in any way let someone know, then they would have killed them."

"Is that how they found Ayden beneath the stage?"

"Yes," said Graham. "When Summer heard what was going to happen, she went to Peter and Peter called me. Peter believed you could protect everyone, Winter, so he told Summer to do what they said. She didn't want to go through with it, but Peter knew between you, me, and the FBI, Ayden could be recovered quickly."

"Thanks for that, by the way," snapped Ayden. "Did you know I was shot?"

"We both were," grunted Winter.

"I know everything didn't work exactly like we planned…" said Graham.

"Didn't work?" Winter twisted more in her seat so she could watch them comfortably. "It was dumb and stupid and idiotic and dangerous, and perhaps the worst plan you could have made. You used Ayden as bait because you thought I could get her back? What were you and Peter thinking?"

"We were trying to save Summer's family at the same time. At least Peter was right about you. You saved everyone, even though our plan failed."

"It wasn't me. I want to make that very clear from here on out…I don't do any of it, so stop giving me the credit."

Everyone was silent for a moment.

"You know," said Graham, "that makes things hard to explain."

"I don't care. God uses me, that's all there is to it. I don't do it, he does."

"Well…Peter was right about…God using you."

Winter clenched her teeth. "That was last year. What about now? Summer?"

"It didn't stop," said Davis. "As soon as they figured out Ayden wasn't the right one, they came back to Summer and pressured her to find out the real name. That's why she pushed all of us away. She tried to distance herself so we wouldn't trust her. She was trying to protect us." Davis squeezed Summer against him and Summer chanced a look at Winter.

"When you called Summer," said Graham, "she called Peter immediately and Peter called me. He already knew about Kaci, she told him after the engagement, but now that Summer knew, if she didn't tell them they'd kill her and her family. Peter called the FBI. They decided to let Summer tell them the truth while the FBI set up an ambush around Kaci. But none of us had any clue Claire was the Acolyte. The ambush was destroyed before it even started."

"By the time I got back to warn them," said Ayden, "Claire, Kaci, Peter, Agent Erickson, and you were gone. All the other agents involved in the ambush were dead."

"It's my fault," moaned Summer.

"We didn't know what to do," said Davis. "But Ayden knew."

"Of course she did," said Winter.

"I somehow knew I needed to find you, that you were missing for a different reason than the rest. I found Summer and Davis right after Peter vanished, and Summer contacted Graham who was already out looking for Peter. I had a hunch how to find you, so we all loaded up in my car…"

"…and that's how we found you walking on the road," said

Graham.

"Now," said Ayden. "That's our story. Your turn. Romania? Are you kidding me?"

Winter sighed and took a deep breath, then launched into everything that had happened to her over the past day.

By the time Winter finished telling her story, they had arrived at the outskirts of Cherithville.

"Where do you want to start?" asked Ayden.

"My apartment," said Winter. "That's where Claire and I met. I heard sounds coming from the back after Claire came out. I think she had Kaci in there. There might be a clue about where to go next."

"What about the rest of us?" asked Graham. "We can do more if we spread out."

"Let's see what we find at the apartment first. Then we'll have a better idea of what to do."

Back at the apartment, Ayden parked her car right beside Winter's unmoved BMW. Lights were still on in the apartment, but after a few seconds of watching, they saw no movement.

Winter opened the car door and put one foot out. "Everyone, stay here until I signal you from the balcony, okay?"

"I'm coming with you," said Ayden.

"No. If anything happens to me, you have to get them out of here."

Ayden narrowed her eyes, but nodded.

As Winter walked the short sidewalk to the stairs, she missed the constant pressure of the ankle holster, wishing she could pull out her gun. But as the thought of having a gun crossed her mind, it was almost immediately dismissed. Whatever she found in that apartment, Winter knew God could take care of it…not her. Maybe there would be a time and a place for guns, but it was not now.

She reached the second-floor landing and stretched her hand slowly for the door handle. She gave it a test twist and found it unlocked. As she eased open the door, Winter tensed herself, ready for anything that might jump at her.

The living room was empty. Winter left the door open and rolled her feet across the carpet until she could peer around into the kitchen. Also empty. She set her eyes on the two bedroom doors, easing toward them, straining her ears for any minute sound. She gently opened Kaci's room first, then her own. Nothing.

Winter ran back into the living room and threw open the curtains of the balcony. She waved at the others in the car and then went back to Kaci's room for a closer inspection.

Cut bits of rope and duct tape littered the floor at the foot of the bed along with most of the bedding, with small pieces of tape still attached to the posts. Drops of blood speckled the carpet and sheets.

Winter knelt at the foot of the bed, reaching out to a spot of blood, hoping for some kind of vision or help to find Kaci. Her finger connected with the blood, but nothing happened.

"What is it?" asked Ayden from behind her.

Winter glanced up as the four others crowded into the room. "Kaci was here. She must have been tied up when I came home, here at the foot of the bed. There's not much blood, so she wasn't seriously injured here. I just pray she's still okay."

"What's that?" Davis pointed closer to the wall on Winter's far side.

A syringe lay discarded by the wall, plunger fully compressed.

Winter reached out for it.

"Don't touch it," said Graham. "There may be prints."

"Right," said Winter. "I need to try to get in touch with Erickson."

"We've tried," said Graham.

"I don't care. I haven't." Winter fished out her phone and swore under her breath. "It's dead. I forgot." She handed it to Summer. "My charger should be in my room, will you go plug it in please?"

Summer nodded, took the phone, and crossed the hall.

"You can use mine," said Graham. "I have his number." He handed Winter his phone.

As the phone rang against Winter's ear, something started beeping in the other room.

"Um, guys?" called Summer.

Davis immediately ran across the hall.

"Any answer?" asked Graham.

Winter shook her head. "I'm going to let it ring a little longer. Maybe he'll get the picture." Winter paused and peered through the open doors into her own room. "What is that beeping?"

"Um," said Davis. "You might want to come in here."

Keeping the phone pressed against her head, she walked across the hall. Davis pointed to the nightstand where a smartphone sat beeping. Winter stepped closer to it to read the display. It showed a phone number she didn't recognize.

The beeping stopped. In Winter's ear, Agent Erickson's phone switched to voice mail. Winter hung up.

"Whose phone is that?" asked Winter.

Graham stepped closer to inspect it as Winter redialed Agent Erickson. The phone began to beep again. Winter's arm sagged and her blood ran cold as she realized what she was looking at.

"That's my number…" whispered Graham, with wide eyes.

Winter hung up and the beeping stopped.

Summer covered her mouth with both hands.

Graham gingerly picked up Erickson's phone by the edges, turning it over in his hand. "There's a note on the back of it. Winter…you'll want to read this." He tugged the sticky note off and passed it to her.

Call me. Claire.

54

Four Years Ago

"Just stay calm," said Winter as they watched the police cruiser roll toward them on the street. "Don't slow down or do anything."

Claire nodded and kept the car at a steady pace. Winter held her breath as they passed by the car, but the officer didn't seem to notice them. Claire flicked her eyes to the rear-view mirror and Winter spun in the seat to try to watch through the rain-blurred back windshield.

"Turn at the next street," said Winter.

"Right."

Winter felt the car slow and begin turning.

Suddenly, the police car's brake lights came on, illuminating the back windshield in fractured red streaks. The top light began to flash. The car began to turn.

"Go!" shouted Winter as she dropped back into her seat.

Claire floored the gas, and for the next moment they were alone on the street.

"Take the next one too…and the next," said Winter. She glanced back over her shoulder hoping the officer wouldn't turn onto their street before Claire had a chance to make the next turn. Claire turned, and if he saw them Winter didn't know. The next street Claire turned again.

"We can't keep this up, Winter. We're going to have to ditch the car."

"See if you can find someplace we can hide."

Claire turned again onto another street. "What about there?"

Winter peered forward to a grove of trees just ahead. To either side of the grove were houses. Winter looked behind them again…still no sign of the officer.

"Stop here. If we stop too close then they'll know we went into the trees," said Winter.

"But if we stop now we may not make it there on foot before they show up, and they'll see us anyway."

Winter chewed her lip. "We'll have to chance it."

Claire slammed the brakes and the car sloshed to the side of the road. With one look at each other, they grabbed their bags and plunged back into the rain. It wasn't far to the trees, but it felt like miles. Winter cast over her shoulder repeatedly, terrified the police car would come screaming down the street and find them. It never came. Still Winter mustered as much speed as possible as she splashed through inches of running water near the curb. Claire was just ahead and broke through the tree line first. Winter heard her stifled scream, but it was too late to stop her own momentum as she followed in Claire's wake, slipping on muddy leaf-covered ground, crashing onto her back, and sliding down a sloppy rut created by Claire all the way down to a concrete drainage slew. At the bottom she slammed feet first into Claire, almost shoving Claire into the raging urban river.

"Are you okay?" Winter asked. She tried to wipe the hair from her face and managed to smear mud across her forehead. With it came the putrid stench of sewage.

Mud plastered Claire's hair to her face, wrapping beneath her open jaw. "Yeah. But they'll find us here for sure. We need to cross."

Winter studied both directions and couldn't make any sense of where they were. She nodded. "Okay, but not here. Come on."

It took Winter a couple of tries to get to her feet, then she was able to help Claire stand. The edge of the concrete riverbed offered the best traction as they ran along it, careful not to step too high up the muddy banks or into the water. Winter's best guess told her they were steadily running further away from Michael's apartment and the searching authorities. The drainage river ran straight, with occasional steep descents, forcing them to slow down and pick their way carefully so they wouldn't fall again. After following it for what felt like half an hour, Winter found a place where the drainage was wider than normal, hoping it was also shallower than normal.

She turned back to Claire and pointed. Claire nodded and jumped into the water first. Winter followed right behind. The first step went to Winter's knees, but as they walked it became increasingly deeper, passing mid-thigh near the center of the trench. The stench stung in her nostrils. Winter had to walk slow, with her legs spread far apart and arms to her sides, to keep from being swept away in the current, and to keep her bag from getting even more wet. Claire climbed out on the far side and extended her hand to help Winter.

"Come on," said Claire, pointing up. "We can't stay in this ditch."

Winter nodded and tried to follow Claire up. Grasping undergrowth and clawing directly into the mud, they eventually overcame the slick bank to emerge at the top. There they found an old run-down house, with cracked windows and a junked car rotting to one side. Claire started toward the side of the house and Winter followed, and they came out onto a street full of old houses, trashy lawns, and cheap vehicles.

"Where are we?" asked Winter, reaching into the current of running rainwater on the street and trying to wash some of the mud from her face and hands.

Claire shook her head and did the same. "Not exactly a part of town we want to hang out in, I promise. We should get out of here."

Claire studied the houses for several seconds and then started walking the shorter distance to the end of that street. What lay beyond the corner, Winter didn't know. She just hoped it was a better neighborhood.

As they walked, they passed a house with a middle-aged man sitting on the porch, his hair long and mostly gray, and his face gaunt and wrinkled. He smiled at them with a toothless smile and crooked his finger for them to come.

"Faster, Claire," said Winter.

Winter started jogging and passed Claire.

The rain finally tapered away, leaving dusk in its wake, and bringing a chill breeze. Winter studied the still-cloudy sky, rapidly fading away into the shadows of night.

"Claire, what are we going to do when it gets dark?"

"What do you mean?"

"I mean…it's not raining anymore and this place gives me the creeps."

As if to accentuate her words, a man walked around the corner of a house as if on an errand, and then stopped to stare at them.

Winter chewed her lip and moved her bag to the other shoulder. "And I don't know how much longer I can keep walking. We've been doing this all day."

"Just a little longer," said Claire.

As they continued, the old houses of the neighborhood became old business buildings, now transformed into seedy places rapidly filling with people seeking to get out after being stuck inside all day. Bars, adult novelty stores, loan shops, tobacco stores, and a hotel advertising hourly rates with several scantily clad women lurking about in the parking lot. As they passed by the hotel one of the women called out to them. Winter forced herself not to look again.

A police car rolled toward them down the street. Winter glanced over her shoulder and saw all the prostitutes had disappeared. Claire ducked into an alley and tugged Winter in. They hid behind a dumpster, peering between the dumpster and the grimy block wall, watching for the cruiser to pass by. When it did, Claire and Winter leaned their backs to the dumpster and sagged to the ground.

"I'm so tired," said Winter, "and cold."

Claire sighed. "Me too."

"I want to go home."

Claire said nothing.

55

Present Day

Winter spun to Summer. "Where's my phone?"

Summer handed the phone to her, still clutched in her hand.

Winter rushed to her nightstand, where Erickson's phone had lain, and fished around until she found her charger end. She plugged in the phone and tried to power it on. Nothing happened.

"Come on...come on..."

"Give it a minute," said Davis.

Winter sighed and watched the phone for signs of life. It seemed to take forever, but eventually the phone screen lit up and the startup sounds chimed through the room. Winter bit her lip, bouncing her legs. When the main screen showed up, she immediately started pressing buttons, hoping to speed up the process. The phone was initially slow to respond, but she managed to get into the contacts and find Claire's number.

The phone rang only once before Claire answered. *"Hello, Winter. I'm surprised to hear from you...didn't expect you to get my note anytime soon. How did you get back so quickly?"*

"Where's Kaci?"

"Calm down, we'll get to that."

"If you hurt her…"

Claire laughed. *"Do you think I want to hurt her? I'm trying to keep her safe…and compliant…until he comes. She's to be his bride. Although, technically, they've already consummated the marriage, though he didn't realize it at the time."*

"Leave her alone!" Winter shouted.

"Winter," Graham whispered. "You need to find out about Peter and where they are."

Winter bit her lip and nodded. "Where's Peter?"

"He's here. He's a gift for my master…the would-be-suitor of his bride. His blood will paint the marriage altar."

A swell of boldness, something she hadn't felt in a long time, tickled in the back of her mind, giving her just enough knowledge to get what she needed. "What about me, huh? Am I not a good enough gift?"

"You are not required."

"But I'm back. Wouldn't you like to know how? I'll find you and God will stop you."

"Your god can't stop me."

"Wanna bet? That's what Xaphan said. God has stopped your master plenty of times through me, and you know it. Without me on the altar, you've failed."

Silence on the other end of the line. Winter strained her ears, wondering if Claire had hung up. What she heard was a long throaty whistle. A train whistle.

Winter smiled. "Now I know where you are. I'm coming, Claire."

"I'll be waiting." Claire hung up.

Winter put her phone back on the nightstand and turned to the others. "A train whistle. That's all I heard. Think…where are they?"

"A train station?" asked Summer.

Winter shook her head. "Too public…but something like a train station. Something with shelter, with walls and doors, to keep Kaci and Peter from escaping. Something away from the public…abandoned."

Graham's eyes widened. He reached out and started snapping his fingers. "Uh…um…there's this abandoned train yard, north of town. Lots of old boxcars on track spurs, and several old warehouse buildings."

"But it's abandoned, right?" said Davis. "No active trains. Winter heard a whistle."

"The yard is abandoned, but the two primary tracks running by it are still active."

"Is that the only place?" Winter asked.

Graham stared at the floor a moment and then nodded. "Yeah, I think so. It would be the perfect place."

Winter sat on the edge of her bed. "Okay. Let me think. We need a plan."

"Let's just go," said Ayden. "We go in there and get them back. What's the problem?"

"No," said Winter. "We need to be wiser than that."

"Wise?" said Davis. "Strange word coming from you."

"Shut up so I can think." She propped her feet on the bed rail, put her elbows on her knees and her head in her hands. "It's been over twenty-four hours, but Xaphan's not here yet. He could have been a thousand miles away, knowing the FBI were hot this year. But he could arrive any minute, so we need to hurry. Okay…so first, Summer, you can't be involved."

"But I want to help! You can't just leave me behind. This is all my fault, and I want to help put things right."

"I'm sorry, but it's not safe, even now," Winter said. "If they find out you told your secret, they still might come after your family. No…you have to be our safety net. You'll stay here with my phone and track all of us." She turned to Davis. "Take all our phones. Make sure they all have one of those tracking apps and that the GPS is turned on. Summer, Davis will take your phone…they wouldn't think it suspicious if he had it. I'll take Davis's phone, and Summer will keep mine here. Graham and Ayden will swap phones. Ayden and I both have phones connected with the FBI tracking system, so if Agent Erickson is compromised then Claire might track us through our phones. We don't want them to know we're coming. I'll write down who has whose phone for Summer. Everyone send periodic texts to my phone here with Summer and check-in. Okay?"

Summer crossed her arms and nodded. Davis extended his hand to everyone and collected phones. He sat on the edge of the bed and began to work.

"What about your car?" Ayden asked.

"Right. It can be tracked too. I'll need to swap with someone."

"You can use mine," said Davis. "We'll ride with you back into campus and trade."

"Perfect." Winter turned her attention to Graham. "We need the FBI. They have far more resources than we do. I don't know what happened to Agent Erickson and Agent Golbeck, but if they're missing then we shouldn't be the only ones looking for them. You and Davis will locate them if possible. If not, find the FBI search team. Bring them up to speed with what's happening. Contact Summer for our exact location and bring them. You're our backup, so don't fail."

Graham shook his head. "I should go with you. I'm the only one trained for something like this."

"No, you're not," said Winter, looking at Ayden. Everyone followed Winter's gaze. "Ayden's been keeping something from us."

Ayden crossed her arms. "My grandfather was a World War 2 veteran and my uncle a Vietnam green beret. My father is a Colonial in the Marines…weapons and tactics instructor. I've learned plenty."

"And," said Winter. "I trained as an FBI field officer last summer. Not to mention, both of us have the gift of prophecy. What we can't handle, God will. But you know how the FBI moves. If anyone can find them, you can."

Graham nodded. "Okay. I withdraw my objection."

"I'm not sure what we're going to find at the train yard when we get there, so you must come through with backup."

"I'll come through," said Graham. "One way or another."

Winter looked back at Ayden. "You and I are going to face Claire and get them back."

Ayden set her jaw and nodded. "Let's go."

56

"You need to understand something," Winter said to Ayden after swapping cars in the parking lot of Davis's dorm and speeding off north toward the old train yard.

"What?" asked Ayden.

"I don't think you're fully aware of what's about to happen. What we're going to face is not human and we can't beat it."

"But I thought I was like you," said Ayden. "I'm a prophetess too. That's what you said."

Winter flicked her head for a quick glance at her and then back to the road. Ayden watched her in the darkness of the car. "Do you even know what that means?"

Ayden turned away. "I've seen you do things I can't explain. If I can do them too, then I'm not worried."

Winter sighed. "You have the gift of prophecy, same as me. I don't know why, but you do…maybe God thought I needed some help. But you have to understand, whatever it is you do, you really aren't the one doing it. It may feel like a super power and it may feel like you're in control, but you're not."

"That doesn't make a bit of sense, you know that?"

"It's like this," said Winter. "God gives you the ability to do whatever he wants you to do. And within that is an uncontrollable desire to do what he wants. So even though it feels like you're making the decision, you're only doing it because at that moment you're so in tune with God your decision is his decision. See?"

"No, not really. Are you saying I don't make my own decisions?"

Winter shook her head. "No, it's not like that. Christians want to get closer to God, right? To become better people...to become more perfect in a way...to become more like God. And a side effect is we start thinking like God. We still think for ourselves, but our thinking is more influenced by him the closer we get to him. With this gift, God unleashes all this power through me, power that is not mine, and it causes a time of extraordinary closeness to God's mind. When this happens, my thinking lines up with his, so what I think is essentially what he's thinking. That's why it works. God uses his power to do what he wants, but it's all done through me...so it can feel like I'm doing what I want."

"But you said before..."

"I know what I've said before, but I was wrong," said Winter. "That's where I messed up. I started focusing too much on me, on what I could do, on what I wanted to do, I lost the connection with God...so it all sort of went away for a while. Just...don't be tempted into thinking you're doing any of it. That's all I'm saying. It's not really you."

"Why the Sunday School lesson all of a sudden?"

"Because that's what Claire wants...not Claire...the Acolyte. It's not human. It's supernatural, so only something supernatural can really stop it...angels, God...whatever God wants, but it's his battle to fight, not ours. And Claire knows she can't win that way, so she'll try to cut it off by making us put the focus on ourselves. Do you understand now?"

"I think so. When you say it's not human..."

"It's demonic. And it's surrounded by other demons."

Winter waited for Ayden to reply, but the car suddenly filled with silent tension. Winter chanced a look over and found Ayden staring blankly out the window.

"Are you okay?"

"Yeah," said Ayden. "It just all of a sudden became very real."

"It is real. And dangerous. But we're not really going there to have a war with a bunch of demons. God will take care of the demons. We just have to take care of Kaci and Peter. And if we can do that without confronting Claire directly, then that's what we'll do."

Ayden nodded. "Why do you keep calling her Claire? You know it's not really her."

"I know," said Winter. "I guess I still believe there's something human there. And thinking of it as human makes it a whole lot less scary."

"Scary?" Ayden laughed. "The unmovable Winter? Scared?"

"Always. What if I told you the more confident I act, the more frightened I really am?"

"Then I'd say we have nothing to worry about."

Winter furrowed her eyebrows. "Huh?"

"If that were true, then you acting frightened must mean you're pretty confident."

"You just keep telling yourself that if it helps."

Over the next hill Winter could see the train yard below.

"We're here," she said as she pulled off to the side of the road.

Winter got out and stood in front of her car. Below them the road they were on teed into another road running east to west. Beyond the perpendicular road stood several old warehouse buildings and numerous rusty boxcars lined up on a patchwork of rail spurs, illuminated by ghostly patches of orange and white safety lights. Just on the other side of the boxcars were two long railroad tracks, stretching in both directions as far as Winter could see, parallel to the road below. A thin mist was forming and creeping throughout the yard.

Above and through all of this, a dark haze clung, writhing and living, silently keeping watch. A protective shell probably already aware of their presence.

But beyond the dark haze…

"Can you see it?" Winter asked, smiling as Ayden came to her side.

"See what? The cloud thing?" Her voice trembled. "What is that? Is that the demons?"

Winter nodded. "It is. But look beyond that. Outside of the cloud…outside of the train yard. Surrounding everything. Do you see it?"

"I don't see anything."

Winter turned to her and placed a hand on her shoulder. "Look again."

Ayden squinted and peered out toward the horizon. Then her jaw dropped and her eyes widened. She took a step back and almost sat on the hood of the car.

"Holy crap! What is that?"

Winter turned back to the train yard, laughing. "That's our back-up."

57

Four Years Ago

"What are you two kids doing here?" a grizzly voice shouted.

Winter jumped awake, first slamming her head into the block wall, then the corner of the dumpster. Claire, who had lain slumped against Winter's shoulder, bolted to her feet.

Winter put a hand to her head and looked up. A wrinkled man with long hair and a long scraggly beard stood over them. He wore a tattered green army jacket and held a ragged backpack in his hand. His wild eyes looked them over as he bared his crooked teeth.

"Get out of my spot!

Claire grabbed Winter's arm and pulled. "Sorry," Claire said. "We didn't know. We were just tired."

"Go sleep somewhere else, lousy whores!"

"Hey! We're not…" said Winter.

"Come on, Winter," said Claire as she picked up her bag and pulled Winter toward the main road.

Winter clamped her mouth shut and shadowed after Claire, glancing over her shoulder to make sure the man didn't follow. He merely settled down by the dumpster where the two girls had been.

Back on the street, the nightlife had roared into full action. Winter scanned either direction, hoping for a quick way to get to someplace safer. Small groups of what Winter took to be gang members strutted along the sidewalk, some casting long stares at the two girls. Music blared from the club across the street…a club with no windows, two muscular men standing at the door, and a neon silhouette of a naked girl on the exterior wall.

Winter checked her phone for the time…three in the morning. She also noticed the battery was nearly dead.

"What do we do now?" she asked, her voice almost a squeak.

"I guess we keep walking." Claire turned back in the direction they had been traveling.

Winter followed, holding her arms tight to her chest and casting quick glances behind. She wanted to run, but Claire's purposeful strides set the pace. Still, Winter kept so close to Claire their shoulders kept bumping together.

Within minutes, a group of gang members crossed the road in front of them and started walking their direction, grinning and looking them up and down.

"Claire…" Winter mumbled, now trembling all over.

"Just act normal." Claire moved to the edge of the sidewalk to let the gang pass, and Winter filed behind her.

As they began to pass, the gang paused. Two of them blocked their path and one of them reached out to grab Winter's arm, yanking her bag away and tossing it to another. Winter tried to jerk free, but he held her like stone.

"Let me go!" she shouted.

Two more had grabbed Claire, and Claire was struggling with all the ferocity of a cornered animal.

"Whoa. Calm down," said the one holding Winter as he put a knife to her throat. Claire stopped struggling, but continued to huff like an angry bull. "You two are new here, aren't you? Haven't seen you before."

One of them laughed. "Fresh girls...just what I was hoping for tonight."

"You one of Luis's girls?" asked one of the ones holding Claire.

Winter couldn't speak, she could only whimper and shake her head. She glanced toward the other side of the street, but the people over there paid them no attention.

"Newbie, huh?" said someone else.

"Let us go!" shouted Claire.

"Come on man," said one of the other guys. "Leave the suicide skanks alone. Can't you tell they're jailbait? Probably just runaways."

Winter tried to jerk away, but the man holding her grabbed her face and turned her toward him, the knife going back into his pocket. "No," he said. "She gonna take the stroll, I'm gonna take a ride. This trick's gonna get her first lesson."

Claire screamed and began kicking and biting. The men cursed and let her go, backing away as if Claire had rabies. The one holding Winter released her face and took half a step toward Claire. As he did, Winter leaned closer to him and brought her knee up as hard as she could. He let go completely and fell to the ground.

"Run!" shouted Claire, but Winter was already running.

They were almost on the other side of the street before the gang overcame the confusion, and the shouts and curses of pursuit began. Winter cast over her shoulder to see the gang closing in, more knives brandished. Guns waving too. They turned down the sidewalk at the next street.

And into the path of a cop, slowly rolling toward them. Claire didn't even stop, but jetted past the patrol car. On an impulse Winter veered into the street. The car squealed to a stop and Winter slammed her palms into the hood. "Help us!"

"Winter what are you doing?" shouted Claire from behind the car.

Two officers jumped out from either side of the car, taking

stances behind the open doors.

"Don't move!" shouted the driver.

Winter flicked her eyes up and saw Claire running again. She looked back to the officers and then over her shoulder, pointing to the street corner as the gang came careening around. "Help!"

The gang stopped and surveyed the scene, two of them taking aim with their guns. They stared a long time at Winter, unafraid of the officers.

"Drop your weapons!" shouted one of the officers as he pulled out his own gun. "Get behind us," he said to Winter.

Winter ran behind the car. She looked back...the gang was slowly stepping toward them. Winter's heart pounded and a cold sweat covered her skin.

"I said drop your weapons!" shouted the officer again.

"Winter!" Claire shouted from further down the street.

Winter turned to find Claire waving at her from the next crossroad. She glanced back at the advancing gang...and then took off running, expecting gunshots to ring out in the night at any moment. As she approached Claire, Claire took off and they both raced down the new street. They turned immediately at the next crossroad, and then three more times without stopping.

Finally, they came to a crossroad where they could see a major road and a traffic light not too far away, hopefully indicating a better part of the city. Heaving for oxygen, they both slowed to a walk, set their faces for the traffic light, and plodded down the sidewalk.

As they reached the larger, busier road, they turned to follow it, just wanting to put as much distance as they could between them and the bad part of town. Eventually the sky began to turn a lighter shade of black that quickly became a distinctive blue.

"I want to go home," said Winter.

"I can't go back."

"I know, but what do we do? We've lost all our stuff...Do you even know where we are?"

"Yes," said Claire. "We're at the edge of town." She pointed ahead and a little right. "There's a river that direction that's the border for the city, and there's a bridge not far from here, I think. If we can cross over we'll be out of the jurisdiction of the police. At least that'll buy us some time. We can hide out somewhere until we figure out what to do next."

"Are you sure about that?" asked Winter

Claire nodded and sped up, walking just fast enough to stretch Winter's legs. Though more vehicle traffic trickled onto the road as the city awoke and the early risers were leaving for work, they never saw another police car. After another mile, they turned a corner and Winter could see the bridge in the distance. It stood like a giant gateway to freedom, with iron trusses arching across the center like an industrial rainbow.

Claire half turned her head to Winter without looking at her. "It'll all be over soon. Then you can go home."

58

Present Day

As they ran down the hill, the premonition soared out of Winter
like a white mist, draping in a single physical line, dipping and floating
through the air like a ghost. The dark cloud hanging over the
compound faded away like an illusion as the white mist pierced it,
leaving the alleys and nooks around the buildings and boxcars clearly
visible. The mist stretched out and the end of it landed by the far
corner of a building a hundred yards away. The tail of the white mist
pulled away from Winter and the entire thing gathered like a spring
into that one place, and then transformed into the little girl. The girl
watched Winter run for a moment and then pointed behind the
building. She dissolved back into the mist, one end stretching
forward in both space and time, the other end gliding back to
reconnect with Winter's mind and pour data in. Winter saw clearly
what lay behind the building and what the next moments were
supposed to be.

Winter peered over her shoulder as she rounded the corner where
the girl had pointed, following the white trail. Ayden ran several feet

behind, sweat already gleaming from her forehead. "Come on," said Winter. "This way."

"I know. I saw her."

The mist pulled away again, gathered, and revealed the little girl, standing by the closed door of a building just ahead. She reached up and quickly traced the word "Here" on the door in red letters. Then she dissolved and disappeared completely.

Somehow Winter knew the girl wasn't gone…she could still feel the premonition streaming into her head, though she could no longer see the connection.

Something pulled at her from within, tugging the pit of her stomach toward fear and despair as if grasped by a claw. Almost immediately the tug dissipated, transforming into hope and confidence. The premonition whispered words of encouragement even as her heart sank again into hopelessness.

Fear and despair fell upon her like an avalanche. All the horrible things she had done in her life paraded through her mind's eye, breaking her heart, filling her with a self-loathing that resurrected old suicidal thoughts. Her strength and will drained away, and she slowed to a walk, fighting the urge to collapse upon the ground and weep. Behind her, Ayden whimpered.

Then the pendulum swung in the other direction. She remembered all God had done to not give up on her, to see something worth saving, and to pursue her in a way no human being had ever done. Her strength surged anew with hope, confidence, and an overwhelming sense of worth. The fatigue in her legs and chest vanished, and she rushed forward again, faster than before. Winter cast a glance back over her shoulder, and found Ayden close on her heels, wide-eyed but confident.

"What was that?" asked Ayden.

"I don't know," said Winter.

The door came within reach, but the premonition did not penetrate beyond it, just like the night Shannon died. Everything beyond the moment of grabbing the handle and pushing the door open lay shrouded in shadow.

"Can you see anything past the door?" Winter asked.

"No. But I'm still getting used to it. Can you?"

Winter shook her head. "But this is the place. Ready?"

Ayden straightened herself and nodded.

Winter grabbed the knob, fulfilling the last vestige of future knowledge she possessed, twisted it and pushed the door open.

The room was black. Not just the absence of light, but a living shadow clawing at them from the opening. The same evil shadow present when Shannon had died. The same shadow that had filled Winter's apartment, that had transformed into the most horrific creatures, just before Claire sent her to Romania.

Winter clenched her fists and her teeth, letting an anger that wasn't her own fill her, letting the power of God surge through her until her skin stretched taut and her ears rumbled. She took a deep breath and stepped into the shadow.

Immediately the shadow fell away like sand, scattering into nothing. Winter could see rows of shipping containers, partially illuminated from above by the few old industrial lights that still worked, which cast shadows of exceptional creepiness in their own right. Winter crept past the first shipping container and glanced in both directions down a long alley of containers. The briefest of nudges told her to turn right.

Near the end of the alley, the space opened wide against the wall of the building. Winter still hadn't heard or seen anything, but she felt confident they were close. This was where she was supposed to go. She didn't have a full-blown premonition to guide her, but the confidence was definitely not her own.

Claire stepped in front of them from the left side of the alley and Winter stopped. Claire narrowed her bright red eyes at them and then turned to walk back to the side. "You might as well come on," she said with a bored voice.

Winter frowned back at Ayden. Ayden shrugged, and then they both stepped boldly forward out of the alley into the open space by the wall. Claire crossed to a crate against a container on the left. Kaci sat on the floor, leaning back against the crate with her arms folded on top of her knees and her head on her arms, unbound. Claire rubbed the top of Kaci's head and smiled.

"Kaci!" said Winter stepping forward, but Claire held a warning hand out to her and Winter stopped. Kaci didn't even look up.

"Where's Peter?" asked Ayden.

Claire studied them both, running her fingers through Kaci's hair. She flicked her eyes to a shipping container next to her, its doors open, but the inside beyond Winter's view.

Ayden took a large step toward the shipping container and Claire shook her head.

"I wouldn't do that…" Claire said.

Ayden paused and stepped back beside Winter.

"What do you want?" Winter asked. "What's it going to take for you to let them go?"

"You think I have demands? I don't want anything. That's not what this is about."

"Then what is it? Why do you want them?"

Claire sat down on the crate, still caressing Kaci's head. "You know the prophecy, don't you? There is to be a child. With Peter dead, there is no one to father the child. And when my master takes Kaci as his bride, then he will become the father."

"Why not just kill her, then? He wanted to kill her last year, why not now?"

Claire shrugged. "He didn't know all of the prophecy then. She'll still die, but only after his child is born. Then the child's powers will be his to control."

Winter shook her head. "You know it doesn't work like that. The child's powers are not its own."

"It can be imbued with other powers. It's a pity you didn't see her in the tower. You might have been proud. She enjoyed it, Winter. She moaned with pleasure…just like you used to."

"Don't let her get in your head," said Ayden.

"You used to be such a good rebel," said Claire. "What happened? Wasn't it fun?"

Winter fixed her eyes on Kaci and stepped forward.

"Don't," said Claire.

"How exactly do you plan to stop me?" Winter said as she took another step. "Talk me to death?"

"Have you forgotten already?"

"No. But I don't think you'll be able to do the same thing twice." Winter raised a hand toward Kaci. "Kaci, listen to me. Just get up. You don't have to stay here. Come with me."

Claire laughed. "She won't listen to you."

"Yes, she will." Winter took another step closer. "Kaci, please. It's Winter. I'm here to take you home."

Kaci lifted her head and it rolled sideways from the weight of itself. Black, hollow skin ringed her bloodshot eyes. She locked onto Winter with a glassy stare. Kaci's mouth hung open and she took long, heavy breaths.

"What have you done to her?" Winter asked

Claire shrugged. "Just a little something to keep her compliant. It has a side effect of heightening dormant emotions. You should know…"

Winter narrowed her eyes. "You drugged her?"

Kaci's face twisted and she screamed. "GO AWAY!"

Claire chuckled. "And guess what emotions she's been struggling with? If you think she'll go with you, then you're completely delusional."

"Kaci, you're not yourself. Just listen…"

"No!" Kaci put both hands to the side of her head and screamed again. "I hate you! Leave me alone!"

Kaci's words plunged into Winter's heart, sending icy slivers through her veins. "I'm sorry," Winter said. "I can explain. Please. It wasn't my fault."

"I saw you! I hate you!" Kaci struggled to her feet, teetering and steadying herself with a hand on the crate. Claire let her go, a bemused smile on her face.

"Kaci, Claire's done something to you. You're not yourself."

"She saved me. You're the one who did it." Kaci staggered toward Winter. "It's all your fault. Everything! You took it all away from me! It's your fault I almost died! It's your fault they raped me in that tower! It's your fault my real parents are dead! It's your fault Peter doesn't love me anymore! I hate you for what you've done!" Kaci teetered forward and shoved Winter in the chest.

"Kaci, no…that's not what happened…" Winter wiped her eyes clear and braced herself as Kaci came to shove her again. Winter stepped back out of the way at the last minute and Kaci almost fell. She caught herself and put her hands back to her head, clenching her eyes tight.

"Do you see?" asked Claire. "She doesn't trust you anymore. She's mine."

"Because of what you've done to her," said Winter.

"It doesn't matter. You can't rescue someone who doesn't want to be saved."

Kaci's moans echoed through the building. Her face turned a bright crimson and her cheeks glistened from the sudden surge of tears. She peeked her eyes open. "Winter? How could you? I thought you were my friend."

"I am," said Winter, reaching out to her again. "I can explain everything. But you're not yourself. Claire drugged you. Just come with me and we'll go to a hospital."

Kaci shook her head. "Why would I trust you again? Why would I go anywhere with you?"

"Please…"

Kaci whimpered and her face drooped. "You took everything…"

"No, Kaci. I didn't. Please..."

Kaci shook her head, then with loud wailing she took off running. Winter grabbed for her, but hesitated, and Kaci disappeared down the corridor of containers.

"Now look what you've done." Claire walked toward them, eyes glowing again. "She won't go far at least. Serves me right for wanting to have some fun before I kill you two."

Kaci's cries reverberated throughout the building, and the further away she ran the more difficult it became to place her location.

Ayden touched Winter on the arm. "Go. I'll get Peter and hold her off long enough for you to find Kaci."

Winter glanced at her and then at Claire. "Are you sure?"

Ayden turned to face Claire and nodded, firming her jaw.

"Remember what I said in the car," said Winter.

Ayden nodded again. "I've got this. Go."

"Get out of my way!" Claire roared, seeming to grow as she stalked forward.

"Go!" shouted Ayden, planting her feet and clenching her fists.

Winter turned and ran.

59

Winter sprinted down the corridor between the shipping containers, swinging her head back and forth and checking her speed at each intersection of containers, searching the shadows for any sign of Kaci. Her cries still echoed, but as Winter neared the end of the lane, Kaci's voice fell silent. Two more intersections later and Winter spotted another side exit. She pivoted toward the door still swaying on its hinges, burst through it, and rushed out into the night, but Kaci wasn't anywhere nearby.

A train whistle cut through the thin air, rebounding through the labyrinth of boxcars and warehouses, making it impossible to know which direction the tracks lay. Winter took a deep breath, the odor of tar and creosote filling her head, and ran to the corner of the next warehouse, mumbling a prayer for some kind of nudge or premonition to know which way Kaci had fled. When nothing came, she chanced calling out, even though she suspected Claire was not alone.

"Kaci?"

Something rattled to her right, one building away. Uneven

footsteps pounded into the night. Winter gave chase, her first steps skidding through the gravel. She rounded the corner of the next building, but no one was there, only lines of abandoned boxcars on neglected rail spurs.

"Kaci? Come back. Let's just talk, okay?"

"Leave me alone!" Kaci's voice bounced around the boxcars and buildings like the train whistle, still impossible to pinpoint, though she couldn't be far away.

Winter rolled her feet heel to toe toward a line of boxcars, flicking her head back and forth, scanning every shadow and listening for the smallest sound.

Whimpering floated through the air, mixed with mumbling Winter couldn't understand, loud enough to be just within reach, just beyond the nearest boxcar. Winter approached it and stooped to peer underneath. Kaci crouched on the ground just on the other side, clutching her head and trembling.

Winter's foot slid in the gravel. Kaci jerked her head toward the sound, screamed at Winter, staggered to her feet, and stumbled toward another line of boxcars.

Winter swore under her breath and looked down the line in the same direction Kaci had fled. The boxcars went too far for her to have any chance of intercepting Kaci. The other direction had only two cars before a break, so Winter doubled back at a run, crossed the track spur, just in time to see Kaci dart through another break between two cars about six away.

"Kaci, stop!"

The train whistle sounded, closer this time, and from the same direction Kaci had run.

Winter launched forward, eyes fixed on the last place she saw Kaci, heart pounding in her ears, lead dragging her stomach down. A fog rolled in like the tide of the sea, black fog, the same fog she first saw from the top of the hill. It swirled around Winter's feet, clinging to her legs like glue, and pulling her backward. Winter clenched her teeth and pushed forward, but the closer she got to Kaci's last turn, the stronger the fog pulled.

Raw despair filled her, dredging up her past, whispering old thoughts of suicide. Only by sheer willpower did she keep pushing forward.

By the time she made the next turn, she trudged as if through mud, weeping, almost ready to give up. Winter gripped the side of the boxcar, pulled, and thrust her head around.

Kaci was there, standing not thirty feet away...beside the live railroad track. The train whistle howled again and the black fog swirled in to surround Kaci, pooling as an impossible sea for Winter to cross.

"Kaci!"

Kaci didn't turn. She didn't move. She just stood there by the tracks, waiting as the fog pawed at her sides.

Winter slogged forward, dragging one leg at a time to ebb foot-by-foot closer, calling upon the old stone casing to protect her heart from the outbreak of poisonous emotions.

"Kaci! You have to listen to me! This isn't you...this isn't what you want to do...trust me, it's not the answer." Winter cast her eyes toward the oncoming train, the light piercing the darkness like a giant star. She swung her feet forward, knees aching from the pressure and muscles burning from exertion, still using the rails of the boxcar for leverage.

Kaci looked toward the train, with no indication she heard Winter at all.

"Kaci! Please! Even if you do hate me, even if you never want to see me again, don't do this! You're not yourself. Fight it! Don't listen to whatever it is in your head!"

The fog jerked Winter's leg backward and she nearly fell. She cried in pain, but pushed forward again regardless, fighting to get closer to Kaci. Now beyond the boxcar. Now crossing the open space. Just a little further. Winter reached out...

"Think of Peter. He loves you...not me. I'm sorry I haven't been the kind of friend you needed. I'm sorry I wasn't there when I should have been. But Peter will be there, for the rest of your life. Remember him...please!"

The train was close enough to hear the chug of the engine and feel the rumble of its presence. Winter glanced back at it, easily making out its shape and estimating its speed. Kaci watched it too...waiting.

Winter took another laborious step forward, slowly closing the gap. "Kaci, please..."

The train was nearly upon them. The whistle shouting in a long continuous blast for them to move. The fog swirled up alongside Kaci, caressing her in long tentacles.

Halfway. Diesel exhaust filled the air. "Kaci...don't..."

The train was there. Kaci cast one broken-hearted look at Winter, and then took a long step into the center of the tracks.

Winter screamed, "STOP!"

Four Years Ago

The road leading to the bridge was broken and uneven, years of neglect making it substandard for consistent commercial travel. As they climbed the arch of the bridge, Winter could see not far away to the north a newer bridge for the main highway, teeming with early morning vehicles, the modern replacement for this forgotten relic. Winter wondered if anyone even used the bridge anymore and why it was still standing, but just as she thought this, a car passed them and crossed.

They followed a footpath built into the side of the bridge, separated from the road portion by a low wall. The apex of the bridge rose higher than it appeared to from the bottom, and by the time the two girls reached the top, Winter's sore legs nearly gave out.

"I need to rest," said Winter.

Claire nodded. "Me too." They both put their backs to the side of the bridge and sat to catch their breath.

Winter fingered her locket, wishing she had something to eat. She peered at Claire and found Claire fingering the green and silver pendant in the same way. Claire saw her watching and grinned. Then both girls started laughing.

"This didn't exactly turn out like I hoped," said Claire.

"You don't say." Winter peered down the footpath of the bridge as another car rumbled beyond the barrier wall. "Do you think if we called Michael he'd find us here?"

"Maybe. But my phone is dead now."

Winter checked hers. "Mine's almost gone too. Not sure it'll make a call."

"What about a text?"

Winter nodded. "I can try. Where are we?"

"The old Trenton River bridge. He should know where that is."

Winter typed in the name of the bridge and sent the text off. "Now what?"

Claire shrugged. "We wait, I guess. If he doesn't show up, then we keep going."

Winter sighed.

"I keep going, then," said Claire with a huff.

"I'm sorry. I just can't do this."

Claire squeezed her eyes shut. "Whatever."

"Come on, Claire. Let's both just go home."

"I can't. You don't understand."

"But I do understand…"

"No!" Claire shouted, then took a deep breath and spoke more calmly. "No, you don't."

Winter turned away, biting her lip.

"I had so much I wanted to do with my life," said Claire. "I wanted to be a ballerina, did you know that? But my dad wouldn't let me take dance lessons. It's not like they couldn't afford it, he just didn't want me to."

"Is that what this is about? Getting back at your dad?" Winter faced Claire.

Claire scowled back at her with red, glistening, haunted eyes.

"No. It's so much more than that. Everything I've ever wanted to do or become has been crushed by him. He took it all away in his selfishness…the one person who should want to love me and provide for me more than anyone else in the world. I can't go back, do you understand? If I go back that means he's won."

"But you can go to the police…"

"And do what? Have him kill my mom before they get there?"

"He wouldn't."

Claire nodded. "He tried once. One time my mom tried to get away when I was little. When he found us he beat her, putting her in bed for two weeks, and refusing to let her go to a hospital. He said if she ever tried anything like that again he'd kill us both and go to jail gladly."

Winter's heart sank. Suddenly she wanted to hug her own dad.

"But I keep pushing him," Claire continued. "And every time I do it gets worse. He'll stop at nothing to make sure we both are his slaves. He's a monster, Winter."

"But…surely someone could help."

Claire shook her head. "No one can help. This is my only chance, do you understand? If I go back, he'll kill me, I know it."

Sirens wailed in the distance. Winter and Claire stood up and gazed back toward the city. Five police cars raced along the road heading to the bridge. As they approached the bottom of the bridge, two of them bounded up the slope while the other three turned to block off the bottom. Tire squeals from the other direction made Winter and Claire turn to look at the other side. Two sheriff cars had blocked the other side of the river.

"Someone must have seen us," said Winter with a whimper.

"We have to get out of here," said Claire, frantically looking in every direction.

The police cars racing up slid to a halt just in front of Claire and Winter. Winter took an instinctive step back, pressing against the rail of the bridge.

Officers jumped out, hands on their holstered weapons. "Hands up!" the nearest one shouted

"No!" screamed Claire. "Leave us alone!"

The nearest officer's face paled and he pulled his hand from the gun, raising both of his hands into the air. All the other officers followed his lead and put their hands out to the sides in neutral positions.

Winter realized Claire wasn't standing beside her anymore. She glanced over her shoulder.

Her heart froze.

Claire stood on the concrete railing, one hand grasping an iron truss, eyes fixed on the officers.

"Claire…what are you doing?" squeaked Winter. "Get down."

Claire shook her head. "I can't go back…"

"Okay, but not like this. Just get down. We'll figure this out."

"They'll make me go back. And I will not go back to him, Winter. After everything he's done to me…"

Winter put her hands up to try to calm Claire. "Then just tell them. They'll understand, maybe they can help."

"We can help," said the officer. "Whatever it is. I understand you're in some kind of trouble. Trust us. Just step down off the rail."

"SHUT UP!" Claire screamed.

"Claire, please…" Winter whimpered. "Let them try."

"Haven't you been listening to me? No one can help me! It's too late!"

"It's not too late. Things can still be what you want. You can still have the life you want…away from him, away from everything. You can start over. Please. Just get down."

Claire shook her head. Her body trembled and when she opened her mouth she began to weep, her face bright red and streaked. "I can't…"

"Yes, you can. Trust me. You don't want to do this. You're my friend, Claire. What am I supposed to do without you? I need you."

Claire convulsed forward, leaning closer to the tress. She bent slightly at the waist, placing one hand on her abdomen, moaning through her sobs. "I can't. It's too late. You don't understand."

"Then tell me! You keep saying that, and I'm trying. Just tell me! What is it I don't understand?"

Claire took a deep breath and straightened up. Her shudders stopped. She stared Winter straight in the eyes, her own eyes sad, apologetic, and appreciative all at once. With one hand still on her abdomen and a calm peaceful voice she said, "I'm pregnant." Then she took one step backward and let go.

Winter reached out and screamed, "STOP!" But Claire was gone.

Present Day

"STOP!" Winter screamed.

Everything froze. Everything...physical. The world transformed around Winter in the space of a heartbeat, a blur of frantic motion filling the distance between her and Kaci. Every shadow had flashed into its true monstrous form, riding gleefully upon the front of the train, writhing upon the ground, clutching Winter's legs, swirling through the air above. Cackling. Shrieking.

Yet the train no longer moved. Even the dust particles floating in the train's light hung suspended in space like glitter. Time had stopped, and with it the veil between the physical and the spiritual had been opened.

"Kaci!" Winter tried to shout. Even the waves of her voice clung to the air, unmoving and silent. Winter searched for Kaci, but the gyrating legion of monsters blocked her from view.

Then a rush of white flooded into the midst of the demons, like an avalanche of snow. The white swirls mixed with the demons, scattering them in all directions, twisting with them through the air, and ripping away those holding Winter's legs. As Winter watched the new whiteness, so similar to the white line she had followed into the train yard, yet more full and more alive, at times she could see arms and legs, sometimes faces so bright she could make little sense of their features. The monsters screamed and struck the white swirls with a ferocity that sent shivers down Winter's spine. As the fight raged around her, a concentration of the white beings filled the space between her and Kaci, twirling and pushing back in all directions to clear the path in an ivory tunnel. Even more white streaks swirled around Kaci, ripping the demons away from her and drawing them into the battle with the rest.

"Winter!" a girl shouted.

Winter turned to the little girl standing just to her right.

"They can hold them back for a moment, but you must save her!"

Winter nodded, glanced at the shimmering tunnel and the chaos above, and ran. Running outside of time felt like running through water without the drag. The air moved around her like invisible gel, caressing her skin, before releasing to remain stationary in its previous timeless state. Sand and dirt suspended in the air pelted Winter in the face. The screech of the demons pierced the air as Winter drew closer to Kaci.

The nose of the train stood only inches from Kaci's shoulder. Kaci's hair stuck out sideways, caught in the rush of wind from the nose, and suspended in the time lock. Winter stepped onto the rail with one foot and placed the other on the tracks in front of the train. She leaned close and wrapped her arms around Kaci, then flung herself backward, attempting to pluck Kaci from the time lock as if pulling her out of mud. As Winter leaned back, straining to wrest Kaci free, she put the second foot back on the rail with the first, bent her knees slightly, and launched backward.

The space around them snapped. The silvery tunnel and the war above disappeared. Winter crashed to the ground with Kaci on top, and the train whizzed by, washing them in a gale of wind and dust, and rumbling the ground like an earthquake.

Kaci's arms flung to either side and she screamed. "Let me go!"

As Kaci lurched off of Winter, Winter jumped to her feet, grabbed one of Kaci's wrists, twisting it like she had been taught by the FBI the summer before. With her other hand, Winter grabbed tight onto Kaci's shoulder and steered her away from the train.

"Sorry, Kaci. But you're not getting away from me this time."

Kaci whimpered as they walked, but no longer struggled. Before they reached the gap between the boxcars, the passenger train behind them had sped away, leaving a void of sound in its wake. Within that void came screaming and scuffling from the other side of the boxcars.

Winter stopped, holding Kaci tight against herself like a hostage, waiting for what she knew was about to walk around the gap between the boxcars. The black mist came first, rolling toward them, but stopping several yards short, billowing into a heap before settling back down and spreading out. Ayden, crawling on hands and knees through the mist, emerged first, with Peter standing just behind her holding a shotgun to her head. The black mist draped from each of them like shreds of skin. Ayden spotted Winter and screamed again, straightening enough to put both hands to her head.

Then Claire appeared, striding out of the mist after Peter, a smirk on her face, with the mist wrapped around her like a cloak. "Enough," Claire said. "Give me Kaci, or you all die."

"You won't kill us," spat Winter. "You wouldn't dare disappoint your master."

Claire stepped past Peter and Ayden, chin lowered and eyes glinting. "Would you like to test that? I answer to a higher authority than him. Breaking you would be so much more satisfying than fulfilling his lust."

"You can't win. You know that, right? You've already lost the war. It's written in the Bible."

Claire shook her head. "Even if you are right, this battle, right here, right now…is mine."

Winter took a step backward, glancing over her shoulder for any possible way to escape. No way could she get Kaci to run fast enough, and unless she left Peter and Ayden here to die, she couldn't leave anyway.

"Let me tell you what's going to happen if you don't hand over Kaci," said Claire. "First, I'll have Peter blow off Ayden's head right in front of you."

Winter stiffened. Ayden pleaded with her eyes, as Peter shoved the barrel of the gun into her head.

"Then I'll have Peter blow his own head off."

"You can't…"

"Then I'll snap Kaci's neck so she crumples in your arms." Claire was only feet away now and still advancing with methodical confidence, the black shroud rippling like water.

Winter took another step back.

"Then I'll …"

"Wait!" said Winter. "Just wait."

Claire paused and tilted her head.

"Just you and me. Nobody else. With all three of them as the prize."

"Seems like a pointless bargain to me."

"Then what are you scared of? If you're so confident, then let's see what kind of power you really have. If you win, you can have them all…even me. You can bring me as an extra prize to Xaphan. But if you lose, then I take them all."

Claire studied Winter, but didn't move.

"Seems like the Acolyte would have nothing to fear."

"Very well," said Claire. "Release her."

"No. Tell him to put away the gun and sit beside Ayden first."

Claire hesitated, then looked over her shoulder and nodded.

Peter's head lolled as he took two steps away and threw the gun to the side. Then he came back to sit beside Ayden, placing his head in his hands just like her.

Winter leaned close to Kaci and whispered in her ear. "Please, just trust me this once. Go to Peter and Ayden. This will all be over soon. I promise." Winter circled Claire, putting herself and Kaci between Claire and the others. The mist swirled to avoid her, like little eddies of water. Claire simply paced away, allowing several feet between them.

Winter released Kaci's arm and gave her a slight push in the right direction. Kaci stumbled away and collapsed on the ground in front of Ayden and Peter.

"Just you and me." Winter faced Claire and flexed her fists.

Claire turned and smiled. "Then let us begin. Which of us will prove strongest? The human…or the Acolyte?"

Winter planted her feet in the loose gravel and squeezed her fists, waiting for whatever the Acolyte would do first. She cleared her mind and focused only on her own inability. If they were to walk away from this alive, then God would have to intervene. She didn't know how he would do it, but he would.

Any moment, Claire would unleash the full fury of that invisible demonic army. Winter could still feel the pulsating spiritual war going on around and above them, though at the moment she couldn't see it. She had never been so frightened in her life, so helpless, so weak. But if God could transport her halfway across the world, point her straight to Kaci, and stop time, then surely he would do something now.

As Winter stared venomously at the creature wearing Claire's form, Claire tilted her head back and laughed. She stretched out her arms, absorbing shadows from the clear air, which clung to her like an ever-thickening robe, swirling and alive. Claire swung her arms to point at Winter.

All the shadows upon her body launched forward like black

daggers.

Winter stood her ground and held her breath, ignoring the almost overwhelming temptation to clench her eyes shut and run. Just before the shadows struck her, a white mist encapsulated Winter, sending the shadows spinning like a whirlpool before flying back to Claire's waiting arms.

The smile slid from Claire's face.

The white mist connected with Winter, feeding her moments of time, pouring foreknowledge into her mind, giving her that life-saving premonition she had grown so used to, but now more mature and sophisticated. It wasn't just knowledge and instruction, it was alive like Winter was alive. It was companionship, help, relief, advice. It was impossible, infinite, and redundant. It told Winter what was to come next, but waited for Winter to command it in what came next; her friend these past few years, a personal assistant or body-guard, already possessing instructions from God, relaying those instructions to Winter, but waiting for Winter to give them back before it would act, in a paradox that ensured unity of will and mind. So she emptied herself of all personal thought, praying whatever she said or did would be exactly the things God would want, knowing if she followed the premonition, they would be.

Claire thrust out her arms toward Winter again, shadows flying through the air with renewed hatred. Winter did the same and the white mist flew forward at her command, meeting the shadows halfway across the expanse, splashing against each other like rogue waves, intertwining in what Winter knew to be a fierce battle she couldn't see.

Claire stretched out her arms, absorbing new shadows and sending them around the embattled knot of light and shadow to Winter's defenseless sides. Winter held her arms in front of her face to block the impact, but new white mist formed upon her arms, shielding her, and the shadows scattered on the shield as if sandblasted.

Claire roared in frustration. The shadows retreated to cloak her again and flow out from her feet like a small pool. As the shadows retreated, the white mist simply vanished.

"How are you doing that?" Claire shouted.

Winter smirked. "I'm not."

Claire cast frantically from side to side, turning a complete circle. "Where are they? Where are they!"

"You've lost," said Winter. "This is a fight you cannot win, and you know it. I'm taking the others and leaving." Winter took a step backward, watching Claire carefully.

"I have not lost!" Claire shouted, and then roared so loud the ground shook as if the train passed by again. Shadows streamed out of the air, attaching to her, growing her into a new creature. They became part of her body, new arms, new legs, absorbed into her flesh. Still the shadows came, unending, as Claire grew to tower over Winter nearly twenty feet tall. Claire's roar became more organic, more wild, a rumble, and out of her mouth glowed the flickering orange light of flames. The red of her eyes shone like embers. Soon the shadows were so thick upon her skin, Winter could no longer make out any human form. Claire's face twisted into something resembling the monsters she had already seen, but older, more intelligent, more dangerous, with nothing human left beneath; a towering shadow demon.

"I am the Acolyte," said a deep, thundering demonic voice from the flaming mouth, trembling Winter's heart and echoing painfully through her mind, a roar and a screech all at once. "I am the Right Hand of Hell."

Winter took another step back, the premonition telling her to stand her ground, but the fear just too overwhelming. As the fear took over, her connection to the premonition severed, and Winter knew nothing stood between her and the still-growing monster bearing down upon her.

"I have taught you sorrow." The monster took a step toward

Winter, the ethereal vortex adding to its bulk every moment. "Now I will teach you despair." The last rumbled words lingered in the air, strengthening, rising in pitch until it became an ear-piercing shriek.

Winter pressed her hands against her ears. "I can't," Winter mumbled, voice shaking, the only prayer she could manage. She took another step back with her numb legs. "I can't do this…"

Ayden, Kaci, and Peter all screamed behind her. The growing shriek pierced flesh and bone, easily penetrating past Winter's clutched hands and boring into the depths of her heart, filling her with a raw fear she had never felt before. She fell to her knees, adding her screams to those of the others.

The shadow demon stepped closer, almost floating above the ground. Winter wanted to stand and run, but the lingering shriek paralyzed every muscle. The creature stooped to look Winter in the eyes with its glowing embers. A shadowy hand lifted and reached to grab Winter by the head. Just before its hand touched, the immediate space around Winter flashed and the creature recoiled as if shocked by electricity.

Two shadowed hands came for Winter on either side, and again the creature recoiled in a white flash just before touching her. The shriek in Winter's ears began to fade away, the fear dissipated. The creature roared again, inches from her face, but Winter heard little. Instead, the heavenly rumble she had come to recognize began to grow in her ears. With the rumble came a new confidence.

She couldn't face this creature. But she didn't have to this time. Something else had taken charge. Backup was coming.

More than the spiritual guardian she had always thought of as a premonition, the full force of the heavenly legion surrounding the train yard approached. She could feel the gathering storm behind her, sense the urgency from the creature in front of her.

Winter planted her feet and stood back up, staring defiantly into the glowing eyes of the Acolyte. The creature began to pelt Winter with shadows that swirled around and clawed for Winter. Anything close enough to touch her was repelled in a flash of light, the guardian still at work, though overwhelmed. Winter stepped forward with confidence under the assailment.

The creature stepped back.

"Whatever power you wield is nothing compared to God's. Whether he fights for me or not, you will lose." Winter took another step, driving the creature back even further. Still it thrashed at her with no result. "But today…God fights."

At those words, wind struck Winter's back, swirling around her momentarily, a vortex of air, and then streaming toward the monster, materializing as a long, gleaming white streak, so bright Winter could hardly look at it. The streak of white struck the shadow demon in the chest and the creature howled. The vortex around Winter spun even faster, casting off another streak of white, and a third.

The creature stumbled backward, shadows abandoning their master, fleeing from its surface, and disappearing like ghosts. The white light began to emanate from within the creature with a glow that consumed the former demonic fire. The streams of light pulsated with bright flashes, and the vortex around Winter spun even faster.

With a loud roar, the creature leaned back, stretched out its atrophied shadowy arms, and exploded.

The remaining shadows cast off in every direction like shrapnel, fading into the air. A blinding light remained in the middle where Claire should have been.

Then the vortex vanished. The white light faded into nothing. And Sophie fell out of the air into a heap upon the ground.

Four Years Ago

Winter ran screaming to the rail. She slammed into it and leaned over, reaching down as if she could catch Claire in mid-fall. But Claire already lay on the rocks below, her body twisted, blood surrounding her head like a halo and mixing with the rushing water to make long streaks of crimson. As the swift current overcame Claire's limp body and washed it into deeper water to float downstream, Winter became aware of the two officers at her side shouting into the microphones on their shoulders.

A hand clenched Winter's arm. She faced the officer holding her tight and wiped her eyes to see him clearly. He watched with a pale, soft face.

"Help her," said Winter. "Please."

The officer firmed his lips, let her go, and then jumped back across the barrier toward his car. He ran to the other side of the bridge and leaned over.

Winter looked back, but Claire was long gone. She trembled and the breath caught in her chest, and she scrambled over the barrier to join the officer on the other ledge. There she waited for Claire to float into sight, long after the officer had already run back to his car. Claire never did appear.

More sirens wailed in the distance, growing closer with each second. Winter stole a glance away from the river and back to the city. Firetrucks arrived at the foot of the bridge. An ambulance approached. More police cars had gathered with the first three at the roadblock and officers now ran along both banks of the river.

No one paid any attention to Winter. Her ears buzzed and her vision tunneled. She sluggishly paced toward the bottom of the bridge, expecting at any moment for something invisible to grab her legs to stop them from moving, for the air to thicken, for the bridge to stretch into the distance…to wake up sweating, panting, in her own bed. Anything but reality.

Patrol cars whisked by. Nobody even glanced at her, no one stopped her, no one spoke. The roadblock of vehicles drew near; still she ghosted past, unchallenged. She had become secondary. Unimportant. Nonexistent. In the way. Left behind.

Walking away was the only thing she could do. It was the only thing that made sense. Putting one foot ahead of the other and moving. Breathing. Living. She summoned all the numbness she could to cauterize the hole Claire had just punched through her heart. All she wanted to do now was hide, to get away from prying eyes, to cower in the darkness, to be alone.

Was being alone so hard to do? Was it too much to ask? She was better off alone. Everyone she loved died around her. It was her curse, her affliction from God.

The cauterized hole bled a little.

A car she thought she recognized slowed down just in front of her and pulled to the side. The driver's door opened and Michael stepped out. He ran to her, wrapping his arms around her and squeezing tight. Winter pulled her arms together and huddled in his embrace, letting the hole bleed openly for Michael to see. Of all people, maybe he would understand. Michael rubbed her back with one hand and her head with the other, never speaking, but letting her release all of the pressure within.

Maybe it was better to be alone. But in this moment, she wanted to be in Michael's arms.

After several minutes, Winter took a long, shuddering breath and tilted her head to look at him. She gazed deep into his eyes, brown eyes glistening with sympathy and confusion. His warm arms caressed her in a way she had never known before. She didn't know why she did it, but it felt right. Winter lifted herself with her toes and kissed him on the lips. He didn't fight or push her away, but returned the kiss so gently it calmed Winter enough she could talk.

She laid her head back on his chest and said, "She's gone."

He rubbed her some more. "I'm sorry. The police...they were..."

"I know. We saw."

"Come on. Let's get out of here before they start looking for you. Okay?"

Winter nodded, letting him lead her back to the car, one arm draped across her back and resting on her hip. She sat down and eased her head against the door window, staring ahead to the chaos at the bridge.

"Why does this keep happening to me?" she moaned. "What's wrong with me?"

"There's nothing wrong with you," said Michael as he put the car into gear and U-turned in the road. "You can't blame yourself for the choices of other people."

"But they don't have choices, don't you see? My mom, Ryan, Claire...none of them really had a choice. They died because of me."

"That's not true."

"It is! God hates me! And he's going to kill everyone I care about, don't you see that?"

Michael took a deep breath and firmed his jaw, but didn't say anything. Winter peered back out the window.

"Where are we going?" she asked when she finally realized she didn't recognize their surroundings. "I want to go home."

"I'll take you home. But I have an idea first."

Winter straightened and watched the unfamiliar surroundings pass by. He drove them through the city, beyond the outskirts, and down an old road leading into the forest. Winter had the feeling she had been here before but couldn't remember it exactly. After several minutes of nothing but trees for scenery, the road widened enough for cars to park comfortably on either side. A bridge spanned the road ahead. Michael parked.

To the right, a wide path led deeper into the woods, and Winter remembered coming here with Claire once and being told to leave.

"Why are we here?" she asked.

Michael opened the door and went around to open hers. "Come on," he said as he gently took her hand.

He led her in the opposite direction of the forest path, to the other side of the road. A grove of trees waited, gravestones blossoming beneath their bows.

"This is the Old Circle Cemetery," said Michael. "The coven here is very old and its members have been buried here for over a hundred years."

"There doesn't seem to be that many."

"That's because many are long gone, existing only in the record books and the stories of family members. That's how Wiccans prefer it. We return our bodies to the dust of the earth as quickly as possible…in other words, we don't use coffins, just wrap the body in a shroud. Most markers are made of wood, and so over time they too return to the earth. Some of these trees were planted to be the markers, the roots nourished from the body. But many former members had family who were not of our beliefs. Many wanted something a little more permanent. Those are the stone markers."

As he spoke, they passed through the center of the cemetery.

Most of the markers, whether wood or stone, were dated from before Winter was born, many of the wooden ones already faded and crumbled where they stood.

"It's a peaceful place, really," said Michael. "It reminds us that we all share the same fate in the end. That we all are part of the earth and that we all return."

On the far side of the cemetery, Michael led her to the edge of a small cliff. A lazy river flowed below.

"Is this…?"

Michael nodded. "The Trenton River. We're a good bit further downstream than in town."

"Do you think…if they don't find her…"

Michael shrugged. "Maybe. We're all floating down the river in a way, some further down the stream than others. Some fated to be plucked from it at earlier points. Me, you…your mom, Ryan, Claire. Look at it, Winter. Watch how the water doesn't stop, how the leaves caught in the current have no choice of where they go except what is fated to them. It is not one leaf's fault when another gets caught at the sides and plucked from the river, and neither should that leaf feel guilty that it's allowed to continue when all others have been removed."

Winter sat and draped her feet over the ledge, wiping a tear from her eye. "But I bet it feels alone."

Michael sat next to her. He put an arm around her and she leaned her head against his shoulder. "It probably does."

"How long do you think it would take?"

"I don't know. But I'll stay with you here and watch as long as you want. Today, you're not alone. And you don't have to be alone ever again."

Present Day

For a moment, all was silent except for Sophie's moans.

Winter hesitated and then ran to her. "Sophie? Are you okay?"

Sophie's head rolled to one side. Her eyes fluttered and opened, gazing past Winter before focusing. "Winter? Where am I?"

"It's okay. I think you're safe for now. Do you remember anything?"

Sophie sat up slowly, placing one hand on her head. "It's gone." She smiled. "I can't believe it's gone. How did you do it?"

Winter firmed her lips, grabbed Sophie by the arm, and tugged. "Don't celebrate just yet, it might come back. We have to get out of here."

Sophie jerked away. "It's too late for me! Run! Run as fast as you can, please! I don't want to hurt you again. Just leave me alone!"

"You're not alone, I'm here. And I'll stay right here with you as long as you need. Come with me."

Sophie shook her head. "You don't know what I've done. It'll never let me go now."

"It doesn't matter what you've done…you can be free from it. No matter what you've done, you're not stuck on a path you can't choose. You always have a choice."

"But what if…"

"No what ifs. Just trust me." Winter reached out her hand to Sophie. "Today, you're not alone. And you don't have to be alone ever again."

Sophie stared at her hand, tears filling her eyes. She nodded once, grabbed Winter's hand, and stood.

"Good. Now help me with the others." Winter turned to run, pulling Sophie behind her.

Peter and Kaci lay on the ground, barely conscious. Ayden was trying to stand, but still shaking.

"Ayden, are you okay?" Winter asked.

Ayden nodded. "I will be." She straightened, and opened her eyes, wincing.

"We need to get them up," Winter said. "We have to get out of here before Xaphan shows up."

"Oh, God," said Sophie. "I remember now. He's coming. He's coming now. He'll be here any minute. We have to hurry."

"What do you mean now?" asked Winter.

"I mean he's probably already here. He was supposed to have been here before you arrived. That's why Culsu wasn't afraid of you."

Winter grabbed Kaci beneath the arms and hauled her to her feet. Kaci parted her despair-filled eyes and eyed Winter venomously. Winter ignored it and huffed. "Stand up."

Kaci found her own feet, but wobbled. Winter put an arm around her and pulled her toward the far end of the line of boxcars. "We'll go this way. If he's looking for us in the warehouses we'll have a better chance of getting away."

Ayden hoisted Peter to his feet, propping him against herself, and the five of them began the long walk to the end of the track spurs, a pace set to Peter's and Kaci's shuffling feet.

As they neared the last two cars, a voice cried out behind them, reverberating through the metallic cars. "Winter!"

Winter turned. Xaphan stood as a silhouette in the distance, near the place she had first passed through while chasing Kaci.

"You have something of mine," he called.

Winter spun back around. "Faster!"

"They won't go any faster!" said Ayden.

Sophie whimpered. "I don't want to go back…Don't let him take me…"

"Just move it, all of you!" said Winter.

Winter chanced another look back and the blood froze in her veins. The shadows were returning, far more than the Acolyte had absorbed, swirling all around Xaphan like a dome, five times as high as the nearest boxcar. As he stepped forward, the demonic mass expanded higher and wider, thickening in the middle, like a shadowy bubble.

"What's that?" asked Ayden, voice almost a squeak.

Turning back to their escape route, Winter found a wall of shadows forming just ahead, expanding in either direction and upward. Winter stopped and looked around. "This way!"

She pulled Kaci back toward Xaphan, to a gap in the boxcars they had just passed, knowing Xaphan had no other gap further back to turn and follow them through.

In the next line of boxcars, Winter could still see the dome growing over Xaphan, now stretching high into the sky and covering most of the boxcars in that direction. To the right, the wall of shadows had grown to block their escape. She scanned both directions for another break in the cars and found one again nearer to Xaphan, but still outside the dome. Winter dragged Kaci toward the gap, not waiting on the others.

The next line of cars provided no relief. The wall of demons still grew, blocking their escape in that direction with no break in the boxcars she could see. In the other direction, the wall had begun to move closer. But another break was there, not yet blocked off.

Winter led them through the final gap into an open yard. Two warehouses stood just ahead with a wide lane between them leading to the road. Before they could get there, the shadowy wall to their right curved to connect with an identical wall they had not seen forming to the left, and surrounded them completely.

"What now?" asked Ayden.

Winter spun in a circle with Kaci on her hip. The dome behind them blocked any escape in the direction too. The shadow wall collapsed in on them, now connecting to the outer edges of the dome, the crescent space of safety shrinking foot by foot. Xaphan was coming, and they had no escape.

"Winter! What do we do?" shouted Ayden.

As the dome of shadows crept closer, Winter backed away toward the wall. Soon they would be caught in the shadows either way, and if something didn't come to rescue them this time, they were all dead. Facing the Acolyte was one thing, but the massiveness of the shadows commanded by Xaphan made the Acolyte seem childish. The angelic army that had given her backup before was not big enough.

Winter shook her head. "I...I...don't know."

"You don't know?"

"I don't know!"

The inky bubble over Xaphan passed through the last line of boxcars, surrounding them completely with thick writhing shadows. As the dome of shadows and the wall converged upon Winter and the others, in a flash Winter's vision switched again and she could see the invisible world beyond the shadows. The mass of writhing demons besieging them, crawling upon one another, flew through the air, slunk across the ground, all in a uniform organized effort to build the perfect trap.

Winter's trembling knees buckled and she fell to the ground, Kaci crashing to her side. The others collapsed on the ground just behind

Winter, and Sophie's whimpers transformed into sobs. The approaching dome stopped and the wall stretched out above them to close in the dome. The demons rearranged themselves so no light penetrated save for the one security light caught in the bubble with them. Beyond the thick ceiling, random flashes speckled the demonic ranks as the angelic legion pounded for a way in.

"No…" Sophie mumbled. "I won't go back…"

Winter held her breath, waiting for the attack and wondering what the demons waited for. Then from the far side of the enclosed bubble, the demons parted, falling away like broken beasts, bowing and cowering as Xaphan stepped through. His blood-red robe brushed the ground and his long brown hair fell unbound across his shoulders. He held his hands out in almost an embracing gesture.

"You brought a legion," he said. "I bring many."

Xaphan's eyes shifted to Sophie. "Come to my side."

"No!" Sophie screamed.

A hoard of demons descended from above, crashing onto Sophie. One demon, larger than the rest, with glowing red eyes, burst from the wall and leaped at her.

Sophie covered her face with both hands. "NO!"

As the black mass of demons consumed her, she shrieked and convulsed on the ground as if having a seizure.

Winter reached out for her, but the thrashing demons pounded her arm away until Winter could bear the searing pain no longer. Her insides writhed as she watched Sophie's body quake and then fall still.

The demons settled down, petting Sophie's face and caressing her body. Sophie's features slid from place as if melting, rearranged, until they formed Claire's face again.

She stood, tilted her head as if to crack her neck, and smiled. "Much better."

The Acolyte stepped over Ayden and around Winter without looking at them, crossed the small gap, and took her position at

Xaphan's side.

"Let her go!" Winter shouted. A cackling, like the rattle of bones, answered from the demons.

Xaphan raised his eyebrows. "My powers have grown since we last met. I have now seen the future and it is full of my victory." He paused and smirked. "It is written on your face that you can finally see my friends. And where you have been rescued in the past, you will die now…because nothing can penetrate the presence and the power of this evil gathered here tonight."

Winter put her arms and body over Kaci, the only action she had left. She glared at him in defiance.

"That is my bride," he said.

"No! I won't let you have her!"

"You don't have a choice." He lifted his arm and pointed at them.

The bubble crashed in. Demons clawed at Winter's skin, pulled at her hair, and screeched in her ears. With each acidic touch, unfiltered despair wormed beneath her flesh like varicose veins; a spreading bleakness like fire in every muscle, leaching out her will to live and laughing at the vileness of her own self-worth.

She could hear the others screaming, even Peter, and then realized she was screaming herself. The relentless bombardment upon her back shoved her flat, as if they were trying to tunnel their way to Kaci. Kaci slipped forward as they tugged at her, and Winter clasped Kaci tighter, collapsing to the ground and pinning her down.

Ayden and Peter inched up to huddle with them, Peter cowering beneath Ayden and Ayden leaning against the opposite side of Kaci, helping Winter keep Kaci from being pulled away. Winter peeked at Ayden, reached out, and grabbed Ayden's hand. Ayden peered back, eyes tired and terrified, tears streaming down her face as shadowy claws left minuscule scratches.

Winter could see her own despair reflected in Ayden's eyes. Her own hopelessness. Her own unwillingness to live. She looked to Peter, and though he clenched his eyes tight, Winter found those same unmistakable emotions etched on his face. As she watched Peter's face contort and twist with the same anguish writhing within her, a whisper of light told her the shared anguish meant the source was not from within.

Then the light whispered what to do about it.

She gazed back at Ayden and squeezed her hand a little tighter. "Pray," she said. "That's all we can do."

Ayden nodded and scrunched her eyes tight. She laid her head against Kaci again and was still. The onslaught of demons screeched louder, piercing Winter with icy shards of vibration. The demons pulled at her, ripping her clothes, tearing hair from her scalp.

Winter tensed against the pain and the renewed despair, and leaned forward to reach Peter, one word repeating through her mind...one word of prayer, *Help*. It was the only thing she could think to cry out to God. It was the only thing she needed.

Winter found Peter's shoulder and squeezed as tightly as she could. His head rolled toward her and his eyes parted slightly with recognition and hopelessness.

"Pray!" she shouted.

Somehow the command resonated behind his eyes. A flicker of life returned. He ducked his head back down...and the legion roared, falling a little into disarray. Winter could hear Xaphan and the Acolyte shouting commands and the barrage reformed.

Winter huddled over Kaci, wrapping her more tightly in her arms and leaning down to place her mouth next to Kaci's ear. "Pray."

The horde pressed in on them more tightly than before, mocking, scratching, choking out the oxygen, swirling, ripping, and compressing them painfully together.

"Remember who you are," Winter said directly into Kaci's ear. "Remember what God has done for you in the past. If you ever believed in him, if your faith was ever real to you, you need to pray now. It's the only thing we have. Please pray!"

As the demons smothered in on them, their collective roar shook the ground. Winter clung tight to Kaci, trembling and weeping.

"Kaci, you have to! Pray!"

Kaci moved. She sat up and connected with Winter, paying no attention to the swirling monsters around them, their faces of ecstasy, the joy of their imminent success, their constant tugging to pull Kaci away…not even seeing them. She leaned forward to rest her forehead on Winter's, locking eyes with her, still glazed, but alert.

"No. We pray together," Kaci said and wrapped Winter in her arms, laying her head on Winter's shoulder.

Winter clung to Kaci and repeated the words, knowing Kaci did the same. *Help us.*

At that the demons scattered like bats as white streaks crashed into the battle, more human-like than Winter had seen them before, yet still somehow ethereal and indescribable. The angelic army poured in like the breaking of a dam, catching the demons up and filling the train yard with swirling combat, shaking reality, and saturating the air with panicked screeching. Winter could look around clearly now, finally able to breathe. Compared to Xaphan's monsters, only a small force of angelic warriors drove them back.

This was not her guardian's work. This was not the backup that helped earlier against the Acolyte, now kept out of the dome by Xaphan's legions. This was something different. The same something that had been at the train…an elite force able to penetrate where the larger army could not.

For the first time, Winter recognized the difference, as if two different angelic armies had converged on the same night for different reasons. But why?

Just in front of her, the Acolyte was growing again into her full demonic presence, absorbing all the demons around her, and pounding back any white light daring to get close. Xaphan raged at her and drew a knife. He rushed at them with a roar as he had done to her before in the tower two years ago.

This time he stopped on his own. His face lifted to look behind

Winter and she saw something there she had never seen before...fear.

Xaphan dropped the knife and backed away. The demons absorbing into the Acolyte screeched and scattered, abandoning the form of Claire, who now stood exposed next to Xaphan, with an equally astonished look of fear upon her face.

Thunder rose up behind Winter, the ground trembled, and with a sigh of silence a large shadow passed overhead. A horse landed between her and Xaphan. A blood bay, with a rider who was just as magnificent to look upon as he was dangerous, wearing armor that gleamed like silver and wielding a flaming sword that sliced through the air like lightning.

More thundered up from behind. A second leaped over them, on a blonde chestnut, bearing a rider just as dangerous, just as magnificent as the first. As the bay reared toward Xaphan, the second rider rushed upon the Acolyte.

Two more horses slid to a halt on either side of Winter. Winter peered up to the one just to her right, an ebony horse as dark as midnight, towering over Ayden and Peter. The gleaming warrior brandished a flaming blade and surveyed the raging battle.

"Prophetess," said a voice from her other side, the same voice she had heard behind her on the road to Giurgiu. She turned to the equally stunning rider atop a snow-white horse stamping the ground, frothing at the mouth, eager to plunge into the battle. He gazed down upon her with silvery flashing eyes, his face like ivory. "This is not yet the right moment in time for us to fight this battle, nor have you begun to command the armies. We are here to buy you freedom, but that is all. Run."

Winter nodded and leaped to her feet, pulling Kaci up, not daring to question him.

Xaphan and the Acolyte backed away against the invasion of the riders and the constant barrage of angelic warriors. The siege of demons roiled in confusion, more concerned with self-survival than with the prisoners.

Ayden saw her stand and followed, pulling Peter alongside and glancing toward Xaphan. "What's going on?"

"Run!" Winter shouted. "I'll explain later. Just run!"

The demonic wall behind them had scattered with the rest of the dome. Now the lane between the buildings lay unobstructed before them.

Standing by the nearest building, the little girl watched, a frown of concern on her face.

"You!" Winter shouted. "You did this? Who are you?"

"Winter!" shouted Ayden. "We don't have time!"

When Winter looked back to the little girl, the girl had vanished.

Winter hefted Kaci's arm over her shoulder and ran. Kaci still stumbled, but found better traction now that she was more alert. The more they ran, the more strength Kaci found.

Xaphan roared behind them, chaos raged, and Winter pushed for more speed.

By the time they reached the road and started up the hill, they were all huffing. Winter still didn't chance a look back, even though the sounds of battle began to fade, even though Xaphan had gone silent. They lumbered to the top of the hill and reached Davis's car, fatigue slowing them down, but there was nothing behind them but silence now. As Winter helped Kaci and Peter into the back, and turned to the driver's seat, she took her first full look at the aftermath below.

She found no aftermath. The train yard sat silent and empty, as if a battle had never raged, as if they had never been present at all.

"Let's go!" Ayden shouted from inside the car.

Winter dropped behind the wheel and they sped away.

66

Four Years Ago

"I want to go home," Winter said after about an hour of watching the river. "Will you stay and watch for her?"

"Of course," said Michael. "I'll stay as long as I have to. You can take my car." He reached into his pocket and dangled the keys in front of her.

Winter shook her head. "No. I don't drive anymore."

Michael sighed and put his keys away. "Of course. I'll call Shannon, then."

As Michael spoke into the phone, pacing among the headstones a little ways away, Winter focused on the slow and steady water below. She didn't know what to think anymore. What Michael said made a lot of sense, but was that really all life had to offer? Was she really just a leaf caught in the current, unable to make a difference in her own life or those around her? Was life that insignificant?

She didn't know why, but the thought that what Michael said could be true made the hole in her heart just a little deeper. Winter folded her arms and clenched her eyes until Michael sat back beside her and she could rest her head against his shoulder again, thankful he didn't press her for conversation.

Shannon arrived ten minutes later. Michael squeezed Winter's hand as she stood to leave. Shannon waited by the running car, staring at the ground with red, watery eyes. She didn't greet Winter and Winter didn't speak; she just got in the car, and Shannon began the drive back to Winter's house. A silent drive, punctuated occasionally by an occasional sniffle or escaped sob from Shannon. Just sharing the air with someone who suffered the same emptiness and heartache as Winter was more potent than any spoken words.

"Thank you," Winter whispered as she got out in front of her house. She gazed back at Shannon, and Shannon smiled for a brief moment, wiped her eyes, and then drove away.

Winter hesitated on the sidewalk, looking from her dad's truck in the garage to the front door and wondering what waited for her inside, what angry words would be hurled toward her, what cuts would be made deeper, and if he would even listen to the crushing of her heart like a father should.

She sighed, resigning herself to the worst and to the disappointment of being cheated again from something good that others had and she didn't. After the brief trudge to the door, she found it unlocked and eased it open to creep inside.

Her dad appeared in the doorway of the kitchen. "Where have you been?" His voice wasn't angry or forceful, just annoyed.

"With Claire," she said softly and clicked the door shut, avoiding his eyes.

Steve sighed and ran a hand through his hair. He went back into the kitchen, still talking from the other room loud enough to make sure she could hear over the noise he made. "Listen, I know you're seventeen and there's not much I can do to stop you from doing whatever you want. And I know I've been busy at work...we've sort of had a problem..."

Winter drifted through the center of the living room toward the kitchen door, skin clammy and sweat forming on her brow.

"One of the contractors messed up, and we've had to call them in to redo the work, and it's pushed back the whole production schedule. Not to mention the storm. I know I was gone before you got up yesterday and today, and I didn't come home at all until late last night. I feel like I haven't seen you in two days." He came back in the living room with a thermos in one hand.

Winter stopped in the middle of the room, heart fluttering. "Dad...I need to tell you something..."

"Listen, it's kind of my fault, so I'm not blaming you and I'm not really angry. I should have called or looked in on you to at least let you know what was going on. But next time you want to go spend the night with a friend, if I've been gone all day could you at least give me a call or leave a note or something? And I promise I'll do the same."

"Dad..."

"I just came back for some more coffee and a sandwich, and to check on you. I'm glad you came home at the same time so we could sort this out. I thought I was about to have to go looking for you, and that would have really messed me up. I've got to get back to work and straighten out this mess." He patted her on the shoulder and crossed the room in three long strides. "Listen, we'll do something fun together when this is all over, okay? I'll make it up to you." He grabbed the door and opened it. As he was stepping out, he turned. "I'm sorry. You wanted to tell me something?"

Winter watched him and bit her lip, wishing he would stay, wishing he would pick her up and let her cry in his arms, wanting just this once to actually be his little girl, for him to make everything better.

Steve checked his watch and glanced toward his truck.

"Nothing," Winter said. "Sorry. I won't do it again."

"Good. I'll probably be late getting home again, so don't wait up."

He closed the door, leaving Winter alone in the house. She stared at where he had been, listening to the engine of his truck rev and pull away and fade into the distance. When all was silent, she lowered herself onto the couch, numb, not knowing what to do with the rest of her day. Feeling helpless and useless, and more unwanted than ever. She picked a spot on the floor to stare at, letting time just tick by, trying to think of something to do.

But the mere act of existing was the only thing she was capable of doing.

Present Day

As the others slept, Winter called Summer to check in and tell her where they were going, then gave Summer instructions to have everybody join them. She checked the fuel gauge and prayed they had enough to get there without stopping. As the night grew darker and the stars speckled the sky, Winter couldn't help trying to catch glimpses of Peter and Kaci huddled against each other, sleeping in the back seat. Ayden sat silent, staring ahead with Winter, until eventually she laid her head to the side and closed her eyes.

Two hours later, Winter reached the town of Grady and guided Davis's car to the well-known cul-de-sac.

"Where are we?" asked Ayden, now fully awake beside her.

"Kaci's house. It was the safest place I could think of to go."

The lights were out and Winter wondered if Summer had called ahead like Winter had told her to. As Winter parked the car in the drive, the lights inside flicked on. Before Winter could get out of the car completely, both Beverly and Chris were there.

"What happened?" Beverly asked as she opened the back door.

Kaci crawled out into her mother's arms without fully waking.

Chris helped Peter out of the car. He seemed to be more awake than Kaci, but still leaned on Chris for support.

"What's wrong with them?" Beverly asked as they walked up the sidewalk to the front door.

"Drugged," said Winter. "I'm not sure what it is, but it should wear off after a good sleep…it did with me."

Beverly eyed her, her stern face softening. "Would you hold the door open, dear?" she asked.

Winter nodded and ran to beat them to the door.

Inside, Beverly led Kaci to her bedroom and closed the door. Chris took Peter to the guest room. Winter and Ayden sat at the dining table and waited.

When Beverly came back in, she didn't sit to question them. "You look like you need something. Hungry?"

Winter shook her head. "I'll take a glass of water, thank you."

"Me too," said Ayden.

"I've been trying to call Agent Erickson since Summer called. But he's not answering," said Beverly as she busied herself filling two glasses.

"Xaphan got to him. His phone was at my apartment," Winter said. "I'm not sure how or even if he's okay. But we'll be finding out soon." Winter craned her neck to look at the lights pulling up into the drive. "I'm pretty sure that's my car now."

Chris went to the door and peered out. He turned to her and nodded, then opened the door as Davis, Summer, and Graham came in. They all looked more confused than anything else. Winter had not told Summer much, only that they needed to get out of Cherithville immediately. They each took seats around the table and Beverly brought everyone drinks.

"What did you find out?" Winter asked Graham.

Graham shook his head. "Nothing. Erickson and Golbeck are gone. I mean, completely gone. No bodies, no anything. Their apartment is like it was never lived in."

"How could that even happen?"

"I don't know. I did everything I could think to find them. I called the state office and the national office, and nothing. My inside contact at the FBI said there was no record of them. It seems everything about Erickson and his work has been expunged, at least as far as I've been able to find out tonight."

Winter closed her eyes and grimaced. "That means Xaphan must have someone in the FBI."

Graham nodded. "It's possible. He may have been working multiple angles to get to Kaci. Now that she's out in the open, he won't take the chance of her disappearing again."

"Then we're on our own," said Davis. "The FBI can't help anymore."

Winter sighed. "After what I've seen tonight, we're probably better off on our own. The FBI couldn't have helped anyway."

"What did happen?" asked Davis.

Winter took a deep breath and a long sip of water, before explaining everything—about the train, the spiritual war she witnessed, Xaphan's power, Sophie and the Acolyte, and their unlikely escape.

"In the end," said Winter, "we never really could have survived. Without the help God sent, we wouldn't be here."

Summer lowered her pale face to lay across her forearms on the table. "What do we do now?"

"I don't know," said Winter.

"Well, we can't go back," said Davis.

"You can't stay here either," said Beverly. "I don't think it matters where you go or how much you hide, he'll find you. There's no running anymore."

They sat in silence for several minutes, and then Chris said, "Maybe you *should* go back. If you have to face him one way or another, pick your own battleground and your own timing."

"What do you mean?" asked Winter.

"If this were a physical war, what would you do?"

Winter shook her head. "I don't know. Retreat?"

"But you weren't the one defeated. Listen, like it or not you're in a war and Cherithville is the high ground. Xaphan has lost a battle...pretty spectacularly I might add...and he'll retreat to regroup and rebuild his forces before he attacks again. You shouldn't give up the high ground by retreating too."

"But he knows who Kaci is now. It may be okay for everyone else, but Kaci and Peter are not safe. They have to disappear. And if they disappear, I have to go with them. It's the only way."

"They can face it now and get it over with," said Chris. "Or run for the rest of their lives. Kaci said at the beginning of the year she's tired of running. I doubt she's changed her mind now."

"But we can't use them as bait!"

"Why not? Would you rather Xaphan come at them from behind or in front? Would you rather them living afraid or prepared? Whether you like it or not, it may be time to stand your ground. What is really your job as a prophetess, anyway? To protect them or to face the enemy?"

Winter pressed her palms into the surface of the table. "To protect them. Obviously. And I don't like this plan!"

"Are you sure?"

"Ye..." Winter let her voice trail away and her vision glazed into memory.

The words of the horseman echoed through her mind as he walked behind her on the road...*You cannot face the legions prepared against you, but the Warriors of the Lord can. An army is being prepared for you to command. They will fight this battle.*

And then again at the train yard...*This is not yet the right moment in time for us to fight this battle, nor have you begun to command the armies.*

"I have to fight..." Winter whispered.

"What?" asked Davis.

"He's right. I have to face Xaphan, not protect Kaci. Maybe not right away. But in the end, I'm the one who has to fight. I'm the one who has to confront him." She looked at Ayden. "That's why you're here. You really are my replacement."

"Don't say that," said Ayden.

"It's your job to protect Kaci and Peter so I can lead the battle. That's how it's always been. Think about it. The only times Xaphan has been defeated were when I stood in the way. And the only times he's actually gotten to Kaci were when you were somewhere else. In the tower...you weren't at school yet. With Claire, you had left town to find me. But as long as you've been around, both last year and this year, she's been safe. I'm the fighter and you're the protector."

Ayden crossed her arms. "Well, I'm not quitting school if that's what you're saying. Go into hiding if you want, but not me."

"Nobody's going into hiding...not yet," said Chris. "We'll get you a new place to live, a duplex or something, where you two can live practically in the same building as Kaci and Peter."

"If the FBI are out of it, then there will have to be some other safeguards put into place," said Graham. "I think I can help with that some. If Xaphan is coming for them, they'll need warning and an exit strategy."

Chris nodded. "Graduation is only a couple of months away, and Kaci would not be happy if she couldn't finish. But I don't think Xaphan will try anything for a little while, not after this. And after graduation, I guess we'll have a wedding. Then we get everyone settled into the new plan. Until then, we'll have to figure out something else."

"To just go on as normal?" asked Summer.

Chris nodded. "Until..."

"Until God puts an end to it," said Winter. "With me."

"It's risky," said Graham. "I'm not sure disappearing isn't a better option."

"Me either," said Summer. "At least for Kaci."

"It can always be the backup plan...part of the exit strategy," said Winter. "But it should be her decision. There's no FBI in charge anymore. She's free. Whatever she wants is what we'll do. Got it?"

Everyone nodded.

"We'll finish discussing this in the morning with Kaci and Peter," said Chris. "As for now, I think we should all get some rest."

"There's a recliner and the couch. But I'm afraid the rest of you will have to sleep on the floor," said Beverly.

Chris disappeared down the hall and returned with three sleeping bags and an armload of bedding. Without waiting for the others, Winter took one of the sleeping bags, flashed a faint smile to the others, and went to Kaci's room.

Winter tossed and turned on the floor deep into the night, long after the household had faded into silence. No matter how hard she tried, she couldn't turn off her brain. She ran through all the possible scenarios of the coming months. She thought about living with Summer again so Ayden could take the duty of being with Kaci. She thought about the wedding. She thought about Graham.

She thought about the prophecy...about the child who would change the world before it ended.

The prophecy also said that Winter would have to save them. But what did that mean? What would she have to do?

Winter became aware of time slipping around her. The purpose of her life and the power of her gift converged upon one temporal point not far away. What had to be done...would be done soon.

Through a part in the window curtains, Winter could just make out a single star, twinkling with the light of a distant fire, connecting with the fire of her own thoughts. Tunneling her vision. Filling her ears. Pulsing to the beat of her heart.

Silent.

Watching.

Waiting.

Winter lost track of how long she lay awake, staring at that star and trying to read its thoughts. Eventually exhaustion overtook her and she drifted away.

And landed on the ridge of a mountain. Two armies approached each other below, one vast and organized, with gleaming black armor shimmering like oil and pikes jabbing into the air. A dark haze hung over them like the haze over the train yard, and they marched out of an inky vortex, spinning red at the edges, but full of an emptiness that sucked at Winter's soul.

The other army advanced slowly, cautiously, a desperate and scraggly force, dented and tarnished. Spreading out as best they could, guarding a green field full of beautiful trees and flowers, teeming with innocent wildlife.

Winter saw people there. Cities. Homes. Lives. They had no idea their entire world rested in the protection of a small army who had no chance.

As the armies drew closer, they each broke into a run, colliding together with a roar. The battle began. Swords flew, bodies fell, and the scraggly army was quickly overwhelmed by the sheer mass of the other army, now falling back toward the world, now spilling out upon the beautiful field.

Winter bit her lip, desperately wanting to reach out, to do something, to help the smaller army, but what could she do here alone on the mountainside? She reached out her arms as if to cheer the army on, and found a staff in her hand. She took the staff by both hands, looked at it a moment, and suddenly knowing exactly what she could do to help, she held it over her head as though to hurl it.

When the staff rose, her small army surged forward. The larger army scattered into disarray, falling victim to the renewed ferocity of the smaller army. Winter wanted to cheer, to jump with joy, and in her jubilation she let her arms down. As her arms fell, the larger army gushed forward again.

Winter shook her head, adrenaline pumping, angry with herself for being so careless. She lifted the staff back high, stretching her arms as if to pass the baton to God. The small army pushed forward, gaining momentum again, their armor gleaming, repairing, shining, like the triumphant victors they were meant to be.

Winter didn't know how long she stood like that, but the more soldiers the small army cut down, the more replaced them from the open vortex, an impossible victory if Winter failed this simple task of holding the staff aloft. Her arms burned, the muscles trembled, and the staff began to sag. As it did, so did her army.

"I can't..." she mumbled through the sweat and tears, through the weariness in her arms. "I can't..." She gave all the energy she had, but her arms just wouldn't respond any longer.

Then people appeared at her sides, clutching her elbows and holding them high.

To her left stood Ayden. Ayden's eyes flashed at her. "Your staff is my staff."

Winter nodded and looked to her right.

Kaci smiled at her, warm and full of love. "You are never alone."

Winter didn't know what to say. She wanted to thank them, but gazing down she knew so much work needed to be done with so little hope. Even with the help of her friends Winter wasn't sure her army could prevail. Something else needed to be done.

The clouds parted above, a window beyond the stars into the radiance of heaven. Winter squinted her eyes against the brightness and could barely make out a being flying within the opening. It was long and serpent-like, made of blue and orange fire. It coiled back and forth in a figure eight, sometimes pausing to watch her with intelligent, golden eyes.

A voice floated down from the heavens, from beyond the creature, a soft voice she had heard before. "The final moments are for you to finish. Be of good courage, Prophetess, and end this war."

Winter gazed at the fiery creature and then back down at the impossible battle raging below, and finally understood what needed to be done.

She turned to Ayden and said, "Carry my staff." Then she turned to Kaci and said, "Comfort the others."

Winter took a deep breath, released the staff, and ran down the impossibly steep mountainside as if gravity had shifted in her favor, setting her eyes on the heart of the enemy army. She reached the ground and gained speed. As her speed increased, time slowed to a crawl. Every soldier in both armies laid down their weapons and watched her run, parting before her like an honor guard, enemies and allies alike. None of them dared to stand in her path as she plunged through rank after rank.

When she reached the heart of the army…when she reached the king's chariot…

Fire…fire…fire…fire everywhere…

The wicked plots against the righteous
and gnashes at him with his teeth.
The Lord laughs at him,
for He sees his day is coming.
Psalm 37:12-13 (NAS)

Winter's story concludes in

Mantle

Winter Book 4

By Keven Newsome

The time has come. Xaphan must be stopped. The spiritual battle rages stronger than ever and Winter finds herself at the center of the storm. Not only are her friends at risk, but Xaphan's apocalyptic plans could destroy the entire world.

To defeat Xaphan and his demonic princes, Winter must relive her broken past. And as the power of the infinite is unleashed, she realizes the last eight years of her life have all been leading to this single moment in time.

ABOUT THE AUTHOR

Keven Newsome began his writing career at the young age of ten by creating fanfiction of his favorite video game. He only wrote four pages, though, painstakingly in King James English since that's how they spoke in the game. It was horrible and he promptly abandoned his writing career forever. Thankfully, some years later, fourteen-year-old Keven disagreed with that hasty decision and discovered writing could actually be fun. Since then he has authored five novels, published four of those, and written and published several short stories. He has also recently returned to his favorite video game and become an award-winning fanfiction author on Wattpad. The four books of his Winter series, *Winter, Prophetess, Acolyte,* and *Mantle,* together have been finalists for seven awards and winners of three of those. Originally from south Mississippi, he and his wife live a nomadic ministry life, followed relentlessly by the collective cries of his fans to finish writing his next book already.

http://kevennewsome.com
https://linktr.ee/knewsome.author

www.ingramcontent.com/pod-product-compliance
Lightning Source LLC
Chambersburg PA
CBHW051206120726
47905CB00004B/1006